Your Face in Mine

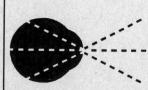

This Large Print Book carries the
Seal of Approval of N.A.V.H.

Your Face in Mine

Jess Row

THORNDIKE PRESS

A part of Gale, Cengage Learning

GALE
CENGAGE Learning·

Farmington Hills, Mich • San Francisco • New York • Waterville, Maine
Meriden, Conn • Mason, Ohio • Chicago

GALE
CENGAGE Learning®

LIBRARY OF CONGRESS CATALOGING-IN-PUBLICATION DATA

Row, Jess.
   Your face in mine / by Jess Row. — Large print edition.
     pages ; cm. — (Thorndike Press large print reviewers' choice)
     ISBN 978-1-4104-7585-5 (hardcover) — ISBN 1-4104-7585-9 (hardcover)
     1. Grief—Fiction. 2. Male friendship—Fiction. 3. Dangerous encounters—Fiction. 4. Large type books. I. Title.
PS3618.O87255Y68 2015
813'.6—dc23
                                     2014038433

Published in 2015 by arrangement with Riverhead Books, a member of Penguin Group (USA) LLC, a Penguin Random House Company

Printed in the United States of America
1 2 3 4 5 6 7 19 18 17 16 15

For my father
Clark Row
1934–2013

多言數窮
不如守中

Words are soon exhausted
Hold fast to the center of all things.
— *Tao Te Ching,* V

And I suggest this: that in order to learn your name, you are going to have to learn mine.

— JAMES BALDWIN

BOOK ONE:
DREAMTIME

1.

It doesn't seem possible, even now, that it could begin the way it begins, in the blank light of a Sunday afternoon in February, crossing the parking lot at the Mondawmin Mall on the way to Lee's Asian Grocery, my jacket in my hand, because it's warm, the sudden, bleary, half-withheld breath of spring one gets in late winter in Baltimore, and a black man comes from the opposite direction, alone, my age or younger, still bundled in a black lambswool coat with the hood up, and as he draws nearer I feel an unmistakable shock of recognition. Even with the hood, that elected shade, that halo of shadow. I don't know whether to call it a certain place above the bridge of the nose and between the eyes, or perhaps something about the shape of the nose itself, or the way he carries it. Or the exact way his lips meet. Or the mild inquisitive look in his eyes that changes as I come closer to something unreadable, something close to surprise. I am looking into the face of a black man, and I'll be utterly honest, unsurprisingly honest: I don't know so many black men well enough that I would feel such a strong pull, such a decisive certainty. I *know* this guy, I'm thinking, yet I'm sure I've never seen this face before. Who goes around looking for ghost eyes, for pleading looks of remembrance, in the faces of strangers? Not me. He's coming closer, and I'm running through all my past at a furious clip, riffling frantically the index cards of my memory for a forgotten slight, a stray remark, a door slammed in a black man's face, a braying car horn behind me on 83 South. He has his eyes trained on me with a faint smile, a smile that dips at the left corner, and says,

Kelly. I'll bet you're wondering why I know your name.

I'm sorry, I say. Do I know you?

Kelly, he says, pursing his lips, it's Martin.

We're alone, in a field of cracked asphalt, dotted here and there with sprays of tenacious weeds, a mostly abandoned shopping plaza missing its anchor tenant. I would never have come here but for Lee's being the closest Chinese grocery to my apartment, an emergency stop for days when I

12

unexpectedly run out of tree-ear fungus or Shaoxing wine or shallots or tapioca starch. Yes, we're in Baltimore; yes, I once lived here, grew up here; but because Baltimore is not just one feeble city but many, and Mondawmin is, to be as honest as I have to be, on the black side of town, in the course of my predictable life, I might as well be on the surface of the moon. As a child I imagined there were hidden places — the tangle of bushes dividing the north and south lanes of the freeway, the fenced-in, overgrown side yard on the far side of our elderly neighbor's house — that held gaps, portholes, in the fabric of the world, and if I crawled into one of them I would become one of the disappeared children whose faces appeared on circulars and milk cartons and Girl Scout cookie boxes, whose cold bodies were orbiting earth as we spoke, and every so often bumped into the Space Shuttle and slid off, unbeknownst to the astronauts inside. How was I supposed to know that I would only have to cross town to find my own gap, my own way into the beyond?

I cross my arms protectively in front of my chest, and say, I know you are.

You do?

Martin, I say, I need an explanation.

2.

We cross the parking lot together, Martin, the black man who used to be Martin, ducked slightly behind my right shoulder, flickering in and out of my peripheral vision. Somehow I'm still possessed of enough of my faculties to remember to grab a shopping cart. The sliding door creaks on an unoiled runner, and we breathe in the comforting sting of Asian markets everywhere — dried scallops and mushrooms, wilting *choi sum,* fish guts in a bucket behind the seafood counter. Mr. Lee looks up at me over yesterday's *Apple Daily* — when did they start getting the Hong Kong papers? — and says, you're too late, the *cha siu bao* are all sold out.

It's okay, I say. I need to lose weight anyway.

Yeah, says his daughter, stacking napa cabbages on newspaper in a shopping cart. You're too fat.

14

Lee gives her a dour Confucian look. Little number three, he says, that's enough out of you. And then, turning to me: is the black man with you? He doesn't speak Chinese, too, does he?

Martin has halted by the soy milk case, reading the labels intently.

Yes, I say. Yes, he's with me. And no, he doesn't.

Tell him we don't have candy bars or potato chips. They always ask.

I give him a noncommittal nod.

My wife was Chinese, I say to Martin, making my way down aisle one, filling the cart with black tree fungus and Sichuan chilies and dried beans and tofu skin. I lived there for three years before I got my Ph.D. She taught me how to cook. My voice sounds bland, conversational, informational: I've been stunned, that's the only way to explain it, stunned back into a certain strained normality. He follows everything I'm saying with lidded eyes and pursed lips, nodding to himself, as if it's exactly what I *would* have done, in his mind, as if he could have projected it all, with slight variations.

Hold on. Your wife *was*? You're not together?

No, I say, no, she died. She and my daughter died. In a car accident.

How long?

I look at my watch.

A year, I say, six months, three weeks, and two days.

Mr. Lee, who has never before seen me speaking English, is pretending not to watch us, stealing interested glances over a full-page picture of Maggie Cheung.

I was in Shanghai and Hangzhou once, Martin says. Only briefly, on business. Loved it. Loved the energy. Wish I could have stayed longer.

He reaches up and pulls the hood away from his forehead. His hair, a black man's hair, of course, razored close to the scalp, with neat lines at the temples and the nape of the neck. The look of a man who's close friends with his barber. I can't help thinking of my own scraggling beard, and the last time I tried to crop it into a new shape, how it looked, as Meimei used to put it, *half goat-eaten.* Fullness of time, I can't help thinking. The phrase just won't leave my mind. *Fullness of time.*

You know, he says. You're a brave man, Kelly. I think I'd have run away screaming. His voice is different. It is, thoroughly, unmistakably, a black man's voice, declarative, deep, warm, with a faint twang in the nasal consonants. It's just a couple of opera-

16

tions, he says. And some skin treatments. In the right hands, no big thing at all. That is to say, it *won't* be. When it becomes more common.

Does it, does it — I'm flailing here — does it have a name? What you've done?

If it had a name, he says, what would that change, exactly? Would it be more acceptable to you? Would it be *a thing* people do? Would it have a category unto itself?

He laughs.

I'm just playing with you, he says. You should see the look on your face. Kelly, of course it has a name. What do you think it would be called? Racial reassignment.

We've stopped at the end of the dried goods aisle, the aisle of staples, and I'm teetering on the edge of the snacks aisle: lychee gummies, shrimp chips, dried squid, mango slices in foil, and three or four rows of Pocky, that bizarre Japanese name for pretzel sticks dipped in coatings of one or another artificially flavored candy. Pocky comes in cigarette-sized packs with flip-top lids, and there is, in addition to strawberry, raspberry, and vanilla, Men's Pocky, plain chocolate, in a distinguished pine-green. It's never been clear to me whether this is an elaborate inside joke on the part of the manufacturer or a sincere message to the

17

consumer. There is Men's Pocky, but not Women's Pocky. Am I supposed to be reassured, not having to make a choice?

Racial reassignment *surgery.*

Yeah, of course, surgery. But it's more than that. It's a long process.

Meaning, I have to say — I strain to form the words — meaning you were always black. Like a sex change. Inside you always felt black.

Damn, he says. You get right to the point, don't you? I don't remember you being this direct, Kelly.

Martin, I say, without quite being able to look at him — I cast my eyes up to the stained ceiling tile, the fluorescent panel lamps dotted with dead flies — we're not going to see each other again, are we? Isn't that the point? You wanted a new life. I'm certainly not going to intrude.

Anyone can get a new life, he says. It's easy to fall off the map. I don't recall you ever trying to track me down. And all of you guys left, anyway. Am I just repeating the obvious here? I never thought I'd see you back in Baltimore. You get hired by Hopkins?

No, I say. I'm not an academic. Not anymore. I work in public radio.

No kidding? You mean, what is it, 91.1?

18

The Hopkins station?

No, the other one. WBCC. 107.3.

Oh, yeah. Right. Way up at the top of the dial. I always wondered why there were two.

Are you a listener?

Heck no, he says. I listen to XM. No offense, I like the news sometimes, but not all that turtleneck-sweater, mandolin, Lake Wobegon stuff. Not my thing.

Yeah. I understand.

You do? You understand?

I read the surveys, runs through my mind, *that's my job, I know the demographics. I could break down our audience into the single percentiles.* Look, I say, I mean, it's not a secret. It's a *problem.* We think about it every day. We want to be a station for the whole city, you know, *Baltimore,* and we're just not. It's an issue. I'm trying, believe me.

He whistles through his teeth. Maybe you're the man for me, he says. I need somebody to help me with this project. This idea I have. A *communicator.* He takes a slim billfold from his front pocket — the long, old-fashioned kind, meant to fit in a blazer — and takes out a glossy orange business card. *Martin Wilkinson, Orchid Imports LLC.*

You changed your name.

19

You know many brothers named Martin Lipkin?

It's just one in a long list of inconceivable things I've had to conceive of in the last fifteen minutes, so I nod nonchalantly.

And what, you sell orchids?

No, no. Electronics. My wife came up with the name.

Okay, I say, nodding again, a yes-man.

So you'll email me? Can I buy you lunch?

Is that really a good idea? I ask him. I mean, I *know* you. Aren't I kind of a liability? A piece of personal history?

I trust you, he says, staring at me, boxing me in, so that I'm forced to look straight at his coffee-colored pupils — just the same as before, at least as far as I remember. Listen, he says, we can act like this never happened. If that's what you want. Either way, you'll respect my privacy. I know that much. So I'm just asking: you want to come with me a little further down this road, Kelly? You curious? You want the whole story?

Keeping my head straight, our eyes level, in this Vulcan-mind-meld game he seems to want to play, I conduct the briefest possible mental inventory of my life: an empty apartment; an enormous, shockingly expensive storage unit out in Towson, filled with boxes I'll never open; a job, if you can call it a job;

a few friends, widely spaced; a 500-page manuscript on two dead poets, gathering dust in its library binding up in Cambridge; a wall of books in five languages I never want to read again.

Yes, I say, yes, I'll have lunch with you, Martin.

See you then. He pulls his hood back up, hunches his shoulders, and disappears through the door, back into the tepid weather, the diffident sunshine, the blank, anonymous world that seems almost to have created him.

3.

When I lived there, in the waning gray years of Deng Xiaoping's senility, Weiming College was a cluster of dark square buildings with tile roofs, in a kind of sinicized Art Nouveau style, built on a bluff over the Yellow River. The architect, a German named Manfred Schepler, had built the college for Seventh-day Adventist missionaries in the 1920s but, dissatisfied with the design, committed suicide by hurling himself off the roof of the chapel into the river. That was the local legend, at any rate. My apartment, a cavernous space intended to house six foreign teachers, looked out over the river, almost invariably shrouded in mist. Swallows nested on a ledge above my windows, and all day long the shadows of their diving flickered across the walls. I mentioned to Wendy that it gave me an odd feeling, being continually reminded of Schepler's suicide, and she pursed her lips and shook her head and said, no, that's not a memory we like to revisit.

Revisit was exactly the kind of word she used all the time when we first met. She added English words to her vocabulary through careful and unselfconscious practice, without the slightest indication of an eagerness, an anxiousness, to learn. In this way, she stood apart from every other Chinese person I knew in Wudeng. There were many, thank God, who were completely indifferent to English, but those who did want to learn looked at me as a kind of mobile language-instruction machine that had to be pumped from time to time with offers of homemade local food and foreign exchange certificates. I barricaded myself in my apartment to get away from them, the first two months I lived there, subsisting on a dwindling supply of macaroni and cheese I'd brought with me by the case from the Park n' Shop in Hong Kong, and watching the VHS movies the previous teacher had abandoned before leaving for a hard-seat trek to Kashgar.

And then she appeared, with her back to me, having a conversation with one of the secretaries in the Foreign Languages office when I was using the ancient mimeograph machine between classes. She saw me in the

23

reflection of a piece of framed calligraphy, she always claims, and turned to me and said, you are the new English teacher. I hope your tenure here is satisfying.

The sensation of standing on ball bearings: *tenure,* in the particular place and moment. Where did this woman come from, I was thinking, whose English was better than any of the teaching faculty's, but who seemed by all accounts to be a student, in gray slacks, too long, with a short-sleeved blue button-down shirt that barely contained her small but noticeable breasts, and a pair of gray steel glasses forked over her long, aquiline nose, that reminded me of an interviewer on a BBC talk show?

Qing Dewen was her name. *Wendy,* she said. My name is Wendy. I never called her anything else.

We were married nine months later, in a small ceremony in my parents' backyard in New Paltz, and then afterward, the following September, in a riotous celebration at the only restaurant to speak of in Wudeng. By then I had become fluent enough in Guizhou dialect to understand the jokes men made behind my back about the red hair that sprouts from the tips of white men's penises. We were a star couple, Wendy used to say; everyone in town knew us, and out-of-towners stopped us on the street for pictures. By then we had moved off campus and into an apartment upstairs from her parents. Her father, Qing Xiyun, had been a well-known poet before the Cultural Revolution; he'd gone to college in Shang-hai and lived there for some years, working for the Cultural Bureau. When the Cultural Bureau was disbanded, he was sent to work in a tractor factory near Xian; that was where Wendy was born. After 1977 he was allowed to leave, but without a residency permit for Shang-hai, he could only return to Wudeng. Now retired, officially, he worked as a night guard at the college. Wendy's mother, too, was retired, but she worked even harder, making hand-pulled noodles at home with two assistants.

That year was the happiest I have ever had. Wudeng then was still a small town, and we woke up with the roosters, the shouts of fruit sellers and dumpling vendors on their early rounds, and gusts of cold air through the windows that smelled like the river. We had a tiny table I'd nailed together out of two packing crates, and every morning we brewed a pot of Nescafé and sat together, reading, grading papers, listening to Bach or Brahms on my CD player from home. In the afternoons, after my classes, I sat with Xiyun on the front stoop, drinking tea out of glass jars, watching the children running home from school. He could quote long passages from Du Fu, Li Bai, Su Shi; and Li Qingzhao, but his favorite was Tao Qian, the first and greatest recluse of Chinese poetry:

> From the eastern hedge, I pluck
>   chrysanthemum flowers,
> And idly look toward the southern hills.
> The mountain air is beautiful day and night,
> The birds fly back to roost with one
>   another.
> I know that this must have some deeper
>   meaning,
> I try to explain, but cannot find the words.

What I loved the most were the times when an old woman from the neighborhood would stop with a load of vegetables on one shoulder and complain loudly about her arthritis, or pass on a shred of gossip, without giving me a second glance, as if my presence was no more remarkable than anyone else's. I felt almost as if I had grown a second skin, or passed into some ghostly state, a hologram. Of course, that was a fantasy. Everyone knew we would leave, eventually, that Wendy had married me to leave. It was almost a point of pride. But in that process, somehow, I had become part of the story.

Would I have wanted it any other way? Would I have wanted to stay for good? It's pointless to dwell on hypotheticals. Modern Chinese law does technically permit foreigners to become naturalized, but the spirit of the law is *jus sanguinis.* The law of blood. Foreign-born children of Chinese parents can give up their citizenship and return, with difficulty, but no Westerner has ever *actually* become a Chinese citizen. There are permanent residency cards for a tiny privileged few — millionaire investors, tenured professors — but for anyone else, for me, to stay in China, even if I could keep a job, would have meant a yearly trip to Seoul to renew my visa. A permanent temporary worker. Wendy and I could have had ten children and it would be the same. Beyond all that, I wouldn't have been able to stand it, as the only one, the Wudeng *laowai,* the Pearl S. Buck of the village — a freak of nature, like an albino, or a six-fingered man. I loved it, but only in the most impossible way; and then I took Wendy away with me. Though she knew it was a terrible cliché, and it was hideously embarrassing, especially in front of my friends, she never tired of saying *America is my dream come true.* We lived in the States for eight years, and never went back to China, even after she got her green card. I don't need to, she said, when I questioned her. I've had enough China for one lifetime.

The great miracle of our relationship was that we rarely needed to discuss anything, our lives so perfectly intertwined. At least that was how it seemed to me. When we moved to Cambridge, on one student stipend and a loan from my parents, she walked into the Yenching Library and was hired as a cataloging clerk on the spot, complete with an approved work visa. Three years later, after I finished my general exams, in the fall of 2000, she said, *I want to go off the pill;* we conceived Meimei just after Christmas.

It's true that she was extremely quiet, eerily so, by American standards, and I had to press her to tell me what she was thinking. At times I grew exhausted and snapped at her, sure she was silently judging me, playing the passive-aggressive. But for the most part she was just watching. The world was new to her. I've never met anyone less inclined to make up her mind about abstractions. In day-to-day life she simply never needed to deliberate.

There's something about you, she said to me, once, after we'd been in Cambridge six months. You're not like other Americans. It's a surprise to me. You're — what is it? Quiet? Cool? Calm?

You tell me.

Bland, she said. Is that right? Not as an insult. As a compliment.

Are you saying I'm more Chinese?

Don't be ridiculous. What does that mean, *more Chinese*?

More like a typical Chinese person.

I don't know any typical Chinese person. But I think I understand you. You're like a character from an old story. Like a monk. A Taoist monk. *Passive*.

That's not a compliment. To an American, anyway.

Careful. Can I say that? Careful?

I am careful. That much is true. I hold back. I reserve judgment. I take more time than I should to consider the consequences, you could say. I was that way in college, before we met, all through our relationship, in the aftermath, and now. My entire adult life.

There's a reason for that, I should have told her. Though I never did. And I can't tell you, either, quite yet.

My apartment — the upstairs floor of a town house on Palmer Street, in Charles Village — is really still just our old house, re-created in miniature. She bought the furniture, re-sanded and re-stained it; she chose the gauzy curtains, the kilim in the living room, the calligraphy scrolls, the old Shanghai movie posters framed above the dining table, souvenirs Xiyun picked up in the Fifties. In the kitchen I've framed three of Meimei's paintings, from what we called her green phase: pictures of horses, elephants, mice, cars, all made of neat green balloons and labeled, helpfully, in her three-year-old scrawl.

The circumstances of the accident were never fully explained, at least in a way I could understand, but the bare outline is this: Wendy and Meimei were driving east on Storrow Drive, on a wet November day, in a car she'd borrowed from a friend, an old Audi station wagon. The brakes failed, or the car hydroplaned, or probably, most likely, both: it crashed through a guardrail, rolled over a narrow strip of grass, and went into the Charles, and they drowned. There's no way to avoid saying it. Wendy managed to get out of her seat belt and into the back, and their bodies were intertwined, of course; she was trying to unbuckle Meimei's restraining harness.

For a month I hardly left the house. My bosses at WBUR — I'd gone to work there two years before, while still working on my dissertation, and had put off looking for an academic job until I realized I no longer wanted one — had given me six weeks' paid leave, and I spent most of it in my attic study, or on the living room couch, compulsively reading. I read *War and Peace, The Man Without Qualities, The Tale of Genji,* the complete *Journey to the West, The Dream of the Red Chamber.* At night, to relax, I watched two or three movies in a row. One night I watched Claude Lanzmann's *Shoah,* all nine hours, and woke up on the couch at noon the next day, freezing, the blanket fallen off, hardly able to move. A friend of mine from graduate school, now a professor at the University of Hawaii, sent me a care package of his own hand-grown hydroponic indica packed in Kona coffee cans; I smoked it twice a day, at eleven and six, to give myself an appetite, and then went out and ate unbearably spicy meals. Shrimp vindaloo, extra-hot. Jerk chicken with pickled Scotch bonnet peppers on the side.

Guizhou-style lamb hot pot. Otherwise I couldn't taste anything at all.

I walled in my life with stimuli, or tried to, anyway; if I had been a different person, or in a different frame of mind, I would have spent all the life insurance money in one go, on a Fiji vacation or a Lamborghini. Grief permanently alters the mind, my therapist said. Don't underestimate its power. He asked me to do a simple exercise. When you wake up in the morning, immediately ask yourself, *what kind of person am I today?* Make a commitment: *I am sad but getting better. I am focused. I return phone calls.* It worked for a while, but I realized, months later, that it made the underlying problem worse. I took small steps; that created the illusion I was getting better.

Grief makes you temporarily invisible: a fugitive in your own place, in your own time. That's not news. What frightened me, when I gained just enough traction to begin to think about it, was that I didn't mind so much. In fact, it seemed like a confirmation of who I already was. Snuggled inside my nearly middle-aged soul, wombed inside my happy fatherhood, was a creature who would use the excuse of mourning just to buy time, until no one expected me to *heal* or *move on.* I thought, for a while, that I would make an excellent crank: bushy-bearded, in a torn T-shirt, getting by on disability or food stamps, walled into my apartment with books and manuscripts. I could teach myself Sanskrit and Tibetan and ancient Greek. I could rot on a bench in Harvard Square, part of a venerable tradition, mumbling fragments of Aristophanes.

Finally, obviously, I realized I had to leave. Cambridge was unbearable; my house was unbearable; and my job, which I had loved, the office of program development and planning, had turned into a pale tunnel of drawn faces and outreaching hands. I had become a kind of obelisk of grief, a freak of disaster, and for young women, especially — women I cared about, and mean no disrespect toward — there was something almost pornographic about the way they looked at me, something almost exuberant about all that horror and pity.

The recruiter — no more than a voice to me, Lois, a woman speaking from Boulder, who did this for a living, matching NPR and PRI stations and staff — said to me, this is a bit of an unusual one. It's a fixer-upper. In fact, it's in real trouble. WBCC, in Baltimore, have you heard of it? Probably not. It's second-tier, community radio, independent license, free-form music during the day — kind of a turkey, if you ask me. They've got big money problems. But look, they need a PM *now,* and they'll take you for sure, experience or no. Have you been? Baltimore's a nice town. Super-cheap. Lots of character. Forty-five minutes from D.C. —

— No, no, I said, I'm from there. No need to explain.

Two days after the funeral, Wendy's father called me from Wudeng, using the new cell phone she'd bought for him online a few weeks before. There was no way for them to come; they'd held their own funeral and put up tablets in the family tomb, with a local Taoist priest officiating. Afterward, he said, someone had asked him if it was appropriate to enter Meimei's name in the family record, given that her father was a *laowai,* that she wasn't fully Chinese. I would have hit him, he said, only your mother-in-law stopped me. I told him, you will not slander the name of my only grandchild.

I held the line for a full minute, listening to him gasping for breath on the other end.

You should come back to Wudeng, he said; you should teach here again. There are always jobs, you know. You could translate. There's the new Honda factory over in Xiling, I'm sure they could use you for something. Native English speakers are worth more than gold now, he said, repeating a constant cliché in the news. Live with us, in your old apartment.

And how could I come back to Wudeng without Wendy? I asked him. How would it look?

You're still our family, he said. You're all the family we have now. American, Chinese, I don't care anymore. I used to hate you for taking Wendy away. Now none of that matters. You still have a duty to us. Not money. I don't care about money. We *need* someone.

I can't, I said. I can't.

Not now. Maybe sometime, he said. The offer is open. You understand? As long as we're alive, the offer is open.

4.

Mort Kepler is already sitting in my office when I arrive, fifteen minutes early. He's given up raking the sand in my miniature Zen garden, and now sits back, one hiking boot propped on the radiator, flipping through the latest issue of *Station Manager* with the tiny bamboo rake still held delicately between two chubby fingers like a cigarette. Sorry, he says, thumping his foot back on the floor. I had the insomnia again last night. Winona kicked me out of bed at five-thirty, and Starbucks wasn't open. So I came to work. Isn't that sad?

Something I can do for you?

Oh, he says, I want to talk about a twenty percent raise and two more PAs for *Baltimore Voices.* That okay with you? Just kidding. Don't look so serious, I'm breaking your balls again. But we should talk about how we're going to present this to the board.

The most regrettable thing about Mort

Kepler is that he's a legend mostly — but not entirely — in his own mind. He spent the late Sixties and much of the Seventies as a *Sun* reporter covering civil rights and the peace movement, and published a collection of pieces, *Notes from the American Front,* that created a bit of a stir in 1981. Later, in the Eighties, he moved to the Pine Ridge Sioux reservation in South Dakota and taught high school English, took up an affair with a seventeen-year-old, Winona, and somehow arranged for her to land a full scholarship at Goucher College, landing them back in Baltimore before the scandal broke. Not long after that he began his career as a public radio host, first on a small Delaware station and now here, where he's become a local institution, on a very small scale. His lunchtime call-in show takes all comers — the Nation of Islam, Pentecostal Israelophiles, 9/11 Truthers, lesbian separatists, Christian vegans. Last year the station spent nearly $10,000 on FCC fines, all of them for *Baltimore Voices;* our PAs can't always tell who might begin screaming obscenities the moment they go on the air. Never mind, Mort told me, in my first meeting with him, it's all part of the struggle, the never-ending struggle.

I was born in 1974, on the day Nixon left

office. He tells this to visitors, sometimes, with a bark of bright anger and amusement. Kids, he says, the world is overrun with kids. We might as well just pack it in.

Mort, I say, I'm sorry, I'm a little foggy this morning. Present *what* to the board?

You didn't get my email last night? Shit! He smacks his forehead theatrically. I'll bet I sent it to the wrong address. I got a bad habit of forgetting the last dot, you know, dot E-D-U? He rummages in his bag and produces a rumpled document, four or five pages, single-spaced. The Outreach Committee's new plan, he says. There are some brilliant ideas in there. We want to start a whole new revamped internship program. That actually brings some interns in the *door* this time.

Good, I say, so I'll look at this, and can we meet tomorrow? Same time? Bright and early?

Okay. Tomorrow's okay. But the only problem is, the board meeting's Thursday. That doesn't give us much time to prepare.

Right, I say, but I have to *read* this, Mort, and make sure I can sign off on it, and then Barbara has to look at the numbers and put them in the budget proposal —

You sure? I mean, we're talking three cents on the overall dollar. The PD's approval has

38

always been pretty pro forma.

Well, I say, look, Mort, I just got here. And if I start doing things pro forma without looking at them first, nobody's going to be very happy.

You mean the board won't be.

Well, them. Them and others.

Sometimes in the middle of conversations like this I have a sense of my body tilting upward, till it's parallel with the ground, and I'm looking down at my own office, like a dream swimmer. I hear a certain throbbing in my eardrums, and I see the serious look on the face of the person across from me — because when people come into my office they're always serious, always wanting something, and yet having to pretend that it's for the good of the station, the public interest, the city, the earth. The cringing, the apologies, the hand wringing, all for a few hundred dollars to attend a conference at a community college in Atlanta! And then I want to burst out laughing. I want to pop open a mini-fridge and hand out cans of Coors Light. We're choking on our own piety in this business, and yet here I am, parish priest of this tiny church of public radio, waving my hands and dispensing indulgences.

Kelly, Mort says, is it all right if I cut the

bullshit for a moment?

Please.

I just want to give you a little feedback on how things are going. Now that it's been a month. I — we — look, we're concerned about the level of inclusivity. We feel, some people feel, that you're not taking the committee structure seriously.

Would you like me to respond honestly? I ask. He nods. Mort, I say, I don't. I can't. And then I do something I've promised myself not to do, in fact to avoid at any cost: I open my top drawer, the locked drawer, and take out a green folder, an as-now-empty folder with the words *Station Audit* in the little plastic window.

Last month we received our disaffiliation papers from NPR. As of December first, they're cutting us off. Chronic nonpayment or late payment of annual fees. Decline in listenership across the brackets. Weakness in local programming. That's what they said. It's all itemized. We're going to have an all-staff meeting next week and I'll give the full presentation.

He's been following me, squinting, mouthing the words.

I knew it, he says. You're one of those fucking turnaround artists. You're Neutron Jack. Look, am I fired? Just tell me now.

Of course you're not fired. You're pro-
moted.

To what?

Director of outreach.

No more committees? *None* of them?

Network policy is that we have to have a
standard governance structure.

Do you have any idea what you're doing?
he says. You're *from* here, right? Didn't you
ever listen to BCC at all, as a *person*?

I listened to my own music. I was just a
kid. Never turned on the radio.

Yeah, he says, addressing the ceiling, that's
just like them. Bring in a PD who's never
turned on the radio.

He looks at me with pure, piggish hatred,
and I have the words right on my tongue,
prepared, a whole speech: *Make me the
scapegoat, make me the bad guy. Shoot the
messenger. Just do the right thing and decide
to keep your station, all right?* I've been
practicing in the shower, behind the wheel,
for weeks, ever since I received my copy of
the report. No station should be allowed to
die, not even the little ones, the redundant
ones, with two hours of bluegrass during
the afternoon rush before the news comes
on. It's a community station; it's the principle of the thing; it's a public resource,
never mind if point-five percent of the

41

public is ever listening. It's salvageable. There are good people here. I look through my partition window at Barbara, her silver hair wound up in a long nested braid: a maniacally effective accountant, a chain smoker, a lover of Mel Tormé and Bobby Darin. I look back at Mort, and the words turn to sawdust in my mouth.

We'll talk more later, I say. Take a deep breath.

What, he says, turning around in the doorway, so that Barbara and half the office can hear, is BCC too big to fail?

The Baltimore I know runs on a north-south axis along three parallel streets, Charles, Calvert, and St. Paul. Beginning at the city line, the anonymous ranch-house suburbs of Towson give way to the ring of neighborhoods where I lived out my adolescence: Mount Washington, Roland Park, Homeland. There is the bizarre Art Deco cathedral of Mary Our Queen and the Masons' Boumi Temple and the enormous empty St. Mary's Seminary, and then farther down the anonymous, faceless stone and brick mansions of Guilford, then the Johns Hopkins main campus, cut off from the streets by a forested median on St. Paul Street and the lacrosse stadium on University Parkway. Until this point the city is really not a city so much as an agglomeration of villages, leafy, prosperous-seeming, and carefully composed. At 33rd Street, which leads east only a few blocks to Memorial Stadium, Baltimore proper begins, first as a long corridor of row houses broken by large avenues, then the canyon formed by Interstate 83 as it cuts southeast just below Penn Station; below that, Mount Royal, clustered around the Washington memorial obelisk, and finally the gleaming steel-and-glass bank buildings just before the Inner Harbor and its shopping arcades and Camden Yards, the new baseball stadium, which to me still looks like an architect's drawing or a hologram.

I moved here when I was twelve and left for college at eighteen, and when college was over there was China, and Wendy, and then graduate school, and Meimei, and WBUR, and in the space of fifteen years I came back only five or six times, each time only when I couldn't possibly avoid it. I did everything I could not to come home for longer than a week; and then finally — just before I married Wendy — my parents retired and moved to New Paltz, and I thought, briefly, that I would never have to see the city again.

Not because I hated Baltimore, not at all, but because, as one of my friends put it, it was a place to be *from,* not a place to belong *to.* When I arrived at Amherst I realized within five minutes that it was pointless to try to explain to a girl from Rye, New Hampshire, what it meant to go to an illegal warehouse show on North Avenue, or why it mattered that my sweater came from Don's Discount in Fell's Point, or why I had a collection of Polish saint cards taped to my wall, since I wasn't even Catholic. I felt, for the first time, provincial. Everyone had a hometown, a story, a past, and it could matter if you wanted it to — if, for example, you lived at 88th and Park Avenue, and your father was the director of the Guggenheim — or not, and I chose, as nearly all of us chose, not. I wanted to be denatured, detached, to luxuriate in my cocoon and emerge an utterly different butterfly. Everyone I knew from home had done the same. To be fair, we weren't exactly locals, to begin with: mostly our parents were academics, teachers, lawyers, scientists, who'd made a life here more or less arbitrarily; whose concerns were global, and who viewed Baltimore and its problems with generic concern, not civic pride. When I saw my friends at Thanksgivings and

Christmases it was as if years, not months, had passed, and we stayed mostly in one another's houses, as if the city might not want to take us back.

By then I'd lost touch with Martin completely. I last saw him, I'm remembering now, on February 12, 1993, the day of Alan's funeral, and that was the first time in months — the band had broken up, and he had all but disappeared, barely even coming to school. I assumed that his life had gone on, as all of our lives did; I assumed he'd disappeared into this new and large and atomized world. It never occurred to me that he might have stayed in Baltimore.

I met somebody, I tell Wendy, in the car, on Charles Street, coasting through one green light after another. An old friend.

How old?

High school. He's changed, though. I wouldn't have recognized him.

That always happens.

No, I'm about to say, you don't understand, but I stop myself.

Anyway, what was he like back in the old days?

That's the problem. I don't really remember.

What do you mean, you don't *remember*?

45

I mean he wasn't that memorable, honestly. I mean, individually. We were in a band together, we played music together. And we hung out. But everyone hung out.

Hung out, she says. I've always hated that expression. It reminds me of laundry.

It's a bad habit, probably, talking to your dead wife, but I do it without thinking, as unconsciously as talking to myself. And perhaps it really is just talking to myself. The Wendy of my imagination is more voluble than the real Wendy ever was, more inclined to keep the conversation going. But she *is* still there. It sounds absurd, but there is another voice, another presence; it answers me, I don't tell it what to say. You could call it my unconscious, but if that's the case, my unconscious is much more capacious than I ever thought it could be. And it speaks better Chinese.

It couldn't possibly have been the way I remember, I've been telling myself. Martin couldn't really have had surgery. Changed his hair, put on makeup, had his skin dyed, maybe. It ends there. The rest was an illusion, drag, a fetishistic thing, maybe. Online I searched for *racial reassignment* and found articles on passing, on Michael Jackson, on Jewish nose jobs, on eyelid surgery in Korea — more or less what one would expect. It

46

doesn't exist. It isn't something people do. There would be an outcry; there would be public discussion. Like cloning, like stem cell research: the technology couldn't just develop out of nowhere. You can't develop a new category of human beings without anyone noticing. Martin, I want to say, is a little unhinged, maybe. Mildly delusional. Or living in some alternate universe, aesthetically, intellectually. It's a great question mark, and that's why I'm going downtown, now, to have lunch with a question mark. This is the story I tell myself.

Tell me about him, Wendy says. Just open your mouth and talk. Maybe that'll help.

He was just this guy I knew. He was tall, rail-thin, absurdly thin, super-pale, not a great complexion. Always wore T-shirts that hung off his frame awkwardly, and he walked with a bit of a stoop. I remember that. Baggy black jeans, Doc Martens, a bicycle-chain bracelet on his right wrist. We always complained that it hit the bass strings when he played, but he said he liked the effect, it was, like, *industrial.* You don't know what that means, do you? You don't know what any of this means.

Don't worry about me. Just talk.

We were called L'Arc-en-Ciel. The French word for rainbow. Didn't I ever tell you this

47

before? It sounded kind of badass if you didn't know what it meant, at least that was the theory. We never recorded anything — anything that made it to vinyl or a CD, anyway. And then a Japanese band came along and stole the name. So there's no trace of us anymore. It was Alan's thing, really, mostly his idea, and he wrote the songs, which were sort of like Jesus Lizard crossed with Devo. Lots of big thumping guitars and high, piercing keyboards. When we played people stood fifteen or twenty feet back and frequently covered their ears, which we took as a compliment. Martin auditioned with "Blitzkrieg Bop," then a Primus song, and then something by Steely Dan, to show he could really play. He was good. You know how hard it is to find a good bass player? It was me on the drums, Martin on bass, Alan on guitars and keyboards and vocals and everything else. *His* band, though it wasn't as if anyone played any solos. We thought nothing was worse than the Grateful Dead — the endless noodling, the blissed-out girls spinning in circles. Alan said, we want to sound like a heart attack. We want to sound like a 3-D nightmare.

Okay. Okay. Enough about the band.

What else? I ask. What else can I say? He went to my high school — Willow, the

Willow School, a private, *progressive* school, whatever that meant, it was just as much of an anorexia factory as the rest of them — in name only. Never had much of a presence there. No clubs. No plays. Didn't even really hang out with us in school much. Frankly, I don't even know if he graduated, either. *Martin Lipkin* — who were his parents? Where was he from? Blank, blank, blank.

A single memory: we dropped him off one night, after a late show, at a row house somewhere off Guilford, a neighborhood I'd never been to before. No one I knew lived that far south; and as I remember it, not just the one house but the whole block was dark, not a lit window anywhere. This your place? Alan asked. Yeah, Martin said, home sweet home, and we waited — polite, well-brought-up children that we were — till he'd used his key and disappeared inside.

How is it, I ask Wendy, that we can spend so much time with people, and know nothing about them? I mean, we were a serious band, for a high school band. We practiced twice a week, Fridays and Sundays. We played shows in Annapolis and D.C. and Harrisburg. It ought to be criminal, how casual we are with our friends, at that age.

You were young. You weren't thinking for the long term. You don't think, when you're

49

a teenager, that anyone ever goes away, do you? Every friend is a friend for life.

I roll to a stop at the corner of St. Paul and Cathedral, and look over at my reflection in a storefront window: an ordinary face, I guess you could say, relatively dark-featured, with a close-trimmed beard and thick eyebrows, the gift of my Portuguese great-grandparents. An unremarkable, unhandsome, inoffensive face. A white face. I should add that now. It would never have made the list before. There are so many parts of myself that I can change, that I have changed, but who spends much time assessing the givens? An unremarkable face of a man alone in his unremarkable car, who, if one observed closely, could be seen talking to himself out loud — not to a speaker-phone, not to a Bluetooth headset, to the air.

I shouldn't have come, I say to Wendy. I should never have moved back here. It was a terrible mistake.

Did you have another choice?

I should have been driving.

Silence. I could snap my fingers and hear it echo: my mind, for a moment, a deserted room.

5.

Aegeos, the restaurant Martin suggested, is in the prime spot — first floor, water side, nearest the Aquarium — in the Harborplace shopping complex where Phelps Seafood used to be. In truth, I haven't been to Harborplace in so many years that I hardly remember what goes where. Locals, by and large, avoid it. Fundamentally it's just a mall with expensive, inconvenient parking, unless you're downtown for some better reason, like jury duty. But of course that's not the reason: to go there is to be reminded, if you're at least as old as I am, that at one time the city's very existence seemed to depend on two long glass-and-brown-brick sheds filled with potted ferns, neon handwriting, and shiny baubles from The Limited, La Sweaterie, and The Nature Company. This was before crack, before AIDS, before the final Beth Steel shutdown, three recessions ago — as if Baltimore has ever come out of recession in my lifetime — and yet year after year the tourists spill across its tiled plazas in waves, buying *Don't Bother Me, I'm Crabby* aprons and twelve-dollar salads, blueberry-flavored popcorn and ships in bottles, and their money, as far as I can tell, gets flushed into the oily water of the harbor, or rather onto the balance sheets of multinationals, leaving not a trace. Of course, now the Inner Harbor has metastasized: where there were once grain piers and hulking warehouses, from Fort McHenry to Canton, you find gleaming condo highrises, marinas, and office towers. But Harborplace itself hasn't changed; in fact, it's become a little tired, almost seedy. Half the interior shop spaces are walled off with paperboard murals: *New Shops & Entertainment Coming Soon!* To walk in here, I'm thinking, is to look at the future in a developer's mind, circa 1978, and to watch the police cars circle the perimeter along Light and Eager Streets, in case Baltimore itself spills in.

Martin is sitting at a window table already — this is the kind of day I'm having — with a salmon-colored legal pad in front of him, looking out over the harbor, which today has a kind of low-wattage electric sheen, and talking into his BlackBerry as I sit down. Tell him that's clever, he's saying, and turns to me and mouths *sorry* — it's clever as a negotiating tactic, but we don't do things that way. You're talking about a currency that lost thirty-five percent of its — yeah. Right. Sheila has the routing number. You don't even have to call HSBC. Just take care of it and email me the confirmation. Got it. Okay. Later. You're not late, he says to me, I'm early. And I apologize. I should have waited at the bar. It's an unfair advantage, sitting down first.

Advantage for what?

He opens his arms wide, so that I can see, at either end of the wingspan of his taupe suit, an immaculate French cuff with an onyx period for a cuff link. You're right, he says. You're absolutely right. I just, you know, I think like a businessman. Instinctively. Like you think like a reporter.

I'm not a reporter.

For good?

Never was. There's no money in it.

He snorts and rubs the corner of his eye with his pinkie, as if bothered by a contact lens or a sudden itch. You work in the nonprofit realm, he says. There's no money in any of it, is there? Wouldn't you like to jump ship to corporate, ultimately?

Corporate radio? I thought it was all run

by computers now.

What about, say, MSNBC?

Why is it, I always want to ask, that strangers assume I'm just waiting for my chance to move to the big time, that promised media-land of fame, wall-to-wall exposure, the news zippers, the endless symphony of dings, bleeps, swooshes, texts, pings, updates, alerts? No one wants a job to keep anymore: I get that. We're all free agents. But do I, in particular, look like I want to be on that treadmill, do I have that look of perpetual dissatisfaction, the hungry one, the up-and-comer? No. It's become a default, I suppose, an assumption, the question that always has to follow *what do you do?*

No, I say, look, I mean, public radio is different. It's a mission. It's about what you want out of your life, I guess you could say. Nobody does it for the money. Really it's a kind of self-flattery, when you get right down to it. But whatever — I fell into it because I need a steady job. It beats pumping gas.

Or working for Fox News.

Right, I say, with a weak laugh. As if that were an option.

It occurs to me that this would be the place where I could clarify what it means to be on the programming side, the administrative side, of radio. But, on the other hand, I'm just enough of an operator not to. It's an old habit, this self-promotion that dares not speak its name. That's how you get into Amherst with an A average.

So what, you just wanted a promotion? That's what this is about, moving back to Baltimore, taking this job?

His BlackBerry buzzes, conveniently, and he checks the screen before shutting it off. I find myself staring, for no good reason, at his ears: perfectly ordinary, like all ears, fascinatingly shell-shaped, overly detailed, a kind of virtuosic molding of cartilage with no obvious rationale. Why do we have earlobes, for example? To be tugged, tickled, pierced? I remember nothing about Martin's ears other than they seemed a little too large for his head, and that he was always tucking his chin-length bangs behind them, especially on the right side. These are the same ears, presumably, only the color has changed.

He's done it; it's real. Here, in the soft mood lighting of an expensive restaurant, and the high, flat light of the sky over the water, in public, framed by two potted olive trees and a trellis of fake grapes, he is inarguable; there are no cracks, no fissures;

he is unquestionably a black man. All at once I feel an intense, pressurized pain in my sinuses, my forehead, eye sockets, across the bridge of my nose: as if my own face has become inflatable and is about to lift off.

You okay? he asks. Hey. Kelly. Look at me. You need a Tylenol or something?

No. I'm all right. Already the pain is receding; I wet my napkin, rub it across my forehead, and it's gone, just as fast as it came.

Thought you were having a panic attack there or something. He laughs, a deep, reverberating belly laugh. Heck, I *knew* you NPR people don't like to talk money, but this is something else.

No, I say, really, it's not about money at all, Martin. I came here because I needed to start over. So to speak. I needed something; this was what came up. I was grieving. That's how it is. Sometimes you have to make quick decisions.

Was it a mistake, coming back to the old town? Too many memories, something like that?

I don't remember nearly as much as I ought to.

Maybe that's a good thing.

I feel bad that we never kept up, I say, trying to sound as loose, as conversational, as possible. It wasn't right, to end things the way we did.

When was that?

When was that? After Alan died, of course. After the funeral. What was that sushi place called, in Towson, the place we ate afterward?

He laughs, weakly, as if I've said something mildly funny, and then stretches out his chin and rotates his head ninety degrees in each direction, a calisthenic stretch, only his eyes are open, peering, checking out the room.

I'm sorry.

Don't be sorry, he says. It's not your problem, is it? Why shouldn't you want to catch up? But listen, here's the thing: if you were me, who would you trust with this kind of information, with this particular secret? It's not like I got one of those scanners and stole someone's Social Security number off a phone call. The way real people do, the standard way. It's not *criminal.* Lord, if it were that easy. Listen, Robin's a good woman. You'll meet her. But she's got a family to protect now. She wouldn't believe it if I told her today. She'd think I'd gone schizophrenic.

You have kids?

Adopted. Twins. Sherry and Tamika. They'll be eight in December. What's wrong? You look skeptical.

I mean, because, biologically —

I'm officially infertile. Unofficially, vasectomized. Those genes are staying put. But look, what I want to talk about right now is *you.*

What about me?

Well, why do you want to get into this mess? Why not just be a good public-radio guy, station director, whatever it is? If it's not the money, then what?

You haven't even told me what you want me to do.

It's right in front of us staring us in the face, so to speak, right? *My* story. I need someone to tell it. To spring it on the world, the way it needs to be done.

What you need is a publicist.

Yeah, maybe, he says. Somewhere along the line. But first I need to have the whole thing worked out. I need a *narrative.* Not just for myself, you see. There are other people involved. Expose one part of the story and you expose it all.

You mean the surgery. The doctors, the hospital, the research —

Of course. And of course you must be curious. But honestly, it's nothing that surprising. Mostly it's been done before. Collagen, rhinoplasty, eyelid changes, voice box alterations. A lot of nipping and tucking. You'd be surprised at how little it takes to make a difference.

And the skin?

Drugs, he says. Dr. Silpa, my doctor, he's got it all figured out. He did decades of research on this stuff. Synthetic melanin. Tailored precisely to the shade you want. It's all proprietary; the patents are in. But look, that's not what I'm talking about; that's just *research*. The technical stuff you can write up in a few pages. What I'm talking about is the story, the emotional logic of the whole thing. That's the crux of the matter. Why me? Why was I the pioneer? In a hundred years this'll be as common as a nose job. But there always has to be a first one. Your job is to prove that I'm not out of my *mind*. Ever heard of Christine Jorgensen?

No.

I'm not surprised. But ask your grandparents — anyone who was around in the Fifties — and they'll know that name. Dimly. Jorgensen was the first person to have a sex change and write a book about it. *A Personal Autobiography.* I got a copy from eBay; it's in my office. I'll show it to you sometime. She was a huge celebrity. When she came back from Denmark — that's where the surgery was — there were crowds at the airport. This was 1952. The tabloids were all over it. She appeared on talk shows. Sid Caesar made jokes about her. She made it a possibility; fifty years later, it's just ordinary business. So I'm the Christine Jorgensen of the twenty-first century. That's the business model. Only now, of course, we have to be global: everywhere at once. Americans are stuck on the idea of race, no question. *Here* we're going to be facing some serious hysteria. At first. But the thing is, there are a hundred other ways to play this in a hundred other places.

Do you have someplace in particular in mind?

He waves a finger at me.

Not till you sign on, he says. Then you get the whole picture.

Sign on to do what? Produce a documentary? Write a book?

All of it. The whole package. I leave the specifics up to you. What I say is, if someone's good at telling a story, the format doesn't really matter. You work in radio, fine. Start with a tape recorder. That's good. People don't notice so much. I mean, *eventually* I want to wind up on Diane Sawyer.

But look, baby steps. You start by doing research. Two months of research, give or take. Here and in Bangkok. You'll be compensated all along the way. *Then* we make a decision about how we're going to blow this thing.

Bangkok, too?

Of course. That's where it all happened! My womb. My chrysalis.

I have to think this through, I say. I mean, I'm *interested.* Who wouldn't be? And I'm your friend. I'm still your friend, right?

You wouldn't be here otherwise, he says.

I mean, *I* wouldn't hire me, necessarily. For this kind of thing. I'm not one of those people with a huge Rolodex.

Come on. You're being modest.

I'd say I know people who know people. At the *Times. The Atlantic. Slate. Politico.* HarperCollins. Simon and Schuster. Are there any sure things in this world? No. Could I make it happen? I guess so.

That's all I need. But my point is, it's *you.* The security has to be absolute. I like to keep things intimate. You're just in the right spot. Couldn't have come along at a better time. I *know* you. Always did. You were always the solid one.

And I have a stake in this story, too.

Yeah, you do. Maybe more than you realize.

He stares at me, and I have the sense — it's something around the eyes, the way the lids pull back — that's he about to indicate something, to make a sign, but he doesn't. Not in any way I can read. What falls into that hole, that chasm, between us? What other than Alan? So that's what it is. And I almost want to blurt out, apropos of nearly nothing, *I'm broken, too.* I'd like to have those balls. But this is me we're talking about, and this is the age of irony, of never making a statement you can't serve up with a sardonic twist. Well, I say, we came from more or less the same place, right? So why you and not me? I mean, not *me* specifically. All of us.

All white people.

Yeah. I mean, out of all the white people on the planet, why would you be the one to go first, to figure this out? That's kind of interesting, wouldn't you say?

Kind of interesting. This is the story of the fucking century.

Our salads arrive, enormous piles of cucumber, tomatoes, olives, dolmas, artichokes, feta, and he gazes at me silently for a moment, until the waitress pulls away.

The future is the future, isn't it? Isn't that

what I look like? And the future is for those who get there first. I'm asking you to think, you know, entrepreneurially. I know that doesn't come natural if you're out of the private sector. But maybe this is your time, Kelly. This could be your moment. God doesn't close a door without opening a window.

You go to church?

Druid Hill Park A.M.E., he says. What, you thought I was going to stay Jewish? Become one of the Black Hebrews, the thirteenth tribe? Come on, he says. Look at me, Kelly. I'm *black.* If you want to be along for this ride, you have to make your peace with it. Black and never going back. Listen to me, I sound like some kind of crazy missionary.

No, I say, not a missionary. A convert. However you want to put it.

To buy myself a moment, I take a sip from my water glass, then tip it back and drain the rest. Nothing, it seems to me, has ever been quite as delicious, quite as necessary, as that glass of ice water, tap water, with its faint medicinal aftertaste: fluoride, chlorine. All the ways we are silently, involuntarily, protected. I think of the bourgeois hippies in Marin County, the ones who refuse vaccinations and believe cancer comes from ra-

63

diomagnetic fields, who buy shipped-in tanks of water, as if they lived in Haiti. How difficult it is for us, for the insulated ones, to understand what it means to risk anything at all. If I could I would run back through the hallway of time and tell my younger self, *stop hedging your bets and learn what it means to have a catastrophe.* But all I have now is the terrible present, the catastrophe over and accomplished, and myself, a squeezed-out rag, a rotten iceberg, and this impossible person staring at me and waiting for me to make up my mind.

Months after the accident, in a particularly courageous moment, I took out the manila envelope of condolence cards, and forced myself to read each one before tossing it into the recycling bin. At the bottom of the stack was a typed sheet of paper without an address or postmark. Or signature. It had been stuffed through the mail slot in the door: there was a rust mark on one crumpled edge. *Emanuel Swedenborg,* it read. *Life goes on even if the vessels that receive life be broken. Life goes into new forms.*

It isn't enough to wait, I'm thinking. In the meantime, I need something to *do.*

Okay, I say, and I hear a little *clink,* a nail, or a penny, dropped into my glass, a signal that time no longer stands still. I'm interested. Count me in. What's the first step, then? Interviews?

Ground rules, he says. Forget you ever knew me before last week. You're a freelance journalist working on a story about black entrepreneurship, okay? Something long, a think piece. For *The New Yorker.* You know what I mean. Act a little naïve, but you still have to know your basic shit.

And how did we meet up?

Through a friend of a friend of a friend. Facebook. LinkedIn. How it always happens these days. First step is you're going to shadow me for a few days. A little tour of my world. Can you take the time off?

I think about Barbara and her silver braids, her enormous, antiquated Dell monitor, and the outrageous numbers scrolling across it.

I'll manage something.

Look, he says, there's something else. I never said anything about what happened to your family.

I'd rather you didn't, if it doesn't come naturally.

No, I was holding back. It wasn't appropriate. But I just have to ask. How are you even standing up? How do you make it through the day?

I don't know, I say, which is, of course, the exact truth. There's no other option, is there? I did all the steps. I saw a therapist. I took medication for a while. You don't just roll up and die, no matter how bad it is. Happiness, you know, it's fragile. Whatever you care about, it's fragile. That's about all I can say. I'm no hero.

Well, now, he says. Welcome to the rest of your life. *O brave new world, that has such people in't!* You know that line?

Of course, I say, startled, everybody knows that line, and then I remember: we read it in high school, junior year, in Mr. Fotheringill's class, "Utopias, Dystopias, and Fantasy Worlds." Jesus Christ, I say, it came true.

Yeah. Without taking the Lord's name in vain and all.

Right. Sorry.

We look at each other and laugh, and I feel tears, fat tears, swelling out of the corners of both eyes: something like terror, and something like joy, for the moment indistinguishable.

6.

As a child I was famous for my lungs: I could swim a length and a half of an Olympic-sized pool holding my breath. On the swim team, in middle school, I won sprints that way, on a single gulp of air, swimming blind, my field of vision turning orange, then black, clamping my teeth around the balloon of air swelling in my mouth. But my favorite trick of all was to pinch my nose and sink slowly to the bottom of the pool, dribbling bubbles like a scuba diver, till I rested, face-up, on the bottom, looking at the surface's glassy underside, the world in reverse. I could stay down there for seven or eight seconds, which in underwater time is forever.

Now, an adult again, I heave myself out of the water, checking to make sure my Downtown Athletic Club guest pass is still attached to my swimsuit, and the bored attendant — a short Latina in a black track suit, who looks too young even to have graduated from high school — leaves off texting long enough to hand me a thick, fleecy towel. I've finished as many laps as I can stand; swimming for exercise — really, any kind of repetitive exercise — bores me to death. What I love about water is being able to slip into it and cut the world off, sealing that membrane of silence. Maybe I was one of those babies who never wanted to leave the womb.

Is it always this quiet in the middle of the day? I ask her.

Nah. Not always. Sometimes there's conventions. But otherwise, I don't know, I guess people have to *work.*

I dry my face, my neck, and work downward, scrubbing my flaccid, untoned arms, my knobby chest with its spray of moles, its odd patches of hair. I haven't been in a pool — haven't been in public, in a bathing suit — in the seven months since August. And like all people of my complexion, who live in northern climes, whose skin barely sees the sun eight months of the year, I've turned the color of white wax or lake ice, the color of an eye clouded by glaucoma.

Martin, in the next lane, hasn't stopped once in twenty minutes. He alternates between freestyle and breaststroke, dipping

68

and ducking his head like an efficient water-bird. I wouldn't call him a natural swimmer — he scissor kicks, and doesn't keep his line straight, veering across into the left side of the lane — but he compensates with stamina. You can see it in his exaggerated shoulders, his fistlike calves. If you weren't here, he told me, I'd go for an hour without a break. It's the only way I can think.

In my bag is the manila folder he handed me as we walked in. Some notes I started taking about a year ago, he said. Thought I'd write a book. Anyway, it might be a place to start. Or it might be pure bullshit.

I dry my hands carefully and open the folder. Ten pages, stapled, like a high school term paper, with his name in the upper left-hand corner.

ON RACIAL IDENTITY DYSPHORIA SYNDROME (RIDS): A SELF-DIAGNOSIS

This paper is offered as an attempt to open up dialogue about one of the major overlooked mental phenomena of our time. I offer it as a personal reflection and an appeal for scientific and pharmaceutical research into this urgent issue.

I have the physical appearance of an African American male. In seven years of living with this appearance, it has never been questioned or found unusual by any of my friends or my intimate partners, including my wife of four years, who is also African American. However, this appearance is based on a carefully created medical procedure that was carried out in Bangkok, Thailand, in 2001–2, by Dr. Binpheloung Silpasuvan and his medical associates. Specifically, Dr. Silpasuvan carried out a series of facial surgeries, scalp surgeries, body-sculpting procedures, and pigmentation treatments, transforming me from my original appearance as a Caucasian-Jewish "white" male into a convincing African American. I returned to the United States with an altered passport and have since presented myself as the child of adoptive white parents, now dead, with no information about my biological roots. This is the story that everyone around me — my wife, my intimate friends, my pastor — takes at face value.

Those are the scientific facts, shocking as they may be. What is even more shocking is the syndrome that drove me to this extreme, costly, and risky decision. I discovered, in my early adulthood (I was twenty-eight at the time of the procedure), that my long history of psychological

70

problems, including depression, agoraphobia, and involvement in illegal activities, was the result of being born in the wrong physical body. I term this "racial identity dysphoria" because I believe it is in many ways similar to the gender dysphoria that is so commonly reported in the news.

What justifies my belief that I was in fact born in the wrong race, as transsexuals claim to be born in the wrong sex? Some will surely believe that this is nothing more than a publicity stunt, or perhaps a perverse expression of "white guilt." The first charge, I believe, is answered by the fact that I have kept my true identity a secret for so long, and that until now I have made no effort to "go public."

Guilt just did not enter into it. Not then, not now. I never felt that it was "bad" or "wrong" to be a white person or a Jew. Of course, I was aware of the history of slavery, the civil rights movement, apartheid, job discrimination, and so on; but I was never led to feel a sense of responsibility or even involvement in the history of black people in America. My father, my only surviving family member (my mother died when I was an infant; he is now also deceased, as of 1995), was a profoundly self-absorbed person, a historian, an archivist, who had very little interest in contemporary society at all. I grew up around black people and have had black friends for as long as I could remember, but I was not, to any great degree, ever made fun of, isolated, mocked, or bullied for being white. In other words, my dysphoria cannot be associated with some trauma, some discreet, explicable, psychological cause, at least not one I can identify. Transsexuals are usually given a battery of tests before they undergo sex-change procedures. Were there to be such a test for racial reassignment surgery, I believe I would pass it.

What I can say is that I always (until the moment my bandages were taken off) knew in some way that I lived in the wrong body. I've spoken with transsexuals (in fact, I came to know a few of them during my time in Thailand, as they are Dr. Silpasuvan's primary base of customers) who've told me exactly the same thing. There is an inchoate sense in which something is wrong long before there is a sense of what could be done to make it right.

It helped (you could say, in a sense at least) that I did not grow up in a judgmental family or a family that really was very

interested in my appearance or what I
might do to modify it. I never experienced
any pressure to dress a certain way or live
up to a certain kind of social appearance.
In fact, whether or not I put on clothes in
the morning was almost entirely up to me.
Furthermore, beginning in my early teenage years, I existed in a social milieu that,
to put it bluntly, tolerated, even encouraged, freaks.

You might have thought that this atmosphere of social liberty (some might even
call it neglect) would have led me to radically alter my appearance in the conventional ways, by dyeing my hair, for example, or getting piercings or tattoos. I
never had any appetite for such things. In
fact, I dressed in a monotonous, unimagi-
native way, barely keeping enough clothes
around to make it from week to week. I
lived inside a cocoon, one could say, poeti-
cally, I suppose, waiting for the real change
to happen.

It was the suicide of my best friend in
the spring of 1993 that caused me to radically rethink the course of my life —

I fold the pages back, quickly, abruptly,
and replace them as they were in my bag.
Martin is as he was, churning through his

daily mile, flashing me the happy grimace of the endorphin addict. My ears fill up with the silence, the ambient non-noise, of all this empty space: lapping water, humming ventilation fans, low, indistinct Muzak, the attendant's flip-flops slapping the tiles as she paces back and forth, waiting to hand out her second towel of the morning. Expensive silence. How much money, it occurs to me just now, we spend to create these sterile bubbles, these vacuums abhorred by nature. How much money Martin spent; and now he wants to be the first with the brick, the needle, to let the pressure out, to let the world come roaring in? It makes no sense; it makes perfect sense. *Look what I've made,* he's saying to me, through the stinging chlorinated air. *I made this. I made this.*

Why have I never had much entrepreneurial spirit, that competitive, world-defining, world-acquiring instinct, so identified with my kind? Wendy always used to find it amusing that young people in Wudeng would come to me for business tips, assuming, in those days, that as an American I would have absorbed supply-side economics in the womb. I had nothing to tell them. This silence, this anticipatory silence, gives me tremors. The future, you could say, gives me tremors. And there Martin is, reaching after it, claiming it, his muscled arms as classic as a Rodin sculpture, or a hood ornament. Pulling me, phaeton-like, with him.

Why, I wonder, why does he even need a story at all? What does he need to explain? Look at his happiness: isn't that reason enough?

— You know what the girl's name is? Finlayson. Finlarson. I think it's Swedish. Anyway, she comes up to me and says, Mr. Perkins, I've got the records you requested now, follow me. And she actually opens up the counter and lets me walk back into the stacks with her. Starts taking down boxes and showing me things. Old deeds, lien records, structural assessments, for the whole area. I wish I'd had a camera, or a backpack; I would have just started squirreling stuff away while her back was turned. And then Vonetta comes around the corner and sees me there and says, *excuse* me! We are *not* allowed to have the public back in here for any reason! And this Finlayson girl says, this is the Office of Public Records, and I'm a state auditor. Can I have your name, please?

I'm surprised Vonetta didn't have a stroke.

She turned purple like a goddamned grape. *Get the hell out of my office!* she says.

Nobody talks to me like that in my office! I am a city of Baltimore employee and a shop steward of AFSCME Local 522! And Finlayson says, I don't care if you're the mayor, I've been instructed to open up these records pursuant to discovery in this case, and if I have to get a marshal in here to do it, I will.

Lee, Martin says, I think you've shot your chances of ever getting anything out of that office ever again.

That's exactly what Vonetta said. She gave me this burning-up look and said, don't *bother* coming in here no more, Lee Perkins, and I said to Karen, looks like I'm going to have to buy you a lot more tickets on that Baltimore–Annapolis bus. And she says, don't bother, just get me a gas card; if I drive I'll get here quicker.

Girl got balls.

She has no idea what she's up against.

Vonetta Harper's going to take early retirement.

Forget that. She's got her little minions, and they're just *trained* in the fine art of playing solitaire and ignoring requests.

What I know so far: Lee Perkins, to my right, is a lawyer, an assistant district attorney, who works on property misuse and real estate fraud. Paul Delacroix, across the table, runs the ESPN office at Camden Yards. Marshall Haber, next to Martin, teaches history at the University of Maryland, Baltimore County. We call ourselves the Chamber of Commerce, Marshall said to me, as we were being introduced. That way we can expense the meal. We're one another's clients. On paper, that is. Or sources, in my case. I view this as research. Weekly research at the DAC. It's on my calendar.

For the most part it's as if I wasn't there at all. I sit back from the table, pad in my lap, clicking and unclicking my pen under the table, but writing only a few words, names, and phrases. When Martin explained what I was doing, they nodded, and Paul said, Martin Wilkinson, spokesman for the Talented Tenth, which produced a mild rumble of laughter.

Kelly, Marshall says, turning to me now, what you need to know about Vonetta — I've tangled with her, too — is that she's the most powerful woman in Baltimore. Hands down. God love her, she may be a tyrant, but she knows everything about everything. You can't register a deed or file a property transfer or a zoning request without her. You know in that TV show, *The Wire,* they had all that stuff about drug dealers and property developers? That was all based on her office. She was pissed because they wouldn't give her a walk-on part. Tried to revoke their filming permits.

That was her one shot at the big time, Paul says. She's too ugly for reality TV, God knows. Else she'd go on *The Apprentice* and be the Bad Black Lady, like that other one, the crazy one.

Let's change the subject, Martin says. We increase her power by talking about her, right? Everyone knows Vonetta's all reputation. A dictatorship of one.

Baltimore, the city of fiefs.

It's not like it's so different other places. All politics is local, you know that saying? Anyway, people fight because the stakes are so low. If you had a *proper* city, you know, a *working* city, where landlords didn't just walk away from whole blocks at a time, and the government wasn't always going around declaring X property derelict and Y property uninhabitable —

You're saying if people actually wanted to live here.

If people wanted to use the *existing* housing stock, and not knock everything down and build another ridiculous condo, or fill in the harbor so they can get a better view of the Domino's sign —

If we had a taxable tax base, and not fifty percent of cash flow in the city in the underground economy —

If the government actually *gave* a shit, instead of just putting up Empowerment Zone this and School of Excellence that —

Well, I guess that about sums it up, Marshall says. Y'all can go home now. I'll just sit down and make sure Kelly here gets all that down on paper. Ninety-five theses on the future of Baltimore.

That's just boring as shit. No way *The New Yorker*'s going to print that. Am I right?

I don't know what they'll print, I say. I'll just write what I hear, and they can sort it out, one way or another.

That's a polite answer, Marshall says, but not a very convincing one. You're saying you don't have a slant?

Not this early in the game.

Well, you must have pitched them something.

I wanted to write about black entrepreneurs, I say, because most people don't know they exist. The culture doesn't seem to allow for them.

Which culture do you mean?

Mainstream culture.

Right, but that's a tricky concept, isn't it? Because you're not just talking about numbers. Believe me. The numbers are on *my* side. People watch sports, the local news, maybe some talk radio, Rush, Howard Stern —

Tom Joyner, Paul says.

— but that's not what you're talking about. Even if you're being as broad as possible, you're still talking about the thinking person's news.

What you saying, Lee says, cracking a smile, black people don't *think*?

You're talking about a minority to begin with, Paul continues, the people who think *anything* about *black entrepreneurs,* who even know for sure what the word *entrepreneurs* means.

Yeah, Marshall says, but it's a powerful minority.

No doubt, Paul says. And that's what *The New Yorker* is all about. Talking to the five percent of the population that makes decisions.

My dad read *The New Yorker,* Lee says. Every week. Read it in the library. Then later my mom started bringing it home from one of the houses she cleaned. We had a stack of them in the bathroom. It all started with the guy who wrote about Arthur Ashe, what was his name, McPhee? My dad *loved* that book about Arthur Ashe. Even made me read it.

It's the exception that proves the rule.

No, Marshall says, it's not that simple, Paul. In a democracy, in an open society, anyone can have an intellectual life. We forget that. Yeah, it doesn't show up in the Nielsen ratings. Those people don't *do* Nielsen ratings. They're not in the focus groups. You know, when I was a kid, when they started busing over on Greenmount, every day I was the first one at the bus stop, and this white lady bus driver — I'm talking about six-thirty in the morning — would be sitting there drinking her coffee and reading *Das Kapital.* I'm not kidding. I never forgot it.

So is that like Huey P. Newton reading *The Republic* or what? Knowledge is power? Paul chortles, leans back in his padded chair, and nods gravely as the waitress sets an egg-salad sandwich in front of him. Listen, he says, biting the tip off his dill spear, I got a new one for you. Power is power, knowledge is, what do they call it? *Edutainment.*

Tell that to the kids at Dunbar.

No, Paul says, but look, I'm serious. You can talk all you want about the intellectual life, and you're damn right, there's *thinking* people everywhere, in every walk, but *The*

81

New Yorker, I mean, pick it up, it's like reading *Playboy* for the interviews, only in reverse, because the thing about *The New Yorker* is that the ads are the porn. You know those little tiny ads they have, like, for the desk that's hand-carved by Shakers in Wisconsin, and costs five thousand dollars? It's a lifestyle magazine for people who think they're too good for a lifestyle magazine. That's some subtle shit right there, but it's the truth.

So what's he supposed to do? Marshall asks. Write for *USA Today?* You think they print fifteen-thousand-word articles about the black middle class?

Kelly, Paul says, you know I'm not casting no aspersions, right? I'm just telling it like it is. We're all in some kind of business. Shit, no, I think this article's a great idea, it's just, you know, don't expect people to line up and start singing "Kumbaya."

They're waiting for me to say something: there's a pocket of silence over the table, the vacuum of a conversation bubble popping, the lid lifted off a foaming pot. Martin, who's said nothing, busies himself with dressing his chicken Caesar, adding extra pepper, flicking a stray crouton off the tablecloth.

I wish I'd brought my tape recorder, I say,

lamely. This is all excellent. This is exactly what I was hoping for. An honest conversation.

Just quote me off the record, Lee says. Please. I mean it. I don't need any more flak from Weinblatt — that's my DA. Anyway, I'm not authorized. You've got to put *an official in the district attorney's office speaking on background.* Don't even call me an ADA, or he'll start doing process of elimination.

Likewise for me, Paul says. I mean, you can use my name, just don't put ESPN in there anywhere. They've got special search engines that find that stuff. If my name's next to ESPN, I'm a company spokesperson. Which would mean my ass, in this case.

You see, Kelly, Marshall says, this is what you're going to get. No offense, people, but look at us, right, prominent pillars of the community and whatnot, and we *still* don't want to be identified as what we are. Successful Black People. You know what my coach at City College used to say? A black man goes downtown and buys a suit at Jos. A. Bank, and you know what it comes with? A bull's-eye on the back.

Marshall, Martin says, finally, and every head turns to look at him. *Mar*shall, he says, again, with a little dip of emphasis, let's not do this.

Do what?

The whole victim thing.

I'm not, Marshall says. I'm making a factual observation. Read the statistics if you don't believe me. Psychologically, black people are less likely to feel secure. *Financially,* black people are less likely to feel secure. Sociologically —

What I'm saying here is, let's take that as understood, okay? Let's treat that as the background. That's what Kelly's trying to do here.

Marshall laughs, an unexpectedly shrill, reedy laugh. I don't know, he says, are we there yet? Can we really treat that as *back*ground? What, because of Obama?

No. Not because of Obama. Because it's a much bigger world than it used to be. Because we have so much more *power,* globally, than we think we do.

This is what you're going to hear from him, Lee says to me. Blackness as a brand. As a *strategy.* I think that shit is stark crazy, but what do I know? I'm just a lawyer.

Jay-Z's doing it, Paul says. The whole global brand thing. You look at the numbers for Rocawear, sixty percent's overseas.

Yeah, Martin says. Jay-Z, that's one model.

But it's so much more than that.

He takes a long sip of iced tea, dabs his lips with a still-folded napkin.

So? Marshall asks.

So? You want me to give away all my trade secrets?

Don't be paranoid, Bill Gates, Paul says. We're not in your business.

Everyone's going to be in my business eventually. But look, that's beside the point. What I'm saying, *now,* is, we need more brothers looking overseas for opportunities. It's a big world full of very small niches.

You know what he does for a living? Marshall asks me. Has he told you what he sells?

Martin exchanges a glance with me across the table.

Electronics, I say. Specialized electronics. I'm not an expert —

Oh, come on, he hasn't given you the sales pitch yet? He sells *unlocked cell phones.* Open-platform computers. Self-replicating proxy servers. Isn't that right? What do you call it, spyware?

Not spyware. He shrugs. Geekware, maybe. Stuff people want so that they can get around Microsoft and Verizon. I don't even understand some of it myself. I have a technical lady out in Mountainview who handles that. Me, I just do the buying and selling. It's low-volume, big-margin sales. My customers are the kind of rich techies who want all the latest gadgets, prototypes, the stuff you can only get over in Asia, but they want it sold to them by somebody who speaks American, who operates with a friendly face. They want to have a *guy.* A hookup. Whatever. I'm not saying it's easy money, but it's not exactly the salt mines, either. Eventually, when the brand's established, I'll sell out and move on. I'm into business, not *a* business. If I could tell one thing to the kids at Dunbar, it's that. Capital flows. Always be on the move.

That Zig Ziglar shit, Lee says. Always be selling. You can get it off a motivational poster.

No, Martin says, carefully, it's not that. I'm not talking some self-esteem crap. And I'm not just talking about *money.* Success is more than money.

Power, then. Influence.

Connectedness, he says. To be intractable. Undismissable. *Visible.*

You writing this down? Paul asks me. Or do you just have one of those automatic, photographic memories?

Marshall fixes me with a newly interested look.

86

You know, he says to Martin, it must be nice to have a Boswell. An amanuensis. That's seriously old school. I should look into getting one myself.

You lost me, Lee says. Ama-what?

Amanuensis, Martin says. Someone who follows you around and writes down everything you say. I could sell you one, you know. A digital voice recorder. I've got one the size of a toothpick for a hundred ninety-nine.

Hear that? Marshall turns to me. You're superannuated, he says, with shining eyes, a pretense of malice that is itself malicious. You're fired. Go home.

7.

I'm going to say something here that should come as no surprise, at least not to those of my generation, born after the civil rights movement had shrunk to pages 263–67 of *American Panoramas,* and raised, for the most part, in the Eighties, watching Bill Cosby sell Pudding Pops on TV: my education in blackness, in the experience of black people in America, began one hot summer afternoon in 1989, in sticky-floored Theater C at the Chestnut Hill Mall 13, with Spike Lee's *Do the Right Thing.*

Of course I had heard rap before. I knew, in a kind of academic way, what a crack addict was, and I knew a great deal about Martin Luther King: my parents' first date was at the March on Washington in 1963. But in the world I lived in before I moved to Baltimore — Newton, Massachusetts, *not* Boston, unless you count the occasional trip to the Aquarium or Faneuil Hall — the only black people I saw regularly were babysitters and maids. My parents were ardent Democrats, classic northeastern Waspy liberals, who nonetheless, characteristically, chose to live in a neighborhood populated with people exactly like themselves — plus a margin of Chinese, Indian, Thai, and garden-variety reform Ashkenazim — for the schools, the parks, the playgrounds, the excellent restaurants.

Of course it wasn't Alabama, it wasn't 1955; there were always a few black kids, a photogenic sprinkling. Tiffany and Wesley Roberts, whose father was Duane Roberts, the Celtics point guard, were one year ahead of me at Passing Brook Elementary. Tiffany was grasshopper-legged, a natural sprinter, an indefatigable four-square champion; Wesley spent recesses under the pines at the far end of the soccer field, trading stickers, buttons, Garbage Pail Kids, baseball cards, Dungeons & Dragons imaginary weapons — whatever currency of the moment.

That was where I came to know him, briefly, in third grade, before his dad was traded to the SuperSonics. He sat hunched over, legs folded, stretching out the hem of his long T-shirt like a table, displaying some treasure — a folder of Reggie Jackson cards from every season, a Don Mattingly rookie card, a mint Topps pack of the 1979 Pirates — and daring the rest of us to make an offer. It wasn't fun, exactly, being so utterly outmatched, but Wesley knew how to work the margins, trading cards he didn't need for the best we had to offer. He stared into space, over our shoulders, reciting statistics in a listless, deadpan voice, showing why his cards were always worth more, had more long-term potential; he used words like *investment* and *dividends.* Today we might give him a diagnosis — Asperger's, mild autism, social anxiety disorder — but no one at the time, as far as I can recall, saw anything wrong. Never did anyone in that circle refer to him as *black.* Creatures of instinct, we didn't care about the color of his skin, or the content of his character; we cared about his stuff. Only later did it occur to me that that was why he sought us out, and perhaps why he became — I Googled him once, in idle curiosity, a few years ago — a venture capitalist seeding start-ups and then selling them to Microsoft. He's grown into his looks now; he and his father have a foundation together that runs after-school sports programs in Seattle.

This was the life I was raised to have, racially speaking, the life my parents had, post-1973, when they left Back Bay for the suburbs: the life of a Good White Person. I was meant to have a few, select, black friends — peers, confidants, individuals — a number of acquaintances, business associates, secretaries, hygienists, a few charities, to which I would give generously, as much as possible, and a broad, sympathetic, detached view of the continuing struggles of African Americans to achieve the long-delayed goals of full civic participation, low birth rates, ascension to the middle glass, hiring equity, educational parity, and so, so, so, on, on, on. I was supposed to live with the frisson of guilt that comes from owning an expensive, elaborate security system, and to mention, at parties, that rates of incarceration for black males are six times the national average. I was supposed to organize for Obama, and own at least ten separate items of Obama paraphernalia, and proudly display my *Yes We Did* postcard on my refrigerator for all of 2009 and 2010, and feel that slow-fading flush of warmth and exultation, as if someone had reached out and grasped my hand, and held it, a squeeze as a substitute for an embrace. This was the life, until a few weeks ago, that I thought I was having. I should have known better.

1989 — a number, another summer — sound of the funky drummer!

What did I hear, that first time, when Donald Harrison's rendition of "Lift Every Voice" ended, and "Fight the Power" roared to life, in a cacophony of scratches, samples, and found noise, before that first deep bass hit, that nearly lifted me out of my chair? Something like the screeching of brakes, something like a jet plane taking off: that's what the Bomb Squad sounded like to a fourteen-year-old in 1989, who was used to the tinny, Casio-looped beats on Eighties rap. Even before the story began, the credits were a body blow — the sheer brightness of the colors, the insistent, defiant, angry sidewalk dancing of Rosie Perez, in a pink miniskirt and tights, in shiny boxer's trunks, bobbing and weaving. Everything that came after was a little after the fact of that first song. *Freedom of speech is freedom of death. Elvis was a hero to most. But he never meant shit to me.*

I was listening. I was paying attention.

It wasn't long after that that the few black kids at Newton South Middle started wearing T-shirts that said *It's a black thing — you wouldn't understand.* By this time I had graduated from the haze of childhood and had begun hanging out, whenever I could, in Harvard Square, and particularly at Newbury Comics, the epicenter of cool. My father was just then negotiating the terms of his new job at Black & Decker in Baltimore — he was, is, an electrical engineer, who invents power-saving devices for small appliances — and I knew my world was shifting, that Newton was already history, *over*, and I started turning my attention to magazines: *SPIN, Rolling Stone, Alternative Press, Maximumrocknroll, Vibe, The Source.* And it was in *SPIN* that I read an interview with Chuck D that contained the sentence *white liberals aren't our salvation, they're the problem.*

It had never occurred to me that I was someone else's problem.

With *Do the Right Thing* came Public Enemy. After Public Enemy came N.W.A., Niggaz With Attitude. And at the same moment, the Native Tongues, De La Soul, A Tribe Called Quest, X-Clan, Del the Funky Homosapien, The Pharcyde, Black Sheep, Arrested Development. Ice-T, Ice Cube, Onyx. In the early Nineties, hip-hop was everywhere but invisible — still controversial, still not quite accepted even as music, still hardly on the radio, and therefore an indispensable part of a teenager's education. By the time I was sixteen I was buying bootleg tapes of every new album, $5 a pop, and I could repeat whole songs, whole sides of albums. It was the omega to punk's alpha, the nastiness to our earnestness. *Ends justifies the means, that's the system, so I don't celebrate no bullshit Thanksgiving.* I listened to it hypnotically, miming the gestures in traffic on the way to school, spraying my imaginary MAC-10 through the windshield. *We're the number-one crew in the area, make a move for your gat and I'll bury ya.*

This shit is pathetic, my friend Ayala Kauffmann said, once, a year later, when I was giving her a ride to school. She was biracial, though it was easy to miss; with a mop of brown curls, a nose ring, and an Indian-print blouse she could have been any other Rebekah, Aviva, or Dasi. Hinjews, Mexijews, Sephardi ex-kibbutzniks — at Willow we had them all. Her father had disappeared when she was a baby, leaving nothing to her, not even his name, and her mother had remarried Ira Kauffmann, a balding, kindly Reform rabbi with fishy eyes.

I mean, she said, I get it. I get De La Soul. Everybody loves De La Soul. But this is just like looking at *Hustler.* It's *gross.* And it's grosser still because it's *you.* Nobody meant this for you. Or if they did, it's just a classic retread minstrel show. *Look at the bad black man!* You're getting played. I can't believe you would pay money for this shit.

I didn't. Well, not much, anyway.

And you think that makes it okay?

Just because you're not listening to it doesn't mean it's not out there, I said. Wouldn't you rather know?

What, this is supposed to be my direct line from the ghetto?

Chuck D says hip-hop is the black world's CNN.

You're not the black world. You're not *black,* don't you get it? And listening to this shit doesn't change that. It just makes you a parasite. It would be one thing if you actually *knew* any black people. And I don't count.

That's really fair. You get to be the authority, but yet you don't count.

You don't get to decide what's fair, she said. Don't you understand? She ejected the tape, before I could stop her, and flipped it into the backseat, among the Subway wrappers and 7-Eleven coffee cups, the broken microphone stand, and the guitar-string envelopes. You get to shut up, she said. That's your special job. You get to not have rights for a change. Shut up and go away and leave black people *alone,* for once.

I didn't listen. Or maybe, in some sense, I did.

At Willow, in place of community service, we had what we called *volunteer jobs,* assigned by the principal's office, six hours a week minimum. And the black people I knew in any true sense — any real recognition, any actual conversation — were all from my VJ shifts downtown: soup kitchen, sophomore year; food pantry, junior year; community health clinic, senior year. Mostly my supervisors were solemn, tight-mouthed men, ex-cons, Vietnam vets, halfway-house residents, who hardly bothered to learn my name; but there were always others, who asked why I wore my hair that way, who wanted to know how many hours of community service I'd been sentenced to, and what I'd done to deserve it; who offered me menthol cigarettes, which I graciously, nauseously accepted, who told me something about doing a month in the hole at Lorton, or being shot out of a helicopter in Khe Sanh.

And then there was James, a category of his own. James supervised a whole crew of prep school do-gooders — PSDGs, that was his term — at the Belinda Matthews Memorial Food Pantry on Saturday mornings, teaching us how to process a hundred pounds of cast-off lettuce, how to stack boxes of government cheese, how to load a shopping bag so it wouldn't split. He stood a head taller than most of us, six-five, in an army jacket, with a shining bald dome, a crocheted skullcap, and a silvery soul patch, like an aging hero from a Melvin Van Peebles movie. He told us he'd been in the same City College class with Kurt Schmoke, then the mayor; after that, he'd turned down a scholarship to Howard, traveled the country playing bass in an R&B band, and spent some time with the Peoples Temple in California, years before Jonestown. But I knew, even then, he said, more than once, I knew that Jim Jones was a crazy motherfucker. It was well *known* that he would screw anything that moved, anybody that came within ten feet. Man or woman. That was how he did it, you know. Everybody felt dirty. Everybody was compromised. Closer you get, the more compromised. So I packed my bags and got out of that scene.

And then what? Alan once asked him. We were on the same shift, in the fall of our junior year; we'd go straight from pitching rotten tomatoes to band practice. What'd you do then, after Jim Jones? How'd you get back to Baltimore?

James palmed a cantaloupe from a wax-board crate, sniffed it, like a chef looking for the peak of ripeness. Son, he said, looking straight at Alan, I did cocaine. Nothing but cocaine for fifteen years. You hear? Bought, sold, sniffed, ate, shot up, smoked, stuck it on my gums, stuck it up my ass once, I was that desperate. Took it into prison with me, took it right up to the moment I left. Fifteen years in the white mountains. Six of them in jail. Then I found God, and here we are.

I guess we should take that as a warning, Alan said.

No, James said, and he coughed, politely, to keep from laughing. I'm not here as a warning. Not to you.

He was a Muslim, though he rarely discussed it; not Nation of Islam, but NBIM, which, he told me once, stood for New Baltimore Integrated Mosque, a special congregation where Arabs and Pakistanis and black people all worshipped together. Occasionally, if I arrived early enough, I found him doing morning prayers outside in the empty lot next to the food pantry's row house. *Inshallah,* he always said, when we talked about how many bags we'd distribute that day, and Alan and I started doing it, too, as a joke, first, and then without thinking. *Inshallah,* we could sell fifteen T-shirts. *Inshallah,* if you get into Wesleyan.

It happened to be in the same moment that I came to know James that I read *The Autobiography of Malcolm X* for the first time, and came upon the rapper Paris, who referred casually to *blue-eyed devils* and *sons of Yacub,* as if talking about his uncle Bill from Indiana. At the Black Cat bookstore on Read Street, I found copies of *The Final Call* and the *New Afrikan Party Newsletter,* and sat reading, for an entire Sunday afternoon, one column of tiny print after another, mesmerized by explanations of how the downfall of White Amerikkka could be predicted by the phases of the sun, how school health clinics and Planned Parenthood were agents of genocide, how black people could use shea butter to boost their natural immunity to AIDS.

There was something refreshing about being called a devil. This was in 1991, at the very peak of the crack wars, when Baltimore was Murder Capital for the first time; I had just gotten my license, and I drove myself, alone, or sometimes with Alan, down to the food pantry twice or three times a week, and the fact of being independent changed everything I saw, as if I had to own the city for the first time, having to find my own parking spaces in it. It wasn't a matter of fear, though I carried Mace with me everywhere, wore my wallet and keys on a biker chain, and checked the backseat and trunk of the car religiously, as carjackers were known to put a gun to your head from behind as you drove. What astonished me was how easily I could slip past the box hedges and pin oaks of Roland Park, the Victorians and Colonials and Tudors prim and quiet, and into the derelict corridors, the bombed-out storefronts, the vacants, the dealers in puffy jackets standing sentry on every corner, the Korean liquor stores with armored grates and triple-thick glass in front of the register. This was a drive of ten minutes. It is still, come to think of it, a drive of ten minutes. This geography, I thought, was a crime. Someone had given me a postcard of Proudhon that I taped to my locker: *Property is theft.* How could it be anything else? How could I be anything other than a criminal, by the fact of my pimply existence?

I even started doing it with Alan. If gay people could be queers, what was the harm? What up, devil? I said to him once, within James's earshot, and James turned around.

Did you just say what I think you said?

You're right, Alan said. It's not funny.

You don't hear me calling anyone around here a nigger, do you?

You could if you wanted to.

Thanks, James said. Thanks for giving your permission.

That's not what I meant —

Lookit here, he snapped. We got a job to do. I watched, so clearly, as all his affection for us folded up in his face like a fan. No names, no name-calling.

Well, we are, aren't we?

Aren't we what?

Aren't we the devil? I mean, aren't we the *problem*?

He shrugged.

Choose, he said. Be the devil if you want. What you are right *now* is a pain in my ass who can't sort tomatoes worth a damn. This look ripe to you? Get back to your job, okay? Just do your *job*.

In October of the following year, our senior year, James was shot twice in the head in his apartment above the food pantry, and the building was torched; when I drove down, that same afternoon, it was still smoking, wound around with police tape, and the roof had caved in. It reminded me of photographs of the ruins of Europe in the Second World War. I recognized one of our weekly clients, Dawson, wheeling a shopping cart filled with neatly sorted bags of beer bottles and aluminum cans. Hell, he said, you didn't know? Motherfucker was selling drugs out of there the whole time. Wednesday through Friday, when the pantry was closed. Went in there one time myself, see if I could get me some extra cans of beans. Didn't want none of *those* kinds of beans, feel me? Yeah, he had a good thing going there for a while.

I don't believe it, I said.

Then forget it, he said. Forget I said anything. Don't matter now, do it? Still dead. Still fucked it up for the rest of us. Got to go down to Jonah House now, stand in line.

I'll give you a ride, I said. It felt, obscurely, like being at the end of a TV movie; I was supposed to have learned something. I was supposed to be changed. Black people's lives, I should have said, facing the camera, are no more expressive of statistics than anyone else's. Who am I, who are *you,* to go looking in this horror for a pattern?

Naw, Dawson said. Can't leave the cart.

Put it in the trunk.

Everything's going to turn out all right, he

said, pushing away from me. Trust in the Lord. You hear me?

When I went to college I snapped out of my love of hip-hop, as if out of a dream. Someone looked at my tape collection and laughed. Who are you supposed to be, homeboy? I dumped them all in a box and began buying CDs instead — Pavement, The Spinanes, Stereolab, Liz Phair. I grew a goatee, developed a taste for expensive coffee, read Baudrillard and John Ashbery, read Ginsberg and Williams and Pound, read Rexroth and Kerouac and D. T. Suzuki, and began getting up at seven-thirty for daily Chinese classes.

Was I fleeing from something? Was I certain why I loved this new language, with its four tones and eighty thousand characters, its unshakable alienness, its irreconcilability with any language, any world, I knew? Is that even a question? Did any of us know why, given all our advantages, our entitlements, our good study habits and chemically inflated self-esteem, we were still so prone to spastic fits of despair, why we sought out more and more exotic ways of getting high, why we wore Sanskrit rings and tribal tattoos, salon-styled dreadlocks and Japanese see-through raincoats? How could it be running away, when it was nothing more than running in place? How could it be guilt, when the air was so thick with good intentions, with accusations and counter-accusations?

All I know is this: when I came home, I never went downtown. I tore my *Illmatic* poster off my bedroom wall and used the back for calligraphy practice. In a fit of orderly pique, I carted off the contents of my high school bookcase — *Invisible Man, Native Son, The Fire Next Time, The Autobiography of Malcolm X, Soul Brother, Black Like Me, Black Ice, I Know Why the Caged Bird Sings* — to the Salvation Army. I waited, listening, for the thunderclap, the world splitting open under my feet, and heard only the tinkling of the Good Humor truck down the block, the moan of Mr. Takematsu's aging lawn mower over the backyard fence. I thought of my parents' earnest faces, of my father, clean-shaven, playing the guitar for my kindergarten class — *If I had a hammer, I'd hammer out danger . . . I'd hammer out love between my brothers and my sisters all over this land* — and their sententious, balsamic-sprinkling, Chablis-swilling, late middle age, their faces puckered with concern over the prospect that I would go off to China and become a mercenary investment banker. How vicious and unfair to blame them for my lack of imagination, with the short and pathetic half-life of my good intentions! When all I wanted, all any of us wanted, was to go back to that childlike state, hand-holding, faces raised to the words of the beatific saint, promising us that this story, like all good stories, had an ending, that everything was going to be okay.

What is there in Mookie's face, when he staggers away from the scene of Radio Raheem's death, picks up the garbage can, and carries it, like a javelin thrower, to its launching point, to the window of Sal's Famous? Why, that is, doesn't he have any expression at all? As if he's watching his life flash by on TV. As if he's watching an old, old movie. His whole body sags with the effort of acting out the script. And I, even then, even at fourteen, knew that I was supposed to hate him, and couldn't. And wanted to *be* him, and couldn't. *Here we go again,* his face says. *I don't want you to witness this.* He is alone. He doesn't want to be the Representative Black Man. But he can't be anything else. The credits roll, I wipe my popcorn-greasy hands on my shorts. I walk out of the theater in a daze.

I've glimpsed something. But a glimpse, as it turns out, is not enough.

I lived in white dreamtime. I have been living in white dreamtime. And the problem with dreaming, the epistemological problem, is: when you think you've woken up, have you really? Is this waking, or a deeper, more profound state of sleep, the state of the most vivid and palpable dreams?

There's something else I forgot. Or, rather, something else I can't remember. I can't remember what caused me to fight the boy; I was seven, we were at some school summer camp, not in Newton but nearby, he appeared out of nowhere, and like that we were grappling in the dust, the only fight I'd had in my life up to that time. He elbowed me in the shoulder, pushed me over, and walked off; I was blinded, howling. That nigger, I said, when my counselor picked me up, and he put me down immediately and pinned me against the wall by my shoulders. Don't *ever* say that again, he said. He had greasy shoulder-length black hair, a knobby nose, a Ziggy Stardust T-shirt fraying at the collar. You understand? Say it again and I'll beat the shit out of you myself. I'll fucking *kill* you. You understand?

How is anyone supposed to understand?

Thus ends my confession.

8.

When I interviewed for the job at WBCC last fall, the Monday of Thanksgiving week, the board could have paid for me to take a cab from the airport, or, more likely — this is public radio — instructed me to take the MARC train and a cab to my hotel. They didn't. Winnifred Brinton-Cox, the chairwoman, met me at the baggage claim and drove me into town herself, a trip of nearly three hours in afternoon traffic. It was a strange and uncomfortable position, sitting inches away from a stranger who was offering me a job; it meant my interview began the minute I stepped off the plane. That was — that is — Winnifred's style. She was born in Negril, moved to Brooklyn as a child, but she still speaks with West Indian flourishes, a kind of expansive, jovial quality combined with a certain stiff English hauteur, and she has a beaming smile that she bestows on all sentences equally, whether she's delivering good news or saying something cruel and gratuitous. Her day job is in community affairs for the Johns Hopkins Medical Centers, which, as I understand it, entails explaining to very poor people why their houses have to be demolished to build the world's most advanced, most expensive hospital. It's hard to be on the side of progress, she told me, when I asked her about it. On the side of development. On the side of the inevitable. But God didn't put me on this earth to be Santa Claus.

It was within fifteen minutes of leaving the airport that she told me the job was mine, if I wanted it; I was the most qualified candidate and the most exciting. What I like about you is that you have an outside perspective, she said. You come from a place of success. Efficiency. A functional station structure.

You make that sound exotic.

You'd be surprised, she said. The question is, are *you* ready to be unpopular? Because let me make a prediction. If you take this job, no one's going to invite you out for happy hour. You might not even get a birthday card.

If you're asking if I depend on my work for self-esteem, I said, the answer is no. Work is work.

You sure about that? she asked. You sure that hasn't, eh, *changed*?

I'd forgotten that in my phone interview with the board, when asked why I wanted to make a move, I'd explained, in the briefest possible terms, what had happened with Wendy and Meimei.

Sorry to be so direct, she said. But I want you to think this through. These people smell indecision, understand?

I'm not undecided, I said, a patent lie. I want this job. I'm here.

Two nights ago Winnifred called me at eight forty-five — on the late side, for a business call, but I had nothing better to do, as she surely guessed. I'm wondering if you could come down for a quick breakfast meeting, she said. Henry's, at eight sharp?

There was no way I could refuse, of course, though I longed for the days of day-care drop-offs and family responsibilities, so painfully, so wetly, that I could hardly hold up the phone.

When I turn around the pastry counter into Henry's seating area I see immediately that this is no ordinary meeting: Winnifred is squeezed into a corner table alongside Walter Avery, the college president, whom I've met only once before, and a tall stranger in a navy blazer and polo shirt, a pudgy, bulbous-nosed man in his forties who looks like a high school football coach, complete with bristly red hair and a sawtooth mustache. They have in front of them a platter of assorted danishes, croissants, pecan rolls, bâtards, and scones, and the table is already scattered with crumbs and wadded napkins lumped from coffee spills.

Kelly, Winnifred says, let me introduce you to Ron Dwyer. Ron, Kelly.

Kelly's a good Irish name, Ron says, pumping my hand.

I think my parents chose it out of a hat. We're Dutch and German all the way back.

New Amsterdam Dutch?

Ellis Island.

I can't imagine why we're having a conversation about genealogy in front of two African Americans, but Ron looks pleased to have the details in order.

Kelly, Walter says, Winnifred's told me that you're scheduled to have a meeting with the staff this week about the accreditation issue, and so I felt we needed to have this conversation first, just so that there's no miscommunication anywhere along the line. I'll keep it simple, because I know you have places to be. BCC has opted to embrace a new arrangement for the WBCC license. This is an opportunity we've been thinking about for a while, and the letter from NPR gave us a window of time. Now we're about to act.

Walter is also a big man, with very wide features — his nose in particular is like a lump of pancake batter dropped onto the griddle of his face — and I have the sensation, at this moment, of being a place kicker facing three linebackers across the line of scrimmage. All three of them have hunkered down at the same moment, waiting to hear what I will say, and I feel as if they could upend the table at any moment and reach out for my throat.

I'm sorry, Walter, I say — what else can I say? — can you clarify that a little? I don't quite follow.

BCC is selling the station, Winnifred says, with one of her characteristic Teflon smiles. It's a very difficult decision, and one I've questioned all the way along the line. But in the end I think it's a disservice to the community and the college to keep things going the way they are.

You can't sell a public radio station, I say. I mean, you know that, right? The FCC —

Walter holds up a long and impressive hand. No lecture needed, he says. We're not selling anything. Winnifred spoke imprecisely. We're *trading* the existing WBCC, 107.9 FM, to WATB, 930 AM, and the owner of WATB, Ron here —

Ron, Ron says, pleased again to be speaking of himself in the third person, only as a representative of PureLine Communications —

— is going to assume the WBCC frequency for a new format.

Sports-talk-traffic-weather.

NPR doesn't license AM-only stations, I say. What's the WATB transmitter like, anyway?

Two thousand watts.

That's a fifth our size, and we're tiny as it is.

Kelly, Winnifred says, let's be honest here. I know this must be a shock, though I did, of course, *warn* you that the situation at WBCC was unstable when you took the job. Baltimore isn't a large enough market for two NPR stations. The letter more or less said that. Our expectation for the new WATB will be more along the lines of a true college radio station, staffed primarily by students and interns with a very small professional leadership.

Hold on, Walter says, we're putting the cart somewhat before the horse here. The first thing you're worried about, no doubt, is your own future and your family's future.

As soon as he says it, an innocent slip, a bit of rhetorical filler natural to anyone who fires people often, the mortification spreads over his face like a port-wine stain. I was very open and honest during my interview about what I called, for lack of a better word, my *life situation.* I thought it would win me sympathy, which, of course, it did.

Okay, I say, trying to distract him. I get what you mean. No offense taken. Lay it out, Walter.

You're a very understanding person, Kelly. And we're willing to offer you three options. One, keep your role at WATB. We will keep your existing contract and renegotiate when it comes up for renewal. Two, take a severance package now. Three months fully paid, COBRA after that, with full TIAA-CREF contributions, the whole nine yards. And a nondisclosure clause, of course. Three, assume a new role at the new WBCC.

What new role?

Assistant PD, Ron says. We're confident that someone as enterprising as you obviously can make the switch to commercial without too much difficulty. Of course, the staff will be much smaller. Most of our programming is national feed. Primarily, you'll be in charge of sales to the local market.

Who's going to tell the staff?

Walter clears his throat. I'm leaving tomorrow for Venezuela, he says. It's a fact-finding trip organized by the mayor. Intercultural exchange. We're thinking about doing a sister city down there. So unfortunately I'm out. Winnifred will go with you, I think, if there's time in her schedule.

I won't do it alone, I say. It's not right. It's immoral. I feel that I was hired under false pretenses, I'll say that right now.

So I assume that means you're taking the severance?

You can say what you want about WBCC, I say, but public radio isn't something to be trifled with. *Morning Edition* is the top-rated morning drive show in greater Baltimore just like everywhere else. There's going to be outrage. I hope you've consulted with your lawyers, because I wouldn't want to be in the crosshairs of an FCC audit over giving up part of the FM dial to commercial radio.

Jesus Christ, Walter says to Winnifred. You told me he'd be glad to get out.

This is all news to me. I didn't hire a stone thrower.

I'm just giving you some advice based on

115

a broader perspective. There have been other cases like this, and they've all been ugly. So, in other words, gird yourselves for some nasty media. *City Paper* is going to be all over this story, no doubt. WYPR will pick it up. NPR stations tend to stick together. The *Sun* will be pissy, too, if anyone over there's still awake. Plus, you know, the whole philanthropy side of things. The Greater Baltimore Commission. The Abell folks. No one's a big fan of commercial radio these days. No offense, Ron.

This, Walter says, thickly, with a susurration in the back of the throat, this, this, what you're saying — this is over a station *no one listens to.*

It's the principle of the thing. Plus, WBCC is weird. It's local color. Turn us on any time of day and you'll hear something you won't hear anywhere else. We're like the homeless guy who sells his little poetry books down on Gay Street, right? No one buys the books, but we'd sure miss him if he left.

I wasn't prepared to do this, he says. Blinking, recovering himself. Because I didn't think it would be necessary, but there *is* a final offer available. Six months' severance with an additional limitation: you can't work in radio in Baltimore again. No station, nowhere. You're out of town. I guess that's not such a dealbreaker for you, is it?

And before you say anything, Winnifred says, beaming again, yes, this *is* hush money, and yes, we *will* sue you if you so much as utter a word out of turn to *anyone*.

Ron pulls at his collar, his Adam's apple protruding, as if he's just swallowed a golf ball.

Who wrote the checks, I'm wondering, and how was it disguised? Perhaps Winnifred has political ambitions and a PAC of her own. Who is PureLine Communications, at any rate? If I were the muckraker I'm pretending to be, this would be the story, and I would be wearing a wire. It all feels so ordinary, so matter-of-fact, this transaction, this yielding up of the comparatively innocent, the unprepared, to the profiteers of this small, small world. Who would have thought that a tiny public radio station you can't even *get* clearly in half the city would be any kind of a prize? Or, on the other hand, perhaps the scandal is that there is no scandal. BCC needs money. WBCC is underperforming. Winnifred is fulfilling her fiduciary responsibility, and who could say otherwise, if WATB really does become student-run, a low-wattage flight simulator, so to speak? Surely that's what WBCC was in the beginning. In that case the real scandal is *us,* the eternally subsidized, the overeducated, undermotivated, the preachy, those who hide their resentments in lectures, who think that the world — in the form of a university, a government office, some fragile and temperamental nonprofit — owes us a living.

Kelly, Winnifred says tenderly, reaching across the table to touch my hand, given the circumstances, I'm sure you understand that we need to have your decision before you leave here.

I realize, only now, that no one has offered me coffee, tea, a baked good from the tray, and my stomach is clawing at me to eat. I'll get something on the way out. Winnifred, I say, I'll be there, but you'll do the talking. After that I'll take the six months. But I'm not signing anything until after I hear *you* tell them what you've decided.

Fair enough, Walter says.

Winnifred appears to have risen slightly in her seat, though it may be just a trick of my perception. You *took* the job, she says. I warned you it might be rough going. And now you want to wash your hands. That's not the mark of a leader.

Winnie, Walter murmurs, you know the man's right.

I'll let you work it out, I say, rising. You

know my terms. Good to meet you, Ron. Best of luck.

It's almost as if I could do this, too — I could be a dealmaker, a manipulator. Or is it just a role we all learn, now, watching TV? I walk along Charles Street, trying to remember where I parked, feeling a little dizzy, short-footed, as if I'm leaning over to one side, and slightly shrunken, as if I've just shed a skin.

9.

In my life I have never heard, never imagined, the sound an office makes when everyone in it is fired at once. Here it is the sound of the live feed burbling over the speakers — Joe Giamelli's taped show *Once Upon a Garden* — and occasionally the automatic scritching of Barbara's fax machine, and the squawk of the walkie-talkie back in the engineers' room, and the emergency frequency beeping every minute or two at Sully Parker's news desk. The machines speak, and I look from one face to another, willing my arms not to cross my chest protectively, to remain open, in a receptive, listening posture. No one looks at me. I count them, once, twice. WBCC has seventeen employees, and they are all, mercifully, present — no one on vacation, no one with a sick uncle in Denver. They are all staring at Winnifred, who has just made the announcement, in a convincingly shaky voice, and now wipes her eyes with a tissue. There is no better defensive weapon than a tissue, it just now occurs to me. Not for nothing does she work in public relations.

How much time do we have? Sully asks.

Winnifred seems in no shape to answer, so I pick it up: Until what, Sully?

You know. Until the final decision is made. Until the ax falls.

Sully, I say, I'm so, so sorry to say this, but the final decision *has* been made.

Bullshit, Mort says. That's so much self-serving nonsense, and you know it, Kelly. It ain't over till it's over, right? He looks around the room, gathering the troops, but there are only one or two muted *yeah*s, a few murmurs, and otherwise silence, thick as before. It's going to be a lawsuit, then, he says. Jesus Christ, Winnie, you sold us down the river, didn't you?

Don't you *dare* use that expression with me, Winnifred says. That's disgusting. You ought to know better.

Well, okay, good, Mort says. I guess you can say you're firing me for cause. Because that's the only way you can do it. Our contracts all say that we have ninety days' notice if our employer files for bankruptcy or goes out of business. That's standard boilerplate.

But WBCC isn't going out of business, Winnifred says patiently. As I've just explained. We're in a transitional period.

Were we just not *popular* enough? Diane Mackintosh, our pink-sweatered musical consultant, asks, her face already red and raw, a shred of tissue clinging to her nose, too. I mean, is that what you're saying here? Basically BCC is giving up on us because we're not *marketable* anymore? Because I have a few things to say about that. Take this off the air — she flaps a hand around the room, at no one in particular — and it disappears. I could show you the stacks of letters saying that we're people's *lifeblood*. That's what I care about. Not about *ratings*. I went into radio to change people's *lives*.

No one is saying the station isn't an amazing resource, I say. It's distinctive. There's so much here to be proud of. And all of you can go on to offer the same content in other formats. Internet radio. Podcasts. Blogs. There's a hundred different venues that didn't exist ten years ago.

That don't pay anyone a salary.

No, I say, you're right. Not yet. The industry's in transition. But public radio was never about institutional support; it was always about listener membership. And

122

WBCC never had the membership dollars, the sponsorships, to work properly, in any case. BCC was footing too much of the bill. It was unrealistic, to be honest. In a down market something like this was bound to happen.

Shut up, Winnifred is signaling me with her eyes, all but mouthing the words.

We had six weeks of pledge drives last year, Sully says. You're telling me we didn't *try*?

I'm telling you that we were in the wrong position in the marketplace.

This capitalistic language, Diane says. It's making me *ill*.

I'm sorry, I say. I'm sorry! I wish I didn't have to be saying these things. Someone should have said them a long time ago. From my perspective, this station has had very poor leadership. Very poor strategic planning. I know it doesn't help now. I just wish I'd had more time. It's a huge waste. I'm so, so sorry.

No one appears to be listening, save for Winnifred, who stares at me with such concentrated fury I can feel it radiating from her body. For a moment I wonder whether she could construe what I've just said as talking to the media, a violation of my agreement, but she cuts her gaze away, flicking me off the table of her mind, and I know how insignificant I am, thank god, how justifiably an afterthought and a minor irritation.

We go to the papers first, says Michelle Berkowitz, who's young, not even thirty, with a communications degree from Northwestern. I've never quite known what she was doing here. There's going to be a firestorm, she says. You'll see.

We can't stop you from doing that, Winnifred says. We can't stop you from doing *anything.* This is a station committed to public discourse, and discourse is what there will be. But in the end it's likely that things will still come out on the college's side. I say this as a matter of sheer practicality. I would encourage you all to think of this as a transitional period to new employment —

Where? shouts Trevor McCloud, our chief engineer. Everyone turns to look at him. His eyes have turned bubblegum pink; spit glistens at the corners of his mouth. I've got two kids in private school, he says, a mortgage, home equity, a car loan. *Where?* In fucking Kansas? In Milwaukee?

Trevor, I say, trying to lock every joint in my body at once, this is incredibly hard, it's a disaster, but we're giving you every minute of advance warning we can. The station won't be off the air for six weeks. You've got skills. You've all got portable skills. I won't say, *it could be worse.* It couldn't be worse. Especially for those of you with kids and houses and families and obligations. But we will do everything we can.

Fuck you, he says. I mean, at least Winnie's *from* here. You're just, what, an import? A scab? What's your job, anyway, in the new scheme of things?

No job. I'm looking for work, just the same as you.

Well, good luck with that, Mort says. Personally, *I'd* give you the highest possible recommendation.

Mort, that's not fair, Michelle says. Stop looking for a scapegoat. Or if you *are* going to look for one, open your eyes, okay? Who do you think made this decision? She turns to me. I mean, it's a sweet deal for Pure-Line, right? They're not putting any cash in up front, are they? For a prime FM license? Just ad revenues? Wow, BCC is *such* the winner in that scenario.

I don't know, I say. I've told you every-thing I know.

If you're fishing for dirt, Winnifred says, you're not going to get it from us. This was a straightforward strategic decision on the

125

part of the college.

Oh, Mort says, what now, Winnie, you *supported* this? This is too much. He combs his fingers through his hair, which he wears Bruce Springsteen style, down to the nape of the neck; along with the open-necked shirts, the arrowhead on a thong, and the single gold loop in the left ear, it's his virility costume, and I won't hesitate to say that I find it deeply satisfying to see it become clownish and transparently sad. This is just *evil,* he says, it's a corporate takeover, a total sellout, and I don't know why Walter thinks he's going to get away with it, but he's not. This meeting is over. I have to go on the air in an hour, and guess what I'm going to talk about? Guess what just happened to your carefully orchestrated PR calendar, Winnie? I can't *wait* to hear what the people have to say.

I have packets for everyone, Winnifred says, standing up, as if on cue, and pulling a stack of lavender folders out of her bag. I'll just put them on the break-room table, and everyone can have a look. Your severance is calibrated to your latest contract. There's a number for the BCC HR department, but don't everybody call at once, okay? Read the materials first. And, obviously, the sooner you can prepare a résumé, the sooner your transition can begin.

A crash, outside the newsroom, in the direction of the engineers' room; everyone jolts out of a collective stupor, and a few run in the direction of the sound, just as Trevor emerges, hugging an enormous outdated computer monitor, trailing cords, like a gigantic tumor, the casualty of some botched surgery, and drops it on the hallway floor. You can take your severance and shove it up your ass! he hollers, at no one in particular. I should have known you people would stab us all in the back.

Easy, man, Mort says. He brushes past me, walking slowly toward Trevor with his palms out, and the tiniest, most imperceptible swagger, as if to say, to us, *see? See what you've gotten us into?* We're all upset, but come on, man. Let's not shit the bed, okay? You don't want to do anything you'll —

You! Trevor screams, turning purplish, the color of an unripe eggplant. Fucking batshit liberals! We had a word for you when I was growing up, you know that?

Trevor, Mort says. Trevor. You can call me anything you want if it'll make you feel better. But not here. Let's go down to Max's, okay? I'm buying. I'm buying for everyone. All right? Can I buy you a beer? Let me buy

127

you a beer.

Fuck you, hymie, Trevor says. Fuck you, kike. As he says the words, his face contorts, a mangling of grief and horror and self-loathing. He's my age, after all, or perhaps five years older, perhaps forty; he's probably never said these words before in his life. Even ancestral rage, I can't help thinking, comes to us secondhand. *Fuck* you! He whips around and throws the 200-volt adapter, concealed like a baseball in his enormous right fist, through the soundproof glass of the broadcast booth. It spiderwebs, sags inward, as if stunned, unsure of how to respond, and then collapses, throwing shards across the monitors and desks and soundboards.

Enough! Winnifred shouts, phone pressed to her ear. I've called the police! Someone behind me is sobbing. I look around at an empty room: everyone has taken cover behind a desk, or rushed into my office, or out into the lobby. *He could have had a gun,* they'll say later, interviewed on the Fox ten-o'clock news. *It was like one of those postal-worker situations.* Police sirens are howling outside, all the office phones ringing at once, the emergency band squawking under its blanket of broken glass. But Trevor is already finished; he's sitting on the floor, cross-legged, like a child in kindergarten, and Mort is kneeling in front of him, holding his hands.

10.

In a cloud of meaty smoke, whooshed away by an enormous ventilation hood, Robin Wilkinson lifts a rack of skewers out of the oven and delicately rotates each one, turning the blackened side up, the raw pink side down, adding sea salt and cracked pink peppercorns from a bowl. When she bends over the counter the front of her dress droops a little too low, revealing the top of a salmon camisole, and she flattens it, demurely, with one hand.

We have a pretty nice grill, she tells me. It came with the house, actually, and so I got really into cooking outside. Not just hamburgers, you know, rotisserie, *churrascaria,* pretty ambitious stuff. And then we got this stove, and I realized we can more or less do all the same things inside. Even more, in fact. I can make *shawarma,* if I want. The kids love it. But it has to cook for at least six hours, and the heat's so high you don't want to leave it on by itself. It's not like a pot simmering on the stove. These kebabs are so much simpler, though you do have to check them. The biggest mistake most people make is putting meat and vegetables on the same skewer. Why would you do that? I've never understood it. Stick a cherry tomato on there and it'll be, just, *carbon*. Okay, that's it. End of lecture. As you can see, when I meet new people, I get nervous. I talk too much.

She slides the rack back in, wipes her hands, and takes a generous sip from her glass. We're drinking a Chilean rosé, Montes Cherub, which sounds like it means *swill*, she said earlier, but actually it's quite good, all Syrah, very dry, really good to start things off.

No, I mean, I say, it's an awkward situation, I guess. Initially. I'm not just any guest. You have to feel that you're a little on display.

Don't you get that all the time, with your subjects?

This is kind of a new line of work for me, actually, I say. Martin may have told you. My background's mostly in public radio —

Right. WBCC. That's a sad story, isn't it? Sad, but typical of this town. No one thinks big here. No one wants to *innovate*. A station like that, it was a resource, and what do we do but sell our resources away?

In the living room, across the kitchen island and down three steps, Sherry and Tamika are playing a tennis video game, bounding across the floor with little white wands in hand. On your *toes,* Martin is saying. See what Venus does? Constantly up on her toes. Your heels never hit the ground. Always ahead of the next shot.

Listen to him, she says. You'd think he actually knows what he's talking about.

He doesn't play himself?

No, of course he does, he's just not, like, an *expert,* exactly. I played tennis at Penn. I guess I'm a little sensitive.

You'll take over when the time comes, I guess.

No, she says, pouring herself another half-glass, no, it's best not to learn that kind of thing from Mom. I don't want to make it an issue in our relationship. No stage parenting here.

Spoken like a child psychologist.

Yeah, well, it's got to be good for something, doesn't it? Are you done with the zucchini yet? She looks over my shoulder, at the counter, and smiles. Martin, she calls out, who is this guy? What, did you decide I need a sous-chef?

I disclaim any knowledge, Martin calls back. We don't talk about food.

Oh, yeah, right. Only the serious man stuff. Money. Power. Race. The big three. I forgot.

I had a good teacher, I say, but a limited repertoire. Half the things I know how to make I can't, because you can't get the ingredients here. Or if you can, it never tastes right. Wendy used to say that cooking an American duck was like cooking a big bag of fat with a little meat at the bottom.

Robin pours the zucchini chunks into a bowl, adds olive oil, balsamic vinegar, a splash of the wine, and mixes everything together with her fingers. I hope you don't mind, she says. I like to get my hands dirty. I have to say, Kelly, you sound extremely well adjusted.

I'm not sure that's such a compliment.

No, it's an observation. We get to make those in my line of work. Notice I said *sound*. And the other observation I was going to make was: it's a lot of change for you, I mean, this tremendous loss, leaving one job and one city, moving home, taking up another job, then leaving your entire line of work.

Baltimore isn't really home. My parents aren't here. And we were never *from* here;

we landed here for a while and then left. I'm not terribly attached to it, honestly. All I really need is a place to keep things.

That sounds very portable and *comme il faut.*

Well, I say, I guess that's right, for the time being.

Robin, Martin says, I'm going to make you send him a bill.

We're just talking.

Anyway, he's supposed to be asking the questions.

I don't think that's what this is going to turn out to be, she says. I think this is going to be like one of those Janet Malcolm pieces where the reporter becomes a character in the story. Like *In the Freud Archives.* I'm just teasing, she says. And trying to show off. Another bad habit.

Not at all, I say. In public radio that's just casual conversation. You'd fit right in.

Well, I'm a listener, she says. Martin's not. You can always tell a Jack and Jill girl from a mile away.

You were in Jack and Jill?

Oh, good, she says, that's one thing I don't have to explain to you about the black middle class. How do you know about Jack and Jill?

My best friend's girlfriend was in Jack and

Jill. When I was in college. Amherst. She had some kind of scholarship from them, too.

And she talked to you about it?

Not really. She just said it was sort of what held her world together. Like a country club, a sorority, the Girl Scouts, all wrapped up in one package. What, it's not supposed to be a secret, is it?

No. I think we mostly assume that no one else really gives a damn. Anyway, it's very old school, very aristocratic. There's color prejudice, too, within the black community. Of course. I don't mean to be giving you a lecture. But J and J — one of my friends used to call it Just Jamocha. Or JSOP. Just Short of Passing.

She stands up straight and does a quick shoulder rotation, as if to punctuate the thought, and I duly notice that her skin is easily three shades lighter than Martin's. In an amateurish way, I would call her medium-light and Martin just absolutely medium, perfectly what one would expect, halfway between, say, Shaquille O'Neal and Harry Belafonte. Robin, on the other hand, has definite pink and lavender undertones; maybe it's makeup, but I doubt it. You could even say that her face shows a certain gray- ness, a kind of pallor, that some light-skinned black women have. As a factual statement. I'm aware, at the same moment, that I would never describe her as anything other than beautiful.

Listen, I say, I don't want to make you uncomfortable. We don't have to be this, this — right off the bat — this —

Anthropological?

Right.

Well, why not? Isn't it true, as the cliché goes, you know, that the color line is all about ignorance? Martin told me your wife was from China, right? Tell me if it's okay to discuss this.

It's fine.

Well, then, I would wager, I would guess, that you know much more about the intricacies of Chinese culture than you do about African American culture. Though one has been under your nose, so to speak, your entire life, and the other one you had to seek out, actively *choose*.

I think that's probably true, I say. On the level of conscious intelligence, factual information, yes, definitely. But then again, if you look at it from my point of view, it's easier to be an expert on China, isn't it? No one expects me to be an expert on black people. Frankly, nobody *wants* me to be an expert on black people. That would be intrusive. That would be weird. It would raise all kinds of red flags.

But I'm not talking about being an expert. I'm talking about basic cultural competence.

Give me an example, then.

Oh, no. She has a high, piping laugh, a practiced laugh, I think, from working with children all day long, full of soft exclamation points. I'm not giving you a test. Anyway, we've got to feed those girls before they collapse. Come on. You can help me set the table.

Look, Sherry says to Tamika, when dinner is almost finished. She points at my hand. He has a wedding ring, too. See? I *told* you that all grown-ups wear wedding rings. They have to. It's, like, a *law*. When you're a grown-up you have to get married.

Who told you that? Robin asks her, her hands paused above her plate. Someone in school?

No one. I just figured it out myself.

It's not true, you know, Martin says. Sherry. Look at me when I'm talking to you. Grown-ups don't have to be married.

Well, you're married, aren't you? Sherry says, looking up at me. Mr. Kelly? You're married, right?

Not exactly.

137

That's the end of this conversation, Robin says. Sherry, you have to learn that there are some questions —

No, I say, it's all right. If it's all right with you.

Go ahead, Martin says. We don't keep secrets in this house.

Well, Sherry, I say, I *was* married, but my wife died. You know what that means, right?

Did she have leukemia?

She died in a car accident.

Sherry scrunches up her nose and squints at me, as if to ascertain, through some secret method, whether this is the truth or another moralistic fable.

Was she wearing her seat belt?

She was.

Then she shouldn't have died, right?

It doesn't always work that way.

Okay, Martin says. Okay —

I hold up a hand. Let her talk, I say. Let her ask what she wants to ask. Sherry, is there anything more you'd like to know?

Tamika, sitting perfectly straight, removing bits of meat from her skewer with great delicacy, looks over at wayward Sherry and all but rolls her eyes. That's enough, Shay-Shay, she says. You don't have to ask him about his little girl.

What little girl? Robin asks. Tamika! She

reaches over and pulls Tamika's chin toward her. What are you talking about?

Nothing, Tamika says, her eyes round, lips making a little *o*. I just thought he had a little girl. I could tell.

You could tell?

I guessed.

Don't guess, Martin says. Never assume. You hear me? *Ask*, little girl. Learn how to *ask*.

Excuse me, I say, and float away from the table, not entirely sure of my legs, over-stuffed and cramping. The thing about grief is that it ambushes you; you never know when the great pleasures of life — a glass of wine, buttered popcorn at a movie theater, driving the Pacific Coast Highway with the windows open, whatever — will turn sour and hollow, and so you stop trusting plea-sure itself, and become wary, overcautious, self-protective. Then that caution, too, falls away; you forget, and learn to enjoy yourself again, inordinately, but you are still vulner-able. That's as far as I've gotten. Still vulner-able. I wander down a hall and find the guest bathroom, exactly as I imagined it would be, lights on, fresh towels, a cardamom-scented candle, a glass bowl of flat river stones next to the sink. All of it has nothing to do with Martin, and everything, these benign surfaces, this domestic anonymity, colored only by Robin's deft touch. Martin, I want to say, you are a sick genius, or as we used to put it in high school, a genius of crack. Where did that phrase come from? Some song, some band's callow humor. Why was it funny? Why is anything funny?

I sit on the toilet, waiting for something to happen; it felt for a moment like diarrhea, or nausea. Nothing. With one sleeve I wipe the tepid coating of sweat off my forehead, stand, zip, and inspect myself in the mirror. The same face, slightly flushed, slightly puffy, a little more obviously graying at the temples than I remember. In the months after the accident I lost fifteen pounds, more or less all my disposable weight, and went around padded in sweaters and wool hats; since then, I've gained most of it back. I am, more or less, the same person I was three years ago, or twenty years ago. After all, Martin recognized *me*. That, in itself, is astonishing.

A year after the accident, I asked my therapist, Dr. Silverstein, if he thought it was odd that while Wendy was constantly on my mind — was speaking to me — I never, ever, thought about Meimei. I kept her pictures around, and her artwork, out

140

of a desire for sheer order, but nothing I did, or saw, reminded me of her. I might see another father exactly my age crossing the street, another three-year-old clutching his hand, and look right through them, not registering a thing. No, he said, refusing, for once, to turn the question back on me. No, of course not. Don't you know it's natural? He seemed quite agitated, as if I'd mentioned, in passing, that I had a loaded pistol in my courier bag, and was thinking of using it. Don't touch it, he said. Don't touch her. Let the wound heal by itself. The worst thing you can do is blame yourself for what you're *not* feeling.

I do think of her now, in roundabout, philosophical ways. I do not remember, say, how it felt to give her a bath, the way she squealed as I scrubbed shampoo into her scalp, and gave her spiky rhinoceros horns; I choose not to remember sailing with her on the Charles, or the way she grabbed my back pockets and hoisted herself up against my legs from behind as I tried to leave for work. Those memories are there, perfectly visible, in their own vitrines, but what I choose to think about, instead, is how it felt to have a purpose in life. I say this entirely in the abstract. When I left Harvard and began working at WBUR it was because I was sick of trying to support a family on the penury of a graduate stipend, plus Wendy's small salary; I wanted a *job* that turned in small, manageable cycles and paid in large fixed increments, not the echoing black hole of a dissertation and the endless anxious scrabbling of an assistant professorship in Bloomington or Columbus or Madison. My wants, my needs, and my obligations were perfectly in sync, in a righteous, time-honored order. Now, by contrast, I'm on a permanent vacation, thrust back into independence. Unneeded, unwanted. Worst of all: *single.*

I'm beginning to sweat again. Even in the unpredictable persona of the grieving husband, the grieving father, I'm wearing out my welcome in this bathroom. And I see, now, in front of me, the opportunity, the necessity, of quitting this charade, this impossible, quote-unquote *job.* I could thank Robin for the lovely dinner, shake Sherry and Tamika's hands gravely, drive away, and never take another of Martin's calls; break my lease, fill my storage unit to the roof, and cash my severance checks nearly anywhere. I could go back into research. The thought has never occurred to me before. Somewhere, somehow, I might cadge a fellowship, a librarianship, an archivist's position; with a Harvard Ph.D., I might even still be able to get a job in a low-level college somewhere, or maybe teaching Chinese at a prep school. There are options. Other patterns might be applied.

I want to ask Wendy her opinion, but Wendy isn't here. I've begun to sense it, more and more clearly, when I roll over in bed to turn the lights out and think of a question I wanted to ask, or in the car, our favorite sanctuary, where I've become accustomed to telling her what I ate for dinner the night before, just to hear her horrified laughter. She's no longer hanging on my every word, you might say. And in unfamiliar environments — waiting in line for my morning coffee at Cross Keys Bagels, on a walk through Fell's Point — she seems altogether gone. It's ridiculous, a sentimental, *Ghost*-like canard, to be abandoned by your lover in the afterlife, and yet here I am. Your brain is wounded, my therapist kept saying, it's traumatized, it has scar tissue, all those things really *exist* in there, not just metaphorically. It has to regrow itself. That's the *time heals all wounds* part. Literally, you have to wait for it to heal, just like a broken wrist. Think about the neurotransmitters restoring themselves, if that makes you feel better. Every time you laugh at some stupid movie, every time you jerk off — in his Argentinean Spanish accent it sounded like *cherk off* — you are rebuilding your capacities somewhere in there. Maybe that will let you be a little more optimistic, okay?

Is it sheer inertia, or some grim, pseudo-Wasp stick-to-itiveness, some shred of Protestant work ethic, or is it simply the desperate need to get out of my own head that sends me out of the bathroom and back into the vast, skylighted kitchen-dining-living room, where Martin now sits alone, draining the dregs of a balloon-sized glass of Cabernet Franc? Sit down, he says. Robin's putting the girls to bed. You feel okay?

Yeah. I just had to take a moment. I guess I'm out of practice being around kids. Kids and their directness.

Practice has nothing to do with it. Two weeks ago I was teaching Tamika how to do a penalty kick and she accidentally did me one in the balls. Full-on. I practically passed out, right there on the field. They ambush you. That's the nature of the thing. You're never prepared.

You take parenting really seriously.

Why do you say that? I mean, is there another way to do it?

No, I say. I mean, you've thought it through. Most fathers just cruise, don't you think? They take it day to day.

I'm surprised you want to talk about this. You looking to get back in the game? 'Cause single people can adopt, too, these days. Especially if you're willing to do it cross-racially.

He meets my eyes, and I think, the strangeness of my life knows no bounds.

I'm a big fan of adoption, he says. A real advocate.

No, I say, I couldn't do that. I'm not thinking that far ahead.

Of course. Enough said.

Listen, I say, and I hate to bring this up —

Then don't. Not here.

Okay.

We stare at each other for a moment. The house uncannily silent: a whispery hiss from the dishwasher, a low murmur of voices from down the hall. I've forgotten this: the quiet of the aftermath, the depth of stillness children leave in their wake.

Fine, he says. You might as well go ahead and say it. Just keep your voice down.

It's just a question. Have you thought about how you're going to tell her? How, and when?

Why? Do you have some advice on that subject?

Of course not.

Then why ask?

I guess I'm wondering if you have a plan.

A plan for what? If she divorces me?

That's not necessarily where I was going, I say, but yeah, okay. The possibilities. The possible consequences. I mean, she's not going to take it lightly.

She won't divorce me.

You're sure of that?

Look, he says, Robin's an extremely subtle thinker. Number one. She's been through all this identity stuff, critical race theory, race and the psyche, race as a social construction. That's more or less all she did in college. And she's accepted that the story of my background, biologically, is totally unknown. It's not as if I've invented fake ancestors.

But you have. Of course you have. I mean, you *look,* you're *designed* to look, like a black man. No one would ask you to take a DNA test to figure that out.

The way I'm going to present it to her, he says, is, look, it was so traumatic, it was such a psychic break, that I repressed it for a long time. That is, I repressed my former self. And in any case, I haven't even gotten to

146

number two. Number two is that Robin Wilkinson does *not* believe in divorce. She's one of those *Dan Quayle Was Right* people. She'd go almost as far as to say that the only reason for divorce is physical danger from the spouse. She's told me, outright, that she won't divorce me if I'm unfaithful.

Are you joking?

You'd be shocked, he says. She plays a good white-liberal game, no doubt, but underneath that she's basically Pat Robertson. At least when it comes to the black family.

Okay. Okay. If that's true. *Even* if that's true. What's the harm in telling her now? We could use her, among other things. She could help us prepare the ground.

Prepare the ground for what? Do we have a plan, Kelly? You haven't even told me yet what you thought of the RIDS paper. I'm assuming that's just being polite.

The paper's a start. It gets you thinking along the right lines.

But?

Well, it wasn't written for me.

That matters?

I lean across the table, dropping my elbow into a pool of harissa without noticing. Martin, I say, speaking in a hoarse whisper, look, I was *there.* I need an honest accounting. I can't tell this story otherwise. I can't make sense of it myself. You have to understand that.

He closes his eyes.

I went through this already, he says, his lower jaw easing forward, the lips drawing back and showing me a perfect row of white teeth, piranhalike. I went through this shit with Dr. Silpa. He put me through my *paces*. I *edited* that part of my life. You understand what that means, don't you? I was sure you'd understand.

In that RIDS paper you're asking people to look at you as a specimen.

I think I'm cool with that. I've thought about it. I'd rather keep it superficial. Fuck it, like the pregnant man, right? Let them think of me as a freak. The real story doesn't lend itself to sound bites, and anyway, it's unnecessary. We need to come up with something that fits in tight little paragraphs, something *anyone* would buy. Not my story, per se. An ur-story.

If I believed that I'd have quit a long time ago.

Look at you, he says, being all caped crusader. Woodward and Bernstein. Or, what is it, Orson Welles? You're looking for my Rosebud?

Martin, I say, seeing stars, or what I

imagine to be stars, little pinpricks swimming like amoebas in my peripheral vision — how can you say that? How can you fucking say that?

He holds up his hands, palms flat: a trainer ready to catch my punches.

Jesus, you're sensitive, he says. I thought the whole Alan thing would be water under the bridge by now. I thought you'd have resolved it, one way or another.

I'm startled to find my eyes leaking tears.

What's to be resolved? I ask. What, was there a note I didn't get to read? Something you want to tell me, Martin?

Fine, he says. All right. You want the whole story? Forget that RIDS nonsense. That was just a feeler. I've got the whole thing for you in a box. On tape.

What do you mean, *tape*?

Tapes. DATs. Microcassettes. I wasn't systematic about it. But it's all there — nearly. Back when I thought I could write it up myself. I used to get up at five in the morning and go down to the rec room and just, I don't know, *narrate.* For an hour or so at a time. Everything I told Silpa. And more.

Well, shit, I say, with a little laugh, I'm glad you're telling me this now. While I still have access to a studio.

Why do you think I hired you in the first place? He slaps me on the shoulder. That's a joke.

And then what? I just transcribe, and that's it?

Of course not. You're the journalist. You get to shadow me and interview me and all. For clarification. And for, you know, the personal stuff. There's things I never recorded because they wouldn't make sense to anyone but me.

And me. And maybe Alan.

Right. And so you'll understand what I'm telling you: don't take notes, all right? Just, you know, *internalize* it. If it doesn't sound right I'll tell you later, when I read the book. Just hang out.

Okay, I say, with an inward sigh. *What kind of relationship is this?* I suppose I'd like to ask. But how can you ask that question without asking, *what kind of person is this?* There's a principle at work here, but I can't wait for it to reveal itself, can I?

Okay, I say, okay, boss.

Boss? I'm your boss? Then we should make it official, shouldn't we? He gets up and disappears into another room for a moment, and jogs back, holding a leather portfolio. How is it that you've let this go on so long? he asks, scribbling a check.

Without a deposit or anything? Remind me to give you a lesson in negotiating sometime. This is just a retainer, okay? Let's call it the first month's pay. Tell me if it sounds fair to you.

I hold out my hand for the check as he passes it across the table, like a playing card, and read the number, $20,000, in one fluid motion, opening my wallet and slipping it in.

My advice is to open a new bank account, he says. Online. Do it as a wire transfer. Use only your initials. HSBC is good, or Credit Suisse. There are tax reasons, but we can talk about that later. I'll call you tomorrow. We have to set up a schedule. And I've got to dig out those tapes.

My breathing feels unnaturally loud; or maybe the room has become quieter; or maybe we've been waiting all this time for a door to close down the hall, for Robin's footsteps. *What is this for, exactly?* seems the obvious question. *What am I worth to you?* But the silence, an almost prayerful silence, closes in around us, and I say nothing.

Don't worry, he says. His face has spread out into a grin, nostrils flaring, eyes jumping: money has come into the room, with its rustle, its electric crackle, and it excites him, shamelessly. It's almost infectious. My wallet, thrust into my front pocket, glows like an orb, a radioactive pellet. This is only a taste, all right? he says. Trust me. You'll get used to it. It's all a matter of seeing things on a different scale.

11.

The only reason to drive anywhere, Alan said, was because you're in a hurry. Otherwise, why not walk? He hated the way I drove, not inordinately slow or careful, but *sensible.* Why be sensible? he wanted to know. If it's two in the morning, and there's no other cars in sight, why not cruise through the red light at North Charles and Northern Parkway, why not pretend, for a moment, that no red lights exist?

He had his own license for less than a month; he totaled the family Volvo in a way the mechanics said couldn't be done, a Volvo with 270,000 miles they'd owned since 1979. Thus for more than a year — the entire touring life of L'Arc-en-Ciel — I drove him everywhere, even to school. It was that or take the bus, Cheryl said. She slipped me a twenty every week for gas money, and when I protested that I had a Texaco card, paid by my parents, she said, consider it hazard pay. Alan and I spent it on coffee, powdered donuts, and leathery slices of pizza from 7-Eleven; pizza jerky, Alan called it, and said it was his favorite food.

We argued about veganism — I was all for it, but he said it was a fool's errand, making a fetish out of purity, as if it was possible to live like the Jains, ahimsically, in the twentieth century — and about whether one should start slow on the stereo, first thing in the morning, a little Nick Drake, maybe, or folky Neil Young, or wake up with a thunderous blast of Antischism or Bolt Thrower or Cannibal Corpse. We argued about the causes of the Civil War. We argued about whether Ian MacKaye was a better singer in Minor Threat or in Fugazi. We argued about the latest articles in *The New York Times* I swiped off my neighbor's doorstep, and whether it was ethical for me to steal a newspaper, even if Mr. Macalester read only one out of three, and let them pile up in a scummy heap on the pavement. But we never argued about — never discussed — the terms, the content, the causes of our friendship. Adolescent boys hardly ever do. They pretend as if the people around them simply sprang out of the ground at random. We never said *I love you,* of course, though we surely did, and when we left town — for the weekend, for the summer, for rehab, for college — we never said goodbye. Not so much as a *see you* or *talk to you then.*

Why does he hang up in the middle of a sentence? people would ask me. Why does he pretend not to notice I was gone? Because he's opposed to time, I answered, in my snarky, sixteen-year-old way. And grammar. He thinks all periods should be replaced by semicolons.

And in the end, of course, there *was* no period, or semicolon; there was just silence. There was just:

I started to worry about him only when he stopped complaining. This was the fall of our senior year, after he and Ayala broke up, after L'Arc-en-Ciel dissolved in a ranting three-day argument, in person, over the phone, via answering machine messages and scrawled notes stuffed in each other's lockers at school. He'd been away all summer at an arts institute at Cornell — the Telluride Institute — and had returned with a dog-eared copy of John Cage's *Silence,* wanting to turn L'AEC into a conceptual rock band, in which one song consisted of nothing but snare-drum beats, and another involved playing only whole-note intervals on a retuned guitar. Martin had gotten heavy into primitive rock — The Stooges, The Fugs, all the Amphetamine Reptile bands, Neanderthal, Man Is the Bastard — and had put a poster up in our practice space saying *Think Smart, Play Stupid.* I was where I always was: I liked chords. I liked melodies. I liked choruses. It was a nonstarter, and it was all over by the end of September, when I watched Alan eat a plateful of cafeteria chow mein without saying a word.

Cat meat got your tongue?

What? he asked. Oh, sorry. I was thinking about something else.

He had lost weight, and he couldn't afford to; we were used to reminding him to eat, on the road and after hours of practicing, and used to making sure he'd taken his insulin and done his blood test. It was a prerequisite for being Alan's friend; his mother, Cheryl, made sure of that. Being diabetic for so long had made him hate food, he said. It was like a malevolent force in the universe, life-giving, life-taking, capricious as the Hebrew God. I looked at him carefully, again, head to toe, and saw something on the papery underside of his right forearm that looked like a dot of blue ink.

What the fuck is that?

That? I stabbed myself with a pen by accident.

I should say, by way of explanation, that though we'd sampled our share of drugs in high school — bong hits, shrooms, black-market ephedrine, and one collective acid trip the summer we all turned sixteen — Martin and Alan and I were mostly bystanders, and in those days heroin and cocaine were all but unheard of, a relic of the Eighties, of *Less Than Zero* and *Sid and Nancy*. The theater arts building at Willow was named for Samantha Dinerstein, class of '88, who overdosed on speedballs her freshman year at Sarah Lawrence. What instinct for self-preservation we had drew the line at snorting, shooting, and sex without a condom, or, in some cases, sex at all.

At Telluride, though, Alan was befriended by a circle of New York kids from Stuyvesant and Saint Ann's, who were hardcore for Rimbaud, Apollinaire, Anaïs Nin, Henry Miller, Kathy Acker. They did a lot of mescaline and hash, but this guy named David kept getting these care packages from a friend in Washington Heights and then disappearing for six or eight hours at a time. Finally Alan asked David directly, and David — who had the longest lashes he'd ever seen on a boy, or boy-man, whatever seventeen-year-olds are — said, there's really only one question. Are you in or out? And handed him a copy of De Quincey's *Confessions of an English Opium-Eater.*

You have to understand, Alan told me, his eyes wide, you have to know what it's *like* there. You're going from building to building, and there's just these miniature canyons, with bridges over them, and you could be reading and not paying attention to where you're walking, and just like pitch into the rail and boom! You're looking down three hundred feet into this gorge, with this tiny little creek you can hardly even see at the bottom. I mean, okay. Everybody knows that kids go to Cornell, the winter drives them crazy, and they jump into the gorges. But it's not like you have to *seek them out.* It's more like Camus: every day you have to come up with a reason *not* to jump. Look, this is what David said to me: the question is why I'm doing it. The question is, why aren't you? If somebody said you could sit at the table with Jesus at the last supper, wouldn't you? If somebody told you you could sit at Buddha's feet in Sarnath, wouldn't you? What if you could talk to a rock in its own language? What if you could become a cloud? What if you could be *whatever you wanted*? What if you had eyes in your kneecaps, your armpits, the crooks of your elbows? What if you had eyes in the soles of your feet that could stare down into the earth's magnetic core? And look, I just thought, this kid is a fucking lunatic, but then that same night I was reading the *Critique of Judgment,* about the aesthetic sublime, and I realized, holy shit, Kant is talking about exactly the same thing. It just all came together. David kept saying, the greatest gift is to take life out of your body and give it back to your body. That's what heroin is. Death in life. And you know what? He wasn't lying. Can you understand how *rare* that is, for someone to tell you something that's one hundred percent the truth?

Are you saying the rest of us are lying?

No, I'm saying that language is never completely accurate. Ordinary language. I mean, this is just basic stuff. Wittgenstein. Quine. Language is all about its own failure. But *heroin,* heroin, is more than anyone can ever say it is. It takes promises and raises them up a level.

By this time I was, I think, Alan's closest friend. But not his only friend. And not the only one he told when he started shooting up. It was a secret, but a badly kept one. In a month it was the general word around the hallways at Willow, and some younger kids, sophomores, began asking him to hook them up. He refused. He wouldn't give it to anyone else, he said, much less sell it, not unless the person was completely and utterly *prepared.* He got packages from New York, sent to a P.O. box in Mount Washington, just down the hill from his house, and he hid them in the rafters in the garage.

All of which is to say that I could have exposed him, reported him, at any time, and so could any number of others. Cheryl was, all things considered, a wise and understanding mother. She had pictures of herself dancing in the mud at Woodstock hung up over the fireplace in the living room. But Alan's younger sister, Rebecca, had just spent a month in Sheppard Pratt over the summer; Rebecca was the basket case in the family, fifteen, bulimic, a cutter, who'd been having an illicit relationship with a thirty-five-year-old father of two. Alan was headed to Harvard or Oxford, in her eyes, already all but gone.

Lots of people have maintenance-level habits, he said, and if you hear otherwise that's just Nancy Reagan propaganda. Look at Patti Smith. Look at Joey Ramone. Look at Wayne Shorter and Jim Carroll. It's not the healthiest lifestyle, but what is?

Methinks the man protests too much, I said.

Meaning what? Meaning I'm not actually aiming to make it past twenty-five?

Nobody does heroin without a death wish. You all but said so yourself.

Okay, he said, well, let me refer you back to *The Myth of Sisyphus,* our text for the day. Who *doesn't* have a death wish? Freud says it's as natural as anything else. It's never felt anything other than natural to me. And yes, you can say, that's just garden-variety teenage angst. Guess what? Rimbaud quit writing poetry when he was nineteen. Keats was dead by twenty-five.

We were raking leaves down the slope of his front lawn, piling them up in a neat barrow at the curb; Cheryl had promised him a theremin if he did all the yardwork that fall. He'd insisted on wearing a pair of oversized leather gloves, claiming he was afraid of getting blisters, and his wrists, jutting out of a flannel shirt, seemed hardly more than bleached bones.

Alan, I said, trying to keep my voice as neutral, as level, as I could, are you listening to yourself? I wish I had a tape recorder. You're becoming a caricature, do you know that?

And you're not, Savonarola?

Forgive me for giving a shit.

Oh, I do, he said. But not for being so transparently *jealous.*

I was jealous of you for getting an A in AP English, I wanted to say. I was jealous when you were fucking Ayala. I was jealous when you were L'Arc-en-Ciel's frontman, giving all the interviews. Do you know all the times I've been jealous? It sounded so petty, and so rote, so *high school.* You're not a genius, I wanted to say, and this isn't your time, or your stage, or your historical *moment,* you're just an embryo, if that, suckling on a nutrient-rich diet of hundred-year-old ideas. Is that what I wanted to say, or what I would say now? In any case, I put down my rake, and walked farther down the hill to where my car was parked, and drove away.

It seemed to me in those purgatorial months between Halloween, when the first of our applications were sent, and April 15, that the hierarchy of our world disintegrated: parents and teachers losing their grip, and then, more disturbingly, losing interest. Like teenagers, they kept to their own rooms and avoided our gaze. You could say some part of it was relief, some part a kind of gallows nonchalance: they had handed us over to another tribunal, and, for the first time, felt that they had been instructed to withhold judgment. My own parents, who had been minimalists in the kitchen as long as I'd known them, took up an interest in northern Italian cooking, and began filling the basement with cases of Barolos, Brunellos, Sangioveses. Between dinner and the end of whatever they were watching in the den — *Masterpiece Theatre, Frontline, NOVA* — they finished a bottle a night, sometimes two. I was playing drums for two new and short-lived bands, The Near Misses and The Wash, and was out more nights than I was home; I might come in at ten and find the dinner dishes still on the table, the candles melted to nubs, and the two of them, my guardians, my progenitors, asleep on the couch in their work clothes, their slippered feet poking out of a plaid blanket. I was never sure whether to wake them or not. I was never sure whether to envy them or pity them. In one way, at least, I had seen the last of them, and I was, for better or worse, alone.

We avoided each other for more than a month, until Cheryl called me to ask why he wasn't filling out any college applications. I think you should ask him, I said, and she began to cry, over the phone, a sound like the plashing of a waterfall, so loud I held the receiver away from my ear. You're his rock, she said, you're his conscience. He brushes me away like a fly.

Look, I said, I have no power over him. You want me to talk to him? I'll talk to him. But it won't make any difference. He's got bigger problems.

Bigger problems than not going to college?

I stared at the touchpad, at its recessed buttons, at its strange and awkward division of the alphabet, and tried to recall the last time that one of our parents — anyone's parents, that is, even Ayala's dad, beloved Rabbi Kauffmann — had tried to exert, to possess, moral authority. All our independence, it seemed to me, had been a smoke screen, a shadow play, and they had bought it, they had inhaled it. We had been granted the status of superior beings.

I can't help it if you're blind, I wanted to tell her, but instead, I said, look, Cheryl, I think you need to draw a line with him. Stop giving him money.

What the hell are you talking about?

It was unbearable, it *is* unbearable, a thousand times more so, in retrospect, that I didn't answer her question. Instead, I got off the phone, making some excuse, another three weeks passed, Christmas and New Year's passed — skiing in Lake Placid, a strange last-minute inspiration of my father's, though I sprained my ankle and spent most of the week in the hot tub reading *Jude the Obscure* — and when I returned our answering machine tape was shredded from overuse, and Alan had already spent two nights in the ER, two nights in intensive care, and was on suicide watch at Sheppard Pratt. Rebecca found him, I was told, or else he wouldn't be alive; she knew immediately it was an overdose, though he'd hidden the syringe, thrown the works out the window, and she said so to the dispatcher. By then, in the space of those weeks, his future had disappeared; the question was his survival.

How else can I say it, other than to say it? That he remade me in his own image. Or that he wanted to, and succeeded, for a while: there was a version of me that *was* Alan, a provisional, experimental second self, that knew all his jokes, all his stock phrases, anecdotes, and allusions. I could have been his Charles Kinbote.

Or is it nothing more than a dodge, a kind of metaphysical excuse, to say that I failed him because I was him? Instead of saying that I failed him by taking my life away and moving on. For the last year of his life, from the time he entered rehab to the day he died, I became terrible at paying *attention* to him. My own trajectory, I suppose, was too absolute for that. I was admitted early to Amherst, my first choice; I won a merit scholarship that, in the end, as my father never tires of reminding me, paid for half of one semester; I gave up playing the drums and started reading and writing poetry every free moment, fascinated by James Merrill and John Ashbery, Frank O'Hara and Kenneth Koch. How's Alan? people asked me, constantly, and that was all that reminded me that he was still alive. You could say that I wrote elegies for him starting in the winter of 1992, that he became *useful* to me before he actually died.

It was the third-to-last day of winter vacation the following year; I was due back at Amherst on Sunday night, with a paper on Giordano Bruno in hand. Alan and I hadn't seen each other since the previous weekend; he was working eight-hour shifts at Borders in Towson and going to NA meetings nearly every night. Called in sick today, he said, when I finally took off my headphones and picked up the receiver. I'm feeling crappy.

And we've hardly seen each other at all, have we? You'll be back at school in a minute and I'll be leaving anxious messages on your machine.

There had been times, that year, when he acted like a jealous, left-behind high school girlfriend, sending me long letters and calling three times a week, wanting to know about my life, my new friends, and I'd all but ignored him, and then long stretches of silence in between, when I'd been the anxious one, calling Cheryl at work — a number I still had memorized — to make sure he was all right.

As far as I knew, as far as I had seen, he was solidly in recovery, after a month of rehab, a relapse in the summer, after graduation, and another month of rehab the previous August. He'd been in methadone treatment but had stopped, abruptly, claiming it was just the same high, that it felt wrong, and then he'd gotten seriously into NA, going night after night, spending hours at coffee with his sponsor, Charles, an ex–Hells Angel and ex-con. It was at Charles's insistence that he'd gotten a full-time job. His letters to me were full of jargon I barely understood: *Working the steps. Having a day. Crazymakers. Restitution junkies.* And — not surprisingly, I guess — his tastes in literature had changed: *The Road Less Traveled, The Courage to Heal, Fire in the Belly, Zen and the Art of Motorcycle Maintenance, Be Here Now, Awaken the Giant Within.* Recovery lit, he called it. When I tried to bring Bataille and de Sade with me to rehab the second time they just chucked the books in the trash. It's like North Korea in there. But over time, hey, you get to like it. It speaks to you. It's sweet and medicinal. Like Charles says, you'll have plenty of time to read later if you can only stay alive.

I have this memory, though it was January, of parking my car with leaves overhead: black-leafed oaks and elders and gum trees, their branches blocking out the sullen sky. I walked across the street to his house in a tunnel of imaginary leaves. The door was open; no one answered my knock. Cheryl was at work, of course, and Rebecca was spending her senior year at a prep school in Colorado. The house felt loose and creaky underfoot, full of odd drafts, barely inhabited. Alan, I called out. Hey, man, put some clothes on, I'm coming up, okay?

Okay.

He was sprawled over the enormous overstuffed couch we'd found abandoned down the street, years before, and hauled upstairs, unscrewing the hinges of his bedroom door to fit it in. There was a slash across one of the arms I hadn't seen before, the stuffing flowering out like a corsage, and hundreds of cigarette burns, as if he'd gotten into the habit of using it as an ashtray. And Alan in a Victims Family T-shirt with a blue-and-white afghan coiled around his waist. Sorry, he said, I would have come down, but I'm sick for real. All out of sorts.

What, the flu?

Who the hell knows. In any case, keep your distance.

You want something? Should I make you some soup?

He fixed me with a one-eyed stare. No thanks, Mom.

I mean *from a can.* It's not rocket science.

What I need is your company, he said. I need your advice on an important metaphysical question. He produced a book with a streaky brown cover from underneath the afghan, a bark-colored cover.

What the hell is that?

Shut up, he said. It's important. Listen to this: *A little knowledge, a pebble from the shingle, / A drop from the oceans; who would have dreamed this infinitely little too much?* What do you think that means?

I'd have to hear the whole poem.

Why?

Because, I said, a line like that out of context could mean almost anything. It's all fuzzy metaphors. Are we talking about the tree of knowledge, carnal knowledge, scientific knowledge? For my taste it's a little too vague. And condescending. Who's the *who*? Who are we talking about?

I could hear myself talking, snappy and dry, squeaky, an irritable pedant already at nineteen. No less of a shell, in my own way, than he was. He stared at me out of dark eye sockets that now looked perpetually bruised. At some point, without my fully registering it, a capillary had burst in his right eye, leaving a red blotch just outside the pupil. Otherwise, oddly, his face looked better, plumper, than it had a year earlier. He was finally putting weight back on, I thought, at long last.

All right, he said. I get it. Due diligence. Okay, the poem sucks *as a poem.* But that's why I read it to you. I'm taking it as advice.

And what kind of advice would that be?

He flipped the book back open.

Young men, he read, *when lifted up may become white swans, grandiose ascenders, "flying boys," just as young women when similarly lifted up may become flying girls, and make love with invisible people at high altitudes. The Jungian thinkers have done well in*

170

noticing and describing this phenomenon, and the phrases puer aeternus *and* puella aeterna *are familiar to many.*

I'm reading this, he said, and I'm thinking, this is about me. This is *my* life. Don't you see that?

Dude, I said, Alan, have you been making love with invisible people at high altitudes? How come you didn't tell me? I want in on *that* action.

He closed his eyes.

I'm not going to respond to that, he said. You know why? You know what I think the problem with college is?

You've never been to college.

I had a summer, he said. Telluride. College teachers, college courses, college texts. I had my taste. And you know what the problem with it is? It's an extension of adolescence. It's just *camp.* It happens too late in life. You know what Charles said to me? By twenty-two every human being should have spent one year in the army and one year doing manual labor.

And how much time flogging Deepak Chopra at Borders?

Don't mock me.

I'm not mocking you. I'm calling you on your BS. Didn't you tell me that's what an addict's friends are supposed to do?

You're not my friend.

What the fuck are you talking about?

I don't mean that in a bad way. I mean it as a factual observation. I honor you. As a former friend. I mean, really, come on, can you see it another way? This is our polite visit in the museum of our friendship.

I'll believe that, I said, when I meet your *new* friends. When there's someone I can hand you off to. And I don't mean Charles.

We're getting off track here, he said. I was telling you something about who I really am. I'm sorry if you don't want to hear it. There's a word for it: that's what I'm learning. *Puer aeternus.* The eternal boy. Peter Pan. Icarus. Et cetera. Listen: the name of this chapter is *The Road of Ashes, Descent, and Grief.* I'm *grieving.* But here's the thing: now I know I'm grieving! And what you know, you can control. What you recognize you have to re-cognize.

Okay, okay. I get it.

You don't get it yet. You think this has nothing to do with you.

Why does it have to have anything to do with me?

Because you're more like me than you want to admit. Because a person only has one chance to get it right in life.

No, I said, I don't believe that, and I'm

sorry if this sounds arrogant, or condescending, or whatever, but neither should you.

For example?

For example, you aren't dead, I said, though you probably should be, and if that isn't a second chance, what is?

Would you do me a favor? he asked. Go in the bathroom. I have to take my diabetes shot. There's a couple of new syringes in the cabinet. Get one out for me, would you? I'm feeling so dizzy I can hardly get up. And then maybe you can make me that soup you were talking about.

The syringes were on the top shelf inside the cabinet, still in their sterile packaging; they were bigger than the ones he usually used, which were no wider than pencils, and their labels, oddly, were printed in Chinese. Did it matter? Maybe adults used larger syringes. What was the other presumption: that he was back to shooting up? I was so angry, so shut out, and wounded, in the way that only nineteen-year-olds home from college can be wounded, that I thought, fuck him if he is. Live and let live.

Where's the insulin? I called out to him. Doesn't it come in a little bottle?

I have it here.

Alcohol pad?

Yeah. One of those, too. Man. All of a sudden I'm *starving.*

All right, I said, all right, dropping the syringe into his waiting hand, I'm going down, I'm on my way.

When I came back into the room I smelled something odd — something sweet, a burnt-sugar smell, out of place. And thought that I must have dropped something on the stove by accident. I left the soup with him and hurried down to check, and then came back, and he had taken a few sips of the soup and fallen asleep. He looked good. He looked happy. I say this not to excuse myself, but because it is merely, entirely, true: there was color returning to his cheeks, or at least that was what I saw. I pulled the blanket up around his chin. I didn't wake him. I watched him for a minute, and then I left. He was only sleeping.

12.

Recording #1 (41:32)
Source: TDK Chrome cassette tape, 90 minutes, condition ++
Labeled side one "Tape 1 PRIVATE DO NOT DESTROY"
Digitized to .flac with ProTools noise reduction
Note: Speaker frequently pauses for intervals of :10 or longer.
To preserve consistency, all such intervals are marked in the text with a space break.

I was four years old before I ever met a black person. Can you believe that?

I remember it so clearly — my clearest childhood memory of all. I guess that's not really surprising. She was sitting at the picnic table on the back patio, where we had meals in the summer. In a caftan, a bright orange-and-red print. She had an Afro. Lots of silver bangles on both arms. I imagine she must have been about thirty. I had no idea where she'd come from. It was the morning; she'd arrived overnight. I came out to ring the dinner bell — it was a big iron triangle, the kind they use on ranches — and I startled her, but then she looked over and saw me and smiled. She had been crying. There were tracks of tears on her cheeks. But when she saw me her mouth split into this enormous grin, the widest mouth, the friendliest mouth, I had ever seen in my life. A slice of the sun. She laughed, and she said, where did you come from? And I just wanted to run to her. Hell, maybe I still am running to her.

You know what the sex-change therapists say? Begin at the moment you knew. But in my case, it's more complicated than that. Nature versus nurture: I've been play-ing that goddamned chess game my whole life. Out of context, or out of nowhere? Out of them, or out of me? By which I mean, of course, good old Mom and Dad. Or Dad, I should say, since she's just a shadow, an afterthought. I was born, wasn't I? Though sometimes it doesn't feel that way. It seems almost like something to mention in parentheses. Oh, yeah, her.

Sometimes, sometimes I wish I didn't remember her, but I do. Just barely. She was incredibly pale, with that light, light blond hair, eyebrows, everything, and the one image I have of her is in our kitchen, this enormous kitchen — it was the conservatory of the house before the commune converted it. She's standing against the windows, her back to the windows, and it's as if the sunlight is coming through her. I remember I was terrified of that. And fascinated. In any case, there's my one memory, and then she was off. Untraceable, unidentifiable, or so my father claimed. I have no record of her whatsoever, not even a picture. I used to beg him to tell me whether I had her nose, or her ears, anything, and he would say, sorry, but as far as I can tell, you're all me. More's the pity. Well, it was the Seventies, wasn't it? On a commune, in the Seventies? Nobody was keeping records.

Big Love. That's what the place was called. It's near Baltimore, actually. Edgewater. I went back there once, a few years ago, out of curiosity. The owners tore down the old house and built this gigantic

Venetian palazzo. Circular driveway, tile mosaics, fountains, the whole thing. And a Maserati out front. But the barn was there: the barn I played in. That's the only way I recognized it. The barn, and the trees, and these little hills looking out on the Severn.

Toward the end we were the only ones there at all. All I ever knew, in those days, was people leaving and never coming back. That black woman — know who that was? Shirley O'Dell. She was a backup singer for Ike and Tina, and later had a disco hit, "Give Me Someone to Love." Her boyfriend, her ex-manager, had come out to Big Love and said he was never leaving. She showed up and they left the next day.

All those communes had the same trajectory — some of them just took longer to follow it all the way through. The guru, the big buildup, high times, donations, crowds, then the scandal, the blowup, people start to defect, the guru takes off, or dies, or whatever, then it dwindles down to the diehards, then the land gets sold for tract housing. Soon there's nothing left but an old farmhouse, or a Home Depot, and a bunch of kids with names like Kali and

Starflower Moonbright scattered around the county. But at least — and it's a huge at least — there was no sex at Big Love. Or, I should say, at least, no sex I ever saw. At some of those places it was open season on the kids. Beneficent may have been downright crazy, but he was no Jim Jones. Should I give you the history, the whole rundown? Silpa wasn't too interested. And maybe it's tangential. But still, it's culturally important. Beneficent Walker, the founder, that was his real name. Ex-Mormon, ex-seminarian, claimed he could speak fifteen languages, started the Church of Universal Holy Kindness. CUHK. He published a book, too, a best-seller: *The God of Now.* No one remembers it these days, but if you ever meet a boomer ex-hippie, chances are they'll have it on an old dusty shelf somewhere, next to Ram Dass and the *Tao Te Ching.* That paid for Big Love, and kept the power and water on for a couple of years, but it wasn't meant to last — he died the year I was born. Spinal cancer, claimed he could cure it through prayer, then changed his mind and decided God wanted him back. Of course, I never knew any of that until later; all I knew at the time was that there was with Beneficent, which was all happiness and harmony and light, and then there was after Beneficent, which was now. We had a shrine to him behind the house, in a Quonset hut, which was supposed to be temporary, until they raised the money to pay for marble. For a while it was Dad's job to keep fresh flowers on the altar and keep the universal flame going. Which meant a new Sterno can every six hours on the dot, day or night. He had me doing it instead, toward the end. Popping off the lids with a screwdriver, flicking a rusty Bic lighter. Five years old.

My mother — she was a devotee from the beginning. Sat at Beneficent's feet, transcribed his talks from reel-to-reel tapes, mimeographed the newsletters. Her name was Katherine; she never told anyone her last name. Straight up refused. It's not even on my birth certificate: Katherine Doe. Like a nun. A bride of Christ. And here's the thing: ordinarily that would just mean she was the guru's secret girlfriend, but Beneficent was celibate, actually celibate; he believed women were serpents, channels of sin. On the other hand, he was a student of religious history. Think of the cults that proscribed sex: the Essenes, the Gnostics, the Shakers. Self-erasing. He understood the value of pro-creation, but his compromise was to make it impersonal and assigned, and my parents were his experimental model. Dad already knew he was gay. And Katherine never wanted children. To say the least. Dad used to say I was a product of pure faith. A prototype.

And Dad? He was a fairy. A flaming queen of the first order. I mean, look, I suppose he could have disavowed me outright. He could have given me up for adoption or abandoned me. He did his duty, but that doesn't mean he was what I would call a family-oriented person. I had to pry the details out of him with a crowbar, and that was just before he died, when he was too weak to resist and I was the one feeding him Ensure through a straw. But the thing about me, the distinguishing feature, you could say, is that I never really cared that much about my genes. Past a certain point. To me it's the absence that makes the difference. I had the lightest dusting of mothering one could ever imagine. Ostensibly the reason was that after Beneficent's death she was completely shattered, and she spent my first few years in and out of a catatonic depression. It doesn't really matter. Somehow I was kept clothed and fed and sane. There were other women around, though I don't remember them, either. Shortly after she left, we left and moved into Baltimore. Big Love was sold; my father got some of the money. I was never quite certain how that went down. He had already finished his Ph.D. at Hopkins — Russian history. And was kept on as a lecturer for a few years. Then somehow, I don't know exactly, he moved into being a librarian. And that's what he was, for life. The Slavic languages librarian. Which is like being the priest of some obscure religion no one actually practices. For some reason you're kept on. You're a relic, but a relic with a continually renewed contract. I mean, this was the tail end of the Cold War. Russian studies was going the way of the LP record. Who would be in there looking for volume thirty of Mayakovsky's collected works? But universities are like that, right? I mean, what is a university, otherwise, than a kind of giant pack-rat collection, betting that all this stuff is one day going to be useful?

So that was his life. It didn't pay much, but what did that matter? Our house was practically free. It was a dump when we

bought it, not much more than a shell.
Enrique rebuilt it from the ground up. That
was Dad's boyfriend, his first one. They
really made a go of it, too: seven years.
These days they might have been married. As it was, he didn't even live with us
— not officially. Dad was afraid the neighbors would object, or at least that's the
excuse he gave. None of the boyfriends
ever lived in his bed. They were always
bickering about toothbrushes and borrowed underwear. It was all part of his
generalized paranoia, and of course that's
why none of them stayed, in the long term.

Paranoia. That was his native condition,
his MO, even before he got sick. I've never
met a person who could read more into
less. He's stopped using my shampoo.
That kind of thing. Maybe he's washing
his hair at someone else's house. At work
he had two officemates, Janice and Philip
— the three of them must have worked
together for fifteen years — and I don't
think they ever stopped fighting. Not one
day. He would come home in tears because Janice refused to water his Virginia
creeper. That bitch has the blood of my
plants on her hands. It was all theater, only
sometimes not. And as a child, how could

I tell the difference? I thought grown-ups were that way. I looked forward to the day I could use foundation and Pond's Cold Cream.

This house we had, this house Enrique built for us, for my dad's specific requirements, had no windows to speak of. It was a row house, of course, but the front window, too, was blocked off; there was this huge built-in bookshelf there instead. You had to have the lights on twenty-four hours a day. I had a window, in my bedroom, the front bedroom, upstairs. But Dad's were covered with velvet drapes, always closed. I'm not kidding. It was cliché piled on cliché. Richard Simmons on TV? Remember him? For a while I thought we had to be related to him. There was no one else I could imagine. This was in the Eighties, after all. No gay men in wide circulation. No Nathan Lane, no *Will and Grace.* And apart from boyfriends, Dad had no friends to speak of. No meals on Friday nights, no Thanksgivings, nothing. If you want one fact about my childhood that matters, there it is: I was alone. But it's too easy to say that. Those words are meaningless, really. There's no adult language for what it means to be alone as a child. Those first years in Baltimore — it was like I was the only child on earth.

Shabazz. I went to El-Hajj Malik El-Shabazz Elementary. I was the first white kid to enroll there in eight years, since they'd changed the name from Paul Revere. Too much, isn't it? But here's the thing: all those horror stories, those urban-pioneer, reverse-gentrification stories, the white kids getting picked on, beat up, you know the drill, none of that happened to me. I wasn't a curiosity, I was a nonentity. I was invisible. Even my teachers hardly remembered I was there. I always sat at the back, I paid attention, I did all the worksheets on time, and in between, when the fights happened, when someone threw a chair through a window, or broke another kid's nose, or whipped out a box cutter, I took cover, mostly. There were always a few of us at the back taking shelter; sometimes we turned the desks over and made ourselves a little foxhole. At lunchtime we hid in the cloakroom or in the bathroom stalls. Those were my friends. The hiders. This was the Eighties; there weren't police in the schools yet. No metal detectors, no security checking bags at the door. And the school itself was new —

new carpets, new paint on the walls, new lockers. But no windows. That was my daily migration, from one cave to another. And you know what? I didn't hate it, at the time. I had no grounds for comparison; I made a life out of it. Frankly, I was glad to be out of the house. I'd never been to school before I entered the first grade at Shabazz. I'd learned to read — somehow I'd always been able to read. I could add and subtract. But I'd never played with a basketball before. I'd never had a lollipop. Never listened to Michael Jackson. For better or worse, that was my gateway into the world. And then, lo and behold! I had a friend. William Thurgood Marshall Hayes. Willie.

As I said — you have to always bear this in mind — I wasn't a threat. I wasn't a symbol of anything, at least not as far as six-year-olds were concerned. In that place, at that time, I was simply odd. Willie kept saying, You'll grow out of it. That was his theory. Eventually, he said, your hair will fall out and grow back, you'll get darker, you'll be just like the rest of us. Small kids anticipate everything adults will ever imagine. Isn't that what Picasso said, return me to the mental world I had when I was five?

Willie was the best. A little kid, like me, small for his age. Small and wily. His father was a wrestling coach at Dunbar; he had a practice mat in the basement and used to put us through self-defense drills. How to get hit. How to fall. Arm blocks and pressure points. To give us inspiration he let us watch *Enter the Dragon* and *Kung Fu Action Theater.* God, we spent hours down there, eating Cheetos and pretending to be Bruce Lee. Willie had two older sisters, much older, teenagers, and they ran an unlicensed hair salon with his mom in the back of the house. His mother was half Cape Verdean, and that was the food they ate. Cachupa. Jagacida. Canja. Canja, especially. It's a thick chicken soup — thickened with rice, like avgolemono. Almost like a porridge. The world's best comfort food. Robin learned how to make it. It was either that or keep making pilgrimages to New England. No Verdean restaurants around here. Anyway.

I mean, the point is, it was a family. Not in the nuclear sense; in the original sense. The elastic sense. No matter what time of day, somebody would be home, the TV would be on, and something would be on the stove. No one once questioned my being there. I could go on for hours. I remember that house better than my own. The orange shag rug in the living room. Herbs in pots around the windowsills. There was an enormous Ali–Frazier poster hanging up in the hall, and another one in the dining room — Ali knocking out Sonny Liston. And a couple of Benin masks, the ones with the enormous foreheads and tiny eyes. We used to do our homework at the dining table, and Willie would go up to the masks and pretend they were whispering the answers in his ear.

My father was relieved by this arrangement. To say the least. I would call him from their phone, and say, I'm staying at Willie's till bedtime, and he would say, good, because there's nothing in the fridge. His mother — Rashida was her name — she even cut my hair, you believe that? The barber's chair was right there, next to the sink; you tilted your head back for shampooing and then swung right around to the mirror on the opposite wall. I wanted it cut super-close, just like Willie's, and she did her best. Kind of a Roman style, is how it came out, slicked down with pomade. Wish I had a picture. That was how I wore my hair all those years. Christ, I mean, you have to understand, I must have had dinner there two or three nights a week. How else can I explain it? It wasn't just that I was happy. It was that I felt human, as if for the first time. Let me refine that statement. I felt part of the human world. And so when Willie told me it was okay, because I would turn black one day, too, I wanted to believe him. Part of me did believe him.

So that's the story of my happy childhood on Greenmount Ave. An accidentally happy childhood. Until I got shot.

There's still a trace of a scar. It was a graze, a flesh wound. Walking home from school. Guy opened up on his girlfriend right across the sidewalk, in broad daylight; killed her, her new boyfriend, I guess he was, and Dwayne Pierce. Dwayne was in third grade with me. I got caught with a ricochet. My leg was a bloody mess, but I didn't feel anything. Passed out and woke up in the hospital. After that a social worker came to visit. I've no idea why. Maybe the school thought I was too much of a liability, too easy a target? In any case, I was moved in the middle of the year to Roland Park Elementary. Dad objected, believe me. It meant he had to drive me to school. One school is as good as another, he kept saying. A boy should be able to walk to school.

Should I move on? Should I skip ahead, a little? Somehow this seems like the place to do it. My father had AIDS. He died of AIDS. In secret, of course. The way he did everything. It was Enrique, most likely, that gave it to him. Enrique died from it, too, back in Honduras, after he left us. But it could have been any number of people. After Big Love, when we moved back to the city, we went through a time when there was a new guy around the house every month or so. He bragged, in the end, that he never once used a condom with a man. He may have been delusional.

In any case, it was all over fast, because he waited too long. AZT was around; the triple cocktail was nearly on the market; but by the time he bothered to see a doctor he had the full-blown disease and it was too late to start. In a couple of months he lost nearly twenty pounds; then he got

190

pneumonia, in November, November of 1994, and died on New Year's Day, 1995. He'd only been diagnosed — what was it? — a year and a half.

And who was I? Who was I, then, the day I became an orphan?

I have to stop. That's a story for another day.

13.

Martin switches the wipers to low against a mild drizzle, a fine mist, brackish with road salt; the residue crusts along the sides of the windshield. Gray-green, featureless April, the woods lining the highway dissolved in fog. Through the car's open vents I can smell the otherworldly scent of thawing earth.

Didn't you ever *meet* my father?

No. I'm sure I didn't.

Short guy, in tennis whites? You sure? Thinning hair, combed back? Gold stud in the right ear? You never came inside the house, not once?

Tennis whites?

He wore them all the time. They were the closest thing he had to a uniform. He was inordinately proud of his legs.

A moment passes. I'm growing aware, every time he stops speaking, of the particular qualities of silence inside this car. A cushioned, baffled, carefully engineered silence. The engine a low vibration more felt than heard. It's just new enough to have a new-leather smell, like a shoe store, but there are other, more prominent smells: Aftershave. French roast coffee. Dry cleaning? Is there a discernible smell from the plastic-wrapped package just behind my shoulder — the pressing iron, the steam, the sleek fabric itself exhaling? A teasing childish voice, asking, *how did this, and this, and this, come to be*?

Maybe, I say, maybe I should start by saying this: I was really shocked to know about your father. That you never told anyone.

He drains his coffee cup and thunks it back into the cup holder, emphatically.

Are you wondering what to say? he asks. Don't say anything. Did I give you a chance to care? Is it your fault you never knew what *nobody* knew? Of course not. He was a gay man in the Seventies and Eighties. Before anybody knew better. He didn't want anyone to pity him. Pity us, he always said. The catastrophe is general.

Not general to you.

Do you want me to say something I don't feel?

His BlackBerry, attached to his belt, buzzes and cheeps, a ringtone meant to sound like late-summer crickets. After four rings, as if coming out of a daze, he takes it out, silences it, and tosses it across the dashboard.

Listen, he says, maybe the way to put it is like this. My childhood — this whole story — it's like its own crazy little bubble, right? An ectoplasm unto itself. That's how Dad wanted it. And I understood him, and I followed the pattern. At first it was just out of shame. Later, toward the end, it was respect. You know the movie *Amadeus*? The part where Mozart dies, and they throw his body into the pauper's grave, the unmarked grave, and shake a little lime over it, not even a coffin? Dad loved that. Do *that,* he said. So I did. As close as you could get in the twentieth century. I kept his anonymity. I kept our big secret, whatever it was, exactly. But that's not the same thing as love. And it's not the same thing as grief, either. You could call it a habit of extreme privacy. Which I'm trying to break. *Slowly.*

I think about Robin — how can I not? — Tamika, Sherry, his house and its shiny, unplumbable surfaces, its granite and tile.

Whatever happened to Willie?

To Willie? You really want to know? It all ended in a fight over Legos. We still saw each other, that first year after I left Shabazz. I still ate at his house once or twice a month. Still needed it, to recharge my batteries. And his mother insisted. Stay friends, she always said. No reason you can't stay friends. She bought us toys to play with together. With what money I don't know. What was she thinking, buying toys that two little boys always have to share? I wanted to take the castle home to my house to play with, Willie said no, it's *my* castle, I shoved him, he shoved me, I cracked my head on the coffee table. That was it. Don't ever let them tell you only girls are bitter in their grudges. We never talked again. And after that, magically, my old neighborhood — that whole world — sealed itself off from me. When I was home, away from school, I was inside the house. Alone again. How was I supposed to know what a mistake that was?

There was no other way, was there?

Of course there was. At that point Dad wouldn't have stopped me from hanging out in the neighborhood. *He* didn't care. It was all me; I couldn't make it work. Not psychologically. It was too much of a break. After I left Shabazz it was as if my whole life was outside the neighborhood. That car ride to Roland Park was like my oxygen line. I was like some fragile plant that can survive only at one elevation. Who was there to tell me that it would take me twenty years to find the name for my unhappiness? That I had *had* everything I needed, and failed to recognize it, and thrown it away? It was a matter of starting from scratch.

But there's a thousand ways of starting from scratch. Is that what you're saying? That this all was a form of rebel —

I'm not *saying* anything. I'm posing a question. An obvious question. Was it me, or was it him? Did my father, effectively, make Martin Lipkin into Martin Wilkinson? Can your white father make you a black man? Or could I have been anybody?

I check the time signature on the recorder: one hour and fifty-three minutes. Is that all? A day, a week?

This is making you uncomfortable, isn't it?

What do you mean?

Oh, come on, Kelly. Your knee's jiggling.

He flicks on the emergency lights and slows the car, easing us off to the side, over the bassoon tones of the rumble strip and into the scabby grass. Across the drainage ditch a fallow cornfield stretches to a hazy, soapy horizon. To our left, the highway divider is an impenetrable thatch of overgrown oaks: the westbound traffic audible but not visible. The Northeast Corridor and

196

its abandoned outdoors.

Let me tell you something that happened when I first got to Bangkok, he says. Silpa's office was staffed by trannies. All different stages. It's common there. Some of them do a little work-for-surgery arrangement. And I was a little freaked out by them. I mean, anyone would be, if you're used to the ordinary, heterosexual world. So Silpa introduced me to Suki. His private secretary. You'll meet her — she's the best. She took me into an examining room and took everything off. Look at me, she said. Really *look*. Take all the time you want. It's okay. It's just hair and skin. It won't bite you.

And?

Well? I looked. I checked her out. I couldn't tell; she seemed one hundred percent. Her face — her breasts — down below — the whole package. I would never have known. It was complete. She was Silpa's best advertisement.

So what's your point?

You know what she said to me? *I don't ever think about being a man. As far as I'm concerned, I never was one.* I looked her in the face, and I just had to accept it. I had to buy it! So this is what I'm saying: what do I have to show you, Kelly?

To convince me it's real? I believe it's real.

How could I not?

To believe it was *always* real. I'm not talking about etiology. I'm not talking about *cause.* We can speculate about the circumstances all we want — later. Right now I'm just talking about the fact of the phenomenon. I was a black boy in a white boy's body. I was a black *man* in a white man's body. Can you accept that, Kelly? Can you really believe it's possible, when it comes down to it? I need to know. Before we go any further, I need to know.

I believe you.

No, see that's not the same. You *believe* it because I'm *saying* it. I'm not asking you to accept the words. I'm asking you to accept the thing itself. The possibility that —

Yeah, I get it. You don't have to repeat yourself.

Which means it could happen to anybody. It could be latent in anybody. It could be latent in you.

What would be the chances of that?

You think it's some kind of genetic freak that so many kids go to liberal-arts colleges, you know, Bennington, Santa Cruz, and come out as lesbians, and then a few years later they're getting the hormone shots and beginning to transition? You think environment and suggestion has *no effect at all*?

Either it's a fad, a style thing, which is bullshit, or it's present in a much higher percentage of the population than we realize. Given the technology, the resources, the access, a change in social approval, it could be ten percent. Seriously. There's research. And if one, why not the other? You have to turn the whole logic around. Not who are you *now*, but who would you most like to be? What is the ultimate form of you? You follow me?

I close my eyes.

Martin, I say, what you're really asking me to say is, you're not a freak. You're not a monster. You are, authentically, who you say you are. You are, one hundred percent, the black man Martin Wilkinson, the man I met at Mondawmin Mall, what was it, six weeks ago? You *are* that man. No one else. No matter what the explanation happens to be, in the end. Is that what you want me to say?

His eyes are shining.

Yeah, he says. I guess that's it.

Then the answer is yes. See? I don't even have to think about it. If you hadn't introduced yourself I would never have known. Isn't that enough? You could have gone on living your life. *You* chose.

I did. I put my faith in you.

And so what do *I* have to do, then, to

demonstrate that I was worth it?

When I know for sure, he says, I'll tell you.

We drive for ten more minutes in silence, and turn off the interstate onto Route 193, the suburban strip outside the old city, passing three intersections, each interchangeable with the last: Wendy's, Best Buy, Starbucks, Walmart, Target, HomeGoods, Bed Bath & Beyond. Since moving to Baltimore I haven't once needed to go to a mall, or any store larger than a supermarket, though in Cambridge, with a household of three, we were forever searching out some bargain outside the city on a gray February Sunday, placating Meimei with food-court egg rolls and new DVDs. In a little more than a year I've forgotten how to drive these four-lane roads, with cars stacked up in the dedicated turn lanes, the traffic signals signaling seven different movements at once. It's as disorienting as a pinball machine. I used to be the expert, the director, the choreographer of our American existence. And now, it seems to me, having stopped growing — shrinking, in fact, as I get older — I need nothing from this America. No economy-sized pallets of paper towels. No *Little Mermaid* bathing suits. I have failed to burgeon.

I look over at Martin, the very essence of

calm behind the wheel, eyes on every mirror, checking his watch. Which of us is the visitor, I want to know, which of us has given up his claim? Instead, I clear my throat and ask: how long are you going to be?

Are you on a schedule? I thought you had all afternoon.

Just for my information.

Maybe an hour and a half. These legislative lunches never run too long.

And what is it you're legislating?

Import-export stuff. Tax exemptions. Inspection issues at the port. I come down here every six months. All part of the job.

We'll have to talk more about that. *The job.* I still don't really grasp it.

Is it relevant? I mean, for this? For the story?

Maybe indirectly.

I'm an open book, he says. For you. For now. Ask away.

14.

During my dissertation-writing years, in my late twenties, I traveled so often between Beijing and Taipei and Tokyo and Cambridge that I coined my own term for jet lag: *the gray hour.* Three in the afternoon, the day after you've arrived, when the last of the morning's adrenaline has leached away, and, in the middle of teaching a class, driving on the highway, picking up a child from daycare, the daylight turns into a gluey fog, your eyes loosen in their sockets, and your stomach begins to burn its leftover acids: because it's three in the morning, of course, according to your circadian clock. Your fuels are spent; your body hardens into clay.

I park on Duke of Gloucester Street, just south of the statehouse, planning to walk downhill to the harbor market for lunch, but when I get out of the car I feel that same unmistakable lurching sensation, my clothes chafing, my shoulders about to give way, as if I've carried two bags of bowling balls up a long flight of stairs. The gray hour. I associate it with a satchel full of unread journals and the taste of the cheap jasmine tea I carried with me everywhere in a jar. On the next block there is a sign for a bookstore-café, the Wickett Arms, with hand-chiseled letters on what appears to be a blackened shield. I cross through the front space, an ordinary-looking room, and enter the café through an open grate in the rear. It's a brick vault, a former prison, with chains dangling from the walls between the fair-trade posters and framed burlap sacks from Costa Rica and Ethiopia. From the teenage girl at the counter I order a double red-eye — having never been able to stand the syrupy texture of straight espresso — and wait for it in front of the pastry case, not trusting myself to sit down and get back up again. Then, waiting for it to cool, still wary of a comfortable chair, I wander back through the shelves, looking for the African American section, and take down a copy of *The Souls of Black Folk.*

I read Du Bois in high school, in AP American history, and then later on in a class at Amherst called "The Concept of an American Minority." I'm remembering, now, something very particular: his description of his newborn son, who lived only a few days.

How beautiful he was, with his olive-tinted flesh and dark gold ringlets, his eyes of mingled blue and brown, his perfect little limbs, and the soft voluptuous roll which the blood of Africa had molded into his features! I held him in my arms, after we had sped far away to our Southern home — held him, and glanced at the hot red soil of Georgia and the breathless city of a hundred hills, and felt a vague unrest. Why was his hair tinted with gold? An evil omen was golden hair in my life. Why had not the brown of his eyes crushed out and killed the blue?

No more evil omens, no more vague unrest.

The body you want, not the body you have.

I could write a brochure.

Fuck, I think. I *am* writing his brochure.

On the same note, who would I want to be? How far does it extend? Could I be, for example, Takeshi Kitano? I've always loved Takeshi Kitano. Something about the weariness in his eyes, and his utterly still face.

204

Or, simply, better looking. Given the chance, I might choose to be handsomer. Better bone structure. A slightly larger penis. From what point do I begin to empathize with Martin? Or does this stretch and distort the very idea of empathy, the powers of the imagination? I have no idea what it would be like to want to be a woman. In my life I've known two trans-sexuals: Donald Hathaway, who was two years below me at Amherst, and who became Dani my senior year, and Trish Holland, at WBUR, who called herself a boy-dyke, wore three-piece suits, and resembled a thinner Leonardo DiCaprio with dark hair. In neither case did I ever feel I had to *understand* them. There is a point where analogies end. Acceptance has to precede analogy. Acceptance is not equivalence.

Acceptance is not enough.

I sip the coffee, now in its proper state, just short of scalding, and with a rush of tingling energy, take out my pen and notebook — a reporter's notebook, which I bought weeks ago and haven't used at all, except to note the dates and lengths of our interviews — and write out a line from the *Tao Te Ching:*

Know the white,
Stay with the black,
This is the pattern of Heaven.

When I was first learning Chinese in college, enraptured by each new character, I used to write famous quotations on little slips of paper and carry them around in my pockets, like fortune-cookie fortunes. At parties, after the third or fourth beer, I would distribute them to friends — girls, especially — making up meanings as I went along. It was one last failed attempt to cultivate an aura of eccentric cool. Later, however, in China, my ability to quote famous proverbs from memory made me a minor celebrity. In restaurants, at official banquets, people would crowd around my table to listen to the *laowai* who could recite Confucius and Zhu Xi. Wendy hated it. They're treating you like a monkey, she said. You're supposed to meditate on these things, not broadcast them like songs on the radio.

But, I persisted once, what if I find them relevant to the situation?

They're never relevant to the situation. They're *timeless*. It's different. You're distorting them. You think you're becoming Chinese, and you're not. You're becoming a parrot.

What would she think of all this? I won't ask myself this question, I've decided. Why should she, in particular, be my tribunal on matters of race? She hated to talk about it. Generalizations of any kind drove her to tears. Once, in a squabble over the remote, I forced her to watch ten minutes of *Chappelle's Show,* some inane skit about white men wearing grass skirts and Latinos playing bongo drums, and she went into the bathroom and vomited. No one I've ever met took the ideal of a colorblind society more literally. In one of her college essays — one I edited, though she hardly needed it — she wrote, *the idea of* e pluribus unum *means that all labels are deceptive. We could even say they are lies. Skin color, religion, and nationality are all beside the point, which is that human beings are individuals.*

She would never have forgiven me, I think, for taking up Martin's cause. If that's what I've done. Any more than she would forgive me, even for a moment, for wishing I was somehow other than who I am, that I had been born in Wudeng. She would never find it funny that I would call up a passage from the *Tao Te Ching* and pretend it matters.

Even if I don't think I'm pretending. Isn't the most basic lesson of Taoism, I would have said, that we should see things from every side? The yin-yang. Complementary forces. Strength flows into weakness, and vice versa. What are ideas of race but complementary forces, constructions that depend on each other? What Chappelle is doing, I told her that night, is just *playing* with stereotypes. Not embracing them. He's making them ridiculous. He's signifying. I got up to pull a Henry Louis Gates book down from the shelf, and she leaped up behind me and ran to the bathroom. When she returned, patting her blotchy face with a damp washcloth, she said, *you* can play. *You* can tell me it's okay. Because *you're already here.* And then she went to bed.

I look down at the characters; I finish the red-eye and contemplate asking for another. It's been forty-five minutes, but I'm not at all hungry; probably I'll just have a dry sandwich from the pastry case.

I look back at *Souls,* at the next paragraph, and the next, not thinking, not stopping, just reading:

No bitter meanness now shall sicken his baby heart till it die a living death, no taunt shall madden his happy boyhood. Fool that I was to think or wish that this little soul should grow choked and deformed within the Veil! If one must have gone, why not I? Why may I not rest me from this restlessness and sleep from this wide waking? Was not the world's alembic, Time, in his young hands, and is not my time waning? Are there so many workers in the vineyard that the fair promise of this little body could lightly be tossed away?

Your self-pity is unbelievable, I tell myself, as my sinuses begin to stick, a little contorted sob rattling in my throat, you myopic, narcissistic, privileged motherfucker, with your brand-new offshore bank account, your severance checks, your sheer, everyday whiteness, your get-out-of-jail-free card, you who can have it both ways, any way you like, but I am still looking toward the wall, so no one can see me frantically scrubbing the tears off, and getting up to slide the book onto its shelf where it belongs.

15.

Recording #2 (24:23)
Source: Maxell cassette tape, 60 minutes, condition +
Labeled side one "Tape 2 PRIVATE DO NOT DESTROY"

I have to say a little more about him. It's not right, leaving off the way I did.

This is the story he always told me: he grew up on a turkey farm in South Carolina. His dad died of liver failure at age six. His stepfather beat him with a rake. He spent three hours a day feeding turkeys and dragging the dead ones out of their cages and burning them. His dissertation was on Alexander II and the freeing of the serfs, and by god, he used to say, I was a serf. By those lights, could I really blame him? He went to Vanderbilt, by some miracle, and then when he was a junior some frat boys caught him coming out of a gay bar with his boyfriend. They were in the classics club together. The frat boys broke both of his legs and left the boyfriend a paraplegic. He used to say, I had a hard time making it to twenty.

But here's the thing: it was all a pack of lies. Except for the part about going to Vanderbilt. His mother — my grandmother — came down for his funeral. From Tuxedo Park, New York. Some of his colleagues posted an obit in the *Times:* that was the only way the family found out. He'd never changed his name, but in every other way he'd disappeared, lock, stock, and barrel, for twenty-five years. I asked her, what was he like, what was Dad's childhood like? and she said, uneventful. When did you know he was gay? Horrified: I had no idea he was gay. His dad, my grandfather, was some kind of executive in the early years at IBM; he had two older sisters, a handful of nieces and nephews. Grandnieces and nephews, surely, by this point. Afterward she sent me a whole file of photos, clippings, the works. His bar mitzvah tallis, his Bible. You should have these things, she said. They wanted to have me up there, a big family reunion, all the Lipkins together again. Thanksgivings, Passover Seders: until I moved out of the house, I got a call, every time.

Of course by then I knew I was Jewish. Part Jewish, of course, not technically Jewish at all, since Mom wasn't. Apparently, he knew that much. But Jewish enough that as soon as I went to Roland Park someone asked me which temple I went to, where I did Hebrew school. When I went home and asked Dad about it, he said, tell them you're a Hare Krishna. He wouldn't discuss it. It means nothing to me, he said; it means nothing to you. Just because you're surrounded by them doesn't mean you're one of them. And so what was I going to do, at age twenty-four, with his tallis, his old yarmulke, from 1958? Eventually I had to mail it all back. It was either that or burn it. His secrets, not my secrets. He was given something; he disowned it. I never had the chance.

What do you do with a guy like that? I mean, I should try to list, now, all of the small kindnesses, the little delights, of our life together. I should try to make him lovable. He was a good cook, of a kind. Much addicted to phyllo pastry, and anything pressed, pickled, or salted. A maniacal housekeeper. A catalog shopper — everything he bought for me came from Lands' End, L.L.Bean, or Sears, through the mail. If the Internet had existed then, he'd have bankrupted himself in an afternoon. He had none of the campy habits you'd expect — old movies, Judy Garland, opera — except he loved ballet. A mad fan of Maya Plisetskaya. He insisted I play the piano. He insisted I learn French. He taught me how to tie a Windsor knot. Which is more than most men can say of their fathers these days. There, is that a good enough list? Because the fact is, I think about him and I'm just blinded, still, even now, with this rage, that I will never know why he pissed so much of his life away on useless, pointless schemes for avoiding companionship and love. You can't simply call it agoraphobia. You can't call it trauma. Yes, maybe he nursed some secret pain; maybe, just maybe, he was abused, or what have you, violated. But I don't think so. He was in full command of his faculties. He knew what he was doing. In the end that was the kernel of his whole being, it was all he cared about.

For the longest time I thought it all went back to Beneficent. And believe me, I scoured the country, looking for any text, any article, something in an archive, a pamphlet, anything. Maybe with Google I would've found something. In any case — and this was later, when I was in college — it finally dawned on me: there's nothing there, really. There's no secret. There doesn't have to be a reason for human perversity; it just is. Spend enough time in Baltimore and you see that pretty clearly. There are people who are just a teaspoonful less human than the rest of us. And you take a decaying city, a ruined city, like this one, where the rents are cheap, where no one's looking over your shoulder, and it's just a magnet for them. Dad was just letting his freak flag fly.

This is what I mean. This is my whole point. About Sherry and Tamika. What do I think about Dad? Does it really matter, now, in itself? What do I do with Dad? is more the question. What did I learn? No mysteries. No questions unanswered. One day they'll know everything. Total sunlight on the whole fucked-up picture. Sunlight is the best disinfectant. Why am I making these tapes? Because now is not the time.

But there will be a time. They won't have to wonder what I was thinking. Call it revenge? All right, then. All right, Dad. That's my revenge.

16.

By the second week of my new life — my
post-work life, my early-bird retirement, as
a friend from WBUR put it, when I for-
warded him the news — I've reached a kind
of equilibrium, if not a routine. There are
still a few hours of work to do every day at
the office, signing unemployment applications and writing letters of reference, packing files into boxes and sealing them for
storage. BCC has hired a new program
director, Ken Wong, a twenty-five-year-old
fresh from the Towson college station, and
Ken's first order of business has been to
blanket the office with the new station's call
letters: *WZAK, the Zak!* — a bolt of yellow
lightning across a royal blue field. On our
desks, overnight, appeared *The Zak!* coffee
mugs and pens, mouse pads and refrigerator magnets, and thus Ken's second order
of business was an interoffice memo posted
on the front door and every other surface:

Throwing away WZAK promotional materials is theft and violators will be prosecuted. This applies to current and former employees. He turned off all our swipe cards, too, so we have to buzz, like deliverymen, and wait for Matilda, the poor security guard, to leave off watching *The Price Is Right* in the maintenance closet and let us in.

But by lunchtime — sometimes as early as eleven — I can clock out, no longer required to maintain even the semblance of responsibility, and to avoid the dread of long afternoons in a silent apartment, I've taken to walking uptown and depositing myself, my laptop, and a stack of books at Century Coffee, a new place just across the broad avenue from the Johns Hopkins main gate. There have been days warm enough to sit outside on the patio, at least for an optimistic hour or two.

And what do I fill my mind with, these days, no longer required to fill out a single spreadsheet or calculate a budget, parse the latest policy change from CPB or come up with a new tack for the grant-giving fundocrats at the National Endowment for the Humanities? For the first hour I put on my headphones, silence the Internet, open the folder on my desktop labeled *Transcripts,* and click on the first file: *4/12/12.*

Sometimes, sometimes I wish I didn't remember her, but I do. Just barely. She was incredibly pale, with that light, light blond hair, eyebrows, everything, and the one image I have of her is in the kitchen, this enormous kitchen, which had been the conservatory of the house before. She's standing against the windows, her back to the windows, and it's as if the sunlight is coming through her. I remember being terrified of that. And fascinated. In any case, there's my one memory, and then she was off. Untraceable, unidentifiable, or so my father claimed. I have no record of her whatsoever, not even a picture. I used to beg him to tell me whether I had her nose, or her ears, anything, and he would say, sorry, but as far as I can tell, you're all me. More's the pity.

You're the Alex Haley to my Malcolm X, Martin said the other day, with a hearty laugh, the Quincy Troupe to my Miles. Don't tell anyone I said that, right?

What exactly does that mean, Martin?

What exactly does that mean? You're my coauthor, not my ghostwriter. I want you to improvise. *Create.* Be a little bit of a myth-maker. Which doesn't mean I'm asking you to lie. Be selective, but don't lie. I don't want to have to sit there while Oprah rips me a new one like that *Million Little Pieces* guy.

Sometimes I wish I didn't remember my mother, but I do. She was very pale, with light blond hair and eyebrows, and the one image I have of her is in the kitchen of the commune where I grew up. She's standing against the windows, her back to the windows, and it's as if the sunlight is coming through

But that's just cleaning up the transcription. An oral interview isn't a story in itself.

My mother was the epitome of a white woman.

Ridiculous, and over the top.

I was an unwanted child.

What is this, Dickens? In frustration, I close the file, clicking *Do not save,* and start again.

I have two vivid memories of women from my early childhood. One is my mother, who disappeared when I was four. She was very pale, with light blond hair and eyebrows, and I remember her in the kitchen of the commune where I grew up. She's standing against the windows, her back to the windows, and it's as if the sunlight is coming through her. I was terrified and fascinated. The other is a young black woman who appeared one morning at the picnic table on the back patio, where we had meals in the summer. She wore a caftan, a bright orange-and-red print. She had an Afro. Lots of silver bangles on both arms. She must have been about thirty. I had no idea where she'd come from. I came out to ring the dinner bell — it was a big iron triangle, the kind they use on ranches — and I startled her, but then she looked over and saw me and smiled. She had been crying. There were tracks of tears on her cheeks. But when she saw me her mouth split into an enormous grin, the widest mouth, the friendliest mouth I had ever seen in my life. A slice of the sun. She laughed, and she said, where did you come from? I wanted to run to her. Hell, maybe I still am running to her.

Transcribing again. I can hear Martin, perched on my shoulder: *I'm not asking you to take dictation.*

But you're a natural storyteller. And you've done this before. Any story improves with practice.

I'm asking you to package me. I want the PG version. Do it this way and you're just asking people to psychoanalyze me. Lose the stuff about my mother, keep the part about Shirley O'Dell. Streamline. Say I have no memory of my mother. Make it easy on yourself. "The first woman I remember in my life was . . ."

People won't psychoanalyze you for idealizing a black woman?

It's simple cause and effect. It's imprinting.

You don't want to be seen as running away from whiteness, as choosing between whiteness and blackness? Is that offensive, or something?

It's complicated.

And what you're asking is for me to *not make this complicated*?

This time I hit *Save,* close my laptop, and leave it out for all to see as I head to the bathroom. Half wishing someone will steal it and put me out of my misery. When I return and find it still there, a mute clam, I switch the music in my iPod to Arvo Pärt's *Tabula Rasa,* prop my feet on the chair across from me, and close my eyes, hoping the shimmering violins can dissolve my misgivings. Trying to forget I'm in Baltimore at all.

Every month or so when I was in college I used to flee to Northampton — or if I was lucky, Boston, or once in a very long while,

221

New York — and spend most of a weekend drinking coffee somewhere, preferably at a table by the window, listening to my portable CD player and reading unassigned books. That was what I imagined adulthood would be like: a man drinking coffee by a window on a city street, an anonymous citizen, lightly employed, a cosmopolite of the world of the tactful and restrained. A world full of acquaintances, in which anyone might show up at any time. In the Nineties it was possible to believe you could go on living that way forever. Like now, I'm thinking, opening my eyes, this very moment, that woman over there leaning over the bar to retrieve an extra stirrer for her coffee looks just like Rina, my girlfriend all through junior year at Willow, her rust-colored hair held back in the same short ponytail, even the same three hoops in her right ear, but it couldn't be, of course, Rina lives somewhere in California, and then Rina turns and sees me and stops short, spilling the foam of her latté down her shirt.

And here you are, she says, when she's deposited her shoulder bag and half-empty cup at my table, and dried herself off, as best she can, in the bathroom, here you are, acting as if you have every right to be in

Baltimore. *I* sent an email around to everyone I still know from Willow when *I* moved back here.

When was that?

Last September. Listen, have you seen anybody? Does anybody still know you're alive?

I pulled up my stakes in Baltimore a long time ago. I'd be embarrassed, frankly. It would be like starting over.

That's ridiculous, she says, and scratches herself between the eyebrows. A gesture I remember, and yet never would have recalled in her absence. It's shocking how little she seems to have changed. Her face is a little longer, thinner; she's wider at the hips, more freckled, her teeth duller. She had perfect, luminous teeth; in the period of a few weeks when I couldn't stop staring at her, as if needing to be always reminded, I was fascinated by them, as much as by her tiny nipples, the size and color of pennies. She selected me, in ninth grade, literally grabbed my hand, at a party, and leaned against me, until I let my hands fall around her waist, and kissed me hard on the mouth. We dated, if you can call it that, for three months; then she went off to camp, had a fling with a counselor, and broke up with me by postcard. A mistake, she admitted later, but I never trusted her enough to try again, and we remained wary friends ever after, until our separate adulthoods swallowed us up.

I'm still in touch with Bill, and Trevor, and Myra — who else? Nellie. That's all. Ayala, too, though she's in San Francisco. But the locals would love to see you. Or at least, Jesus, know that you *exist.* But enough on that sore subject. What the fuck are you doing these days?

I give her the briefest version of recent events I can, and as I'm doing so, I notice a silver band on her ring finger, engraved with a serpentine pattern.

That's brutal, she says. I heard about it on the news, of course. And you want to know what my honest reaction was? I couldn't believe BCC was still around. Even in high school it always sounded so *ramshackle.*

Rina, I say, you didn't tell me you were married.

Oh — this? I'm not. I was. Lauren and I are separated. Married at Big Sur, before the ban, which means we'll have to get a legal divorce. I think. Actually, it's a little up in the air.

Rina came out as a lesbian in college, at Mills; I still remember the letter she sent

224

me, with a picture of her girlfriend, who wore a flannel shirt and looked like Fred Savage. Then, the last I heard of her, she wrote me again, over email, in 1999 or 2000, saying she was dating a man, Kevin. This was in San Francisco; they were partners at a start-up, something to do with simplified credit card transactions. *I'm done with labels,* she said. *I think that's the way the world's headed, anyway. Love who you love.*

That must be hard, being in limbo that way.

It's not as if we have actual assets to fight over. Or kids, thank god. Which reminds me. I heard, you know, about your wife and daughter. It filtered through the grapevine. But I didn't know where to find you. I thought about calling your folks, but then I realized they'd left, too. I should have sleuthed around more. Nobody gets lost these days.

Well, I say, I didn't open my mail for a month, nor look at my computer, so I wouldn't have seen it, anyway. Though I know that's not the point. You meant well.

It's nice of you to say that.

Listen, I say, desperate to find another topic, Rina, have you heard anything about Martin?

Martin Lipkin? No. Other than that he's gone.

What do you mean, *gone*?

I mean he left the country. Disappeared, straight up. Someone really tried to find him — I think it was Trevor, out of curiosity, this was years ago — and the deal was that his father died when we were in college, of AIDS, as it turned out, and then sometime after that Martin left. The house was sold. He went someplace in Asia, too, I think. Singapore or Shanghai or something like that.

Really. I had no idea.

You were his friend, too. You haven't heard from him in all this time, right? No Facebook, no nothing?

Not a word. Not since Alan's funeral.

I think he took it really hard.

I guess.

Kelly, Rina says, reaching a coffee-spattered hand across the table and laying it across mine, it's incredibly good to see you. It's, like, life-affirming. I really thought you'd go down some kind of black hole after what happened with your family. You were never exactly Mr. Chipper.

I became resilient. It happens. Traveling helped. Losing Alan helped. *Helped* isn't quite the right word, is it?

That sounds very wise.

She hasn't lifted her hand; in fact, she moves her thumb slightly, almost imperceptibly, under my palm. Passing a pulse.

You know where I'm living now? Glamorous quarters. Over my mom's garage. It's a full-on apartment, at least. They renovated it when I went away. You should come over for dinner. I have a separate entrance; you wouldn't have to see them.

I wouldn't mind. It's been years.

No, you would. Early Alzheimer's is no joke. Mom can be nasty. Paranoid. And she throws things. We've had to clear out all the vases, all the tchotchkes. Everything she hasn't already broken. And she's stopped speaking English. It's all Bulgarian now. Lots of complaining about Zhivkov and Brezhnev.

Which is why —

Yeah. Of course. Why would it be any other way? It wasn't for the weather. I mean, the job's great. McKinsey is great, when you're doing contract work and not trying to climb the ladder. In San Francisco I'd still be busting my ass eighty hours a week. But fuck, I never thought I'd move back to the East Coast, let alone *here.*

I'm really sorry, I say. Jesus Christ, Rina. I mean, I had no idea.

It's not the kind of thing you put in the class notes, is it?

I don't read the class notes. Though Willow still finds me, everywhere I go. I don't know how they do it. I'd have to change my name.

You'd have to do more than that. Go to ground, like Martin. Or have a sex change or something.

Yeah. Maybe that's the answer.

Look, Kelly, she says, and squeezes my hand again. I'm a little out of practice with the games and all, and plus, I don't really have time to do a whole dance, but I would really like you to come over. Soon.

How soon?

How about in three hours?

When the unavoidable time comes — after we've picked at our linguine long enough, and started a second bottle of Sangiovese, gulping at our glasses too eagerly, as if it were Kool-Aid; after she's switched the music from Nina to Billie to Ella, and gone from room to room lighting candles (trust a lesbian, she says, candles are *essential*) as night comes on; after she comes around the table and leads me to the bedroom, by one hand, undoing her blouse with the other — it happens so quickly, at least by comparison to the buildup, really in the length of one thought, one agonizingly guilty thought: how wonderful to feel a woman's curves, to have a body spill out, present itself, the breasts penduluming into your face, the alert nipples demanding to be tongued, the satisfying handfuls of her hips, her ass, her unshy legs gripping me, her hand finding me and guiding me into her. My eyes are closed; I look up for a moment; her eyes are also closed. We are two bodies having sex with a multitude. We have abandoned the present. This is my first time since Wendy; I ought to be weeping, to be curled up in a fetal ball; but as it turns out, I've waited long enough, the body's mourning period has passed, unnoticed, and now it cries out for something new, as bodies always will. We twist, and wrangle, on one side, then the other, winding up with me on top, her chin raised, her jaw working, as if readying to spit something out. Eyes closed again. Who do you want me to be? her body asks. I bend down and kiss her neck, work up to her ear, drop my hands under her back, coil my fingers around her shoulders. Robin's shoulders. Whose else would they be? Robin's breasts, rising up at me; I bury my face between them. With my eyes closed, I taste them; I pull out, move my face down, burrowing, moving my chin past her thatch of hair, inhaling Robin, tasting Robin, unembarrassed, undisgusted with myself, for the moment. What can I do? Someone once said — in high school, in college? I was drunk at the time, I was sprawled on a smoky carpet — *the cock is its own compass.* I'm with Robin, as long as my eyes are closed. I'm on the verge of saying it. Back on top of her, in the long arc of orgasm, when all our perversities are unleashed, I can taste her name. But I don't say it. I collapse, like a corpse, and sleep it off, and it's past midnight when Rina nudges me awake.

I'm going to take this as a compliment, she says.

Do you want me out of here? I should go.

Eventually. Before morning.

She's propped on one elbow, in a T-shirt and boy shorts, looking amused. I'm not even going to ask, she says. I'll take it that was a long time coming.

The first time, actually.

Jesus Christ. That's not funny. How the hell do you feel?

I don't know. I'm not awake yet.

Take it easy on yourself. They say it can be like starting the grieving process all over again.

I don't think so. It needed to happen. Even Wendy said so.

What do you mean?

Oh, I say, lightly, she used to visit me. We had conversations. Up until a few weeks ago, actually. And shit, she *scolded* me about not wanting to date. It was a major topic of discussion, believe me. You surprised?

Kelly, she says, remember? I spent the last decade in *San Francisco.* You'd have to work a lot harder than that to surprise me. Half my friends out there have astrologers. More than have health insurance.

Can I ask you an awkward question?

Is there any other kind, at this point?

You were thinking about someone else. So was I. So who was *your* someone else? Who was my body double?

Oh, she says, at first I was thinking about you. Remember that time we tried to have sex, back in ninth grade? God, I was *terrified.* I was thinking about how glad I am to be thirty-seven and not fifteen.

Seriously?

Come on, it's different for women. Do I really have to explain this, Kelly? I wasn't treating you like some blow-up doll. I was *synched* with you. Yeah, okay, I thought a little about this guy Brian. My last fling, before I moved back. What about you, though?

Someone I just met.

A possibility?

Definitely *not* a possibility.

Well, you're allowed to feel guilty, she says. Like it or not, you're still recovering. You're still in the process. You can't just decide that all of a sudden you're free of it all.

But if I didn't know I'd had these feelings —

Oh, come on, don't be ridiculous. You *knew.* She was just in the general class of *women I'd fuck if I got the chance,* and now she's moved up the ranks to *women I wish I could fuck right* now.

She's the wife of a colleague.

And?

And, I say, and, I think that, on principle, she'd rather jump off a bridge than sleep with a white man.

Man, Rina says, that is *hot.* A holy vow. It's like lusting after a nun. No wonder you're all skeevy about it. Go take a shower. Towels are on the chair. Go home and go to sleep. In the morning it'll all feel like a vague and pleasant dream.

We should get together again. Just to hang out, I mean. Let me buy you dinner sometime?

And then more kabuki sex? She reaches over and runs her fingers through my hair. I don't know, Kelly. Maybe this should just be like one of those little winter-break hookups in college.

I don't want to wait another fifteen years to see you again.

You won't be in Baltimore long, she says. That's my prediction. In the end it was never much more than a way station for you, was it?

I don't like to think of it that way.

Look, it's too late to be sentimental, isn't it? Of course you feel bad. We all feel bad. I mean, why did we leave, any of us, in the first place? Because of the crime. Because of the *unsolvable social problems.*

Which is just another way of saying —

That we don't want to look at so many poor people.

So many poor black people.

Yes. It hurts, doesn't it? In high school, you can feel optimistic about it. It's a *project.* But then after the project's over, and they're still poor, and it's the end of the Nineties, the greatest postwar expansion, blah, blah, blah, Sandtown-Winchester, economic development zones, and they're *still* poor, what do you do then?

You move to fucking Boulder.

Boulder, Portland, Santa Monica, Burlington, Park Slope. And look at me: I can't wait. As soon as I can, I'm going back. Don't get me wrong: I'm still putting my shoulder to the wheel. I was McKinsey's charitable-projects girl for two years. Twenty hours a week at the Oakland Partnership. But at least then I got to help poor black people and still live in paradise.

Rina, I say, how did we get this way?

What way?

The way you say, *it hurts to say it,* but it actually doesn't. The world is full of people apologizing for saying unconscionable things they actually mean.

Well, she says, I'd rather be cynical than self-deceiving, the way most Boomers are. I'd rather be mean and accurate. Like the line from the Liz Phair song. You know? *Obnoxious, funny, true, and mean?*

I want to be your blowjob queen.

She throws a towel at me.

You had a thing with Martin, too, didn't you? I ask, trying to be casual, as if I've just remembered it. Jesus, I forgot about that.

A *thing?*

Well, didn't you?

We hooked up once. One night. Sophomore year. So?

That was all?

Yes, that was all, she says. Now tell me: why are you so interested in Martin, all of a sudden?

You remember that song by the Pageboys, "Of All the Lost Ones"?

Of course. I loved that song. *You were the most lost of all the lost ones.* So?

So — okay. Forgive me for being schlocky, but that was him. He was always the most lost. And now, still, he's the most lost. The weakest link.

The weakest *living* link.

Yes. Right. It bugs me. It's always bugged me. How hard do you have to work, in 2012, to be utterly untraceable? So, you know, I'm just trying to jog my memory. I mean, he was slippery. It's hard to recall just what he was like.

He was a normal high school boy, Rina says, as I remember it. In that way. In that he was too eager. Sticking his tongue down my throat like he was trying to get my tonsils out. Grabbing me between the legs, groping around for the right button to push. You really want this kind of detail? It doesn't, like, turn you *on,* does it? Because that would be weird.

Trust me. I'm utterly unmoved.

I was really into him, she says, always was, and frankly I also always assumed he might be gay. In that he didn't have much time for any of us. And he was cute, in his own gangly way, and in a band and all. And the bass is a very phallic instrument. He just didn't *try*. Didn't wear deodorant. Didn't try to get rid of his acne. Kind of an enigma, really. But so that one night I guess someone had dragged him to the party at Ayala's house, and we were both drinking gin and Sprite, and somehow we wound up together in her dad's garage. You remember what it was like? That old Morgan he was always rebuilding, and the couches? So that was where it happened. Once I gave him the signal he was all attention, put it that way. Really wanted to have sex. Really, *really*. He might have been a virgin, for all I know. But we didn't have a condom or anything. So in the end he went down on me, and then I gave him head, and that was more or less it. We wound up sleeping all night back there. That enough for you?

That's plenty. Thanks.

Part of his mind was always elsewhere, she says. But in that sense he was just like Alan. Only the elsewhere was different.

What does that mean?

Well, she says, scratching herself between the eyebrows again, think about it. For Alan the elsewhere was death. We can say that for sure. But Martin wasn't one of those suicidal emo boys. He just wanted to be, I don't know, *elsewhere.* Far away. On some other planet.

Or to be somebody different.

Yeah, she says. Oh, wait! Fuck. I completely forgot. I *did* see him again, once. Just for a moment. God, that was years later, wasn't it? Nineteen ninety-nine. It must have been 1999, because that's the year Mom was diagnosed. I spent a month here, going around to nursing homes and things.

And?

Well, it was downtown, on Charles Street. Near that bookstore with the café, what was it called? The one across from the Walters. Anyway, it was definitely him. But he looked like a different person altogether. He was wearing a suit and carrying a briefcase.

Did you talk to him?

No! I mean, that's what makes it so strange. I rolled down the window and called out to him, and he didn't even look my way. Then, I mean, I pulled over, and got out of the car, and yelled, *Martin! Hey, Martin!* And he turned around, stared at me, I mean, obviously recognizing who I was, and then walked away. No smile. No wave. I was stunned. But then — I mean, I was busy. I was stressed. I just put it out of my mind. At the time I was *sure* it was him.

And I was sure *he* knew it was me. But later, you know, I started to wonder. I mean, who the fuck would do that? *I* never did anything to hurt him. Maybe he became an assassin or something. He looked like he might be going to kill somebody. But whatever it was, it was permanent. I feel sure of that. Whatever it was, we'll never know.

You're sure it was 1999? And he looked exactly the same? I mean, his face, his skin, everything?

Why would you ask that?

No reason, I say, trying to keep my face blank. Just looking for all the available information.

17.

Of course I remember you, Steve Cox says, over a stormy cell-phone connection, filled with flurries and zings of static. You know what I remember? Your face. You have a very open face. Or at least you did. Very — I don't know. Vulnerable. Not rigid. What's a word for not rigid? Flexible? No. Soft? *Permeable.* Not the kind of person an attorney gets to meet very often. I could tell instantly that you didn't deserve to be wrapped up in — well, what you were wrapped up in. And anyway, the details were pretty memorable, Kelsey. I see a lot of hinky stuff in here, but even by those standards. Say, did you ever think about that Costa Rica deal I told you about?

It's Kelly.

Sorry. I'm terrible with Christian names. Guess it comes from a lifetime of X v. Y. Kelly *Thorndike,* I have that right? How's your wife?

I'm having this conversation in the entry-way of my apartment, cradling the phone against my shoulder.

Long story, I say. She's not in the picture.

My condolences. Personal and professional.

I'm actually calling about something unrelated, I say, a completely different subject. I need someone to do a private investigation. A background check.

Employment? School?

Employment, I guess you could say. Loosely speaking.

The more you tell me, the more I can help you.

Okay, I say. Actually, cancel that. Call it a missing person instead.

Silence.

You still there? Steve?

I'm waiting.

It's an odd situation, I'll grant you that.

Life is full of nothing but. Listen, Kelly, you've got my full attention. Pen poised and ready. Pad on my desk.

The name's Martin Lipkin, I say, with a slight hiccup, a juttering of the chin. He was a high school classmate of mine. Willow School, Brooklandville, Maryland, class of '93. Last known address somewhere near Greenmount Avenue in Baltimore.

Last time you saw him?

Nineteen ninety-four. February. In Towson. That's a suburb.

I know where Towson is. Any sense of his plans at that time? I mean, you used the phone book, right? I'm not going to do one PR search and get his number?

No trace. I've looked everywhere I can think of. And no one I know from Willow has seen him, either. Not in fifteen years.

Anything else?

I can get his yearbook picture. I'll send it to you. And, oh, yeah, there's a very small chance — just the smallest possible chance — he might be using a different name. Martin Wilkinson. His mom's last name. You could search for both. It's a shot in the dark, but there it is.

So let me ask you one last question. What's your instinct? You think he might have moved to California? Alaska? Is he playing in a band somewhere? Doing porn? Selling drugs? He in prison? Selling real estate? Or just, you know, a bad correspondent? You think I'll find him with a wife and two kids out in Hunt Valley, just trying not to be noticed?

He was slippery, I say. Always kind of a mystery. Kind of fascinated by disguises. I think he could have made a really concerted

241

effort to hide his tracks. Not even necessarily for any good reason.

You know what my retainer is, in that case? I'll pay it.

Then you must have had a good divorce lawyer. Better than mine, anyway. Listen, I'm telling you, if you ever have a moment. *Costa Rica.* There's still parcels left. The country doesn't even have an army.

It's my turn to be silent, as he rattles on, his voice weaving in and out, packets of data colliding and falling apart.

Was he another depressed case, like your other friend, maybe? Be honest. Makes my life easier and saves you money. Could he be dead, you think? Homeless shelter? Halfway house? Because in that case you could spend everything and get nothing. You know how hard it is to get dental records on paupers' graves? DNA on a John Doe?

He's alive, I say. Definitely alive. Though that doesn't mean you'll find him.

18.

Recording #3 (34:56)
Source: Sony cassette tape, 90 min-
utes, condition +
Labeled side one "Tape 3 PRIVATE DO
NOT DESTROY"

When did I first know I was white? Not at
Shabazz. No, sir. Of course I knew I was
the color white. I knew I wasn't black. I
knew I wasn't Mexican or Korean or Puerto
Rican. But when did I know I was white,
as a thing in itself, as something to be? At
Roland Park. At Willow. At Roland Park, at
Willow, where there were other white
people.

The funny thing is, it was all a little artificial
at first. I had to be told. When I arrived at
RP, I spoke, effectively, black English. Not
consciously. Not at home. But I had a
school vocabulary; I addressed the teach-

243

ers as they expected to be addressed. Where Darnell at? He on the jungle gym, Miz Dixon. It's just idiom, after all. Any child can pick it up. And at Shabazz no one thought it was funny; no one thought I was funny. Sad, maybe, a little, but not funny. But at Roland Park the teachers were in a panic. The second or third day — I'll never forget this — they had a meeting with me, my teacher, the principal, Dad, of course, and a speech pathologist. Martin, Mrs. Richards said — that was my teacher — it's not wrong to speak that way if you want, it's not hurting anybody, but there's such a thing as standard English, and that's what we speak at this school. We don't want you to be uncomfortable here.

I'm not uncomfortable, I said.

And we don't want you to make anyone else uncomfortable. Without meaning to. Ashante, for example. You like Ashante, right? Didn't she share her cupcake with you at lunch? You don't want her to think you're making fun of her. That's when I started to cry.

What was I supposed to think? And Dad, I

looked over at Dad, and he was just kind of puzzled and amused. Don't worry, he said. You want your little chameleon to change colors. He'll change soon enough. They didn't think that was funny. But you know who really took offense, after all that fuss? Malik Williams. Remember him? His son was in my class. The *Sun* columnist, the first black columnist they hired, though he lasted all of five minutes. He was an old-school firebrand, an Al Sharpton wannabe, with a big head of dreadlocks and a beard. Scary Rasta style, though he was local — West Side through and through. He was fired in a plagiarism scandal, accused of stealing copy from some other columnist in Atlanta. Of course he sued, and lost. Major news in Baltimore in the mid-Eighties.

In any case, his son, Stokely, came home and told him that there was a white kid at Roland Park trying to talk like a brother, and he just hit the roof. Demanded a meeting with the principal, wanted to meet with Dad, too. He called it cross-racial experimentation. Wrote a column about it, too. What kind of perverse linguistic experiment is going on at Roland Park Elementary School? Why are they teaching white children to speak pidgin Black English? And Stokely — God, he was such a nice kid — he was really caught in the middle. He even said to me, Dad told me I should give you a beat-down. He was the tiniest kid in the class. Couldn't have beat me in arm wrestling.

But it worked: after that I shut up. Stopped talking in class altogether. No one said anything about it; I think they were relieved. Took me almost an entire year, most of third grade, and then, when I opened my mouth again, I was white. Dad was right. I hardly remembered being at Shabazz. To spare myself from having to explain it, I used to tell people I'd been at RP since kindergarten, and hardly anyone ever questioned me about it. I mean, I was happy, wasn't I? You know what it's like there: it's a good school. A little island of happiness with a well-fortified PTA. Those jungle gyms get repainted every year, and that library has story time in three different languages. They don't sell off the new textbooks and use the old ones at RP. I'd send my kids there in a heartbeat. Those were the happiest years of my life, you could say, once I settled in. So to speak. Third grade up until middle school. Well, it's a latency period, isn't it? In more ways than one. Transsexuals, you know, they say the same thing. Prepubescent children are allowed to be androgynous, to a degree. They can play at cross-dressing, they can engage in all kinds of imaginative fooling around. Or, in some cases, they can just be nothing. Ungendered. Sexless, curveless, living only in their heads. That must have been me. Once I knew I was white — once I was told, once I was reminded — I just sort of relaxed into being nothing at all. I spent no time outside in the neighborhood. None at all. If I played outside of school, it was at friends' houses. Or on Roland Avenue. For a few years I spent every afternoon till five at the Roland Park Library, across the street from school. Dad picked me up there. And then when I was a little older I started taking the bus down to Hopkins to meet him on campus. It was a pretty genteel existence, comparatively speaking. Roland Park blots out the rest of the world pretty damn well.

And then I went to Willow. There was no option, really, at that point. Dad wanted me to go to Northern Middle, but the guidance counselor at Roland Park had some kind of private meeting with him and convinced him that he didn't want a dead son. What was allowable, what might slip under the radar, at Shabazz, was not to be tolerated after grammar school. Thus our apartheid system proceeds. So I was set up with the SSAT, and went on interviews, all kinds of aptitude tests, and Willow was the one that wanted me.

I'll never forget the first time Dad took me out there. It was in April, early April, just this time of the year. Trees bare, chilly, rainy. We came up the driveway, past the horse barn, past the pasture, the lacrosse field, the other lacrosse field, you know, rounded the top of the hill, saw the lake, the theater, and the trees all around, trees that seemed unending in every direction. I mean, talk about a brand. Talk about impact. The Willow School. As in, you are going to school in the enchanted forest. And that was before I even saw the swans. Who goes to a school with swans? People call it a country club, it's not a country club. It's a sacred grove. How can you not feel special? How can you not feel, like, elected to be there?

Up to that point, believe me, I had worked

hard, so hard, at being average. I followed football, baseball, and basketball. It drove Dad crazy. I listened to Z100. Whatever the big movie was, I wanted to go. After *Top Gun* I had the little bomber jacket and the aviator glasses. Frankly, I would have been happiest in the suburbs. I had a friend, Carl, whose dad lived out in Owings Mills; I had a sleepover there once. Typical ranch house, basketball hoop in the driveway. We played In the sprinklers and went to Chuck E. Cheese's for dinner. I thought that was paradise.

So you can see: Willow was a shock. Whatever it was, it wasn't normal. Look down the hall: you've got the pimply eighth-graders hunched over their Magic cards, you've got Sheila Puchner practicing her Ophelia monologue, Dr. Kendricks arguing with Jason Kornbluth about the Second Law of Thermodynamics. You've got kids learning to play "Epistrophy" on the xylophone and kids sneaking out into the woods to smoke clove cigarettes. God, I hated it at first. I'd worked so hard not to be a freak, and here I practically had to be one.

19.

Martin takes the topmost styrofoam box from a stack of three, opens it, and hands me a blue crab still in its death clench, brick-red, crusted with Old Bay. I've already spread the *Sun* across the picnic table, unpacked the cheap Chinese mallets and bamboo picks, the potato salad and tepid complimentary cans of RC Cola. What's your strategy? he asks. Pick and accumulate? Or pick and eat?

Pick and eat.

Davis, he shouts over his shoulder, don't think that just because I'm eating I'm not watching you. I'm *watching*.

We're in Druid Hill Park this time, at the picnic tables on a rise overlooking the basketball courts. Half past noon, late April now, a muggy spring Saturday. On the far side of the park drive is the reservoir, and beyond that, the fringe of the downtown skyline. I imagine I can see the shot tower, that old Civil War relic, off to one side. Davis, Martin's little brother — Big Brothers Big Sisters of Baltimore — is running wind sprints across the court, a long, thin shadow in gray track pants and a Golden State Warriors shirt. Every so often he stops and smears an arm across his eyes. He hardly seems winded.

He's sixteen, Martin tells me, six-six, rear guard, great rebounder. Plays for City College High School. Doesn't need to be coached, thank god, 'cause that's not my thing. I'm here for the bigger issues. Life issues. Kid lives with his mom and three little ones. Older brother's in federal prison in Richmond. Under the three-strikes system, interstate transport of narcotics, that's twenty years. *This* one, though, he's supersmart, 3.71 GPA, three AP classes. He's going places. But he has to be watched. Mom's supportive and all, but she's got two jobs and a so-so boyfriend.

And what do you do, exactly?

Honestly? I bother him. That's my job. He gets a call or text from me at least every other day. We have Wednesday-night dinners twice a month. I come to his practices. I've been to his parent-teacher meetings when Laronda can't make it.

That sounds more like surrogate father-hood.

No doubt. It bugs him, too. He's embarrassed to be seen with me. So be it. Everyone his age should have a persistent dickhead like me tapping him on the shoulder. On his own, remember, Davis's life expectancy is ten years. BBBS is double-teaming him, me and another guy for when I'm out of town. The program needs a big success. Harvard. Stanford. There's matching funds at stake.

Teeth clamped around a finger of crab, working it doggedly from the claw, I'm trying to remember the first time I saw Martin in ninth grade. It must have been at school, but I have no memories of him at school; what I remember is the first time he appeared at band practice, in the early spring. Alan and I had been fooling around in his basement for a few weeks; we didn't have a name yet, or a single finished song, but it was permanent enough that I'd stopped lugging my kit home every time. We hadn't decided to formally audition bassists, but somehow Martin knew about us, and simply appeared, one Sunday, in stone-washed jeans, Converse high-tops, and a plain white T-shirt tucked in at the waist. His bass — painful as it is to remember — was an

Ibanez, sky-blue, with a lightning-shaped head, and he wore it, as he always would, too high, at belt level.

Penny for your thoughts, Kelly.

I'm just thinking about what a dork you were when we met. Or, rather, what a dork I *thought* you were. A music nerd. You were really into jazz fusion. Weather Report, Jaco Pastorius, all that junk.

That was all Willoughby's doing. Dad's last boyfriend. *He* was the one who turned me on to playing the bass. Dad would never have paid for music lessons, but Willoughby was right there, after all, a house fixture. He made me practice on a fretless bass before I even got to *see* a normal one. I could play the Allegro from *Eine Kleine Nachtmusik* on that thing. And after that it was all Seventies stuff. Steve Swallow, Ron Carter, Jaco, Genesis, Oregon, Pink Floyd. You could say it taught me to respect the instrument, I suppose. It gave me technique, though of course it wasn't the technique that really mattered.

I would have said — looking at you — that you'd never heard hip-hop in your life.

I *hadn't* heard hip-hop, he says, wiping his mouth delicately with a napkin and reaching for a third crab. Not in my conscious mind. Of course, it was there when I was at

Shabazz. It was on the boom boxes. Kool Moe Dee, Roxanne Roxanne, Run-D.M.C. Probably I liked it as much as any kid. But that was *rap,* that was a dream, a lost era. We did breakdancing, too, when I was at Shabazz. Was anyone talking about breakdancing in 1991? It was just *humiliating.* Even when you guys listened to it I never paid attention. Public Enemy, A Tribe Called Quest, NWA: I missed all that stuff. Didn't want to touch it. You can understand why. All those layers of repression, all that impacted shame.

And then what happened?

He laughs and spreads his hands out on the table, putting his thumbs down on the newspaper, now patterned with concentric spills of soda, crab juice, and brine. Why does this have to be a story about hip-hop? he asks. I mean, sure, *later* I listened to Biggie and Puff Daddy and Tupac and everyone else. But that was never my thing, really. Not exactly. For me it was reggae.

Reggae?

The house of blackness has many doors. Not everyone chooses the same way in. Jazz. Blues. Plantation hollers. Talking drums. Dance. Masks. Drag. All the different forms of the diaspora. Robin taught me that much. What I liked about reggae — what I didn't like about rap — was that you just couldn't beat it down. Even when it was angry it was still happy. It was still *music.* The thing is, too, reggae tells a story. I mean roots reggae, the real stuff, not that Beenie Man crap on the radio now. Reggae is its own world. A direct relationship to Africa. A direct descendant from the kings and queens. It's a whole cosmos. Next to that, hip-hop is pretty weak. In my view. But I didn't come to realize this until much later. When *I* was alive again. When I was receptive.

After high school. After Alan.

Yeah, he says, you're right. We're jumping ahead. But you asked the question.

You said *you were alive again.* Meaning what?

He turns and looks again at Davis, who's doing a through-the-legs dribbling routine from one side of the court to another. His nostrils flare. An extra shot of oxygen. The throb of energy a moving body, a child's body, *this* child's body, throws off.

Meaning I was my true self, he says, meaning I was the person I am now, in embryonic form, anyway. This is hard for you to hear, isn't it? How could it not be, right? But listen: high school was simple. I was in a band, thanks to you guys. I was some kind of punk rocker, indie rocker, by association, anyway. And the rest of the time, heck, I was *studying*. I'll say one thing for Willow: all that shame, all that passive-aggressive, no-discipline, high expectations and no consequences stuff, it worked on me. I couldn't look at Mrs. Walbert's face when she was disappointed in me; she puffed up like a soufflé. So I *learned* chemistry. Whatever it was, whatever they put in front of me, I soaked it up, thank god. Don't you remember that I won the Latin prize three years in a row?

To be honest, I say, no. I'd forgotten.

No, in high school, by that time, I'd found a niche. I was a busy little beaver. Up until the riots, at least, I was actually *happy*.

What about the riots?

Okay. Okay. Here we are. The final, the last, affirmation of my whiteness. He laughs, suddenly, as if he's startled a flock of flamingos. You know what it's like, talking to you? he says. It's like what they say in AA about the trapdoor. You know that expression? You think you've hit bottom, but you've only hit a trapdoor.

Maybe that's what memory is like, I say. And think: maybe that's what friendship is like.

Yeah, he says, the past is a black hole and all. No worries. You'll find a way to stitch it up. Don't look so sad, Kelly.

I'm thinking about '92. No happy memories there.

No, he says, so let's be like the Special Forces and get in and get out, okay?

Davis climbs up the stairs from the courts, slugging from a bottle of Gatorade the color of antifreeze.

Have a seat, D, Martin says. Kelly and I were just talking about you. About colleges. You know, *he* went to Harvard.

Davis gives me the barest possible recognition, a tight little nod, and sits on the other end of my bench, making a triangle of the three of us. He has an impassive face, rounded around the mouth, and ears that seem too small and too high, little doughy squiggles above his long temples. A slightly goofy-looking kid, used to avoiding an adult's gaze.

Grad school, though, I say. Pretty esoteric stuff. Chinese poetry.

I thought you were a reporter.

Kelly's had many lives, Martin says. Like a lot of people. Like me. It's the nature of the times. That's why it pays to have options.

Does he sit and declaim like this all the time, I'm wondering, or is it just for my benefit? Look, I say, I really don't know anything about the college game these days. Other than it's harder than ever. You taken the SATs yet?

PSATs, he says. SATs in the fall.

Test prep this summer, Martin says. After his defense clinic at Auburn. You get your mom to sign the form?

She's in Atlantic City. With Manny.

How long?

He shrugs. Aunt Doris is watching the kids, he says. Manny's talking about getting a catering job up there. Keeps saying he's going to move us all up there for school in September.

There's no jobs in Atlantic City, Martin says. Economy's dying. Now that there's slots at every racetrack in the tristate. Plus Foxwoods. Plus the hurricane. I wouldn't worry about it.

He's got a friend, though.

A friend's not a job. Job's not your mom taking her babies out of Baltimore.

A fire engine races by on 29th Street, barking and screeching, sending a flock of tiny birds up into the air, where they form a cloud, a disk, and then drop all at once back onto the grass. Davis discreetly flicks through the messages on his phone.

Where else'd you go to college? he asks me.

Oh — Amherst. You know where that is? In Massachusetts?

Where Emily Dickinson's from, he says, expressionless. We just did a unit on her. That's a real place? I mean, it's still there?

Yeah. Actually, it hasn't changed that much. The buildings, I mean. It's still a quiet little town. Great school, though. Really small classes. Why, I'm thinking, can't I squeeze out a sentence longer than three words? Nobody falls through the cracks there, I say. You can't be anonymous. You get all the attention you could ever want. On the flip side, you're stuck with the same four hundred people for four years.

He gives me a look halfway between astonishment and disgust.

Four hundred people in the *whole school?*

Davis, you have got to understand, Martin says. The really good places are small for a reason. Lots of advantages to that. Plus, it's a tiny school sitting on a mountain of money. Get into Amherst and they'll give you a full ride. Books, travel, everything. It's the all-star league of the mind. Here, show Kelly that video you made.

I deleted it.

BS, man. It's on YouTube.

My data plan's off.

Okay. *Fine.* Martin takes out his phone,

taps the screen, and hands it to me. I book-marked it, he says. It's Davis in front of a wavering camera, in an alley, or an abandoned lot, with two girls flanking him in matching black hoodies and pink wide-frame glasses. The audio isn't tracked with the video, and I can hardly hear the beat through the phone's tinny speakers, but I can hear Davis's piping, slightly flat falsetto: *I willed my keepsakes signed away — what portion of me I could make — assignable and then there interposed a fly — with blue uncertain stumbling — buzz between the light and me —*

That was his class project, Martin says. For the Dickinson unit.

He's gay, I'm thinking. For what good reason? Because he sings too high? Because he's secretive and drawn into himself, because of the way he folds his legs, the delicacy of his fingers tapping the table like a keyboard? He's gay, and Martin doesn't know. Is it true? Would it matter, even if it was? All Martin's trying to do is get him through twelfth grade. And give him the chance to unmake himself.

By the time he's in college — say, three years from now — Martin will no longer be just *Martin*. The truth will be out. And another avenue of unmaking will be open.

I look at Martin's face, and at Davis's.

The truth is, I'm thinking, it could be almost anyone. There's a fly beating against the glass of this thought. If the hole is deep enough. If the wanting is bad enough. Did I think we were special? Was Martin special?

Mom's asking when I'll be back, Davis announces, chin buried in his chest.

Okay, Martin says. Got to clean all this up first. Want some crabs? There's extra.

Mom does that, he says. Cleans them and all. Makes crab cakes.

Stay just as you are, I want to tell him. Don't go anywhere. Don't go.

20.

The second night of the L.A. riots, April 30, 1992, was also the night of L'Arc-en-Ciel's biggest show, at the Spring Fling at Johns Hopkins. We were supposed to show up for sound check two hours early, but by four-thirty we were stalled in Alan's living room with the TV on; our amps and cases stacked in the hall, my station wagon unloaded. Reginald Denny's beating — the white man yanked from his cement truck, kicked, struck with a brick, left lying with his long blond hair splayed in blood on the asphalt, all filmed in the shaky lens of a helicopter camera — played in an endless loop on all four stations.

Alan sprawled across the couch, guitar in his lap, fingering chords silently and staring at the set list he'd written inside the back cover of *Heidegger: Basic Writings.* Martin had gone to the bathroom and never returned. I sat curled up in an easy chair, smoking one of Ayala's Camel Lights from a pack she'd left on the mantelpiece. I hadn't smoked since one obligatory trial cigarette in sixth grade; in fact I hated smoking, was opposed to it, considered it a form of mass corporate poisoning, an addiction factory, but I needed something to ease my ratcheting heart, and we didn't have any weed in the house, and drinking was out. It was bad luck to drink before shows. And in any case my personal feelings about smoking, as about anything else, had never seemed more irrelevant, more like piss in the ocean.

I had been sitting, immobilized, for the better part of an hour, watching plumes of black smoke rising from South Central, lines of policemen with shields and shotguns, spidery looters carrying stereos and sacks of diapers through shattered windows. I had a splitting headache. I wanted to break my sticks, take a kitchen knife and slash my drum heads, or pour gasoline over the whole kit and set it alight, if that wasn't such a cliché. Instead, I concentrated on each inhalation, trying to measure out a lungful of smoke, swallowing the dry cough and the urge to spit.

We can't just play a fucking *show,* I said to Alan. Right? I mean, what do they want us to say? *Happy fucking spring?*

He got up and turned off the TV.

What the hell are you doing?

Enough, he said. Enough is enough. Just sit tight for a second.

I stood up to stretch my legs, and saw a flicker of movement in the window: Martin was standing on the front lawn. He'd taken his shirt off and hung it around his shoulders, and he stood, hands on hips, staring up at the mulberry tree that hung over the side of the house, now just beginning to bloom.

When Alan returned he held out a record for my inspection: Fugazi's *Repeater,* lyric sheet turned up. "Styrofoam," he said.

There are no more races to be run
There are no numbers left to be won
We are all bigots so filled with hatred
We release our poisons like Styrofoam

This is what we're going to do, he said. To start with. Hold still. He popped the cap off the Sharpie and wrote something in block letters on my forehead. Now you do me, he said. Martin! Come here!

Bigot, Alan's forehead said.

Mine said *Racist.*

Martin's: *Burn This.*

The songs we played, without more than a fifteen-second pause in between, were our angriest, loudest, most dissonant. That was all: three songs, and then two tall guys rushed the stage; one threw Alan off, into the crowd, and the other leaped over the guitar amp and then tripped on the drum riser and knocked three teeth out on the edge of the bass drum.

It happened, as they say, in slow motion, in a kind of sludgy, badly colored filmstrip: Alan balling up around his guitar in midair; Terc kicking a third guy off the stage as he tried to climb up; a complete stranger running right at me, *for* me, fists outstretched, and falling, and rolling across the stage with his hands wrapped around his face, blood running through his fingers. My crash cymbal was in my lap, the snare under my feet; a guitar cord whipped through the air; Martin's bass cabinet groaned as someone knocked it over. Sirens; squawking megaphones; I pushed the hardware away and scooted off the stage to the left, thinking I would circle around and find Alan out front, and promptly, as I reached the stairs, tripped myself, and planted my elbow in a row of stage lights. I still have that scar.

21.

Young man, says the elderly woman in the salmon suit next to me, nudging me with her elbow. Young *man*. It's your turn.

She hands me the collection plate, full of bills, of course, fives and tens and a few folded inconspicuous ones. I'm on the aisle, and the deacon is already waiting beside me. I balance the plate on my knees, trying to let nothing drop, and reach for my wallet. Three bank receipts, a misplaced Acme Coffee Frequent Flier card, and a twenty.

In goes the twenty.

Did she notice? Her eyes stay locked on the choir, which is cooling off after a fast "What a Friend We Have in Jesus." The deacon, who can't be less than eighty, puts his hand on my shoulder as he shuffles to the next row. Possibly for balance. And at the same moment Martin, packed in with Sherry and Tamika and Robin in the row in front, turns around and gives me an assessing look. You okay? he mouths.

I nod and smile.

What else can I be here but a quiet, insignificant alien, an observer, a gap in the fabric? There are the women with enormous hats, great tilted slabs of taffeta and satin; there are men with two-toned shoes and matching purple ties and pocket squares; the choir wears burgundy robes with kente-cloth scarves; and the minister, Dr. Reginald Charles, looks a little like Samuel L. Jackson with deeper-set eyes and without the indignant stare. The air is thick with the smell of gardenias and hyacinths and musky cologne. And those of us without fans are fanning ourselves with our programs. It's hitting all the marks, as Martin said it would, when he gave me the address over the phone yesterday. Don't come expecting to be surprised. Moved, maybe. Overwhelmed. It's not about subtlety. Sometimes even Robin gets a little embarrassed. She's not sure she wants you to come.

Tell her I'm really looking forward to it, I said.

Yeah. I'm not sure that'll help.

We're near the end now, after a sermon that must have lasted forty-five minutes; I followed the first half, a reading of the parable of the talents as a message about financial security and self-sufficiency, but lost the thread somewhere in Paul's letter to the Philippians, and even the woman next to me, who had punctuated every other sentence with *Mmm-hmmm* and *Tell it* and *Yes, Lord,* lowered her chin and began to list against me toward the end. And then sprang awake, and up, with the first chords of "Forever Praising Him," the burbling of the fretless bass and the snap of the electric snare.

Here's the thing: I don't follow the rituals, I'm shaky on the good news, but I know the music. Contemporary gospel is just a hair away from Eighties pop R&B, and if you grew up, like I did, with Whitney Houston, Janet Jackson, El DeBarge, Jermaine Stewart — *we don't have to take our clothes off to have a good time* — then the sound of this music, minus the choral singing, the multiplied voices, is the sound of MTV in 1986, all squiggly neon lights, shoulder pads, pink lipstick. It's *The Cosby Show.* Irrepressible happiness. *Teflon* happiness. And I don't mean that in a bad way.

At several points along the way, in fact, I've been wiping tears out of my eyes.

I get this way in churches. And synagogues. Partly because I associate them with funerals and weddings. But mostly because, like many areligious people, I secretly love the idea of church. Human beings need rituals. I took an anthropology of religion course in college — the professor was a lapsed seminarian from Ghana — and I remember him saying, *we're only a hundred years removed from an absolute reliance on sacredness, at most. That's a hundred years versus a hundred thousand years of human development. Sacredness doesn't disappear; it migrates into the realm of the absurd. Going to the gym. Putting on makeup. Collecting wine. Riding a speedboat.*

I'm staring at the back of Martin's neck.

If you had nothing — if you started from nothing — and came upon *this,* a fully formed world, based on the idea of not enduring, not even resisting, but actually *refusing* pain, not sitting and waiting for the spirit but actually embodying it, loudly and clearly, every week, whether you feel like it or not —

It could be anyone.

Young man, the woman next to me says again, when everyone is standing, embracing, collecting hats and purses, I could use a hand getting up. She holds out her hand, I take it, and her grip locks against mine; under the loose, ashy skin, speckled with liver spots, her frame is rigid, the joints welded by sheer determination. Help me with something, she says, reaching into her handbag and producing a smartphone in a pink rubber case. Check and see if there's a text message on there, would you do that for me? My grandniece just had a baby and said she was sending me a picture. I can't read the buttons. All I do is, people call me and I swipe the thing and talk.

I open the phone, and indeed, there's a text from Kimmy, *grandma sylvie we luv u heres the newest member of the family thomas javon turner,* and a picture of a swaddled newborn in someone's arms, with pasty black hair, narrow cheeks, and puzzled green eyes.

Oh my, Sylvie says, when I hand back the phone.

Looks like my little one, I'm about to say. Because he does look a little like Meimei: that same grayish skin, and the wide, startled look, melatonin and pupils meeting daylight for the first time. But that would be a weird thing to say. A bad omen. Congratulations, I say, instead. That's a beautiful baby.

Sister Sylvie, Martin says, I need my friend back now, if you don't mind. But she's already turned away, under the spell of life.

■ ■ ■ ■

It was Alan's decision, Martin says. He was
the one who found the marker. He was the
first one to do it. I know he wrote that it
was consensus. It wasn't. *I* wasn't comfortable with it.

Slowly, pensively, with a rounded, overfed
gait, we're crossing Taylor Park, which leads
from Martin's neighborhood to the far side
of the Maryland Institute campus and the
expressway. For lunch Robin made blackened snapper, quinoa salad, and miniature
quiches with kale and bacon. It's the one
decent meal I've had in a week. There are
chickadees and killdeer skittering overhead
and the trees are just furred with green. A
moment of fragrant life, life springing underfoot.

Then why didn't you say anything?

What was I supposed to say? I just wanted
to play the show. Maybe with a dedication
to the victims. Something neutral.

That's your big realization? That you felt
nothing? During the riots, when the rest of
us were so outraged?

You want to know what it felt like? Think
about it. Think about everything I've told
you. Forget who you thought I was. Can

you imagine the sheer oddness that I was feeling, the sense of not being where I was supposed to be? And where *was* I supposed to be? That's what I'm talking about. I was stunned. I felt sick. What I did *not* feel was some righteous sense of *us* and *them*. I felt — you want to know what it was like? Remember that ectoplasm thing I was telling you about? So this was like that — like being an egg. Someone picks up an egg and taps it on the edge of a bowl. Tap, tap, tap. Testing. How hard is it going to be? How much force is required, to break that egg? Every egg is a little different. Too hard, and you spill it everywhere. Too soft, and it'll take you forever. There's a thrill in that moment of *testing*. You want to know what it was like? It was *exciting*. It was *stimulating*. You think that's sick? That's how it was. I feel my insides coming out and I didn't know whether I was supposed to cover up the wound or just let go. Was I supposed to be the guy with the brick, or the guy on the ground?

Those were the only alternatives?

In that moment, yes.

I don't think so. I don't agree.

Oh, come on, he says. *Remember*, Kelly. Put yourself back in that moment. He spins around and takes a snap at me, one hand half fisted, the other slapping his shoulder. You're telling me that there wasn't part of you that was saying, *don't hurt me! Don't hurt me! It wasn't my fault!* I'm not talking about logic. I'm talking about brute visceral response. You *were* Reginald Denny. How could you not be?

How would you know?

I was there. You were *crushed.* You and Alan both. *Disappointed.* In that moment there was no subtlety, no nuance, right? Savagery. Primitivism. The great American nightmare. *Help! There's a big black man with a rock!*

And you would have been Reginald Denny, too.

This is what I'm talking about! Do you see it now? He bends over and palms an imaginary rock, tests its weight, squints at me, measuring me as a target. I could feel — I could feel my own hand with the brick and my own head as the target. Total cognitive dissonance. It was like I was having a stroke. And you know what I did? Did you ever wonder where I was, when the fight was going on? I *ran.* Unplugged my bass and hopped off the stage and got the heck out of there. I wound up in some dining hall, still carrying the bass. Reading the flyers, trying to look nonchalant. Then I came back and found you. By that time the police were cleaning up. I pretended I'd gone for help. Not my most courageous moment.

We weren't supposed to be courageous, I say. We were ambushed.

Oh, come on, he says. Look, I loved Alan as much as anyone. But he was asking for it. I mean, this was *Hopkins.* He wanted to see what it was like to be Abbie Hoffman. He thought it was funny. Don't you remember, Kelly, how happy he was? He kept flipping down the mirror in the car, trying to get a better look at his black eye. Laughing the whole time. Remember how he insisted we all take pictures afterward? And then he wrote that piece for the *City Paper.* It was his little excursion into the life of a provocateur.

And what about the music? What, you're just embarrassed by it now? Just a passing phase?

Stop here for a second, he says, extracting his phone from his back pocket. Robin's texting me.

We've crossed out of the park onto Wilbur Street, a long row of low-rise public housing units, single-family, built to look like Eighties condos — all angles and planes, brown metal sheathing and slabs of brick. Just about every building I can see, down to

274

Pennsylvania Avenue, has that boxy Seventies-Eighties look, with the windows high up and long blank walls facing the street. Even the New Evergreen Baptist Church across the way is built in modernist-bunker style. Which means, of course, that they were all built after the riots, in place of the old ornate row houses and tenement houses and shop fronts burned or condemned as blight. A small banner strung up over the rear entrance to the church reads

EVERGREEN BAPTIST HEAD START
GETTING OUR KIDS
"FULLY READY"
FOR KINDERGARTEN

You know where we are, right? Martin says, thumbing away at the screen.

Yeah.

Two blocks that way is the Royal Theater site. And the new Billie Holiday statue.

The Old West Side is where we are. Baltimore's Harlem. We took a Baltimore History elective in high school that included a tour along Pennsylvania Avenue — Thurgood Marshall's birthplace, the churches and improvement societies and lodges where Du Bois, Marcus Garvey, Philip Randolph, and King once spoke. The Baltimore

Masjid, the Ideal Savings and Loan. It was like visiting a parking lot and looking for a cathedral. A few of the original church buildings survived; the rest were just points on a map, now abandoned storefronts, Dollar Stores and Foot Lockers, without even historical markers, just handwritten notes from our guide, an elderly man from the Urban League who wore a fedora and walked with a cane.

If you weren't from Baltimore, I'm thinking, and you arrived here, out of nowhere, you'd be utterly lost. Not a Target in sight, no supermarket, no ATM, no Dunkin' Donuts. Not a food desert so much as a desert, period. No commercial signifiers, none of the reassurances of home. Pick a random block here, I'm thinking, or in Philly, or Detroit, Cleveland, Bridgeport, Milwaukee, St. Louis, any of the lost cities, the gutted and ruined cities, and you may be in the one place left in America with no solace left at all, not even the satisfaction of opening your wallet.

Let's turn back, I say. Back to the park, okay? We're not going anywhere in particular, are we?

I'm going to say something that's going to break your heart, Martin says, after we've walked a few minutes in silence, crossing DeVine, circling the park's southern edge. I *tried* to care. I really wanted to get into it. I mean, I could see it in your face, Kelly! I used to watch you almost crying when you played the drums, do you know that? You were *transformed.* I took home our practice tapes and listened again and again. What the hell was I missing? Well, I never got it. I liked *being* in a band. And it's not like the bass parts were difficult. But I never drank the Kool-Aid. I never thought of it as *art.*

Well, okay. I don't know if I'd call it art, either.

Don't apologize, he says. Don't do that. Look, Kelly, I'm not asking you to be ashamed. I'm not asking you to disown anything. It's not your fault. There was nothing wrong with L'Arc-en-Ciel. There was nothing wrong with any of it. Look, it's your own history, your *being,* for god's sake! It just wasn't *mine.*

As if a camera has just swung out in front of us on a boom, as if we're being filmed for some documentary, I'm suddenly aware of what a picture we make: a black man and a white man, same age, side by side, close enough to imply a certain friendly intimacy. A conversation in low voices.

Define that. Define my being.

You know what my father said, the first time I played him one of our tapes? He said, Jesus Christ, it's like you're trying to invent music all over again. Without knowing how. And isn't that true, just a little bit? What did Alan know about playing the guitar? A couple of chords and a lot of screwing around. What do you have to have, to pull that off? That special self-righteousness. That arrogance. That *cocoon* — that special Willow feeling, you know what I mean? — that sense of being the arbiter of all things. That, that *transparency*. That sense of living in a world of hypothetical questions. I could go on and on. What would it feel like to start a riot? You see what I mean?

And that's your definition of whiteness?

Let's put it a different way, he says. Why did you leave Baltimore, Kelly? I'll tell you why. Because you felt you could. Right? You felt that freedom. Much as you loved it. There was nothing here for you. Why stay in a city that's a ruin? A broken city, a looted and betrayed city, with all these vacants, all these empty lots, a city that bulldozes its beautiful theaters? Why stay, if you have the option of leaving? It's a stupid rhetorical question. You left because you couldn't stand looking at all those hopeless poor black people anymore.

What do you do when someone quotes you back to yourself, practically speaking, more or less, without knowing it? A little knot has lodged itself in my esophagus, enough to breathe, but not to speak, not for a minute.

And what about you? I manage to ask, finally.

What about me? He could go on talking like this for hours, I'm thinking, extemporizing this way. He's leaning into it. I *couldn't* leave, he says. Even when I had the chance. Drawn back like a homing pigeon. From wherever I happened to land. Even Bangkok. And I *love* Bangkok. But wherever else I was, I just felt eventually like the earth was going to swallow me up and bring me back here. I just had to go deeper and deeper into Baltimore. *Bind* myself to Baltimore. Hopeless and fucked-up as it was. But then I realized something, and it's business school 101. One man's vacant lot is another's man's gold mine. Absence and anonymity: that's the twenty-first-century recipe for success. I was going to be a black man one way or another, but I wasn't going to just up and disappear because my city's off the map. Because, truthfully, the world is going to come to Baltimore one day. The world *is* Baltimore.

Hold on. I scrabble in my bag for my notebook. Let me write this one down, okay? I'll have to use that line in the book.

He loosens his collar and glances at me sideways, as if we've become sparring partners and he's waiting for an unexpected move.

I didn't make that up, he says slowly. Alan did.

When was that? I never heard him say that.

Later. After you left. When Cheryl used to bug him about applying to college. He would say, *I don't need to go anywhere. The world is Baltimore.*

I stare at him, my mind buzzing with the white noise of the traffic below, for a moment not quite digesting the words.

What, you mean, after he was back from rehab? When I was away at Amherst?

You thought we never saw each other, Kelly?

He never mentioned anything about it.

Maybe he was afraid to freak you out. He knew I was changing, that's for sure. Changing into *what,* of course, is a different story. But he knew something was happening.

My chest has become a giant ticking clock, a wound spring releasing itself in tiny increments.

Where was this? At his house?

280

I don't remember. Who cares? I saw him there; he came downtown; we had lunch together; we hung out in Fell's Point a couple of times at night. He needed help. I tried to help. I took him to a methadone clinic. Hell, I took him to get an AIDS test. This really bothers you that much?

It's just all news to me. He never *told* me that he'd seen you. Aren't I allowed to be hurt by that? It's a betrayal. What else could it be? I *wanted* to know what happened to you. I was curious. I didn't abandon you; you abandoned *me*.

Isn't that a little strong, Kelly? *Abandoned?* I don't recall you wanting to hang out so much senior year. After the band broke up. I don't recall you leaving me a lot of messages. Did you ever ask him about me, directly? Did you ever mention me in his presence?

How was I supposed to know he had seen you? Anyway, it wasn't the first thing on my mind. He was *dying.*

He wasn't *dying.* He died.

However you want to put it.

No, he says. It's different. His death was a discreet event. Not natural. Suicide is never natural.

Didn't he ever say, *you should call Kelly*? Didn't he want to know why you'd dis-

281

appeared like that?

Haven't you been listening? He detaches himself from the railing, finally, and begins walking back to Pierson Street, his street, pumping his legs, hardly looking back to see if I'm following. He knew there was something going on with me, he says. He kept talking about my *journey*. To tell the truth, it bugged me. All this New Age stuff he picked up from NA. The hero leaving home. The three obstacles. *Growth.* God, he went on and on about growth. Of course he was right. I was able to see that, later. After I stopped being angry. I realized he never really *wanted* me to be like him.

It took me a long time to see that.

He gives me a look, over his shoulder: *you, too?* And then, with recognition, or pretending recognition, he nods.

I mean, he says, in a sense you could say it was Alan that gave me permission. He opened that door. He said, *there's more than one way to live.* He was into radical solutions, after all. No halfway measures.

No, that's true. No halfway measures.

Rolling toward us on Howard Street, slowly, deliberately, is a Baltimore Police squad car, with two shadowy figures underneath the mirroring glare of the windshield. The

282

driver's-side window rolled down, a beefy, red-haired forearm adjusting the mirror. And without touching his body, without looking over at him, I feel a change in the envelope of energy around Martin, a crackle of static electricity: and I draw up my breath, stiffen my spine, and open my hands, keeping them in plain sight, keeping my gaze straight ahead, an unworried, unselfconscious man, as I imagine a black man would always have to be, though I've never imagined it before in quite this way. It occurs to me that in a way, on this street, in this odd place where pedestrians rarely stray, I am his alibi. There is a percentage by which a white man and a black man walking together by Tilson Falls Park are less likely to be stopped than a black man walking alone. You could do a study. You could measure it. This is the calculus that a black man lives with every day. This is a theory I've always understood but never experienced, not once. And, too, it occurs to me, as it should have, long ago, that there's a reason Martin puts on a suit and a silk tie every day when he leaves the house, whereas I, in my current state, have worn the same hooded sweatshirt, the same jeans, the same black Converse, for three days running. Were I a black man, it occurs to me, working or not, in this city, I would have a dry-cleaning bill. And I want to turn to him, though I won't, and say, *I understand the part about hypotheticals.*

I realized something recently, I tell him, instead. Two times nineteen is thirty-eight. We've outlived Alan by exactly one lifetime.

Didn't he always say that he could die at sixteen? Martin says. Having lived a long and happy life? That was his downfall, that Ian Curtis crap. Self-pity. Self-aggrandizing pity. It made him vulnerable. He didn't value life enough. He just *gave* it away.

Deep in my chest cavity, in some un-mapped region, some imaginary town down a side road from the pancreas to the bile duct, a church bell is tolling, a deep, sono-rous vibration, traveling across a lake, up forested hillsides. Something is waking up. A disturbance, an alarm. He knows some-thing. What does he know?

What's your point?

He stares at me and begins walking even faster, almost at a jog. We're going some-where with this story, I can't help thinking, and he doesn't want to get there, either. But there's no other way.

I don't have a point, he says. Just a good memory.

22.

Recording #4 (1:04:34)
Source:
(1) TDK Chrome cassette tape, 90 minutes, condition –
(2) Sony cassette tape, 60 minutes, condition + +
Labeled both tapes side one "Tape 4 PRIVATE DO NOT DESTROY" "Tape 5 PRIVATE DO NOT DESTROY"

This part has a soundtrack. Bob Marley, "Exodus." One of the greatest riddim tracks ever. [hums] Bum, bum-bum, bum-bum, bum-bum, bum-bum-bum. Listen to it. Whoever's listening to this, if anyone ever does: if you don't have it, go out and get a copy. You should have it on as you listen to me. One layered on top of the other. Don't worry about the words just yet. Just the bass and the drums.

What do you hear? Walking. Moving. The song is taking you somewhere. Right? Don't you want to go? Doesn't everybody want to go? Move. Move. Move.

So what happened from, say, 1994 to 2000, in my life? The lost years. Six lost years. What happens when someone goes out of sight, in this day and age, in this economy, in Baltimore, when they make every effort not to be found? When they have no visible means of supporting themselves? Well, okay. I'll spell it out.

Pot.

I was running pot in its second heyday, when it was the chronic, the KGB, the Super Sticky, the Buddha, Sour Diesel — when the demand was skyrocketing and the supply, at first, was not that great. Most of what was on the market in 1994 was Mexican junk. Mota. People were adding other stuff to it just to get a buzz — meth, mescaline, even PCP. The Colombians weren't in the market yet. Escobar didn't believe in pot. Too much volume. And the American and Canadian growers were just coming in on a large scale. It was just the beginning of hydroponics, aeroponics,

286

when costs were coming down and all those years of hippie research were finally paying off. That was when they invented the Sea of Green and the Screen of Green — autoflowering, cloning, using colloidal silver to feminize the plants. You could put in $50,000 and get yourself a house, racks, trellises, grow lights, carbon scrubbers, ozone generators, seeds, buckets, motion detectors. The whole package. The challenge was all in distribution. You had dealers everywhere, of course, demand was out the window, but most smokers were still used to paying twenty or thirty bucks a bag for total garbage; the high-end stuff was still a niche product. Friends selling to friends. There was a lot of paranoia about expanding your field. What we were doing was like Starbucks. Create a market, then feed that market. Convince people to spend four bucks on a Frappuccino instead of a dollar on coffee, then make sure that Frappuccino is everywhere they want it. In the mall. In the grocery store. Buy bulk and corner the wholesale market.

Seymour was the one who got me going. He was my lodestar, my mentor, my launch pad. My compass. I probably wouldn't be alive today except for him. We first got together in '94. First time I met him — it was at a party somewhere, I think at Willa Rodriguez's mom's place off Coldspring — he was just back from Miami. Kept going outside to make calls on his cell phone. It was the first time I'd ever seen anyone — other than a banker, maybe, or someone on TV — with a cell phone. The old squarish kind with the huge battery. So I asked him: who do you have to call so desperately, man, at two in the morning?

And he said, You really want to know?

Yeah. I really want to know.

You're graduating high school, right? You have a job?

That was it for me. Curiosity killed the cat.

Before him I'd never really known a white criminal. Of course I'd known dealers, or at least knew of them, around the neighborhood when I was younger. But Seymour didn't do anything at the street level. He didn't have turf. His dad was some kind of banker at Alex Brown; he grew up in Roland Park, got kicked out of Boys' Latin and then Dartmouth for dealing. Then his family cut him off, and he basically went to ground, went AWOL, and climbed up the ladder of the business — developed his own sources, his own clientele, all up and down 95. Maine to Florida, the Appalachian Trail of weed. I must have smoked two or three hundred different varieties with him. He got product from everywhere — Colombia, Peru, Thailand, Afghanistan, Nepal, Jamaica, Humboldt, Salt Spring Island, Paraguay. He carried around metal suitcases full of samples in the back of his Saab, and would go around having tastings, four or five stockbrokers or doctors or what have you at a time. Developing customer profiles he wrote up on his PowerBook. With him it was all classy, down to the way he dressed, super-put-together, all blacks and grays, Banana Republic style.

And so a month after I met him he had me signed up as a courier working the New York–to–Miami route. Trying to crack the distribution nut, break into the regional business. We drove these vans that old Cuban ladies took back and forth, visiting family. Pick up the abuelas on 125th Street and Lex, stop overnight at a Motel 6 in

Richmond, drive all the next day and night to Miami, do the drop-off, pick up more abuelas on Calle Ocho, stop at a Motel 6 in Charlotte, same time, same station, and when you get back to New York take the van uptown to Inwood, leave it in this garage overnight. The chassis, the floorboards, the hood, the wheel wells — we could carry five hundred pounds and all it cost was a little extra gas money. Kept it at a cool 67 the whole way. Made sure the tires were solid, tested the lights, did everything to make sure we never had a stop. Because the thing was — no matter how hard we tried, how many air fresheners and pounds of coffee — you could still smell it. The abuelas would get all giggly before we stopped for pee breaks. You can't have all that sticky bud in an enclosed space and not smell it. Triple-bagged Ziplocs and all. I would do three runs and then take the bus back to Baltimore and have two weeks off. A thousand dollars a run. Tax-free. It was a genius operation. White kids saving money for college; old Cuban ladies visiting their sisters; never had a cop give me a second look.

So anyway: that went on for two years.

The entire time Dad was sick. Easy work, easy money. Then — overnight — the whole thing disappeared. The vans, the company, the garage up in Inwood: poof! Never knew why. Seymour thought they'd found an easier route. Shipping containers, maybe even commercial air. There were FedEx people involved in those days, before the company came down hard on side deals. All those big planes carried a little extra weight. In any case, for six months, I was shit out of luck, workwise. Seymour had left town; I didn't know if he'd ever be back. I'd saved a lot of my cash, and of course I had the house outright.

So what did I do? I went to school. UMBC. Econ 120, Accounting 120, Con Law, and "Introduction to Holocaust Literature." I registered late, and all the intro English courses were full. So instead I had Dr. Klefkowitz in this little tiny room with eight other kids. Klefkowitz must have been at least seventy. And he had the numbers tattooed on his arm. Never said a thing about it, but he didn't hide it, either. He looked at me as I was leaving on the first day — I was the last one out of the room — and said, excuse me, Martin Lipkin, may I ask, you are a Jew?

My father was Jewish, I told him, my mother wasn't, as far as I know, I never went to synagogue, never had a bar mitzvah. I know a lot of Jews. I don't know. Am I a Jew?

He shrugged. You're asking me? Don't ask me. Ask a rabbi.

I don't know any rabbis.

Well, he said, maybe you'll read these books and feel something.

We read — who did we read first? Primo Levi. Elie Wiesel. Borowski. Danilo Kiš. But the best one was this guy I'd never heard of, Bruno Schulz. Who wasn't even really a Holocaust writer at all. I mean, yes, he was killed by a Nazi. But everything we have that he wrote, just two little books of short stories, was written in the Thirties, before the Germans invaded Poland. He never wrote a thing about the Nazis. All his work was about his childhood and his family. And his debates with God.

I'm not much of a reader. God knows. I mean, since high school, when that was my job, when I read everything. My adult store of knowledge, like Seymour used to say, is all from the school of fall down six times, get up seven. But there was this one story by Bruno Schulz that changed my entire life. Really not the whole story. Just one page. For years I had it taped to the wall in my bedroom. Then I had a guy at Kinko's do it in tiny print and laminate it on a card. So, okay: the story is called "Tailor's Dummies." The father is this older, crazy guy, a hermit, like Dad, not incidentally, who has this thing about mannequins. Dummies. He sees life in these artificial things, these, you know, made-up forms of human beings. That's his project. This is the father talking, giving his treatise on dummies and what they mean. I had to order a new copy on Amazon; it just arrived yesterday. Hold on, I'll get the page.

"The Demiurge," said my father [MW reading aloud], "has had no monopoly of creation, for creation is the privilege of all spirits. Matter has been given infinite fertility, inexhaustible vitality and, at the same time, a seductive power of temptation which invites us to create as well. In the

293

depth of matter, indistinct smiles are shaped, tensions build up, attempts at form appear. The whole of matter pulsates with infinite possibilities which send dull shivers through it. Waiting for the life-giving breath of the spirit, it is endlessly in motion. It entices us with a thousand sweet, soft, round shapes which it blindly dreams up within itself.

"Deprived of all initiative, indulgently acquiescent, pliable like a woman, submissive to every impulse, it is a territory outside any law, open to all kinds of charlatans and dilettanti, a domain of abuses and of dubious demiurgical manipulations. Matter is the most passive and most defenseless essence in cosmos. Anyone can mold it and shape it; it obeys everybody. All attempts at organizing matter are transient and temporary, easy to reverse and to dissolve. There is no evil in reducing life to other and newer forms. Homicide is not a sin. It is sometimes a necessary violence on resistant and ossified forms of existence which have ceased to be amusing. In the interests of an important and fascinating experiment, it can even become meritorious. Here is the starting point of a new apologia for sadism.

"My father never tired of glorifying this extraordinary element matter. 'There is no dead matter,' he taught us, 'lifelessness is only a disguise behind which hide unknown forms of life. The range of these forms is infinite and their shades and nuances limitless. The Demiurge was in possession of important and interesting creative recipes. Thanks to them he created a multiplicity of species, which renew themselves by their own devices. No one knows whether these recipes will ever be reconstructed. But this is unnecessary, because even if the classical methods of creation should prove inaccessible for evermore, there still remain some illegal methods, an infinity of heretical and criminal methods.' "

We barely discussed "Tailor's Dummies" in class. It was just before midterms and Klefkowitz had already told us Schulz wouldn't be on the test. Too hard, he said. Too weird. I think I was the only person in class who read it. And when I did — after I'd looked up what Demiurge meant — my whole body lit up like a lightbulb. I mean, I didn't know what it meant vis-à-vis Martin Lipkin. So I went to Klefkowitz, to his office hours, and asked him, what the hell is this? Is this Judaism?

No, he said. I mean, yes. In a sense. But no.

Well, which is it?

He got up from his shelves and put his fingers on this fat purple book — I saw the spine. It read *The Zohar.* To me that sounded like something out of *Ghostbusters.* Then he turned and sat back down. No, he said, really weary, you have to find that out for yourself.

Well, what does this part mean? Even if the classical methods of creation should prove inaccessible for evermore, there still remain some illegal methods, an infinity of heretical and criminal methods. What kind of heretical and criminal methods?

Then you know what he did? He slid his chair over to me and put his hand on my face. Like he was a blind man.

You'll figure it out, he said. The important thing is, you felt something.

All I was really doing in college was thinking about college. As a marketplace. As the final nut to crack in the world of large-scale pot retailing. Seymour kept calling me — he was living up in Burlington by then — new product was coming online, hotter and hotter stuff: cyber-pot, we used to call it. But college networks were so insular. You had to find a way to override all of that and cut out the middleman. So we invented this thing called the Little Green Bus. Maybe you heard of it, at Amherst? It was a college-to-college van service, staffed by students, coordinated by students. By this time the Internet was really up and running and I put the whole reservation thing together that way. Except for the payment. No one would use credit cards online back in those days, so I had to hire a girl in Catonsville, a friend from my econ class, to take orders over the phone.

Anyway: you wouldn't believe how popular we were. We had three routes: the long one, Duke to Burlington; the short one, Burlington to Princeton; and the east-west, Harvard to Oberlin, stopping at Amherst, Cornell, and Kenyon. And our drivers — well, they were paid a percentage of sales. Some of them made enough for college themselves doing it. We couldn't pack the vans tight enough. Everyone knew what the Little Green Bus was for. The weed had a brand name: we even had custom-made horns that played "Brown-Eyed Girl." I swear to God, there were places — Sarah Lawrence was one — where we'd sell out the store and have to send an overnight driver down from Burlington to restock for the rest of the trip south. And we were doing it with a fifteen percent markup for convenience. No one cared. The product was awesome. The whole thing was a guerrilla sales company before the concept existed. Word of mouth. No advertising. No corporate address. All the fleet management was done by a guy Seymour knew in Hartford: he painted the vans, he fixed the vans, he provided the gas cards for the drivers. We paid him in cash. No taxes, no filings. The credit card account went to a Mailboxes place on York Road.

It was genius, and it lasted three years. Longer than we ever imagined. Right through the millennium. Finally, one of our drivers had an accident — in an empty van, by some miracle. Taking it in for service. Rolled it over on 91 near New

Haven and ripped the chassis open. Bricks of weed all over the shoulder. Seymour sent the guy bail money and then somehow got him on a plane to Honduras. No names, no evidence, but the whole network had to go overnight. We left fifty thousand dollars out on the road, plus the value of the vans. Just abandoned them wherever they were. One guy drove his off a pier into Lake Erie. Another took his out to Moab, got all the pot out, and then torched it in a bonfire out in the desert, or so the story went.

And all this time Seymour was in Vermont, running the wholesale operation, and I was still here, in Dad's house, running Little Green Bus and picking up checks from that mailbox out on York. We talked only on pay phones, like real drug dealers. And I was getting a little paranoid, with hundreds of thousands of dollars of cash in the house. Because that's how much it was. I kept my expenses basically at zero. Survived on Chinese food and those bagged premade salads from the supermarket. Still drove Dad's old Scirocco. Wore two pairs of black jeans and a black Carhartt hoodie. But the isolation was wearing me down. Alan was long gone.

Everyone else from Willow was out of college by now and living in Brooklyn or Berkeley or China. I hadn't made hardly any friends at UMBC, and I wasn't playing music or going out much. The work was seven days a week, twenty-four/seven; I had to carry two pagers and a cell every time I left the house, even to walk around the corner.

So, to make a long story a little shorter: I bought a gun. Not for any good reason. We made no enemies. No turf wars. Never sold shit in Baltimore; Hopkins wasn't even on our radar. Nobody was going to try to rob the house; it was still the fortress it always was. But living alone so much of the time — and watching too many movies, too much bad TV — makes anyone crazy. You get so you can't even make conversation with the girl giving you change for a meatball sub at the deli. Everyone starts giving you these big eyes. So I bought one gun, a Glock. Kept it under my pillow. Then Jonas, the guy I bought it from, offered me a discount on a hot double-barreled Mossberg. I kept that one next to the front door. If I had to I could kill someone by shooting through the door. Then another Glock to keep under my seat in the car. Then a little gun, a Walther PPK, .25 caliber, that I kept in my waistband wherever I went. Then, just for the hell of it, I bought an AR-15 kit gun off the Internet. Screw-on silencer, extra-long clip. No special reason other than that any kid who grew up watching *The A-Team* wants one of those things. I just wanted to take it out to the range and see the look on people's faces. Hell, going to the range had become my only means of entertainment other than jerking off. I had an unlimited pass. In a couple of months I'd gone from just another unarmed Joe Schmo to the owner of my own private arsenal.

And then Seymour came for a visit. Just stopping through. We hadn't seen each other face-to-face in nearly a year. He came through the door and took it all in with one look. I was holding the Mossberg in one hand and a bottle of NoDoz in the other. That was my drug of choice in those days. Espresso wasn't strong enough. Epinephrine freaked me out. Coke and meth were too dangerous. So I'd take six NoDoz at a time, ground up in a Mountain Dew.

Look at yourself, he said. This isn't just pathetic. It's dangerous. This isn't the business we're in.

How do you protect your money?

I hide it, he said. I launder it. I can teach you all that shit. Why didn't you just ask? You need a course in Drug Banking 101. But first you need a vacation. Callie's taking over Little Green Bus. You're coming back with me to Burlington, right now.

And you know what? I knew he was right. I had to get out of town. Baltimore was killing me. That house was killing me. All Dad's things were still around: his pictures, his records, his clothes in the closet. I still slept in my old room, on the same bed I'd had since middle school. I was turning into some kind of pale underground fish, you know, the kind that live in caves, that never see daylight in their entire lives? I was turning into a bat. My skin kept breaking out. I hadn't had a girlfriend in years, but I was watching porn and jerking off four times a day. It was deforming me, all this easy money. It was warping my spirit. Ultimately, I'd screw up somehow and get caught. Or go crazy. Or get so sad I'd kill myself. Or do it by accident, cleaning my guns. Seymour made me get rid of them before I left. One by one, we filed off the serial numbers and threw them over the Tydings Bridge into the Susquehanna. I cried, doing it; it was like killing kittens. Those guns were innocent. They were the only family I had. Then I curled up and fell asleep in the back of his Wrangler and woke up the next morning in the Green Mountains.

I know it's silly. I know it's a cliché. But I'm not afraid. I'm not deceived. No one would tell this story for me. Listen: when I was in Burlington, this was in the spring of 1998, April, May, I was there for a month, and it seemed like every house I went to, every car I hitched a ride in, this song was on the stereo. Okay. Big whoop. Crunchy granola folks like Bob Marley. But everywhere, and the same song. That bass line was in the air; it carried me. Days and nights blurred together. I was carrying around fifteen thousand dollars in a little Mountain Gear backpack. Bricks of dirty twenties. Seymour had made up with his girlfriend, bought a new house with her, and he kept saying, look, let me show you what it's like here, you'll never want to be anyplace else.

It was pretty great. No matter how high you are in Vermont, and I was high, you feel as if you're just getting healthier every day by breathing the air. It's like air conditioning for the soul. Anywhere you walk in Burlington you can see these amazing mountains, Mount Mansfield, the Green Mountains, and then there's the lake right at the edge of the city, and everything just feels washed clean and new. I suppose it reminded me a little of what Big Love was like, back in the day. Wouldn't want to live in Vermont, god knows, but it's about the best place in the world to recharge. And Seymour had this amazing house, a modern place, all wood on the outside, huge windows, beautiful trees all around, cedars and hemlocks, with a sauna and a hot tub on the back patio. His girlfriend — I think her name was Amy — was this incredibly beautiful half-Japanese, half-Mexican girl, still in college, who was some kind of professional vegetarian chef and also a harpist. She would make us these incredible meals, huge salads, fresh soups, sushi, cold noodles, homemade tofu, and then go off into her studio over the garage and play the harp all day. It was the first time I'd ever really tasted food in my life. Seymour took me downtown and bought me all new clothes — lots of linens, and a couple of really beautiful suits, from this tailor he knew, a Czech refugee named Jaroslav.

You know what I'm trying to show you? he said. It's very simple. You want to know how I hide my money? I don't. Nobody bothers rich people in this world. Yes, there's some basic mechanics involved. You've got to get that dirty cash into bank accounts. I mean you. Starting now. We've got to work on that. But the most important thing is, you've got to live like you've got nothing to hide. No fear. And for god's sake, live like a grown-up. Don't know what couches to buy? Get a decorator. Better yet, marry a decorator. Don't know what suit to wear to a summer wedding? Go into Bloomingdale's and ask. You'll put it together soon enough. That's your work from now on. Worried about getting a life? Forget that. Get a *lifestyle.*

I was listening, but at the same time I wasn't really listening. You could say I was storing it up for later. His life wasn't my life. I was still an egg. Still cracking. The chrysalis. It was all coming together, but I couldn't see what it was. I was just walking around with a gigantic rock in my gut. Seymour knew it, too, and he kept saying it was a matter of changing the formula. He had a whole room full of bud, in glass jars, all labeled, sources and dates — his apothecary — and his philosophy was that there was a blend for every psychic condition. That was what he was working on: weed psychiatry. First he had me on "Questioning," then "Anxiety Detox," then "Clarification." I smoked it, I used his atomizer, ate it in brownies, ate it ground up and sprinkled on rice; I got high in the sauna, in the hot tub, in the woods, sitting in his massage chair — I was his guinea pig, in other words, and it wasn't working. What happened instead, not surprisingly, is I started to forget things. Whole conversations, whole days. Names of people I hadn't thought about in months. I thought I had early-onset Alzheimer's or something. And then I came to my senses and I knew I had to leave.

In the end it was very simple: I packed up and took a taxi in the middle of the morning, when everyone was asleep. That was the last I ever saw of Seymour. I went and knocked on this girl's door. Carolina. We'd met at a party; she'd made it clear that she'd give me the time of day whenever I asked for it.

Come in, she said, I was just about to do some peyote. Want to come?

Three days later I woke up in a field, soaking wet. It was just before dawn. Half in, half out of my sleeping bag, my hands spread out on the grass, drenched in dew, smelling of clover. My backpack was gone. My money was gone. I knew that immediately. Seymour was gone. And this is what it was: we know where we're going, we know where we're from. We live in Babylon, we're going to our fatherland.

I picked up my arms, I swear to god, I looked at my hands, in the dawn light, you know, the blue light turning to daylight, and I saw myself getting darker, saw my skin turning brown, all but the palms of the hands, and I knew, I knew, swear to fucking god, that I was emerging, all wet, as what I was always meant to be. I had no fear. I stood up and started walking. I went back to Baltimore; I got my savings out from all the places I'd stored it, the rafters, the basement, safe-deposit boxes, dummy accounts. I did what Seymour told me to do. Found the right lawyer. Put on a golf shirt and flew down to the Caymans with a big fat cashier's check. And then when I got back to Baltimore I opened the Yellow Pages, and looked up plastic surgery.

23.

Six weeks ago, when we met the first time, when I handed her the tacky laser-printed business card I'd just made — *Kelly Thorndike, Freelance Journalist* — Robin made a quick notation on her phone and said, I get an interview, too, right? Want to set one up? My schedule's pretty full.

Mine's not, I said. Send me a time.

Done, she said, and the next day her assistant emailed me a date at the beginning of May. *Lunch 12:45-1:50.* I wrote it down on a Post-it and stuck it on the window next to my desk, and nearly every day for weeks I wanted to call her and suggest another time, tell her I'm traveling, that my deadline was moved up — to find a polite and neutral way to cancel. I am not a practiced liar. I am not an actor. With Martin there as my alibi the whole enterprise makes sense; without him Robin and I will just be two people, two adults, out for lunch, in the ordinary everyday world. Two adults with some business to discuss, some matter at hand, but not without a mild frisson of companionable attraction, a little light-hearted flirtation. Nothing is more terrifying for a conspirator, I'm realizing, than the temptation to relax.

Let me put it another way.

Part of getting past the first stages of grieving, my therapist told me, is learning to surprise yourself again. In a traumatic event, your senses shut down. Taste, smell, temperature — you forget to wear a hat when it's five below. Bite into a piece of sushi and it's like eating a sponge. Then, gradually, it all comes back, but it's different. There's a reset button. Like pregnancy. Or chemotherapy. Ever seen someone whose hair has all grown back a different color?

I've never in my life been attracted to a black woman. Not at all. Not ever. You could call it simple socialization: that in those defining years, thirteen and fourteen and fifteen, the bodies I saw, the faces I saw, were white girls, skinny white girls, by any historical standard — the standard being somewhere between Molly Ringwald and Kate Moss. Girls whose breasts disappeared in the palm of your hand, whose hips, whose asses, described a gentle curve, a suggestion of something, you could say, more than the thing itself.

And that's still my type, if I have a type. Not long after my dinner at Martin's, not more than a few days, I found one of the sites I look at when I need to remind myself to jerk off — which I've had to, ever since the accident — and nothing worked. So I crawled into bed, with half a hard-on, read a chapter of a Paul Bowles novel I'd had on my night table for months, and finally smoked the end of a joint I'd kept in the freezer since Christmas, a last-ditch effort at deriving some sense of pleasure from the world. It happened quickly after that: I could describe, in my mind's eye, every part of Robin, the shape of her kneecap, the frictionless skin at the very base of the thigh, the taste of her as I put my mouth between her legs. I came explosively.

And is it really so surprising? I asked myself a few moments later, after I'd tossed away the tissue and pulled up the sheet, my heart still pulsing away as it did, does, after sex, the real kind. How else is there to say it: Martin has everything I want, everything *any*one wants, even if he took the strangest, technically impossible, route to get there. Of course I look at his beautiful wife — his poised, put-together, self-assured, hyper-confident Doctor Mom — and want to fuck her, to bend her over, to shove her up against a wall. Lust is circumstantial and unfair. I'm not sorry. We know enough now, adults that we are, evolved people, not to have to apologize for our fantasies. Of course it occurs to me now that I wasn't ever attracted to black women partly because no one ever would have wanted me to be, because it's inconvenient, unsightly, because the image it brings to mind, let's just say it, is the master and the slave, Sally Hemings and President Jefferson. Lust is circumstantial and politically inconvenient. So is love, for that matter. When Wendy I were first together, one friend said to me, in a drunk late-night overseas phone call, *I never thought you were the Suzie Wong type.* Another said, *how long have you had yellow fever?*

So since my night with Rina — two weeks ago, and we've had dinner twice since, like any old friends stranded without much companionship, the tension broken, thank god — I've tried not to worry about Robin. People have crushes, I've been thinking, and that's what it is; why make it sound more profound, more ominous, than that? What's going to happen, in any case? *I'm in love with you, and by the way, your husband's really a*

312

white man, so what's the difference, anyway?
She's the Pat Robertson of the black family.
And a shrink. Let her set the boundaries.
Take notes. Make it all on the record. And
move on, and maybe try not to see her
again.

Don't sit down, Robin says, when I open
the door to her office. I'll just be a second.
She's already changed into Lycra pants,
track shoes, and a fleece pullover; now she's
slipping in contact lenses, using a compact
mirror and one long, delicate pinkie. Her
nails are very short, I'm noticing, with a
dark plum-colored polish, almost black. You
okay with walking? she asks. I always walk
at lunchtime. First, because I sit all day.
Second, because there's no decent food
around the hospital. That's what happens
when you tear down a neighborhood. Fancy
MRIs, world-class surgery, but you have to
walk a mile for a decent sandwich.

As long as you give me a head start.

Don't worry. I don't power-walk with
company. Just like to get out of my doctor
drag and be a civilian again.

Her building isn't the hospital itself but
one of its many satellites — the Hopkins
Hospital, since I lived here, having become
a city within a city, taking up a twenty-block

square above Oldtown and Butchers Hill. The view from her window takes in the entire horseshoe of the harbor, from Canton to Federal Hill, with Patterson Park on one periphery and Camden Yards on the other, and stretching out to the tankers dotting the gray-green Chesapeake three miles away. The accumulated brightness of it all — the window, the sunburst-patterned rug, the enormous Jacob Lawrence prints above her desk, the clutter of toys and blocks and tiny plastic chairs around my feet — is making me a little dizzy.

I always tell people not to sit down, she says, because otherwise they try to be polite and break one of the little people chairs. It's not a kindergarten class where the parents come in for conferences. In here it's me and the kids only. I do consulting with the grown-ups next door.

What kinds of cases do you handle?

What kinds of kids? Every kind. I get referrals from all directions. Schools. CFS. Primary-care doctors. Juvenile Justice. The courts. Adoption agencies. Homeless shelters. All the way from mild adjustment issues to full-on psychosis. There aren't enough child psychs in this world to let me be picky. She directs me to the door, waves to her assistant, and we're in the elevator on our way down. Like this morning, she says, two appointments. Just to give you a sense of the range. First one, hyperactive mom, lives in one of the new Ritz-Carlton condos over near the Domino's sign. She works in D.C., has a nanny seven to seven. Single, Dad's already remarried and lives in Spain. Wants to know whether Jacob — he's three and a half — needs Ritalin because he keeps breaking his toys. That's number one. Number two, she's eleven, six foster families, raped by an older foster brother two years ago, prematurely pubescent, getting in trouble hanging out with boys after school. She's a candidate for early pregnancy for sure.

It's pretty much the whole demographic slice.

You know who I don't see? The suburban middle class. I mean, obviously, given where I work. But my kids break high and low. Because that's who lives in Baltimore these days. You've got profoundly wealthy people in Guilford, old-line Wasp money in Roland Park, yuppies of all kinds around the harbor, and then profoundly, profoundly poor people, black, brown, beige, and white, too, of course, everywhere else. What you don't have are teachers, nurses, firemen, shopkeepers, managers, what have you. *They* live in the county. And, of course, they don't get to see a mental-health professional more than once or twice in their lives, because their HMOs don't cover us. Medicaid, yes. The prisons, yes. Rich people, yes. Baltimore is like a big donut with the middle shot out.

We've come out on the corner of Wolfe and Orleans and now turn down North Broadway, a broad avenue of neat brick row houses that descends slowly to Fell's Point. You like Broadway Market? she asks. It's soft-shell season, you know. Or we could go to Bertha's, but I think it's overrated. Or the brick-oven pizza place.

No, the Market's fine.

I like eating standing up. Don't know why. Some people can't take it. But again, I'm sitting all day. Standing up and reading the newspaper and listening to adults talk. Between work and home I get a little starved for conversation, as you can see. So listen, what was it you wanted to ask me? You must have questions.

Oh, I say, you're answering them. Mostly I just need background. Who you are, what you think about the life you lead.

Nothing about how I met Martin? That kind of thing?

Of course. That, too.

And you're not going to ask for my take

on black entrepreneurship?

Definitely.

She bursts into laughter. I'm just giving you a hard time, she says. Listen, I could rattle off opinions for hours, so let me get some hard facts out of the way before I forget. About Martin, first off. We met in church. He probably told you that. And it was the first time I'd *been* to church in about three years; I was there for my friend Kara's daughter's baptism. He, at that time, was quite the faithful churchgoer, and my god, a single man, looking like him, with a job, with a *wardrobe,* and without a mother in law — there were crowds. It was like the Google IPO. But our eyes met, la, la, la, we clicked, it all happened fast. It was very efficient. Small wedding, up on Martha's Vineyard. You have to keep it small when there's no family on one side.

So you wouldn't describe yourself as very religious?

Are you talking about in a black context or a larger context?

Is it different?

Of course it's different. The black community still treats the church as central. You can't *be* black, in a certain sense, without a relationship to the church. An appreciation for it. I've got that. But if you're talking

317

about a deep, personal, everyday, transcendent need for prayer and reflection, an immersion in the Bible, I mean, *faith,* then no. I'm culturally Baptist the way lots of Jews are culturally Jewish. It's imperative to me that the kids are raised in the church. Not because I'm so convinced of the moral edification it offers, but because it grounds them in the community and the tradition. It's all about integrity and wholeness for me, not Jesus and Jehovah. Maybe you got a sense of that the other day.

I did.

You should come again. You'd be welcome, you know.

I will. It's on my list.

She laughs again.

What, you don't make lists?

My whole life is lists. It's just that there's something so earnest about you, Kelly. You *want to understand.* You're like one of those skinny college kids in plaid shirts in 1961, listening to Mingus or Smokey Robinson or something and trying to be hip. Can I be honest here? I keep thinking I'm being played. That's my cynical, heard-it-all, twenty-first-century reaction. It's like you've been in a bubble the last, oh, thirty years of your life.

I don't want anything from you, I would

so desperately like to tell her, to reassure her, just an hour of polite conversation, for now, and in the long term, perhaps, your forgiveness, your acknowledgment that *none of this was my idea.* The problem is that I'm trying too hard to do a good job. I'm trying so sincerely to be fake. And now I'm stuck.

So, I say, in your view, there's just no excuse, anymore, for a naïve perspective, an innocent question?

There would be if you came from, say, Sri Lanka. Or Mars.

Then the white observer, the interlocutor, is in kind of an impossible bind, right? If I'm cynical and worldly I get called out for making assumptions and appropriating a black perspective. If I'm innocent and careful I get called out for false naiveté. Not much wiggle room, is there?

We come to the corner of North Broadway and Baltimore. Here the grassy median gives way to a cluster of trees, a small plaza, benches, now filled with dog walkers, neighborhood wanderers, residents in scrubs uncoiling in the unfamiliar sunlight. Underneath the trees there's a small, improbable statue, hardly more than life-sized: a mutton-chopped man in a frock coat, turn of the century, Theodore Roosevelt style. *LATROBE* inscribed on the marble behind him. Baltimore is full of these unexpected, anonymous tokens of a forgotten civic life.

Oh, Kelly, she says, and turns to look me full in the face for the first time. Are you really asking me, a black woman, about wiggle room?

Then I'm just supposed to stay frustrated?

Something like that.

The light still isn't changing; I wonder for a moment if it's broken, if we should just leap across, but of course what's really happening is time is growing elastic, stretching out like taffy, in the course of an awkward, unexpectedly terrible, somehow ruined, encounter.

You know what amazed me about Martin, when we met? she asks. That he could talk to anybody. I mean, that should be *my* forte. But Martin is a true genius at giving people the benefit of the doubt. It must come from a business background. To him anyone is a potential customer. Or investor, or partner, or something. But that's not the point, really, because that makes it sound mercenary, and it's not. He has the rare gift of turning self-interest into something that's almost like a Christian virtue.

Whereas you?

Whereas I just carry around *baggage,* I guess. I mean, you wouldn't know it, would you? I am the *epitome* of a black upwardly mobile female blah, blah, blah. But as it turns out I can't hold a conversation with a white person for more than five minutes on the subject of race. Maybe those two things go together.

Finally the light turns green, and she sprints across, lock-legged, stalking fury and frustration. I follow two steps behind, and not until halfway down to Pratt does she give me a sideways look. Sorry, she says. I'm upset. I'm uncomfortable. It's no excuse for acting like a baby.

Something has passed between us, I'm just beginning to realize, in that half-block, that fifty yards of uneven and rutted city pavement. Her face, uncomposed, is trying to regain control of itself. In a different age, in a Victorian novel, I would say, *my dear lady,* and touch her elbow, or offer her a handkerchief. I have the urge to be gallant and rise above it all. But we live in an age allergic to suppositions. The pause we're in now is the one where she's expected to say, *These cases are really getting to me, I need a vacation,* or, *I had some bad news before we left the office,* or, *My allergies are acting up and my sinuses are killing me.* She's not going to offer an explanation; I know that much. We've passed beyond social lies.

Where we've arrived, on the other hand, is an open question.

It seems to me, for a moment, that Martin's decision — that Martin's real existence, the real fake black man that he is — has, subtly, indefinably, already seeped into the world around us. That we are living in an ersatz twenty-first century.

You know I spent every weekend down here? I say. Fell's Point was my stomping grounds. The best record store in Baltimore was two blocks that way. Reptilian Records. I spent every spare dollar I had in that place. Between that and the Salvation Army and the vintage store down on Aliceanna and Charm City Coffee down on Thames — that was the circuit. And Jimmy's. That was the only place we could afford to eat.

Mom and Dad didn't give you much of an allowance?

I wasn't really into capitalism. I used to wear a button that said *Property is theft.* Which is easy to say, of course, when your basic needs are all paid for. But at least I was consistent. I don't think I owned a single new piece of clothing until I went to college.

Saved your parents a lot of money.

In theory, but all of it was poured back into music in the end. *That* was the property

I cared about. Drums, cases, cymbals, sticks, gas for when we went on tour. It was a pretty expensive hobby.

What kind of a band were you in?

I'd have to know your point of reference. Ever heard Fugazi?

Fu-what?

Helmet? Jesus Lizard? Jawbox?

I had a roommate at Spelman who was into the Red Hot Chili Peppers and Jane's Addiction.

Okay. Well, we were like Jane's Addiction without the funk, and the falsetto voices, and all that L.A. druggie attitude.

But all Jane's Addiction *was* was funk, and falsetto —

I think I'd have to play it for you. We had a lot of dissonance, a lot of noise, but still *songs,* in the end. We were political and artsy. And for a while we actually had a following. Put out three EPs and one LP. Toured all around the East Coast.

This was all in high school? Any chance of a reunion?

None, I say, keeping my breathing steady, because our singer — his name was Alan — he died of a drug overdose. In 1994.

An overdose?

The nonaccidental kind. He'd already been hospitalized once for depression. A classic late-adolescence bipolar shift.

That must have been devastating. And it was here? No wonder you never wanted to come back.

It was all too convenient, really. Because my parents moved away. With that, and Alan's death, I fell into this groove of thinking I didn't belong anywhere. Right around that time I was getting fluent in Chinese, and all my energy was wrapped up in that, and hanging out with kids from Amherst who'd gone to prep school in Switzerland — it was just easy to think I was some kind of cosmopolite, some Salman Rushdie character, on the run, a homeland that doesn't want me back. I mean, not literally, but —

No, I understand what you mean. Kind of. I read *Imaginary Homelands,* too, and it kind of sounded awesome. Like the fatwa was the perfect excuse. Everybody wants a fatwa from their parents at a certain age.

Well, my parents had nothing to do with it.

That can't quite be true.

No, really. Their emotional lives are just barely above room temperature. Some parents of only children are like that. You must know what I'm talking about. I mean, they can get into the act when they have to.

When the accident happened, they were there, after a fashion. Because, literally, I had nowhere else to turn. Our friends were wonderful friends, but it takes more than a good friend to help out in that kind of catastrophe. And in the larger sense, I mean, all those years we were in Baltimore, my parents were just so much on the periphery of my experience. And they knew it. They couldn't control what was happening to me. Baltimore was way too much for them to handle. New Paltz is exactly their speed. My mom practically runs the library — she volunteers nearly every day. The highlight of their week is singing in the Unitarian Church choir. The truth is, they find parenthood exhausting, and I'm just me, not some kind of train wreck. They made it extremely easy for me to feel like an orphan — a cultural orphan.

I hear you.

You do?

Does that surprise you? Do you even know where I'm from?

Here, I thought. Was I wrong?

I was born here, she says. In my grandparents' house, while they were still alive. But we left when I was two. Then Champaign-Urbana, where my dad went to grad school. He a civil bureaucrat; he did fiscal planning, bond issues, that kind of thing. He got to like small towns. College towns. Places where the voters weren't too dumb to pay for a first-class sewer system or a new gym floor before the old one wore out. First Gambier, Ohio. That was middle school. Then Bennington. You're looking at the valedictorian of North Bennington High School, class of 1994.

Bennington. No kidding.

My dad loves sweater vests, Vivaldi, and *Wall Street Week.* Does that surprise you? He likes to talk about Mom's ancestors who fought in the Revolution. The *American* Revolution. Of course, there's more to it than that. Before I was born, in the Sixties, he lived in New York and drove a cab and played trombone. He was a Manhattan School of Music dropout, a free-jazz cat. Albert Ayler, Noah Howard, Malachi Favors, Archie Shepp, Pharoah Sanders — he was up there with all those guys. Then, so the story goes, he got into an argument outside a club with some black nationalists, not the Panthers but some splinter group, undisciplined, who said the trombone was a bourgeois instrument only fit for Dixie parades. It wound up with one of them grabbing his bone and beating him over the head with it. He woke up in the hospital.

Two weeks later he'd moved back in with his parents and enrolled at Morgan State in accounting.

A one-eighty-degree turn.

He's not the demonstrative type, she says, but when I told him I was going to Spelman he actually broke down and cried. Why, he said, why, why, when you could go anywhere? Why *now*?

And what did you say?

Because I wanted a vacation, she says. I wanted to see how it felt not to be one of two or three. I mean, I shouldn't complain. My mother didn't miss a beat. She did my hair right, every day, made sure we read Hughes and Dunbar and *The Autobiography of Malcolm X*. She found the nearest church with a decent gospel service and got us there at least once a month. And in the summer we were in Oak Bluffs from the minute school got out. It was her parents' house, and their money that paid for college, too, so Dad actually didn't have much say in the matter. Of course, afterward I went to Cornell for med school. But he still doesn't understand Spelman, and doesn't understand why I want Sherry and Tamika to go there. To him blackness just isn't a useful category. He'd rather talk about Seneca and Marcus Aurelius. *Dignity,* that's what he cares about. I tell him, Marcus Aurelius was George Washington's favorite writer, and I'll bet he liked to read him sitting at his desk in Mount Vernon and looking out over the slaves' backs bent over in the fields.

We've come down to the flatland, the ragged end of Fell's Point, even now dotted with derelict storefronts and shifty, dusty bodegas, shoe stores whose window displays haven't changed in twenty years. It's as if there's a law in Baltimore that gentrification can't extend more than five blocks in any one direction: a poor city with a pox, an acne spray, of gentility. Chugging past us, though it's lunchtime, is a school bus filled to the brim, little faces with bright yellow polo shirts squashed against the windows. Girls and boys just a year or so older than Meimei. Kindergarteners. A field trip, is my first thought, but then I remember seeing a headline in the *Sun* about cutbacks and reductions making kindergarten part-time. They look — is it possible for five-year-olds to look? — weary, and resigned.

You know what I've been thinking about? I say to her. The future. The world's future. I mean, you have to ask yourself, is this world we live in, is this Baltimore, sustainable? I'm taking for granted that in fifty years this spot will be underwater. You have to accept that part. But in the *larger* sense, I mean, look around you, can you see anything that isn't some kind of danger sign, some kind of warning?

You really want to know my answer? It's embarrassing.

Of course I want to know.

Well, she says, it's Martin. Martin is what gives me hope. I mean, look, I'm a suburban girl. I would never have come back here without him. What I was saying earlier — he has such tremendous confidence. And vision. You know what he says about Baltimore? Have you heard him on this topic? The great thing about a city like Baltimore is that you can get lost here. No one's paying attention. Where did life begin? It began in the tide pools. The places where things wash up and just *sit* and get forgotten. That's what cities are like. We see the donut-hole economy, the collapse of the middle class, the radical disparities of wealth, and he just sees windows, windows, windows of opportunity. I don't even know what they are. I probably don't *want* to know. People talk about the gray economy; well, I know that what he does is gray. But I trust him. He says, *the twenty-first century is all about informal networks.* All I say is, don't sell drugs. Don't sell drugs, don't sell guns, and don't sell human beings. But intellectual property? Patents? Copyrights? Proprietary information? I could give a damn. If it comes down to asymmetrical economic warfare, I'm all for it.

The small ax.

Trust a white boy to know his Bob Marley. Yeah. The small ax.

A dusty red Camry festooned with bumper stickers pulls alongside us and slows down — practically, it seems, at my elbow. *U.S. Out of Iraq Now. I Love My Country, but We Should See Other People. Nader/LaDuke 2000. I Was at Woodstock and I Vote.* Some people just can't keep their clichés to themselves, I'm about to say, when I glimpse Mort Kepler through the glass, putting a hairy elbow over the passenger headrest and twisting his head, owl-like, to stare at me. As we walk toward the car — too late to change directions, too late to say *excuse me* and sprint over — he leans over and rolls down the window.

Kelly! Thought you'd have left town by now.

Good to see you, Mort. How's things?

Figuring out just how far I can stretch my Social Security.

He has a mad grin affixed to his face, a rictus of a smile.

Aren't you going to introduce me to your friend?

Robin Wilkinson. Mort Kepler.

Gamely, she reaches through the window to shake his hand. Big fan, she says. Sorry you lost your show. I'm sure it's only temporary, right? You'll be back soon somewhere.

Well, he says, still smiling, your friend here didn't make it easy for me. Not to be rude or anything. Just so you know who you're associating with.

Nice to see you, Mort, I say, taking Robin's elbow. And we leave him there, blocking traffic, his emergency blinkers on. Do me a favor, I tell her, don't look back for a minute. Ignore him.

He was really hostile. I'm surprised.

Did you ever *actually* listen to his show?

A few times. He struck me as a sort of sweet crackpot type. I always pictured him with a beard, for some reason.

Do you ever notice how easy it is for people his age to be angry, and intrusive, and *cruel,* and act like they're doing you a favor? Or, alternatively, like it's all your fault?

Well, it was the We Generation.

The Me Generation, you mean.

No, the We Generation. As in, *we did*

everything right and you guys came along and screwed it up. As if we voted for Reagan.

She tosses me a smile, sideways, as if to say, this is fun. Too bad we can't be friends.

We're crossing the street now to enter Broadway Market, with all its attendant smells, the fresh-roasted coffees, the deli meats, Old Bay, Belgian fries, fresh bluefish and dolphin and skate. I remember, out of nowhere, Adele Patinkin, who I dated for a few months at Amherst, and how we used to go to the Kosher Kitchen every Saturday night for havdalah, the end of Shabbat service, and how a painted box of spices went hand to hand around the room, everyone getting a whiff of cloves and cinnamon, nutmeg and cardamom. Reawakening to the world. Food, it seems to me, and the smell of food, is the world's great consolation prize, its way of saying, *things can't possibly be so bad.* I fall into step after Robin, who looks from side to side, grinning, nearly licking her parted lips, flooded with voracious and well-earned desire, who has forgotten me entirely, for the moment, and I realize that I'll have to come up with some excuse for having no appetite at all, for needing to leave, abruptly, for needing to sit in my car for fifteen minutes before I can drive, waiting for my starved hands to stop shaking.

24.

Out of sight, behind the forsythias at the far end of Paul and Noreen Phillips's front lawn, the children are singing "Human Nature." There must be fifteen of them, in a crowd of forty adults, and for the length of the party they've been out in the grass, unattended, with a separate buffet and drinks table, playing hide-and-seek, having somersault contests, dance contests, cheerleading demonstrations. Sherry and Tamika among them, of course, almost shoulder to shoulder, clearly sisters, with identical coils of spaghetti braids that never come loose, no matter how vigorously they roll on the grass. Now the whole crowd has disappeared into the gloaming, the pastel May twilight, and snatches of warbly harmony come floating across the grass:

Reaching out to touch a stranger
Electric eyes are everywhere

— I've been trying to remember the first time I ever saw his face, Marshall Haber is saying. It wasn't at the convention. Before that. It must have been in some TV interview, because he was talking. Sitting down and talking. No idea what he was saying, but you could just tell from his manner, his posture, that he had something going on. You could tell by the way he folded his hands in his lap. *Control.* No unnecessary movements. Right? And this is when he wasn't even a senator yet.

Yeah, that's what people always say, Lee says. The aura and all that.

I'm sitting at the edge of the patio, facing out, fallen into shadow. It's the moment at a party where the detritus of paper plates and napkins accumulates on every surface, second or third drinks are in hand, and everyone over the age of twenty-five is sitting down and unlikely to rise anytime soon. Ten minutes ago Martin and Robin and I were sitting here in a tight circle, eating shrimp and grits, but she took a call from work and disappeared, and the Brain Trust filtered in, overfed, almost limping with the extra weight, everyone shaking my hand, Paul even slapping me on the shoulder. *You* again? Where's your notebook? Is this on the record?

I wouldn't call it an aura, Lee says. That makes me think of a halo, you know? It wasn't that he was trying out for sainthood. You didn't get an MLK vibe. Not a Jesse vibe. That's the thing: he was already *beyond* that. People called it post-racial; it wasn't post-racial. It was post–*race as an issue.* There's a crucial difference there. It was, like, say you call up a lawyer because you need to hire a lawyer, and then you walk into his office, and he's black. Didn't sound black on the phone, didn't see a picture, no warning, and then he's right there, and he gives you this look, you know, he sees you're off guard, and his look says, *you got a problem with that?* Not in an aggressive way. In an informative way, an appraising way. Like, *is this going to be a problem?* That's what he was like, those first few years. After the speech. *Hello, America, I'm going to be your next president. I'm the best man for the job. I happen to be black. You got a problem with that?*

I got a problem with the phrase *happen to be,* Marshall says.

Okay. Okay. That's your job. His job was to use the language of the moment. And white people, excuse me, Kelly, but white people, dominant-paradigm people, they *love* to say, *he happens to be from Mexico.*

She happens to be a lesbian. They happen to be part of a polygamous macrobiotic cult. Because it makes it all random and unintentional. *I happened to fall down and break my ankle.* It all seems so *unfair* that way. You don't have to draw any connections, just look at what's in front of you. *We're all the same. God just happened to hit you with the ugly stick.*

You know what I'm tired of? Paul says. I'm tired of interpreting *the meaning of Obama.* Shouldn't we be over that by now, now that it's a done deal? A president should not mean, but be.

The Obama era. The Obama years.

Keep your powder dry and your drones in the air.

Bet he contemplated using a drone on John Boehner once or twice. Or Grover Norquist. Or Scalia.

Clarence Thomas. Silent but deadly. Shit, Thomas *is* the drone. The stealth bomber of the white right.

Y'all bringing me down, Paul says. You hear that singing? None of these kids were even *thought* of when that song was on the radio. For them it's ancient history. It might as well be the Beatles. Or Elvis.

Don't you know kids don't listen to the radio anymore? Marshall says. For them it's all about *Glee* and *American Idol.* They like a song, they pick it up. Doesn't matter if it's from yesterday or 1930. I like that. It's an eclectic era. Take what you want, the rest is dross.

It's because the music they're putting out today is crap, Lee says. All the Nicki Minaj, Lady Gaga, Beyoncé stuff, with the Auto-Tune and the electric beats, all that fizzy special-effects nonsense.

That's not fair to Beyoncé, Martin says. She's the real thing. She's a throwback.

Says the man who listens to Joni Mitchell. Paul leans over and looks at me. Kelly, has he told you about that? Better make sure you get it down on the record so he can't deny it later. First time he picked me up in his car, what was he playing? *Blue.* Thought I was going to shit my pants. Seriously, that was some country stuff. So country it was like, not even twentieth-century, like, *medieval.* Like there should be recorders and harpsichords on it. And he tried to get off telling me it was Robin's tape.

It was.

I don't care if it was Jesus Christ's tape, I would have tossed it out the window after two bars.

Plenty of people think Joni Mitchell's cool, Marshall says. Herbie did a whole album of her songs. Ain't you ever heard *Mingus*?

Yeah, I heard Mingus.

No, *Mingus,* her album, you ignoramus. That's some whacked-out Seventies material on there. Cassandra Wilson's early stuff comes right out of *Mingus.*

Problem is, Martin intones, Paul, all due respect, you don't know your musical history.

But back to Obama —

Seriously?

Yes, *Paul,* Martin says. Seriously. Let him finish.

Before I was so rudely interrupted by Michael Jackson and the henchmen of pop-culture distraction, Marshall says, let me just say that what Obama is *not* is a proxy. He doesn't carry the bag. Not for the white liberal establishment, not for Israel, not for Charlie Rangel or Tavis Smiley.

He carried the bag pretty damn well for Goldman Sachs. Or he let Geithner carry it.

Then he sicced Elizabeth Warren on Geithner's ass, Paul. It's that *Team of Rivals* theory you were telling me about.

Martin scratches his chin.

You ever read those Joseph Campbell books, *The Masks of God*? he says. Robin hooked me up with those when we were first going out. It's totally fascinating stuff. Anyway. Somewhere in there, Campbell says that the earliest kind of kings in prehistory, in the very early Egyptian, Sumerian, Mesopotamian states, were sacrificial kings, that is, they were put to death by the people and ceremonially buried in order to appease the gods.

I don't like where this is going, Lee says.

Okay. Okay. I'm extrapolating a little. But get this. Obama's just an extremely, extremely smart guy. An intellectual overachiever before he was a political overachiever. And he's also, just to put it mildly, a hybrid. A mongrel. A cobbled-together person who's *chosen* his categories all the way along. You got me? That kind of person is always going to be a natural skeptic.

A master of the mask.

Yeah, but here's the thing. A skeptic is not a cynic. Not necessarily. So Obama, he understands something about the essential nature of being president that the rest of us don't. Being president means being at the center of a circle whose radius is infinite. You're the center of an incalculably complex system. Responsible for everything, in control over almost nothing. Now most presidents are essentially just showboats who are very good at projecting leadership and pretending to have a hand on the helm. They sleep well at night. Dubya was one of those. So was Reagan. So was JFK. And then there are the really deep political minds, the Machiavellians. LBJ. Clinton. But Obama is something else again, because he understands the symbolic role of the president is a *tragic* role. That puts him in a different category.

Lincoln.

Yes. And not because he's freeing any slaves or even because he's the first black et cetera. Because he wears that mask. He has that look all the time, a kind of noble dread. He's a sacrificial king, the still center of the churning world. Call him whatever you want, but he's older than old school. He's the most *primal* president we've had in my lifetime. And the thing is, it's all contrived. It's constructed. And we're okay with that. It's artificial *and* sacred.

Do I feel, or is it just my hyperattentiveness, that there's a palpable shift in the room, a feeling that someone's just gone too far? Not that Martin's wrong; that he's too literally right, too eager to spell it out. There's a kind of malicious energy in his voice: *I know you too well. I know you better than you know yourselves.* Lee purses his lips and nods. Marshall takes out his Black-Berry and absently spins the wheel with his thumb.

That's some deep material you got there, Paul says. Kelly, you sure you ain't writing a book on this guy? 'Cause I think fifteen thousand words isn't going to cut it.

Martin avoids my look, dusts off his lap, and stands, collecting napkins and cups. Gentlemen, on that note, I have to run off and find my wife, he says. You should do the same. Don't let them get lonely.

They're not lonely. They just don't want to listen to us.

So listen to them for a change.

What, Marshall says, they're paying you now? Must be nice. He's getting up, too, and now everyone does, stretching, loosening collars and belts. Got to get the kids to bed, he says. Soccer starts at eight tomorrow. No sleeping in these days.

Coffee in a paper cup and muffin crumbs in your lap. That's Sunday brunch in my house.

Tell me about it.

And I leave them there, as I have to, before they notice and ask the inevitable question, *do you have kids, Kelly?* I wouldn't do that to them. It's kindness, I'm thinking, slipping away, toward the kitchen where the

341

women's high voices ring out. Not to make them apologize for their lives without meaning it. I never would have been able to apologize for mine.

Peter Joseph, it was explained to me, used to be on the board of the Urban League with Martin, and also had a fellowship with the Greater Baltimore Commission the same year as Robin; he's a venture capitalist who made his money on the West Coast — an early investor in Yahoo! — and who now is developing a biotech startup in Harbor East. The party is for Renée Jackson, a City Council candidate with bigger plans. What plans? I asked, and Martin said, national plans. We added a House seat to Baltimore City in the last redistricting.

Isn't that a bit of a stretch, from not even being elected to the City Council?

Watch her, he said. Watch and learn. We shook hands with her as we came in, all together, and then she disappeared into a crowd, every head angled toward her. Short, slim, very erect, in a navy Hillary-style pantsuit, her hair swept back and folded into a sort of a crest — my god, I said under my breath, she's younger than I am, not even thirty, maybe.

She's an Iraq vet, Robin told me, handing

me a glass of white. There's serious political traction there. Great family, too. Her dad's a pastor; he was up on the dais when you came to church with us.

Yeah. Martin pointed him out.

And her mom's some kind of an heiress from Atlanta. Real estate money. They're a Spelman family, too. In fact, I interviewed her. Not that it made any difference. She has a law degree, too. Finished her service working in-house at the Pentagon. Seriously, she's someone to know.

So why aren't you in there, pressing the flesh?

Robin doesn't need anyone's favors, Martin said, in my other ear. I hadn't noticed, but they were flanking me, providing security. She *dispenses* favors. The second-highest-ranking black woman in the whole Hopkins system. One of these days she's going to cash in and work in administration.

What he means is, Robin said, in his rich fantasy life, I'm going to sit behind a desk, push paper, and pull down something in the high six figures. In reality, it'll be a cold day in July.

As she was speaking she laid her hand on my forearm, a purely affectionate, nominal gesture, but in the flutter of a heartbeat I felt Martin's eyes angling downward, noting, noticing, as he noticed everything. And the envelope surrounding us, the membrane of convivial warmth, broke in an instant.

There's food, right? I asked. Sorry to be so abrupt, but I'm starving. Something about Sundays — I always feel as if I don't eat enough the rest of the week.

Is there food? Are you kidding? Robin laughed at me, her teeth — not blindingly white, not iridescent, but perfectly proportioned, stainless, neatly arranged — on full display. I don't know where *you* come from, she says, but among black people a party from five to eight means serious food. Didn't you see the Melba's catering truck? Noreen doesn't mess around. She's from South Carolina. Low-country food.

Shrimp and grits?

Like you've never had it before. Go eat. She waved at me. We'll catch up with you later.

Just after I've dumped my plate in the garbage a little girl darts across my path, a blur of pigtails and blue satin, thigh height, poking a smartphone screen. She's half, I can see that in a second, all Chinese features around the eyes and the mouth, but with an extra broadness in the nose and warm peach tones in her skin. Tall for her age, too. The one time we visited Wudeng with Meimei people came up to us on the street and said, *so tall. So fair. So tall.* Though Meimei was really particularly neither. And one old woman, a shopkeeper, said, American-born Chinese girls always have enormous breasts. Too much milk! Don't give her milk. Give her tofu. We all laughed.

I stand there, still by the garbage can, transfixed for a moment. Her mother comes trailing after her, so obviously Chinese, so obviously transplanted — the same dress pants with chunky black heels, the same long ponytail — that I don't have to wait to hear her piping voice speaking Mandarin and her mother answering back. They see me looking at them; how could they not? And the girl pulls her mother across the room and asks, holding out the phone, in her most polite four-year-old's voice, excuse me, can you please take a picture of me with my mommy and daddy? I want to show my baby brother, he's home with the babysitter.

We descend into the living room, with its faux-retro shag carpet, its leather couches and wall-sized TV, its woven baskets and Kara Walker silhouette and Basquiat poster, a room that announces optimism and arrival, a room that makes *me* wish I had money to give to someone. And I shake the father's hand. Willard, friend of Peter's, partner at Accenture. We take photo after photo. Isabella with Daddy, Isabella with Mommy. Mommy and Daddy holding Isabella up in the air like a cheerleader. Isabella *Chang-Thomas,* she tells me proudly. Finally she loses interest and runs off to join the others, still out on the lawn, and Willard moves off to grab more Lowenbraus, and I turn to the woman, Shen, and say, almost in a whisper, a conspiratorial sotto voce, *wo nu'er jiao Meimei.*

Conjugating verbs in Chinese is much looser than in English, and depends much more on context. In English you would have to say *my daughter's name was.* Or *my daughter's name is.* In Chinese the verb by itself seldom has so much power. To be technically correct I should have said, *wo nu'er jiao Meimei le,* the *le* indicating a finished action, or, even more unbearably, *zhiqian wo you jiao Meimei de nu'er, danshi yinian qian ta sile.* I had a daughter named Meimei, but she died two years ago. But you don't introduce yourself to a stranger this way in any language. Much less the parent of a young child, whose body hasn't yet acquired the solidity, the independent gravity, the fixed status of a separate human be-

346

ing; who is still for all intents and purposes an extension of your own body, an extra limb.

Your Chinese is excellent, she says. Where did you learn it?

Wudeng, in Hunan, on the north shore of the Yangtze. And where are you from?

Shaoxing. But I met Willard in Shanghai. And where is your family now?

Out of town.

But you live in Baltimore? How does your wife stand it?

What do you mean?

The Chinese families here are so *provincial.* She wrinkles her nose. No one speaks Chinese to their kids. All they care about is soccer and getting into the right private school. We bought my parents an apartment in Shanghai, and we're there nearly half the year.

Noreen Phillips appears out of nowhere — it helps that she's no more than five-two — takes her arm, and says, sorry, Kelly, but I'm going to be rude and steal Shen away for a moment.

Not at all, I say, grateful not to have to come up with a reply. And they leave me there, no drink in hand, temporarily unable to move, staring up at an enormous African mask mounted to the wall: a man's face, with upraised eyes, his chin sticking out, mouth open, as if he's trying to swallow raindrops.

The morning of the accident, Meimei was playing with a red boa from her dress-up bin, tying it around herself and twirling through the house, scattering downy feathers everywhere. When I finally returned from the funeral home, after making all the arrangements, it was mid-morning the following day; I'd been up all night in the chaplain's office at the hospital, waiting for the bodies to be transferred, signing paperwork and trying not to fall asleep. My parents had arrived after midnight. They brought me into the house, all but holding me up at the elbows, and the feathers were everywhere, like a trail of rose petals. We tended to leave her messes till the evening, when we had time to get out the vacuum and clean up. My mother disappeared into the kitchen and brought out a broom, and I said, no. Leave them there. And they stayed for weeks, blowing into clumps, gathering lint.

I had no interest in the future. The future was erased. When you have a young child your world is their world: Meimei's friends' parents became our friends; Meimei's school was the hub of our social life; Meimei's needs were our needs; all with the promise that *this is a full and justifiable life,* this is a rationale for staying alive, a bridge to the future, and the arguments and complaining and sorting and competing — speak only Chinese at home? Speak Chinese with Mom and English with Dad? Buy an apartment in the city, or a house in the suburbs? Settle in Boston, or move somewhere with an actual community, like Flushing, or Vancouver, or L.A.? — were just the pulsing blood of that life. Without it, then, now, I'm a dry sponge, I'm thinking with a kind of muted, helpless rage, I'm like this guy, waiting for rain that never comes.

Deep in my pocket, now, against my thigh, my phone comes to life, actual life, with three short buzzes.

Where are you? Didnt leave, did you? Were in the back, come join. M

Beyond the pool, the outdoor bar, and the second buffet, at the far edge of an amoeba-shaped patch of grass, I find Martin in a teak easy chair, his legs up, like a mogul, one hand thrown easily over a half-drunk vodka, the other toying with his phone. Robin is gone. How did he do it? I wonder. How did she allow him to disappear so ostentatiously, to sit and — to all appearances — sulk in a corner?

Sit, he says, and slings his feet to one side, giving me a square foot of the end of the chair. Where the heck were you? I thought maybe you'd gotten cold feet or something. *I* wouldn't want to be you at this party. Always hate having to go where I'm constantly introducing myself on a Friday night. It's too much like work.

This *is* work for me.

Well, okay. That doesn't mean you can't have a good time. I should have had you more under my wing, had you meeting people. That would have been the polite thing, right? But I figured it would be just as good to have you be a fly on the wall. You're the writer. You have to have your own point of view.

I'd be an outsider no matter what.

You sound offended. Isn't that the whole point?

No, I say. Look, I'm not offended. Just a little tired. A little overwhelmed. All this double vision. This double life. You're used to it. You *chose* it. I'm just a visitor here.

He gazes at me for a second.

Like on *Seinfeld,* he says, that one where Kramer gets an intern. You know what I'm talking about? Kramerica Industries. You get to live inside my craziness. Well, no worries. It won't last forever. You've got your finger on the button, frankly. *You're* the one who has to write it all up.

My mouth hangs open for a moment, and then I start to laugh. Sorry, I say. It's just the last comparison I was expect —

You're forgetting how much of the Nineties I spent *inside.* In that crap-ass old house turned crash pad. I watched so much TV it would make your eyes bleed. Kept it on during the day, while I was answering calls and fiddling on the computer. It's an easy way to neutralize bugs and wiretaps. Damn, I must have watched every episode of *Seinfeld* and *Friends* six or seven times. I'm a walking encyclopedia of about six years of pop-culture detritus. JonBenét Ramsey? Monica Lewinsky and Linda Tripp? The O.J. trial? I watched every *minute* of the O.J. trial on Court TV. What I wouldn't give to expunge all that nonsense from my brain. While you were in college becoming fluent in — how many? five? — languages, I was at home selling drugs and watching *Oprah.*

This last line booms out across the pool, and I look up, wondering if anyone is paying attention. The crowd is beginning to thin out; I can see a couple inside through the French doors, the woman jingling her keys, wishing Paul and Noreen into view so they can say a quick goodbye.

Martin, I say, are you afraid, at all, of what's going to happen? Of — losing *this*? Has it even crossed your mind?

Because what? People won't talk to me once they know?

You think they will?

Frankly? It's immaterial. We won't be able to stay here for long. We'll have to relocate to someplace with more privacy. Once the payouts start coming in we'll get a place in L.A. or New York. Maybe one of those towns in Westchester or North Jersey or Connecticut. There's going to be paparazzi. At least for a while. Sherry and Tamika will go to prep school. Maybe Europe. Or, ideally, Asia. Someplace that teaches Mandarin and has tight security.

That's a little dramatic, don't you think?

Well, okay. Presumptuous, anyhow. First I have to convince Robin that it's all okay. You're not wrong, you know. I'm concerned about it. I need her on my side. Publicly *and* privately. I've got to strategize that part. But that's my concern, nothing for you to worry about. You'll get paid no matter what. As long as this is a viable operation, you'll get paid.

Speaking of which, I say, I've been thinking that after we get back from Bangkok

352

Where do you want to be? Where does a writer like to be a writer these days? Want me to rent you a studio in Brooklyn? Or Paris? Short-term apartments are a breeze in Paris. Though if I were you I'd stay in Thailand. Get a house on the beach in Pattaya, or Krabi. For what you'd pay for a studio in Park Slope you could have your own beach house in Pattaya with a staff of six.

I'll take care of it.

You're turning down free rent? If I were your wife, I'd say that's a terrible fiscal decision.

It's such an odd and hurtful thing to say that I shrink back, as if he'd pinched me on the arm.

No, no, no, he says. What I meant was, you need a friend, Kelly. A second opinion.

What I need, I say, is my own time and space.

Because you're ambivalent about signing on? *Still?* I thought we went over this. I thought you gave me a pledge.

Martin, I say, stretching out my legs, who wouldn't be ambivalent? Who, in their right mind, would be one hundred percent *in*?

Can you think of someone? Maybe you should hire them instead. I mean, have you considered the long-term implications of this, the things they're going to say about you? This is going to make Malik Williams look like Mister Rogers. What you're talking about — one way of looking at it — is that this is the most fucked-up reverse-eugenics experiment since Tuskegee. You're going to be accused of some kind of bioethical genocide. Trying to destroy race as a category.

I'm not on a mission to destroy racism, he says, and I'm not on a mission to destroy races. What *I* think is that people should have options. I believe in free choice. That's the American way, right? I mean, not now. Now it's purely a matter of speculation. The technology has to develop, the procedures have to develop, the processes have to get streamlined and *affordable.* I'm like a hand-lathed Daimler-Benz back in the 1890s, twenty years before Ford invented the assembly line. Maybe I'll never even see it in my lifetime. But you want to know the essence, the kernel, of this thing we're doing? It's just that. Choice. Options. All that outrage, all that kicking and fussing, it's always just a period before the whole thing gets absorbed and normalized. All that energy has to be expended.

Okay. Okay. Anyway, beyond all that. Beyond the theoretical questions. You've been incredibly generous to me. And you're promising more —

I am. You want specifics, now, finally? Let me break it down. Fifteen percent of the whole package. Interview deals, photo deals, the book, the movie. Whatever else. Corporate sponsorships. Other relationships. We'll get it on paper when there's some product from your end. For now it's a handshake deal. But this is what I mean: serious money. Money for you to have a fresh start.

Can I be completely honest? It's freaking me out a little. The numbers. You know I'm not a money person. But the check, the offers, the *language* you use: it's disturbing to me. It doesn't feel right.

Because?

Well, if I knew that, I'd have said it already, wouldn't I?

You think I've got some hidden agenda *other* than my hidden agenda? Some meta–hidden agenda? I think you've been dipping into too much postmodern theory. Foucault will screw you up. I learned that after one semester in college. You're always looking for the man *behind* the man behind the curtain.

Well — and here I give him my best teacher's laugh, my seen-it-all Harvard laugh — one of my professors said, you can hate Foucault, but you can't argue with him. In other words, just because you're not paranoid doesn't mean they aren't out to get you.

Listen. Maybe we should turn this conversation around. I mean, look, you've heard just about every bad thing there is to know about me. What about you? What's the worst thing *you've* ever done, Kelly? Isn't that fair game?

Nothing I'm too ashamed to admit.

Seriously? No secrets, in a whole thirty-odd years of life? Never cheated on Wendy? Or anyone? No secret girlfriends, no escorts, porn habits, nothing?

You make me feel like a Puritan.

And what about what happened with Alan?

My face turns hot, then cold; my pulse skitters in my wrists. What do you mean? I say. What happened with Alan when?

Oh, come on. You mean you didn't see my car? *Really,* Kelly? You didn't see it?

See it when?

See it pulling up behind you when you left? When he OD'd, when you were in the house to see it? I mean, evidently. When I

356

went in it couldn't have been more than five minutes later, and he was gone. I mean stone-cold *dead*. I kept meaning to ask you about it. I thought you'd come forward. Even at the funeral, I was expecting you'd say something.

I thought Cheryl found the body.

I was there, trying to call her, when Cheryl came home. It's all in the police report. You missed us both by less than fifteen minutes.

He looks at me blandly, splaying his fingers across his knee. Something about his posture reminds me of a Roman fresco: a philosopher lounging about, toga thrown across his legs, pointing a languid finger at the heavens. Stress him, I'm beginning to see, and he becomes more relaxed. More at one with his own certainties. While I have hot crabs of panic crawling over my face.

You've waited all this time to tell me that I'm a liar? Or, what, a murderer?

You tell me.

Seriously?

Seriously. That's not a rhetorical question. *Tell* me, Kelly. Whatever it is. I'll take it. I'll take your version. I'm not into justice on principle. But I'm still waiting for an explanation.

The backyard has emptied now; a young woman from the catering staff circles the

357

pool, stacking abandoned glasses in a bus bin. On the far side of the house, soft screeches and pounding feet: the roundup of the children has begun. Every animal, every being, is ignoring me. This is what I tell myself. No one, no one but these two people, has any interest in what I'm about to say.

It's very simple. I went to see him; he looked bad. Tired. Said he needed his insulin shot. I got him the needle and went downstairs to make him some soup. When I got back upstairs he was asleep. He'd cooked up and hid the evidence; I realized that later. So I left. End of story.

And you never told anyone — because?

I raise my hands over my head in a parody of a sleepy stretch, trying to slow my breathing, to give myself a window of coherent thought.

Why the fuck do you think? Because of *this*. Because of how you reacted just now. I didn't want to complicate things any further for anyone. He died by his own hand. By choice. Whether I was there or not didn't matter. He would have just gotten up off the couch and found the syringe himself. Maybe not that day. But the next day, or the next. Believe me. He was ready to die. He *wanted* to die. In his mind it was as good as done. Was it selfish? Of course. I take full responsibility for that. Was it criminal? Was it *immoral*? I don't think Alan would have wanted me to fuck up my life because of an absolute, incontestable accident. With the wrong DA I could have been accused of involuntary manslaughter. Do you know that? I could have spent five years in jail.

You talked to a lawyer?

Years later. In graduate school. After an acute attack of conscience. And you know what he said? He said, you've suffered enough. Go live your life. And so I did.

An enormous lump rises and beats in my esophagus, a vibrating tumor. I feel like a bullfrog.

And so I have to ask you. Are *you* going to let me live my life, Martin?

He gets up and throws his arms around me, around my arms, confining me in a reckless hug.

I want to do more than that, he says. I want to *give* you a life. You've had too much wretchedness for one already. Let it go, man! We both ought to let it go. Don't you think? We can help each other *do* this thing.

Is that what all this has been about?

Of course not. What am I, some kind of stealth therapist, some self-help guru in disguise? This is about business. This is a *transaction.* But sometimes in a transaction more than just money changes hands.

So you *can* buy happiness, after all. What a relief.

Don't start on me with that liberal BS. Money isn't happiness. Money is *life,* the energy circuit, the good and the bad. Turn the circuit in your direction and you get happiness. But it's never just about accumulation, it's about use. Use value. You feel me? The way things are going, I could probably retire in five years and play golf. Do I look like someone who wants to spend the rest of his life playing golf and avoiding capital gains?

See? You are a self-help guru. With a clientele of one.

Well, hopefully not just one, he says. Listen, is this enough? I'm worn out. Worn out and *revivified,* true. But I need some sleep. Bangkok's in three days.

That's not quite enough, I say. I need a commitment from you. No — more than that. I need an oath.

An oath?

This dies with us. Saying the words, I feel like a character in a Hitchcock movie, like the hapless tennis player in *Strangers on a Train.* This conversation never happened.

He grins at me. Yeah? Okay. Scoot over.

360

He reaches down and rolls up his right pants leg, flap over flap, tighter and tighter, a tourniquet he pulls up over his knee. Right above his kneecap is a wavering of the skin, a ridge of scar tissue in the shape of a parenthesis.

Eight years old, he says. Corner of Lorraine and Barclay, right outside New Po Shun Carryout. The bullet hit the back of my leg and passed out here. Missed the knee by an inch. Otherwise I wouldn't be walking. If it had nicked the femoral artery I'd have bled out before the ambulance arrived. As it was I spent a good ten minutes with my hands wrapped around the base of a pay phone before they picked me up. One ambulance, two paramedics. Policeman finally put me over his shoulder and drove me to the hospital himself. Black policeman. Weren't so many in those days. Put my eyes against his neck. I fell asleep and dreamed my father was carrying me. My *real* father, not the one back at home. I dreamed up a black man to be my father, right then and there. Tall. Kept his hair in a close Afro. People called him Eight Ball. Wore two silver rings on his left hand, index and pinkie fingers. Smelled like baby powder and witch hazel. Always picking me up. Always putting his hand over the top of my head, like he was measuring my height. When I woke up in the hospital, when I woke up from that dream, I hated my life so much I wished I had died.

So what are you telling me, Martin?

I swear an oath to you, he says. Swear on this scar. Will you take my word? Jesus, I sound like Gandalf. But I mean it. Take my word?

Only later that night, at the blurring edge of sleep, as a police cruiser passes silently under my window, lights flashing, do I bolt up in bed and see what he has done. The double bind. I'm not his employee now. I'm his servant. His dependent. If it weren't wrong, if it weren't terribly, terribly wrong to say so, I might almost say that Martin Wilkinson owns me.

In Maryland, there is no statute of limitations for involuntary manslaughter. I learned this from Steve Cox, whose office, above an antiquarian map store in Harvard Square, had a sign that advertised *All Legal Questions Answered $50.* He had a silver mustache, rimless glasses, and wore, in the middle of winter, a guayabera with a pocket protector. Every surface of his office was crowded with Mexican curios: dancing skeletons, carved santos, miniature sombreros. It doesn't look great, he said, when I finished my tale of woe and he'd checked the state database on his computer. Maryland's common law, and the definition of manslaughter is wide open. The prosecutor might get hung up on establishing cause. But I wouldn't bet on it. You'd be looking at ten years in one of the state prisons down there — Jessup is the biggest. Not happy places. Good behavior, no previous record, you might get it down to three to five. Maybe even a suspended sentence, five years' probation. But then you're still a felon for life. Does anyone else know about this?

No.

You sure? You never got drunk and told some nice bartender, some girl you hooked up with in college? Ever taken acid? People tend to confess crimes when they're on acid. Happens all the time, don't ask me why.

Never. Never.

Well, okay, then. The best thing is to keep this tamped down for good. You married? She know?

No, I said. Not exactly. She's from China, I added, as if it helped.

Don't tell her. Think divorce. Think blackmail. Hate to put it this way, but that's the situation you're in. Give you another piece of advice? Quit drinking. Or at least take it one drink at a time. Don't take drugs. Avoid anesthesia. Keep it straight and sober. Keep it till your deathbed. Either that or move to Costa Rica. I've got friends in real estate there. Set you up real nice for next to nothing.

The standard explanation I've given myself is simple: when I heard the words from Cheryl, when she called from the hospital, my mind went black, my throat filled with cold sand, I nearly passed out, and it wasn't until hours later that I realized I'd never said to her, *but I saw him only half an hour before that.* It wasn't a conscious omission. It wasn't an omission at all. I had lost my mind; I had lost my memory; all I was thinking of was how to live the next seventy-two hours, how to make it to the funeral.

As it turned out, it fell to me to drive Cheryl and Rebecca there. She wasn't able to drive herself, she said; she couldn't be trusted behind the wheel, after two days of Valium- and doxepin-induced sleep. They sat in the backseat, as if I were the chauffeur: collapsed against either door, their black dresses folded about them, like dying crows. Rebecca and I nearly carried Cheryl into the service; Rabbi Kauffmann and I nearly carried her back out again. She clung to my neck like a cramping swimmer reaching up for air. She said, *you were his better self. If only he had listened to you more.* She said, *something of him lives on in you.*

Afterward, because there was no wake, because we were all back from college and hadn't seen one another and needed to confirm, as all mourners do, that we were still alive, Ayala and I and Rina and Trevor and Jake spread the word that we should gather at Kanazawa, the nearest place we could think of to the funeral home. Martin was there, of course. I hadn't seen him in eighteen months. I wouldn't see him again for eighteen years. He wore black jeans and a black polo shirt with a navy jacket over it, an outfit so frighteningly ugly it almost seemed it had been planned that way. His face looked like it had been scrubbed with a Brillo Pad: exceedingly pale and raw, which made his nose seem larger, or perhaps he was having a late growth spurt. At the entrance to the chapel we'd hugged, awkwardly, a first in our lives. Thank god, I'd said, thank god you're here, and he said, why wouldn't I be? Why wouldn't I be, Kelly? But then the music had started — the first song was "Freak Scene," by Dinosaur Jr., from a mix tape Alan had made for

Rebecca just a week before — and I hadn't had to answer.

There was no table large enough for us, so the waitress gave us the tatami room in the back, and we took off our shoes, gamely, and sat cross-legged, as if we were kindergarteners again, playing duck, duck, goose, and ordered large bottles of sake, proving once and for all that we *were* sophomores in college. I sat at one end of the long table, and Martin at the other, saving us from having to talk to each other.

Why did I think we were angry with each other? We had fallen so thoroughly out of contact that it seemed there must be a reason, though we'd never fought, or even disagreed, since the band broke up. Maybe it was still that. That could have been the reason I gave myself. But the look he gave me wasn't the wariness of an old wound; it was fresh outrage. As if he wanted some kind of an answer. Finally, I thought: he blames me for not seeing it coming. For not warning Cheryl. For being too busy being who I was supposed to be, for not dropping out, if that's what you would call it, for not going into full-time mourning before the fact. For not being self-evidently shattered. And I thought: fuck you, Martin. Fuck you and get me out of here. At the end of the meal we hugged once again, even more awkwardly than the first time, our arms curved into stiff hoops like jai alai baskets. I'll see you, he said, and ambled down the sidewalk in the opposite direction of the parking lot.

I've lived with this guilt for so long — nearly twenty years — that I've accepted it as a condition of living, a solid vestigial node, like a tumor, like a bullet lodged near my spine. Has it cast its own pall over my life? Of course. Is there a certain relief in knowing that someone else knows?

There would be, if that person was an impartial listener. A therapist. Wendy. Why, again, did I never tell Wendy? Not because I was afraid she'd betray me; because she would have been appalled that I avoided the consequences. To her the shame would have been unbearable. She would have wanted me to confess.

Did I say I've been living in white dreamtime? The time in which all crimes are historical. *Back then. Lessons learned. Things are different now.* Who would have thought that history could whip around, like a dangling snake, and bite me across the knuckles? He owns me, I'm thinking. His way or three to five in Jessup. Of all the ways

I expected to be transformed by grief, by loss, by a *catastrophic personal loss over which I had no control,* this was never one.

The thing about blind spots, someone told me once, is you don't see them.

So listen, Cox's voice is saying now, on my voice mail, which I'm only listening to now, having fished my phone out of my jacket to charge it before bed. I found something. Took me nearly a month to confirm it, but here we are. Martin Lipkin, aka Matthew Wilson, aka Mark Wilbury, aka Wilbur Martinson, Internet aliases including Body-More, Grnmnt10234, XcashKingX, and Alan93. Served eighteen months at Northern State Penitentiary in St. Johnsbury, Vermont. November 1998 to May 2000. Credit card fraud. Identity theft. Story was, he worked for a business that leased ATMs to gas stations, and figured out a way to get the card numbers out of the machines in his spare time. Pretty minor-league stuff. Or it would have been, if the purchases hadn't been so large. He maxed out every card he found — tens of thousands of dollars, maybe two hundred thousand altogether. Strange thing was, the purchases were all overseas. No cars, no jewelry, no Xboxes or WaveRunners. Nothing that could be seized. In fact, the D.A. never discovered what it was he was buying at all. That's why he served his full sentence. Kid had no traceable assets, nothing with which to pay a fine. Of course, insurance covered the banks' losses. Probably ruined a few people's credit ratings, though. And after release, he skipped parole and disappeared. There's still a warrant out for him in the state of Vermont.

I need to hide, I can't help thinking, I need to leave, I need a conduit, a way out. I need to become not me. As I settle back into bed, beyond sleep, I feel myself grasping Martin's hand at the edge of a cliff, the wind behind us, straining my calves to stay upright, and then, by some wordless signal, we jump at the same moment, jump over the thick shining waves, the stone-dark bottomless ocean.

■ ■ ■ ■

BOOK TWO: EXODUS

■ ■ ■ ■

1.

Out of a dream of my childhood, a hike up Mount Cardigan on a bright autumn day, scampering up a long granite face at a gentle incline, bursts of October light filtering through canopies of yellow and red and orange — I open my eyes to the sun streaming through a gauzy curtain above my bed, the shutters drawn back, the branches of a rubber tree thrusting up into a pale sky strewn with jet trails.

Five or six different species of birds are singing all at once, competitively, trying to drown one another out. An avian pep rally. It's the sound of mid-morning, they're saying, the day fully established, the hard business of seed cracking and grub probing under way, and I look down at my watch and see *10:30.* Someone should have come to get me by now.

But since they haven't, since the day seems unscheduled — not that Martin ever gave me an itinerary, an agenda, not that I have any proof of being here other than a stamp in my passport and a boarding pass jammed into a shirt pocket — I sit up in bed and take a long breath, a waking breath, whatever that means. When you wake up in a new country, I'm thinking now, your senses are the sharpest. Newness, to the touch, to the nose, to the tongue, is a series of small insults. I ought to be paying full attention, I'm on retainer, after all: a professional visitor. A professional *writer*. Why is that so hard to say? I should be taking everything down.

The room — which was dark when I came in, past midnight, and I tumbled into bed without even turning on the bedside lamp — is much bigger than I imagined. The bedroom opens into an alcove with a writing table and a couch, and the look is Thai Resort Classic, even I can see that, all teak and rattan and silk, lustrous green-and-gold scarves hung on the walls, a pair of brass kneeling monks on the coffee table, an antique-looking map labeled *SIAM* over my bed. Thorough, expensive, and generic: too perfect, like a stage set for one of those reality TV shows where I'm a strapping nitwit from Des Moines, a doe-eyed dental hygienist from Wilkes-Barre. On the writing table, in a square glass vase, a bouquet of orchids, of course, bound up with pencil-thin shoots of yellow bamboo. The room smells of incense and also something drier, more chemical: wood polish. Antiseptic. Pledge, Dettol, Febreze. Someone has put a lot of time into this, I'm thinking, a room that says, *you are having an experience. You are getting what you paid for.* Without demanding of you anything at all.

Someone downstairs — the birds have died down for a minute — is speaking Japanese.

It's been years, and I hardly studied it conversationally, mostly just scholarly Japanese, the stock language of articles on Asian literature and linguistics, but I can pick out a few words, here and there, the shape and direction of the sentences. *Of course we pay for . . . the airport . . . no visa requirements . . . full private bath. Yaha. Yes, Yaha.* What does *Yaha* mean? I wonder. *I will mail you the brochure!* he says, whoever it is, speaking formally, as to a client, a customer. *Call me back!* I can almost hear the bow. In Japanese, even speaking on the phone, you bow.

A secretary, I'm thinking. An assistant of some kind. Maybe, from the sound of it, a separate business on the side. Nothing unusual about that. Just that Martin didn't mention it. But who thinks of everything? In a place this size, would I expect to be all alone?

The house belongs to him. I'm remembering this now. How, in the car, pulling through the gate, Martin couldn't resist a proprietary smile. You get sick of staying in hotels, he said. No matter how nice they are. And in any case I have business interests. Makes sense to maintain a presence. An address. I let clients stay here sometimes. These perks, you know, in the business world, sometimes that's all that matters. People are shallow. Sometimes all they want is a gesture.

It's a pretty elaborate gesture, I might have said, though just to make an obvious point.

Now I'm up and moving around, feeling a hollow cramp of morning hunger, postflight hunger. My laptop bag is on the writing table, untouched. My suitcase stands to one side in the bathroom, or dressing room, since it has mirrors, a chest of drawers, a pressing stand. Empty. Someone came and put my clothes away while I was sleeping, and added a bathrobe, a set of blue silk pajamas still in their plastic wrapper, a pair of plastic flip-flops and a pair of leather thongs, and, as I see when I open the closet, an off-white linen suit, more or less my size. Or, when I slip on the jacket, almost exactly my size, the cuffs only an inch too long. What is this, I want to say to Martin, Fantasy Island? Or callbacks for a Tennessee Williams play?

On the other hand, it's a pretty nice suit.

I need coffee. Coffee, a few words with Martin, a plan for the day. I shrug the jacket off, leave it hanging on the doorknob, choose what seems to be the most neutral outfit, a black polo shirt and jeans, and slip out the door, in my stiff new sandals, into the blue-tiled hallway, open to the outside, with tall arched windows at both ends, and down the stairs, only dimly remembering where to go. When we arrived last night the house was dark, floating in a constant hum of crickets or katydids, and there was only Phran to greet us, a short, stocky man, very brown, in a blue sarong and a Dallas Mavericks T-shirt, who carried all our suitcases upstairs at once. Now I come into a kind of central gallery, a breezeway, done in the same blue tiles, and, following a smell of coffee, flowers, and overripe fruit, into a large, open kitchen, or kitchen/office. At the kitchen end a woman in a blue smock dices vegetables with a cleaver, her face covered with a surgical mask; at the other end, along one wall, sits a bank of three computer screens, and a short, slender black man in front of them, his dreadlocks done up in a knot atop his head, tapping a pen on the desk and speaking, into a headset mic, in the voice I heard upstairs: perfect, unhesitating, native Japanese.

And so on instinct, as travelers do, as scholars do, as a matter of habit and protocol, when he says *sayonara odeshka* and turns to me, with a broad, bloodshot smile, I say, in Japanese, good morning, I am Kelly Thorndike, may I have the honor of your name?

God! he says. You startled I. Sorry. Pleased to meet you.

His English has an overloud, exclamatory, gummy quality to it; it takes me a minute, as if two frames of a photograph have to be overlaid, and then I realize he's speaking with a Jamaican accent, a kind of effortful, labored accent, like Philip Michael Thomas on *Miami Vice*. I'm Tariko, he says. The office boy. Head Web lackey and secretary of all things Orchid. Did Martin tell you who I am? Your Japanese is not bad!

I feel, for some reason, the urge to wring my hands, and simultaneously the need to sit down; inside and outside my body, the world for a moment has the consistency and smell of melting candle wax. Behind me I hear the *skitch-skitch-skitch* of plastic sandals, and the woman in the surgical mask appears, carrying a plate of three croissants and a cup of something dark and milky. Sit down, please, she says, and gestures to a small side table. Helpless, boneless, I follow her, and when she pauses for a moment before leaving, I take a bite of croissant and chew it with my eyes closed, trying to remember what a croissant is supposed to taste like.

Tariko, I say, finally, which are you?

Which am I what?

Which were you, to begin with?

Oh! That. Should have introduced I properly. I'm transitioning, of course. Originally Tariko Ogawa, from Kanazawa, Fukui Prefecture, and in six months, Ras Leon Coxholden, from Spanish Town. I'm the first. The first Japanese, that is. To go all the way.

Well, I say, it's very convincing. And then, in Japanese: When I heard you upstairs, you sounded completely Japanese. When I came down here, you looked like a Jamaican. No doubt at all.

Dr. Silpa is a miracle worker. By Jah's grace.

Would you prefer it if I spoke only English?

If you don't mind. I have to use Japanese on the computer, of course. Talking to potential clients. And brethren. But otherwise I try to stay with English. Part of my process.

Are there Japanese Rastafarians?

Of course, Japanese Rastas! I'm second generation. He reaches over to the table and flips open a thin wallet and shows me a much-creased, laminated picture. Bob Marley, in his late stage, raccoon-eyed, slack-jawed, his dreadlocks thick and tumescent, shaking hands with a tiny grinning shaggy-haired Japanese man in a tie-dye T-shirt. My dad ran the first Reggae Sunsplash. Nineteen seventy-eight, he says. Took the first Japanese pilgrimage to Ethiopia. No, I'm dread as they come. One hundred percent Nyabinghi, I-tal from birth. So it's natural, for me. This project. This *journey.*

His smile has a certain infectious warmth; it exudes contentment, confidence, ease. *Why make it so hard?* that smile says. The mark of a natural salesman. He could sell junk bonds, burglar alarms, time-shares, used cars, Mormonism. Whatever it is, I'd think about it for an extra moment. I'd be tempted.

You'll have to forgive me, I say. I'm a little out of my element. Martin didn't tell me that anyone else would be here.

I'm not surprised. We're a bit of a state secret. But look — take your time, man. You just got off the plane. Take it *easy*.

He turns back to the computer, and I take another three bites of my croissant and a sip of coffee. Bite, breathe. Bite, breathe. Out on the street, out of sight, a motorbike roars by, unmuffled, loud as a chain saw. The sunlight pouring in through the doors has a pale, dusty tinge, and I'm beginning to realize that among other small insults, the day is taking on real heat, massive, physical, dry-season heat, not the plangent tropical skin bath I expected. We can't see anything but the garden, of course, but I can feel an echo, a restlessness in the air, a subaural buzz, the resting tone of the vast city. After a day or so I won't even notice it anymore.

What does it mean, I ask myself, that Martin didn't tell me? Did I really think, did he really lead me to believe, that he was the only one? Out of the whole world, out of all the possible variations? The first American, maybe. The first white to black? And then, as Americans do, I didn't stop to consider the rest of the world, all the other possibilities?

Tariko, I say, I have a question.

Yes?

In Japan, is it a secret, too, what you're doing? No one else knows?

Of course it's *secret,* he says, smiling broadly, as if it's the most foolish question in the world. Or else why wouldn't you have heard? News travels fast in the first world.

And when you go back?

Never going back. Not me. No point to it. At the end of this I'll be in Jamaica for good. Jamaica in body, Zion in soul.

And your clients, your potential clients?

They know what's on the site. Haven't you seen it? We're still updating all the time, but there it is. He gestures me over to the screen and clicks the browser's refresh button. That, and only that.

A dark blue screen appears, with a line drawing of an orchid unspooling in white across it, and then, at the bottom, like credits in a movie, one line comes into view, fades, and is replaced by another:

Who Are You?
When You Look at Yourself in the Mirror, Do You See . . . You?
Do You Dream in Another Language?

Do You Dream of Starting Again in a New Skin?

Start Here.

The Orchid Group invites you to consider the possibilities of a new you: an entirely different appearance, from skin to hair to physical features of every kind. At the frontiers of reconstructive and reassignment surgery, we can accommodate the needs of clients who feel that their psychological health depends on a radical physical transformation other than gender. We are a full-service healthcare provider, based in Bangkok, that offers psychological assessment and counseling, lifestyle enhancement, language and dialect tutoring, sequential transitioning care, and a full range of surgical procedures under the leadership of Binpheloung Silpasuvan, M.D., Harvard Medical School, former Assistant Professor of Plastic and Reconstructive Surgery, University of Rochester. Our staff are native speakers of English, Thai, Japanese, Korean, Spanish, Tagalog, French, German, Italian, and Russian. All of our services are offered in complete confidentiality. We offer payment plans and loans through HSBC, Thailand, Ltd.

The text block fades, replaced by a mosaic

of smiling faces: an African woman, very dark, with a kente headband; a dashing, square-jawed Asian man with a pearly grin; a strawberry-blond girl, Swedish or Polish or maybe Russian; a thin, ashen-faced hipster in an Oxford shirt and enormous square glasses. As I watch, each photo dissolves into a new one: an Arab man with a goatee, a severe-looking Latina with arching eyebrows, a Native American man in a suit, a Filipina or Indonesian woman in a hijab, a teenager with a Jennifer Grey nose and bobbed curly hair, a Chinese kid with dyed blond spikes and *Thug Life* tattooed across his breastbone. It's exhausting, trying to label them all. To enumerate the possibilities. Like a Benetton ad, of course, that's what anyone would say, only hitched to the mathematics of a Fibonacci sequence. A difference machine. A deck of cards that always reshuffles itself. A self-reproducing maze, a cancer cell, adding a new layer at every turn.

This Isn't You Seeing Tomorrow
This Is Tomorrow Seeing You

That's what you call it? A radical physical transformation other than gender?
Yeah. Doesn't sound quite right, does it?

But right now we don't really have any choice in the matter. You can't say *race,* otherwise the hounds will be at your back. Can't say *ethnic.* Same thing. It's confusing, no doubt. I'm the one who's here answering the phones all day, trying to tell people we can't make them into a dwarf, can't make them six feet tall, can't make their penis two feet long. It's time to lift the veil, if you know what I'm saying. I guess that's your job.

So Mr. Wilkinson told you that part.

Of course. The whole marketing plan. The computer pings; a chat box has opened up with a line of Japanese. Tariko glances at it and makes a kind of twenty-first-century shrug, slightly shifting his weight back toward the screen: *are you more important than what my device is telling me?*

I'll let you get back to work, I say, but Tariko, one more question.

Of course. Anything.

How many of you are there?

Of me? Of us? Prototypes, you mean? Two so far. Officially.

Including Mr. Wilkinson?

Including him, three.

Will I get to meet them all?

You already have.

I look over at the woman in the mask,

back at her dicing, now, but still within earshot. Julie-nah, Tariko says, don't be shy. Take that thing off. Come here.

When I turn in her direction she's already slipped her mask down under her chin, and looks so much like someone I should know that for a moment I wonder if she's famous, or, say, an Amherst grad, a WBUR employee, a Harvard woman? She has any Korean woman's pencil-straight black hair, held back in an ordinary high ponytail, but very light skin, a little more pink than I would have expected, a thin, aquiline nose, a wide mouth, full lips, and round, curious hazel eyes. I would have guessed, in another circumstance, that she was biracial. In truth, if you dyed her hair she would have no discernible Asian features at all.

Julie-nah, she says, hands tucked beneath her breasts. Kelly, right? You're Martin's biographer? Welcome. Make yourself at home.

She speaks with the flat, disaffected politeness of a gallery receptionist in Chelsea, and then looks over my head at Tariko, as if to say, *can I go now?*

Julie-nah's mad because you took her spot, Tariko says. She was hoping to write the big book on RRS. From a scholarly point of view, of course. She's a *professor.*

But also a participant?

I put the question to the air halfway between them, expecting Tariko to answer, but hoping Julie-nah will.

Anthropologist, he says. This is fieldwork. We're her tribe. Like getting tattoos if you work with the Maori.

I was an academic, too, I say, turning in her direction, still feeling, against all indications, that I know her, that we should already be acquainted. At Harvard. East Asian Studies.

And? She's back at the counter now, still chopping. Whatever she's preparing could feed fifty.

And I left. Went over to journalism. Public radio.

Why? Your adviser didn't like you?

No. Not at all. It's such a direct question, coated with insult, that I have to swallow a moment before going on. I needed money; I had a baby daughter. There weren't any jobs out there I wanted to take. We didn't want to leave Boston. And anyway, I was done with what I wanted to do. One book, one area of research. I was exhausted.

Every life takes its own pathways, Tariko says. Right?

Right.

No, Julie-nah says, wrong. She turns to

face us, her mask slipped back on, with a block of tofu in one hand and a cleaver in the other. What do you know about *every* life? Either one of you? What do you know about your own lives, for that matter? *Pathways.* There aren't any pathways. Only patterns you don't recognize yet. If you knew it was a maze, you wouldn't take the bait, would you?

There's a certain refractory gleam in her eyes, a light thrown off from another source: the look of a fanatic. The absolute certainty and the oblique carelessness, the gnomic casting away of words. It repels me like a force field. I take another sip of coffee, stand up, and walk the other way, through the hallway and out the open door.

This is morning, I tell myself, for the fourth or fifth time. This is Thailand. The yard is as manicured as every other part of the house: an undulating lawn, close-cut, and enormous, almost comic plants spilling over the neat borders of piled river stones. Thick shrubs with heavy, shiny, waxy leaves, ginkgo, bougainvillea, ferns, camellias. Here and there are enormous ceramic jars, as big as bushel baskets, filled with water, lotuses blooming from lily pads on the surface. I look into one and see tiny goldfish, or what I assume are goldfish, flicking about, some no bigger than my smallest fingernail. Phran stands barefoot at one corner of the garden, near the wall, gathering mangoes with a long two-pronged hook. The mangoes — entirely green — fall into his palm, one by one, and he tosses them easily into a bushel basket. Seeing me, he smiles and raises his free hand in a half *wai.* How you sleep? he asks. Sleep okay?

Excellent, thanks.

Want anything? Kitchen?

Julie-nah gave me breakfast.

At this he says nothing and returns to his work, peering up into the tree's canopy for hidden fruit.

There's something deeply wrong, enormously, intensely wrong, but here, in the sunlight, the smell of the bougainvillea, and the faint rumbling of the city outside, a blast of tinny Thai pop from a car radio, a shouted exchange in the street, two friendly voices singing at each other, it fades, without disappearing. A faint, barely noticeable, smell of rot, an open latrine somewhere on the premises.

It's been so long, nearly five years, that I've forgotten the simple gladness of waking up in Asia. *Not at home, not at home,* the little song my heart used to sing, every time the plane landed in Beijing, Hong Kong,

Tokyo. As if I'd gotten away with something. Of course, I had gotten away with something. I had escaped. I *have* escaped. Even if only hypothetically. A hypothetical escape from an actual crime. Why did that never enter into it? Why, in all those years, did I never pause to consider myself a fugitive, if only in my own mind? Not once. Because I was so sure that no one knew?

On the far corner of the garden, across the driveway, is the spirit house for the property, a miniature temple, white with a red roof, set on a pedestal, and hung with orchid garlands as offerings. *San phra phum:* the name comes back to me from the *Lonely Planet* I read on the plane. Every house in Thailand has to have one, no matter how humble or small. The roof, with its curlicue edges, each side curving toward the sky, always reminds me of flames licking upward. Every house is a house on fire. As the Buddha said in the Fire Sermon. You should regard your own body and everything around you as if it were on fire. Was it the flames of desire, or the flames of impermanence? Or both, or are they one and the same? The result is the same. Every house is a house burning down.

Leave. The word hovers in the air, as if the bushes have breathed it. What would I need? Just a quick trip back upstairs: my passport, my wallet. The envelope of baht Martin handed me in the airport: spare you an ATM charge, he said. Here's some walking-around money. We're somewhere out in the suburbs; it might take me an hour or two to find a taxi. But how hard could it be? Twenty U.S. dollars and a universal gesture, the flattened palm rising up to the sky. There are alarm bells ringing across continents in my brain.

Phran touches my sleeve. He's come up next to me on the grass, silently, and holds out in his palm a dark purplish fruit cut in half. *Mang kut,* he says. Thai fruit. The inside looks like a peeled head of garlic: little white sections, half-moons, in a woody shell. Gingerly, I take two. They dissolve on the tongue — isn't that the phrase? — like very soft pineapple, or a lychee, with a chewy, nutlike piece at the center. Amazing, I tell him. He hands me the rest. Eat more, he says, and gestures with the folding knife in his left hand.

Something's happening, I notice, too late, as I pop the final section into my mouth. A counterreaction, a sour liquid rising in my throat and pooling under my tongue, and at the same moment my knees tremble, a definite, single knock, a jolt, a need to sit down. An allergy? I have no allergies. No intolerances. Not even, when it comes to food, any very strong dislikes. My stomach, now, has woken up, something is happening, it's beginning to turn. No so much nausea as dizziness, disorientation, as if my blood is being drained and diluted, half-strength.

The gray hour.

And with this thought, as if on cue, Martin's Mercedes comes rattling through the gate, its mirrored windows glinting, his arm reaching toward me in a lazy wave.

2.

We didn't bargain on this happening, Martin says, as we pull back out of the driveway, nearly colliding with a vendor pushing a handcart of green coconuts. We thought we vetted her carefully. I mean, as much as we could, in complete confidentiality, without a Korean speaker on staff. Silpa put her through the whole battery of presurgical tests. We read her academic papers. Man, *that* was hard going. *Cyborg Reveries: The Post-Racial Holodeck. Kimchi Tacos and Rhizomic Koreanness.* Hired a guy in Seoul to follow her around discreetly for a couple of days. Interviewed her supervisor from her postdoc at Brown. You know she was at Brown? Girl's got serious credentials. Woman, I should say. *Colleague.*

Though the driver has the air conditioning running full blast, I've rolled down the rear window, wanting the fresh air on my face. The initial dizziness has passed; now there's just a prickling weak feeling every-where, and the same sourness on my tongue. Pre-nausea. I need something to grip, tightly: first the door handle, then the handle above the door, the one ordinarily used for hanging dry cleaning.

Kelly, you all right? You look a little green.

I think it's just jet lag. Usually it hits me the first afternoon. Guess it's just coming early.

Oh, yeah? I've got some pills for that, if you need them to sleep.

This isn't jet lag, I'm thinking. It's conceptual lag. We pull around a corner and through another gate, between high stucco walls, emerging into a bright shout of sunlight and a clamoring four-lane road. On the far side there's a village of shacks with flat corrugated roofs, an outdoor mechanic's shop, a food cart with plastic tables set out in a long line, inches from the traffic. An elderly woman in another white surgical mask unhooks a chicken and hacks it into pieces, paying no attention to the whining motorbikes and pink taxis nearly brushing her elbow. Above the village, on rusting steel struts, an enormous Pepsi billboard, freshly pasted, with a woman glancing out over her shoulder, her face framed by a dark fringe. It's Jennifer Love

Hewitt, I'm thinking — thin, pale, pouty, obscenely high cheekbones. The text is in Thai, of course, except for one word: *Aum.* When I look again the eyes stare back at me. Not Jennifer Love Hewitt. Not Jennifer anything.

But did you get a sense of *why* she wanted to do this?

Martin pulls at his earlobe, as if testing whether it will stretch. Yes, he says, I mean, *yes,* we thought so, and no, as it turns out, not at all. She started off saying that it was a scholarly project. Immersion. That's what anthropologists do. She's been studying body modification for years, you know, sort of shopping around, looking at tattoos, scarification, revirginizing, eye surgery — you know that's huge for Koreans, right? — and when she found us, she sort of realized that this was it. She wants to drop a bomb on the whole scholarly world. More power to her, I said. But then she came in with these pictures — she wanted to be a cross between Kate Moss, Mariel Hemingway, and Gwyneth Paltrow. I mean, the whitest of the white. We're talking about stuff Silpa hadn't even really considered. She wasn't satisfied with wearing contacts the rest of her life; she wanted retina replacement. Freckles. She wants to be the kind of white girl who doesn't tan. White like in an Ingmar Bergman movie. White like she's lived on some island in Maine her whole life.

And Dr. Silpa agreed to do it?

For him it's sort of the final frontier. Whiteness is tricky, too, you know. Look what happened to Michael Jackson. Of course, I mean, his methods were crude. But no matter what, it's always about taking something *away*. You practically have to go back into the gene pool to make it right. The basic technology is simple, as I understand it, but it can only do so much. To get that ultra look, that Tilda Swinton thing, you have to go in there and strip all the melanin away. It's practically like introducing albinism. I don't understand the chemistry; Silpa can explain it to you. But Julie-nah — aren't we supposed to be calling her Julie? — she said, no matter how much it costs, no matter how long it takes. Here's one thing we found out: she's not living on a professor's salary. Her father was an executive at Samsung. There's serious money there, though she's done all she can to hide it. Never talks about him. Never talks about her family at all. No phone calls home, nothing.

Our driver, a different driver from the one the night before, is sucking on a piece of sugarcane as if it's a cigarette. Tall, gaunt, very dark, with charms tattooed the length of both forearms, and a Bluetooth headset blinking on his right ear. This is Kham, Martin says, following my gaze. Kham, *ni kheu peun khung chan* Kelly.

Sawatdi krup, he says to me.

Sawatdi krup, I say, automatically, and turn to Martin with what I hope is a politely questioning look and not blank astonishment.

You speak Thai?

Some, he says. Not as much as I'd like to.

Anything else you want to tell me? While we're on the topic of surprises?

He laughs and leans back in his seat, and for the first time, I take in the whole picture: white baggy linen pants, woven sandals, and a loose, silky, salmon-colored shirt. Half exclusive spa, half Third World oligarch. But whatever he thinks he's trying to be, it's working. Something about him is un-clenched, slackened, unwrapped, unwound.

You're looking for an apology, he says. Okay. I didn't give you the whole picture. It was kind of a need-to-know situation.

I didn't need to know that there were others?

Did you press me on the specifics of what was going on over here? I didn't hear that.

We had all that other drama to work out, remember?

It changes the whole picture. If you're not the only one, I mean, why talk about just you? Why not make it a group portrait? Because you're the first American? Because you're the first *African* American?

Because I'm the leader. The instigator. The public face.

The owner, you mean.

He unscrews the top of his water bottle deliberately and takes a long swig, the cords in his throat distending with the effort.

You're going to deny it?

Deny what? he says. What does *own* mean, exactly, Kelly? Non-Thais aren't allowed to own majority shares in Thai companies. Silpa's name is on the incorporation forms. President, founder, and CEO. And I wasn't the only one to capitalize it, either. I'm a minority shareholder, actually. Twenty percent. Officially, I'm a board member. And an independently compensated spokesperson and PR consultant. And anyway, five percent of the shares are compensation just for participating. For being an experimental subject. Tariko and Julie-nah each have five percent, too.

So who else is involved?

You mean where did the actual *money*

come from? Lots of places. Silicon Valley. China. Russia. Oman. Mostly that was Silpa's doing. He has some very loyal customers from back in his sex-change days. People came from everywhere. They say that in the area of genital reconstruction — shaping the penis, making the labia — he's the best that ever was. Other procedures, too; off-the-books stuff, things that aren't supposed to be possible. And total discretion. Don't bother him asking about it. The point is, the money's there. In his world, money's always there.

And all those people, whoever they are, they know what the Orchid Group does?

Not in any detail, he says. We're not talking about active investors here, Kelly. They trust Silpa. That's the main thing. They know it's some new initiative of his, some new procedure, and that's about it. The actual money amounts to them are pocket change. Two million here, three million there. We're talking about people that place hundreds of bets like this. Silent partners. Some of it actually came in in cash. And in gold. Stock swaps, other kinds of things. Thailand's a good place for assets to hide.

Then what do you do, Martin?

Run the website. Run the housing. Where you're staying, I mean. People who come to

Bangkok for this kind of work can't stay in the Dusit like they're getting a nose job. The privacy has to be absolute, for one thing. And we're talking about six months, at a minimum. Eventually we'll have houses all over the city. I tell you, as much as anything these days, I'm a real estate investor. Can't tell you how many places I've looked at. And staffing. Gardeners, cooks, drivers, secretarial. Tariko won't be around forever, more's the pity. There's plenty of Rastas in Thailand; I keep telling him he should stay and open a backpacker café or something. But for him it's Jamaica or nothing.

We've pulled out of street traffic and up onto an elevated highway: *Chalern Maha Nakhon Expwy,* the sign says, in English and Thai. From this height, Bangkok looks almost a little like Los Angeles: blue-tinted office buildings, sullen concrete apartment blocks, billboards for Minolta and Pepsi and the iPhone, shopping malls with garish neon signs, palm trees poking their dandelion heads up everywhere. Only it never ends. I sit up straight, my stomach lurching, and twist around, taking in the three-sixty view. The city stretches out, edgeless, bordered by its own haze. I count what look like six separate downtowns. The traffic shifts and slings around us, fast even by Van Wyck or 405 standards, something tense and manic in the way the taxis swap lanes, six inches closer than American drivers would allow.

Fourteen million people, that's the conservative estimate, Martin says. And it's flat. Nothing but rice fields to hem things in.

Uh-huh.

Look, I've been to any number of big cities. So have you. On a certain level, as a businessman, you don't have to tell them apart. You don't *want* to. One five-star hotel is as good as the next. You just want to make your point and get home. But I'll tell you something: you'll never find a big city, a megacity, less *anxious* than this. What I realized, right away, once I got here: these people know how to live. It's like Paris, only with humility, or Tokyo without that robotic politeness. Thailand was never colonized, right? So there's no inferiority. They never got all wounded and fucked up, like the Indians, the Africans, the Arabs. Thai culture is like a cell; it works through osmosis. There's a flow, a give-and-take. That's the Buddhist way. So you get these amazing secretaries who speak three languages, can run a spreadsheet like nobody's business, understand foreign exchange and how to get stuff through customs, use smartphones and listen to Dvořák, and then you get to talking with them and you realize they believe that their family apartment is still haunted by their grandfather's ghost, and they have to go pay five thousand dollars to a monk at some wat in the middle of nowhere, upcountry, to perform a remote exorcism or some shit like that. And the thing is, it's all okay! It works! These are some seriously unconflicted people, that's what you have to understand. We like to think we're comfortable with absurdity. They don't even see it that way. It's all continuity to them. Frankly, I *aspire* to the Thai condition. Not that I'll ever get there.

Speaking of which, I say, you have to tell me who I'm talking to. Martin Wilkinson, the figure at the center of my book, the *person,* or Martin Wilkinson the businessman?

Are they different? They're not different.

I didn't sign up to write *Iacocca.*

You don't have to. It's a compelling story in itself. Look, either way I'm selling the concept, aren't I? Why should it surprise anybody that I have some skin in the game? So to speak. Anyway, look, Kelly, take your time. Remember: we're here for as long as you need. And really, what I wanted to talk with you about *now,* before you meet Silpa, is you. How you're doing. How you're *feeling.* I dropped a hell of a bombshell on you and we haven't even hardly discussed it.

Of course, I'm thinking, of course he would wait until the very last moment to bring it up. On the plane, I came prepared to talk — notepad, laptop, iPod, and all — but as soon as the dessert course was cleared he popped two pills with a double Glenlivet, reclined his seat, turned on his side, and slept till we landed. Whereas I drowsed into my headphones, fitfully, finally giving up and reading the *Lonely Planet* nearly cover to cover. He's avoiding something, I thought, staring at the magenta hump of his shoulder, the thin Thai Air blanket wrapped around him like a fashionable winding sheet. Abiding. It's an *Art of War* move. I had to smile at that. At least, I thought, I know *how* I'm being played.

I'm doing okay, I say. I think I'm adjusting. To a different scale of things. More dimensions. More questions.

What the hell does that mean?

It means, I say, trying to sound only a little irritated, I'm working through osmosis. Like you said. Bit by bit. You expect me to be coherent? I just got here. It's three in the morning my time. Don't ask me to explain it now.

Fair enough, he says. I won't rush you.

After forty-five minutes, through two major traffic jams and three slowdowns, after I've rolled the window up and down five times, trying to balance the slamming heat and the roiling in my stomach, we pull off the highway into a bustling concrete-block commercial area, the buildings all about six stories — a furniture showroom, a motorcycle dealership in bright yellows and reds, a 7-Eleven, a glassed-in restaurant with an English sign saying *Halal Huice Coffee House.* This is Bangkok, then, I'm thinking, the everyday city, the city as it is, not as the tourists or city planners wish it was. Not as I or Martin wish it was. Now that we're off the highway the traffic has slackened to a manageable six lanes, a constant stream of buses, pink and yellow and green taxis, tuk-tuks, and the omnipresent whining low-cc motorcycles. If I have dreams about Bangkok, I'm thinking, they'll be signaled by the buzzing of motorcycles.

We're here, Martin says, as Kham pulls to a stop behind a delivery van unloading bundles of bamboo. Sandwiched between a food stall and a cheap clothing store, set slightly farther back from the street than one would expect, there's a set of shiny marble steps and a blue-tinted glass door with a white orchid and a circle of Thai script, including the letters *M.D.* Some of the tint has peeled off.

What does the sign say?

Silpasuvan East-West Medical Research Institute. Or something like that.

Not looking for off-the-street customers, are you?

We're not looking for customers, period, Martin says. They find us. He laughs. All the great companies start in garages, don't they? This is our garage. Look, man, don't be nervous. He doesn't bite. Geniuses, real geniuses, are nothing to be afraid of. Up close, anyway.

Based on your vast experience?

He stares straight ahead.

I've known two in my life, he says.

Who else? I ask. And then, as soon as the words have sounded, I know.

Do I really need to spell it out?

No.

Two is enough, I think, he says. For any one lifetime.

We cross through the doorway into a gust of cold, sterile air, hospital air, and remove our shoes, as one does everywhere in Thailand. Neat rows of shoes, expectantly, around every entranceway. With his big toe Martin scoots me a pair of black Chinese cloth slippers. Suki, he calls out, and from the end of a long corridor a tall, pale Thai woman in a royal blue business suit comes hurrying toward us, clacking her heels.

Mr. Kelly, she says, holding out her hand, and simultaneously I feel the thickness of the fingers, the mass of the knuckles, and look up at her cheekbones and the wideness of the jaw. A ladyboy, of course, as Martin said. A trans man. I've forgotten all the words. Very glad see you, she says. *Sawatdi kha.* Come this way, he's waiting.

Suki is our one-person office staff, Martin says, a little too loudly, as we follow her back to the elevator. She's been with Silpa forever. Since before he scaled back. Dr. Silpa was the number-one MTF doctor in Bangkok, isn't that right, Suki? That's male-to-female.

I was his patient, she says, holding the elevator door and ushering us in. Before that. A satisfied customer.

She smiles, widely, openly, and I note, as I never would otherwise, how difficult it must be to get up in the morning and lipstick yourself perfectly, pencil in the daggerlike eyebrows, spread the mascara to its right thickness. Which is not to say she's different from any relatively flashy woman in any office. Or, rather, she is: but only because she has nothing to do with me. The thing about ladyboys, I read in the guidebook on the plane, is that they're not *trans*sexuals in the accepted sense of the word, they're not passing, they're truly a third gender, with its own variety, its own continuum of appearance and attraction. This isn't for *you,* her body says; this isn't open to your scrutiny. These are just tools used for another purpose.

I think they say heat wave tomorrow, Suki says. The elevator is tiny, barely three inches above her head. Forty-two. You want to sit outside or inside?

Outside.

Too hot for Americans. She giggles.

My friend here gets a little carsick, Martin says. *Agan kleun hyan.* He needs the fresh air.

What I notice first about Silpa — what I remember, even now, as a thought process, an unfolding observation — is, my god, he's *small.* He comes through the sliding glass doors, winds his way around an enormous slate planter filled with birds of paradise, and then emerges onto the terrace, where we're sitting, next to a low gurgling waterfall, drinking iced jasmine tea, a tiny, very dark man in a lab coat, dark suit pants, and black rubber slip-on shoes that make no sound at all. A narrow, delicate face, high cheekbones, unnaturally large goldfishy eyes, long lashes. If I were to stand up — I'm not tall myself, five-seven on a good day — he would come up to my chin. I'm not sure he's even five feet tall. Don't get up, he says, waving us back down. At ease, at ease. He cups my outstretched hand, surrounding it with ten fingers, only momentarily, and lets go. Kelly Thorndike, he says. What a pleasure. Thank you for joining us here. You must find this whole phenomenon somewhat improbable.

It takes me a moment to respond. He seems to be in no hurry.

I did, I say, finally. When I first met Martin. Now I almost take it for granted.

Isn't that astonishing? he says. Your mind takes only a moment to acclimate. Modernity at work. *All that is solid melts into air.* You know that quotation? Marx? Sometimes I think I should have that on my business card. Even if it makes the investors uncomfortable.

Martin gives a short chuffing laugh. I don't think anyone would mistake you for a Communist, he says.

Really? You never know. They are still everywhere, you know. Radicals and dreamers.

Suki comes clacking out onto the balcony with a fresh pitcher of tea, and hands Silpa a note, which he glances at, folds, and slides into his shirt pocket, so smoothly that it almost seems rehearsed.

I was thinking, Kelly, he says, earlier today, about how I wouldn't want to have your job. I mean, on a practical level. There is too much to say, isn't there? I mean, what question should you ask me first? Where do we begin? The conceptual level, the cultural level, the actual nuts-and-bolts part? You have complete access, you know. We are going to do this once and do it right. Want to watch some surgery? Fine. No confidentiality laws here. Want to interview the staff? No problem.

I've been trying to place his accent, and now I'm hearing it: upstate New York. Rochester, I remember; he did his residency at the University of Rochester. There's that slight midwestern nasality, the crisp, definite, let's-lay-it-out tone of an actuary or a school principal. And, at the same time, the wry melancholy that comes from surviving nine months of lethal winter, the heaps and barrows of snow, the rusting city with its empty museums and obsolete innovations. This is a Thai man, of course, and we're in Bangkok, in the throbbing heat of mid-morning, birds chattering around the edges of the roof, but if I turned ninety degrees and listened to him without looking I could swear we were standing in a silent white-tiled hallway, next to the emergency eyewash station, watching snow fall over a parking lot in a blue-black winter afternoon. He has a little winter madness in his voice.

I appreciate that, I say.

I'm not sure that I'm doing you a favor.

No, in a way, it is. I mean, my focus is still on Martin. Of course. So all this stuff, this operation, as you say — it's all about explaining the process step by step. It's not a magic trick. It's not science fiction. It's not, like, an *illusion*.

He stares at me again for a long moment.

No, he says, no more than anything else.

From a Buddhist point of view.

I suppose. I would have said from a human point of view.

Well, folks, Martin says quietly, if you're going to keep philosophizing, I'm going to be on my way. More houses to see. I only came to introduce Kelly, in any case. He hitches up his elbows and makes ready to stand, with a wry, ingenuous smile. I knew you would hit it off, he says. Now you see, Kelly, why I said you had to come here? I mean, I may be the face, but Silpa's the voice. I prove that it's possible, but only he can prove that it's *right.*

He's like a fawning graduate student, I'm thinking. A disciple at his guru's feet. That combination of terror and glee in the presence of the master. Okay, I say, trying, again, not to sound as annoyed as I am. Should I take a taxi back?

No, no. Silpa says. One of our drivers will take you.

Best not to take a taxi in Bangkok, Martin says. Not on the highways, anyhow. The drivers are all on *yaa baa.* Burmese meth. It's like letting a toddler onto the Autobahn.

Silpa smiles, a wide, still smile, as if to say, *you said something.* No agreement or disagreement, no concern or unconcern. And Martin walks away, silently dismissed.

For lunch, he says, we have to go *outside,* meaning out of the building, away from the groaning traffic on Sukhumvit Road, and down a series of narrow alleys to a bigger alley, a side street, properly speaking, where cooked-food vendors have set up plastic tables from one sidewalk to the other. You can call it a Thai buffet, he says, gesturing

411

up and down the row of stalls. Whatever you like. Shrimp? Barbecue? Whole fish? Papaya salad?

You pick. Surprise me. I still have moments of dizziness, the world sliding around at the very edges of my peripheral vision, but my stomach seems to be settling, now that I'm back on the ground, at street level.

Good. Smart man. He leads me from one huge tray to the next, pointing and calling out to no one in particular. There are heaps of fragrant long beans and Chinese broccoli, enormous prawns swimming in a marigold-colored curry, shrimp poking their feelers out of piles of grated mango, crabs, eels, whole fried frogs, chicken wings, duck webbing. When we finally arrive at our table there are seven dishes waiting for us, magically, steaming hot, with a basket of sticky rice in the middle, and a sweating bottle of Pellegrino with two plastic cups.

Do we pay afterward? I ask him.

Oh, he says, they have me on credit. I come here nearly every day. Every month or so I settle up my bill, and then they get a big tip for Songkran. That's Thai New Year, you know. It was just three weeks ago. The end of the dry season. You don't mind eating here, do you? I dislike restaurants. Anyway, Thai food has to be eaten outside.

It reminds me of where I lived in China.

Of course, he says. In hot weather you are supposed to live outside. Do everything outside. When we lived in Rochester, in the summer, my wife and I, we used to shock the neighbors when we did the dishes on the back porch. Bucket of dishes, bucket of soapy water, and the hose. That was our *sala*. People used to come over and tell us to put screens on our windows. Because of the mosquitoes! I said, look, do you have malaria here in Rochester? Do you have dengue fever? Fire ants? Pythons? To them it was as if we'd stepped out of *National Pictographic*.

National Geographic.

Right. And speaking of pictures, I have something for you. He reaches into his briefcase — in all this time I'd hardly noticed him carrying a briefcase — and hands me a slim, heavy, blue three-ring binder. Unmarked on the outside. I open the cover and read, in large bold letters, *Case History of Martin Wilkinson*.

I had Tariko put it together, he says. Took quite a bit of time, but I think it will make your life much easier. I'm quite proud of it, too. You could say it's my *Dora*. My most famous case. Though probably more successful than anything Freud ever did.

Because the criteria are different?

Excellent question! He beams at me, like a professor who's discovered a bright student in office hours. Who can say, if we want to get terribly theoretical, how much aggregate happiness we could provide to the world, if we gave people the option to be something other than what they are? But watch out, the food's getting cold. Eat this. Here. He passes me a bowl of finger-sized fish, served whole, tails facing up. They're marinated in lime leaves for twenty-four hours, he says. Put the binder away. You have plenty of time for that later. Take ten minutes and just *eat*.

At the other end of the block, where the street meets another broad avenue splashed with midday sun, there's a low, disorganized clangor: a sound of cowbells and paint buckets and frying pans pounded by amateurs, with no beat. A stream of red-shirted marchers comes into view, carrying signs, banners, and flags — also red — flooding the sidewalks and spilling onto the pavement. Air horns begin shrieking. The people around us look up for a moment and return to their food. Silpa scoops up a hunk of rice and rolls it delicately into a perfect ball.

Who are they?

Oh, he says, the People's Party. On their

way to the parliament building.

Do they do this all the time?

There's a crisis at the moment. A look of sour boredom appears on his face; then he shakes it off, as if reminding himself who I am. With the prime minister. About rice and the commodity market. Frankly, I'm no expert. You'd do better to read the *Bangkok Post.* But are you interested, really, in politics?

As context, at least.

Deep background, as the reporters say? He laughs. Well, Kelly, I have a deep-background question of my own. I've been waiting a long time to ask you this, and I can hardly stop myself.

Go ahead. Why wait?

Did you ever find out what the *miao* character means?

I look down at the binder, which I've placed under the table, between my legs, as if the answer is hidden somewhere in there. And then, without wanting to or meaning to, I begin to laugh: a deep, froggish belly laugh, rising up from my diaphragm, a sound I don't think I've ever made before. A group of businessmen stooped over bowls of noodles at the next table look up at me with wary curiosity.

It's publicly available, you know, Silpa says.

Only if you have access to the right database.

That part was very simple. That's what assistants are for.

I can't stop myself from laughing; I wipe the tears away with my sleeve. Dr. Silpa —

Just Silpa. Everyone calls me Silpa.

What could you possibly want out of my dissertation?

He gives me another of his bland, detached smiles.

Homo faber, he says. We are what we make, right? We are what we produce. Look in that binder and you will find me. How do I come to know a person — a writer, a scholar? How else? You think I'm interested in you as a hired hand, an employee. I'm not, really. That's just circumstantial. Do you know what the Buddha says about karma? If you brush by a person on the street, that's because you knew them in five hundred previous lifetimes. You think you just met Martin out of nowhere, for no reason, in some parking lot in Baltimore? Life doesn't work that way. You *present* yourself to us. We present ourselves to you. It's an opportunity, not an accident. So the question is, what next?

You make it sound like a conspiracy, I say.

And as soon as the words are out of my mouth, I realize that that's exactly what it is. For a moment I feel the sour taste of Phran's fruit under my tongue again; to squelch it, recklessly, I take a forkful of ground-pork salad, dotted with red onion and tiny green chilis. Why not? I'm thinking, as the white heat shoots up into my nose, my sinuses, my eyes leaking tears. If I'm going to get burned, I'm thinking, without quite knowing why, let me be completely burned. Nothing left.

Silpa rummages in his briefcase and hands me a packet of Hello Kitty tissues.

No, he says, still smiling. The laws of the universe aren't a conspiracy. But they are laws.

3.

In the morning, after ten hours of dreamless sleep, I stay in my room, reading, till eleven. Phran brings me a thermos of chamomile tea and half a loaf of milk bread, still in its wrapper from a Chinese bakery. For your stomach, he says, tapping the thermos. Julie-nah made.

It's been a cloudy morning, with intermittent bursts of sunlight; now a soft rain is falling. The beginning of the monsoon season, I guess. I set the binder down on the writing desk, open my laptop, let myself down into the swivel chair, and switch on the light.

CLINICAL REFERRAL
Patient: Martin Lipkin
Evaluated by: Jorge Lopez, M.D.
Assistant Professor of Plastic and Reconstructive Surgery, Johns Hopkins Medical Center

April 24, 2001

Dear Dr. Silpasuvan,

I'm writing to refer the above-named patient, Martin Lipkin, to you for evaluation at Mr. Lipkin's request. Mr. Lipkin contacted me at the GRS clinic because he was unable to find any other surgeon in the United States who was willing to do a consultation on his condition.

Mr. Lipkin is a twenty-eight y.o. male of Ashkenazi Jewish (p) and unknown-other Caucasian (m) descent. At my request, previous to our consultation, he was evaluated by the GRS clinic psychiatrist, Dr. Tomasi, and found to be suffering from mild but detectable clinical depression but otherwise free from psychological factors that would constitute comorbidity. He is not suffering from any physical complaints other than occasional insomnia and anxiety that he describes as "not debilitating." He is a recreational user of marijuana but almost never drinks alcohol and does not use tobacco. His family medical history is almost entirely unknown. His mother and father separated when Mr. Lipkin was an infant. He is not in contact with his mother. His father (according to Mr. Lipkin) died of AIDS-related septicemia in 1995 at age fifty-two and left no extant medical records.

Mr. Lipkin believes himself to be suffering from what he himself has titled "Racial Identity Dysphoria Syndrome." That is, he believes that he was born into a physical identity of the wrong race. He states that for as long as he can remember he has had a vivid but obviously repressed sense that he is living in the wrong body and has recently realized that he is, in fact, internally, African American. He wishes to seek out options for surgical reassignment so that he can appear physically African American.

To my knowledge (and as I informed Mr. Lipkin) there is a) no such diagnosis, and b) no surgeon in the world who would perform any procedure based on such a diagnosis. When he inquired whether it would be possible to pay for cosmetic surgeries that do exist, I told him (as I believe to be true) that the standards of care in plastic/reconstructive surgery would make it nearly impossible to find a surgeon to provide reliable care under these conditions. Mr. Lipkin is a very well informed patient and a very persistent self-advocate and that is how he brought your name to my attention.

It is my understanding that since leaving U of R (where you doubtless knew my former mentor, Martin Trumbull) you established a clinic in Bangkok for radical psychosomatomic disorders. I was not able to locate any recent publications of yours on the subject, but Mr. Lipkin showed me your website, and since I know that you had excellent training, I am recommending Mr. Lipkin to your care with the strongest possible reservations. I refuse to believe that any such syndrome can exist. Notwithstanding Mr. Lipkin's evaluation, I believe he is suffering from some kind of intellectual or cognitive (if not technically psychiatric) delusion. I do not believe that Mr. Lipkin is a good candidate for surgery of any kind.

Yours sincerely,

J. Lopez

Preliminary treatment plan

Patient: Martin Lipkin (Goal Identity: Martin Wilkinson)
Lead physician: Binpheloung Silpasuvan, M.D.
Agreed to and witnessed March 2, 2001

Mr. Lipkin (hereafter Mr. Wilkinson) has agreed to the following surgical procedures in order to achieve his stated goal of a new identity, "Martin Wilkinson," an African American male, appearance determined through MorphTech software and certified as the final version by himself and Dr. Silpasuvan.

1. Mr. Wilkinson will receive subcutaneous injections of melanotomanine (afamelanotide sulfate) three times daily for one month, together with daily UV exposure sessions, to stimulate melanin production, beginning immediately.
2. Mr. Wilkinson will be scheduled for initial facial surgery in six weeks, assuming no contraindications from the above treatment. This surgery will involve alteration of the palatine and vomer bone structures and the addition of muscle mass to the orbicularis oris (upper and lower

lips), as well as ordinary rhinoplasty with nostril augmentation. Recovery time from surgery is estimated to be one month.

3. Following successful recovery from facial surgery, Mr. Wilkinson will proceed with the "Real-Life" transitioning plan agreed to with Dr. Silpasuvan. This transition period may take up to four months.

4. Mr. Wilkinson will be scheduled for hip and buttock augmentation following the completion of the above recovery period. This procedure will involve collagen injections to achieve the desired appearance, as well as extensive scar corrections to make the augmentation as invisible as possible. During this procedure, any existing skin abnormalities, discolorations, etc., will be identified for further treatment or treated in situ if possible.

For the above treatment, Mr. Wilkinson has agreed to pay Silpasuvan Medical Associates a flat fee of USD $100,000 in three installments.

Racial Reassignment Surgery: Possibility and Reality
Binpheloung Silpasuvan, M.D.

Cosmetic surgery for the purposes of changing one's racial or ethnic identity has been an established practice in Western medicine for more than a century, since the first cosmetic rhinoplasties were performed by Jacques Joseph in Prussia in the 1870s. However, medical professionals in the cosmetic surgery field have long avoided referring directly to the racial or ethnic implications of popular and widespread procedures, for understandable reasons. The purpose of this article is to argue for a new era of honesty and demystification about the potential for altering one's identity through cosmetic surgery and related practices, on the one hand, and on the other to introduce the obviously controversial idea that there may be a need to invent an entire new category of cosmetic surgery, Racial Reassignment Surgery, to meet the demonstrable psychological needs of contemporary patients.

The best way to introduce this second theme, I believe, is to make reference to a theoretical case study, which I have assembled as a composite of many patients

I have met in the course of my practice. For the purposes of this case study, the patient is a young British man from London, with characteristic normal Caucasian features, who grew up in a public housing estate among West Indians, works as a DJ playing dancehall music, and is exclusively attracted to West Indian women. This patient displays a strong desire to reduce his feelings of isolation and stigmatization through a change in physical appearance so that he may "pass" in that community.

According to current clinical practice and social reality, this person would be treated in the following way:

1. If seeing a psychotherapist, his struggles with identity would be treated as psychopathology and not referred to a surgeon.
2. If consulting a plastic surgeon, he would be told that no surgical alterations to his features are possible (or even legal).
3. In his community, he might be encouraged, at best, to adopt temporary, expensive, and inconclusive approaches, such as changing his hairstyle, using tanning products, colored

contact lenses, and so on.

Is there another way to approach such a case? Consider the following recent medical advancements relevant only to this particular case:

1. Radically improved understanding of the melanogenic process and the use of peptide-based agents for skin darkening (Silpasuvan 1994, 1996, 1997)
2. Reconstructive techniques specifically designed for Negroid features (Cavell 2001; see also specifically Worth, "The African American Male Face: A Surgeon's Analysis," 2004)
3. The development of artificial cartilage and collagenoids applicable to permanent solutions for face alteration (Teng 1992, Silpasuvan 1998, Worth 2000)

Although there are several substantial obstacles still in place, such as the inability to perform hair transplants without immune rejection (Covington 1999) the answers to this patient's needs, so to speak, are staring us in the face: it is possible to initiate a regime of decisive racial reassignment through surgical means, which in tandem with other forms of treatment commonly used in sexual reassignment (voice lessons, for example) could be considered a new field of potential relief for such individuals. And, from a practical point of view, as the world becomes more and more interrelated and national and geographical barriers less substantial, the desire for these procedures will doubtless become more and more acute in the next century.

Subject: JAMA editorial submission
Date: Wed, 27 Aug 2008
 11:40:54-0400
From: Freedmark, Gary
 <freedmar@jama.org>
To: Silpasuvan, Binpheloung
 <silpa@orchidgroup.com>

Dear Dr. Silpasuvan,
We read your editorial submission, "Racial Reassignment Surgery: Possibility and Reality," with interest. However, we are not able to publish it at this time. While the topic you raise is potentially significant to the global medical community, we feel there is no substantial clinical evidence that would warrant raising this inflammatory possibility in

the current media environment. If you have clinical evidence to share, however, please do so in the form of a full-fledged article.

Cheers,
Gary Freedmark
Associate Editor

"Real-life" transitioning plan (RLTP)

Martin Lipkin (GI: Martin Wilkinson)
May 4, 2001

PHYSICIAN STATEMENT
Mr. Lipkin/Wilkinson is an Ashkenazi Jewish/Caucasian American male transitioning to African American (black) male identity. In keeping with the RRS-SOC (Racial Reassignment Surgery Standards of Care, B. Silpasuvan, 1999) he is required to carry out a period of psychological transition during the surgical alteration of his physical identity. Because RRS is an experimental procedure approved only for specific use in the Kingdom of Thailand, RRS patients (unlike gender reassignment patients, as specified in the WPATH Standards of Care, 2001) are not expected to reveal themselves or "come out" during the course of the transition. The adjust-

ment, then, must be an internal one, based on the responses of strangers to one's new racial status. It is furthermore recommended that this process of transition be conducted in a location that is similar to one's home city or community but *not* the home city or community, to reduce the risk of accidental "outing" or self-revelation.

After consultation with Mr. Lipkin/Wilkinson, I have determined that the appropriate period for the RLTP in this case is six months. This is due to financial and practical considerations having to do with the availability of surgical facilities in Bangkok and the expense of the "real life experience" (RLE) away from Mr. Lipkin/Wilkinson's home.

Before leaving Thailand for the United States, Mr. Lipkin/Wilkinson will receive at least one month of intensive skin pigmentation treatment as described in the Preliminary Treatment Plan. Together with regular shaving of the head and some minor daily makeup application, as well as changes in wardrobe and some preliminary speech therapy, he will have achieved a simulacrum of the appearance of an African American male. All of these appearance alterations are reversible, should Mr. Lipkin/Wilkinson choose not to continue with the treatment.

PATIENT STATEMENT

I left America as the white man Martin Lipkin. I will return as the black man Martin Wilkinson.

I have chosen as the site of my Real Life Experience Philadelphia, the City of Brotherly Love.

For the duration of this Experience I will be a lifelong Philadelphian. My childhood home was the North Allen Projects, now demolished, at the corner of 11th and Poplar. I attended William Penn Primary School and Polytechnic Academy in Center City. And then, as a scholarship student for track and field, Lycoming College, one of a handful of black students on a leafy campus in coal country, five hours from the city. This may explain minor irregularities in my habits of speech. My father died of lung cancer when I was a child; my mother moved to Florida with my two younger sisters after I went to college.

I cherish my earliest memories of home, like the Marvelettes playing on our tiny AM radio in the kitchen. Sitting on a plastic chair on our tiny concrete balcony while my mother plaited my sisters' hair into cornrows. Chicken and waffles on Saturday mornings. And the terrors: stuck in the never-working elevator for two hours one morning. Hearing gunshots in the hall, hiding under the table, hiding in the bathroom, turning off all the lights so they'd think there was nobody home. Never coming to the door when the police knocked afterward.

All these things made me who I am.

Young, unattached, successful, owner of my own consulting firm — branding and product development — I live in a condo in Center City. I drive a leased BMW. Without family in the area, having lost most of my childhood friends to crime, prison, or simple drifting and dislocation, and simply too busy with my work, I have a very limited social life, which I am seeking to rebuild.

My childhood church was the Church of God in Christ and His Disciples, a storefront church, at the corner of Cambridge and North Percy. It burned down when I was in college. Therefore I am a new member of the choir at Elon Baptist. Starting with the Saturday-night services — the beginner's choir. From there I find my way into other service opportunities in the community. The Urban League. Big Brothers Big Sisters. I volunteer my time as a computer specialist and financial counselor.

I don't follow music or movies very closely. Though of course I loved hip-hop in my youth, I now tend toward neo-soul and jazz vocals — John Legend, Esperanza Spalding, Macy Gray, Erykah Badu, Cassandra Wilson. You'll usually find my radio tuned to R&B 100.3. Though when I'm especially stressed (this goes back to my track and field days) I put on Schumann or Brahms or Vivaldi. My high school coach, Pop Garfield, was a Brahms devotee; he used to make us listen to the First Piano Concerto before meets. Play like geniuses, he always said.

I have a credit card at Lord & Taylor. I subscribe to *Black Professional* and *Vibe.* My look is understated but right in all the details. A black silk Balenciaga pull-on over Emporio Armani pants on a Sunday morning. A Brooks Brothers double-vented suit, warm brown, with a chartreuse pinstriped shirt and a blue-and-green paisley tie. Gold cuff links with tiny emeralds. I keep my head clean-shaven and occasionally stop in at South Street Barbers for a straight-razor shave.

I may advertise myself on dating sites or even contact a matchmaker. I would like to meet a woman much like myself. Eventually, I would like to get married. With one caveat: because of a rare genetic disorder, I can't have children. Biological children. So — and this is what I'll tell the matchmaker, or write in my profile — I'm hoping to find a black woman open to adopting a black family.

On a tattered legal pad from my suitcase I make a list:

Martin Lipkin
Matthew Wilson
Mark Wilbury
Wilbur Martinson
BodyMore
Grnmnt10234
XcashKingX
Alan93
Martin Wilkinson (Philadelphia version)
Martin Wilkinson (Baltimore version)
Martin Wilkinson (Bangkok version)

How many more, I'm wondering? How many more could there be, between Northern State and Bangkok, between 2001, say, and 2004, when Martin married Robin, and they adopted Sherry? How many versions are there now? If I did a Yahoo! search for all the Martin Wilkinsons in the Northeast

Corridor, would they all be him?

But that isn't the point, it's not germane, I can hear him saying, it's just routine corporate secrecy, for one thing. Just like Apple hiding its latest version of the iPhone. After all, what was the word Tariko used? Prototypes.

The body is raw material; the story is raw material.

What is it that he's really been telling me all this time?

I flip back through the pages — mostly scrawled notes, nearly illegible, from when I was listening to Martin's tapes the first time, before I got down to the hard work of transcription.

— even if classical methods of creation should prove inaccessible (furthermore?) there still remain some illegal methods a (finitude?) of heretical and criminal methods

It isn't that difficult, I'm thinking, is it, to tell people what they want to hear? To mold a story to the listener's ear. This is a kind of fiction that really has legs. The customized memoir. The Novel Genome Project. What did he say to me, back when he handed over the tapes? *You're the Alex Haley to my Mal-*

colm X. A black man, I'm thinking, is the perfect vehicle, the vessel for every American desire, the vector for every narrative. It's almost tempting to keep this project secret ad infinitum.

In a sense, publicity is the kiss of death.

Goddamn, I almost say out loud, Martin, you're a fucking genius. I roll out of bed, my gut vibrating, as if I've been kicked. The nausea is coming back now, in a hellish green wave. I drop down in front of the toilet, shoving back the seat with a loud *clack,* but the bubble lurches to a stop in my throat and refuses to move. Enough, I would say, if I could speak. Enough! I split my mouth with a fist and drive the index finger back until it scrapes my tonsils. And then vomit in a great whiplashing heave.

4.

From: Kelly Thorndike
  <kthornd@gmail.com>
Subject: postcard from Bangkok
Date: April 14, 2013 8:07:08 PM EST
To: Rina T
  <rtarkowsky@mckinsey.com>

It's been four days. The place I'm staying is this beautiful, large, landscaped house, sort of stucco-like, Miami-ish, on the outskirts of the city. Although it's hard to say "outskirts" here, because Bangkok is the kind of city that feels like a village on the street level almost everywhere. China is like this, too, of course, but because it's never truly cold here, the outdoor life is much more permanent than in the China I know. Everywhere you look there's a food stall or an outdoor market or a pedicab vendor, or all three. Where there are sidewalks, the sidewalks serve two or three purposes; other places (like out here in the burbs) the action just spills into the road. You see people washing dishes and chopping vegetables, arranging flowers, eating, nursing, just chilling with the newspaper, their toes an inch away from the traffic. And it's all rather orderly. There's something about being an American that just imposes the frame of poverty and desperation on any scene like this. But Thailand's not Cambodia. Or Burma. In fact, it's full of illegal Cambodian and Burmese refugees, according to the *Bangkok Post.*

And then there are the ghastly avenues and expressways like any Western city, only twice as large, eight or ten or twelve lanes across, always streaming with traffic, and impossible to get across all at once, so you wind up stuck in the traffic meridian with trucks practically scraping your nose. Thank god I only had to walk a little ways, around one neighborhood where the guy I'm interviewing lives. You don't want to try to get anywhere substantial on foot. The scale of the city is just madness, and I say that judging by the cities I know a little better, Beijing and Shanghai and Taipei and Tokyo. I asked about taking public transportation and my driver just laughed. It exists, of course; there's an elevated train, the Skytrain, very neatly designed, but it only covers about a fifth of the metro area, if that. How would Tokyo work without a subway? With pink taxis, eight every block. From this guy's house to his office took an hour and a half, and that was a lucky break, I was told.

Here's something I read in a tourist brochure, and I don't know if it's true, but it sounds right. When Thais decorate a room, inside or out, they start with the plants first and then add the furniture and whatever else. In the house where I'm staying you can hardly walk around without banging your shins against planters and bowls and these huge clay tanks for lotuses and little winking fish. The small streets, the village city, is just overrun with plant life, and the absence of it makes the large, grandiose public spaces unbearably dusty and sick.

Speaking of sick, I had a very odd attack of jet lag/motion sickness/vertigo when I arrived. This is so much more than you asked for, so feel free to stop reading now. What that forces you to notice, of course, is the most momentary kind of experience, like the quality of the air brushing against your face. (If you're outside, or anywhere near a major street, it's not good.) But then when you come back to yourself there's this feeling of relief and possibility and gratitude as well. And I'm beginning to grasp why people show up here and feel a certain kind of giddiness. My guy is one of those people, an American businessman who came here and started a whole new enterprise. Can't say anything more, because I'm only just getting the bits and pieces of the story myself and anyway it's under wraps for the magazine. But here's my stupid theory, for better or worse. The sensory range of Thailand is very, very wide. It's there in the food, in the aesthetics, the temples, the color schemes, and also of course the way the city reproduces global images so perfectly but not quite.

But it doesn't push itself on you. There's a kind of dreamy slowness there, too. Not like India. I was in India only once, visiting a girl I knew in college on the way home from China, and I found it unbearable, the way my taxi was surrounded by beggars at every traffic light. I can see how one could show up in

Thailand and think, I could do this. Not Bangkok, maybe, but from what I've read there are thousands and thousands of *farang*s living out in the countryside and in the beach towns, whole colonies of German men with Thai wives who have taken over villages in the remote interior. For all the overwhelming qualities as a whole picture it's remarkably unthreatening. And then, of course, there's the lack of resentment, the lack of anger.

Rina, I have to say, it's good to be talking to you this way. A little outside of myself. And the situation. I'll keep going, if you don't mind. Don't feel obligated to keep reading, though.

Thailand is one of those places that is so much itself that it makes the rest of the world seem impossible. Let me tell you what I mean. The first day I was here, on the way home from a meeting, I told the driver I wanted to stop and get some coffee. So he took me to this bubble tea place — I guess that's what he thought I meant by *coffee.* Right off one of the main avenues, across the street from a gigantic shopping mall, underneath the Skytrain. So you've got the ten lanes of traffic ripping by, the sidewalk is elbow-to-elbow, the sunlight cutting in and out between the buildings, the humidity descending in waves, and then inside this place it's like a walk-in freezer crossed with a pediatric hospital, all white tile and big splashes of color, you know what bubble-tea drinks are like, Technicolor froth with those strange black balls at the bottom. Full of teenage girls in spike heels and big chunky bracelets and those ripped-up asymmetrical sweaters that look like knitting accidents. And then I see — after I ordered my plain, unsweetened oolong tea, which made the twelve-year-old at the counter very sad — a little sign at the front of the place, over a booth, with a picture of a man wrapped in what looked like swaddling clothes, and in English and Thai, *These seats reserved for monks.*

Do you see what I mean? It doesn't have to be so radical a shift, necessarily — not halfway across the world. I mean a place that doesn't lack anything, that doesn't depend on a relation to somewhere else. You might even say that about the West Coast, about Berkeley or Mountain View or Seattle, as versus the east. Honestly, if you can live in Berkeley, why would you want to live somewhere else? You get me?

I'm not being very coherent, am I? Let me put it this way: when I left college, when I went to China, what I was looking for, without knowing it, was a place that made Baltimore seem like a bad dream. The quality of not being able to square one reality with another. That's what I wanted. And I got that. Then — mostly because Wendy needed it — I agreed to go back. (Not to Baltimore, but close enough.) I was altered enough. Or at least I thought I was. Then, of course, I flunked out of grad school, effectively, and Meimei came along, and it didn't matter anymore. Life was life. Now, of course, all those bets are off. I'll say this: it doesn't just go away, that need to erase one reality with another. Or, better yet, find a way to make them overlap. There's a claim on me that hasn't gone away. I think I'm beginning to understand how money is really made. Sounds crazy, doesn't it?

There's a little gulping sound coming from my laptop, some kind of alert noise I must have turned on once without realizing it. It's coming from a browser window I left open to Facebook while I was typing this email. Someone is pinging me, I think that's the word. I was never one for instant messaging or chat rooms and never even try to find people that way, and luckily, I'm in a chat-averse age group, the last ones who prefer an actual conversation to little furtive messages skittering across a screen. I click on the flashing blue dot, almost vibrating for my attention in the corner of the screen.

Robin Wilkinson
>What's up Kelly? How's BKK?
Kelly Thorndike
>Hey! I didn't realize you were on this thing.
Robin Wilkinson
>Tamika showed me how to use it. Heard you were a little under the weather? Not turista I hope ;(
Kelly Thorndike
>No it was just a little disorientation I guess. Martin has been very helpful & the staff here are great. I'm extremely well taken care of.
Robin Wilkinson
>He keeps telling the girls he's going to bring them out next time.
Kelly Thorndike
>Not you?

Robin Wilkinson

>Can't with my schedule. Not enough staff drs to cover for that long. Plus I need to be reachable all the time.

Kelly Thorndike

>Got it.

Robin Wilkinson

>Anyway. Makes int'l travel almost impossible. Anyway, not my thing. Drives Martin crazy. Would like the girls to go, though.

Kelly Thorndike

>Sorry to cut you off, it's the nature of the device I guess.

Robin Wilkinson

>Had a strange dream about you the other night.

>Still there?

Kelly Thorndike

>Just waiting, sorry should have prompted you.

Robin Wilkinson

>Not much of a dream, really. We were at one of Sherry's swim meets, and she won a lot of blue ribbons (guess there's a first time for everything), and for some reason the announcer said, over the PA, "And now introducing Sherry Wilkinson's parents, Robin, Martin, and Kelly." And you were there, in the bleachers, sitting next to us. Is there something you want to tell me,

Kelly? Talk about journalistic overreach.
Ha, ha, ha.

Kelly Thorndike

>I think that's supposed to be ROTFL.

Robin Wilkinson

>It's just a matter of time before there's
"Jenny Has Two Dads and a Mom."

Kelly Thorndike

>Love makes a family, after all.

>That didn't come out quite right.

Robin Wilkinson

>My! Had to hold my breath for a moment
there.

Kelly Thorndike

>Sorry. That was supposed to sound
ironic.

Robin Wilkinson

>Give me another minute.

Kelly Thorndike

>Still there?

Robin Wilkinson

>Do you want to talk about it?

>Maybe I should start. I'm the one who
crossed a boundary.

Kelly Thorndike

>You don't need to be clinical about it.

Robin Wilkinson

>Let me put it this way.

>When I first met you and saw you and
Martin together, I sensed there was a lot

of intimacy. Not sexual intimacy. It set off kind of a red flag for me.

Kelly Thorndike

>I don't know what to say.

Robin Wilkinson

>It's been eating at me all this time. And I never do this with Martin. I don't second-guess him. I don't even inquire too closely. That's not my role. We've been together long enough. His schemes always sound crazy. That's the nature of the business, I guess. But this was different. Not sure why.

Kelly Thorndike

>Because I'm white?

Robin Wilkinson

>I'd like to think I'm more subtle than that. Anyway. I Googled you. And the one thing I can say for sure is that you're not a magazine writer. Or if you are, you're the secret kind that never publishes anything online. Or anywhere. Yeah, I know, you said you were just getting into the business. I don't believe it. Maybe that's unfair. I'll take it for granted it's unfair.

Kelly Thorndike

>You're just trying to be protective.

Robin Wilkinson

>That's very diplomatic of you. Anyway. The point is that I did some more kicking around online. And then, I'm not proud,

but anyway, in our personal finances. Which normally is Martin's thing. And I came across this thing, purely by accident, a credit card update email from a Web hosting service for something called "Orchid Enterprises." So I looked up the URL, and bam.

>Still there?

Kelly Thorndike

>What are you telling me?

Robin Wilkinson

>What am I telling you? It's your turn to start talking.

>Seriously? That's how it's going to be?

Kelly Thorndike

>We can stop anytime. Look, I'm sorry. This is going to sound awful, but Martin's my source.

Robin Wilkinson

>Whoever you are, Kelly, you are a piece of work.

Kelly Thorndike

>and my employer.

Robin Wilkinson

>Okay. Okay. I'm over it.

>Do you think it's going to work?

Kelly Thorndike

>Is what going to work?

Robin Wilkinson

>Whatever these "procedures" are. I

mean, have they tested them out? Are there any actual cases involved?

Kelly Thorndike

>Yes.

Robin Wilkinson

>How many?

Kelly Thorndike

>Enough. There's proof.

Robin Wilkinson

>I looked up Silpasuvan. He's been at this awhile. Can't believe some of the stuff he's published. I'm not in the field, but I would imagine this would be raising red flags with the bioethicists.

Kelly Thorndike

>Things are a little different here as far as that goes.

>Can I ask you a question?

Robin Wilkinson

>Since we've come this far.

Kelly Thorndike

>What are you going to do with this information?

>You there?

Robin Wilkinson

>I don't know.

>Nothing.

>Look at how tired I'm getting not even bothering to punctuate anymore . . . I told Tamika that if she ever sends me an email

looking like this I'll take away her phone.
Kelly Thorndike
>I'd call you, but my phone doesn't work here.
Robin Wilkinson
>Not sure I could take hearing your voice right now.
>I'm a human being, after all.
Kelly Thorndike
>?
Robin Wilkinson
>Believe me. I love my husband.
>Where are you right now, btw?
Kelly Thorndike
>In my room.
>It's 1 a.m. here.
Robin Wilkinson
>Is Martin home?
Kelly Thorndike
>Not sure.
>Want me to check?
Robin Wilkinson
>Forget it.
Kelly Thorndike
>Go on.
Robin Wilkinson
>
>
>
Kelly Thorndike

>Think the program is freezing.
Robin Wilkinson
>No, I'm here.
>As I was saying, I love my husband, but he treats me like Wonder Woman. I don't give him any reason not to.
>Neither one of us is really good at the whole vulnerability thing, putting our guard down.
Kelly Thorndike
>I get that.
Robin Wilkinson
>Accepted a long time ago that when he's with me he's 100 percent and when he's traveling we hardly even talk.
Kelly Thorndike
>Are you asking me?
Robin Wilkinson
>Are you telling me?
Kelly Thorndike
>What time is it there, it's in the middle of the afternoon, aren't you at work?
Robin Wilkinson
>Just got back from a conference in D.C., doing laundry, waiting for the girls to get off the bus.
Kelly Thorndike
>What are you wearing right now?
>Sorry that's not what I meant to say.

Robin Wilkinson

>

>

[Robin Wilkinson has left the conversation]

5.

Late at night, a knock on my door.

I've fallen asleep sitting up in bed with the binder across my knees, open to an article about maintaining airway access during rhinoplasty. Trying not to think about Robin. My laptop is closed, shut down, sealed in its case. I won't go back online till morning. Whatever that was, it's over. Can't touch it. I erased my browser history, my message queue, did a Privacy Purge of my profile. And I'm sure she did the same. I imagine us clicking the same buttons, clawing our way back. Erasing our histories. You could call that a kind of romance.

And now instead I'm thinking, for no particular reason, about Paul Phillips. *Fuck you, hymie.* BCC has been closed now for three months: did he find another job? I ignored the outburst and wrote him the most glowing recommendation I could, then mailed it to his home address, in a box with his kids' gap-toothed school pictures, his autographed Ravens helmet. The restraining order wouldn't allow him within a hundred feet of the building. Is it guilt, this feeling? At being a pawn, a bystander? Something irretrievably done, or still undone? In a thicket of wondering I drifted off, and now I'm pulling a shirt over my head and wiping the spit from the corner of my mouth. Hello? I say, as softly as I can manage.

No answer.

I open the door six inches, and Julie-nah glares at me. Skinny jeans, bare feet, her hair loose and spilling over her shoulders. As if she's just come from a walk on the beach. Under one arm she's got a small steel thermos.

Can I help you with something?

You can let me come in, she says, softly, almost mouthing the words. I open the door all the way, and she slips inside so quietly I hear her hair swishing by.

Keep your voice down, she whispers. I don't want *them* to hear me. Do you have some music you can turn on or something?

I take my iPod from my carry-on, plug it into the clock radio by the bed, and put on the last thing I was listening to: Miles Davis's *Porgy and Bess*. She gives me a skeptical look and takes down the wall-mounted remote control that operates the ceiling fan. At the highest speed, a gale-like wind so strong we have to move out of the way, it has a mellow but discernible hum, a drone beneath the music, an extra layer of tubas and baritone sax under Gil Evans's orchestration.

Sit there, she says, pointing to the far side of the bed. I'll take the chair. We can't be too close to the window.

Were you a spy in a previous life?

I was a teenager. She sets the thermos down on my bedside table, pulls the duvet off the bed and capes it around her shoulders. A rebellious teenager, she says, with a very angry father. You get used to a clandestine existence. It's the Korean way. Every house is its own little dictatorship, and every dictatorship has dissidents. Just like every ship has rats. Anyway, it doesn't matter. How are you? I heard you were sick.

I think it's just jet lag. Super-intense jet lag. I'm not used to traveling anymore, I guess. It's all in my head. I'll be done with it soon enough. What's with the thermos?

I made you some congee. For breakfast. That thing is guaranteed to stay hot for twelve hours.

Seriously?

Tariko told me you were married to a

Chinese woman. I thought you might want some comfort food.

That's a pretty nice thing to do for someone you don't know very well.

Forget it. Around here, if I didn't cook, I'd just *congeal.*

For the first time since we've met she looks at me directly, squarely, absorbing my gaze.

What are you thinking right now? she asks.

The same thing I thought when I first saw you. That you look amazingly, *amazingly,* familiar. Like someone I went to school with. Not a specific person, I mean: you could have been any number of people I went to school with.

You went to Amherst, right? And before that, a prep school? East Coast?

Yes.

Then it's not surprising, she says. When I first went to Silpa, I brought him college brochures. Colgate. Bowdoin. Mount Holyoke. And the L.L.Bean and J.Crew catalogs. Plus some things from Ireland and the UK. And Sweden. But mostly it was a northeastern college look. A Nantucket look. An *I-just-went-for-a-refreshing-swim-in-Barnegat-Bay* look. An *I-played-field-hockey-for-Choate* look. You know what I mean? You've got the pinkish tone, the flush, the vivacity, and

455

then that kind of transparent marble-ish glow underneath. Like layers of parchment. Or raw pastry. Delicate but fiery. You want to surround it with plaid kilts, with pink and green. Stick a gin and tonic in there somewhere. Raise a flag to it. You know, like a girl in jodhpurs and the red riding coat and the black helmet, the high boots, the gloves, who turns and gives you this wink, like *I really like to take it in the ass.* That kind of thing.

And how did you — where did you — I mean, you were trying, in a sense you were trying, to replicate *me.*

Your perfect ideal complement. That is, if you were a little taller and more athletic. And blonder.

And richer. I've never even been to Nantucket.

Well, she says, in the actual terms of the project, variables of wealth don't enter into it. Explicitly. But really, you *should* go. I've never understood this false modesty, this *amnesia,* white American liberals have about your own origins. Koreans don't have that problem.

Maybe because they don't have so much recent history to be ashamed of.

Maybe, she says, creasing her eyebrows, as if we're two earnest young intellectuals at a cocktail party, as if to take this conversation to a new plateau of absurdity, like a layer of meringue atop buttercream frosting.

Julie-nah, I say, I think I understand about Tariko. And I've heard just about everything there is to hear about Martin. But you haven't actually explained, yet, why *you* want to do this.

Why do you care? You're not writing my biography.

I open my mouth, then close it.

Is that it, then?

Is what it?

All this hostility, all this alarm? What, because I'm working with Martin? Four days ago I had no idea you existed.

That wasn't hostility, she says. That was intellectual honesty. And, honestly, concern for your sake. Because you don't know what you're getting into. Why *you* matter.

You're the second person who's said that to me today.

Was the first Dr. Silpa?

How did you know?

Because he's as uncomfortable with this whole scenario as I am. It was Martin's idea. I'm opposed to it, completely. I don't believe in recruitment. I think it's insane.

Recruitment for what? I'm about to say, but before the words have emerged I stop

457

myself, as if I've just heard an echo, an alteration or blurring of the sounds themselves; I draw half a breath, and then stop, involuntarily, almost burping in my attempt not to speak.

Are you okay?

Explain that. Explain what you mean, please.

I mean recruiting you for the program. You understand that, right? That's what he wants to do? I mean, do I need to be more blunt? He wants you to have the surgery and become Chinese.

Her face, Julie-nah's impossible face, becomes painfully, unbearably clear, clear in every pore, every fleck, every tiny mole, her molded lips slightly parted now, waiting for my answer. I've heard the words, and now the meaning comes racing around her head, a solid thing, in her unsubtle way of putting it, *and become Chinese,* like a rock on a string, and I spring backward, feeling my face flattening, as if I've just pancaked against a wall.

Fuck, she says. Fuck. Fuck. Are you telling me you didn't have any idea at all?

My heart, but not just my heart, the entire chest cavity, all that spongy and pellucid and semirigid tissue shoved together, is thrashing around, my diaphragm doing contortions, sending showers of sparks across my retinas, and the only thing I can do is lean over and put my head between my knees. Am I going to throw up again? My throat still feels scoured with bile.

Kelly. Kelly. Talk to me.

Can't, I say, through clenched teeth. Can't. Give me a minute.

Should I call Silpa? Seriously. Do you need an ambulance?

No ambulance, I say, gasping, actually gasping for air. It's like a bad Steve Martin interpretation: Steve Martin kicked in the balls, that windbag of a mouth and the Pinocchio nose.

Jesus. Jesus Christ.

Just stop talking for a second.

Okay.

I'm thinking of a woman on a bicycle, with my eyes closed, head still between my knees, my neck now starting to cramp. Not a real bicycle, a bicycle painted in watercolor or some kind of very light oil, in a sketchy, Toulouse-Lautrec kind of a way. *Cyclos Le Monde,* the poster says at the bottom. She's wearing a blue beret and an improbably long skirt. It's a piece of generic decorative kitsch, really, something you might find at Pier 1 or Pottery Barn. Where have I seen it before, and who gives a shit? Somehow, attached to this horrid image, is a kind of explanation of my life. I suppose this is what they call déjà vu.

I need some air, is what I'm thinking. So I slowly pull myself up to a sitting position, stand, and move over until I'm directly under the fan, looking up, taking the wind full in my face.

Take your time, Julie-nah says.

Through the rushing air her voice is pleasantly obscured, a weak signal.

Collect yourself, a voice says. Collect what? My arms, still miraculously attached, move up and down of their own accord, testing the edges of the airstream. For a moment I imagine myself as a wind sock, snapping in the breeze.

Was it staged, I'm thinking, right from the start? Did he follow me, did he track me down? How many hours, how much combing the Web, would he have had to log, to know enough about me, to profile me as a candidate? Was it research, or was it just a hunch? Or a hunch that turned into an obsession? Are we talking about the cynicism of the entrepreneur who takes a chance on a random reunion, or an actual pathology, a conspiratorial, manipulative, two-a.m.-in-the-basement, caffeine-twitching madness?

Heretical and criminal methods.

Martin, I say, mouthing the words, almost. You found me. It feels good to say it. Who else would have believed you? With the evidence of, what, your own body? Before-and-after pictures? When something was missing, or, rather, when everything was missing? — a coherent plan, a shred of evidence, of preparation, of anything other than Martin himself, his own body? And the story.

Who would have believed that story, other than me?

Why pretend it was a coincidence? I clench my fists. If you brush by a person on the street, that's because you knew them in five hundred previous lifetimes. Karma locked us together. Here I am, I'm thinking, forgiving him. Almost out of a sense of duty. What did I want to say to him, when I watched him walking away on that street in Towson in 1993, after the funeral? *We still have each other.* Men, heterosexual men, can't say such things, can they? Not at age nineteen. So we have to think of other, harmful ways to say it. We have to harm each other to make our dependence clear. *Puer aeternus. Pueri aeterni.*

Did he know I'd been to China? That I had married Wendy? Did he know I'd

watched their coffins go into the cremato-
rium one after another, the ashes mixed?

He knew he could draw me in somehow.
That's the kind of sick genius he is. He
knew I'd be lost by now, and ready to jump
out of my skin.

Martin, I say, mouthing the words again,
maybe you're right. Maybe I'm just raw
materials, too.

And then another voice, Wendy's voice,
unmistakably: *you've been inside yourself far
too long. Time to come out. Time to come out.*

Well, I'm just going to talk, then, Julie-nah
says, after a few minutes have passed and
I'm still staring straight up into the fan's ro-
tors, as if dangling from an invisible noose.
Maybe it'll help. I doubt it, but just maybe.
So look. You have to understand that for
this thing to work, this enterprise, they need
to have as many successful models, prototypes, whatever you want to call them — us
— as possible. And in particular what we
don't have is anyone transitioning *to* an
Asian GI. *Goal Identity.* Has Martin told you
that term? Anyway, it's a real stumbling
block. Granted, the candidates are going to
be rare. For the moment. But you can't
launch a product like this in Asia with the
implication that somehow Asians aren't,

well, as desirable. You need that press conference and it needs to look like the world. So it all started back in January, when we got a call from Martin. A conference call. Silpa was there, too. He says, *I've got the perfect one, but he's not there yet. He needs some coaching —*

Julie-nah, I say loudly, so she can hear me, that's enough. I get it.

You do?

Yeah. I lick my lips, readying myself for the lie. I suspected it all along.

Then maybe you're a better candidate than I thought.

Instead of answering, I step out from underneath the fan, my body flushing with warmth, and cross the room to switch it off. Miles's muted trumpet trickles across the room — it's a cliché to say it, to even think it, but what else can you say? — like smoke.

What would it be like, I'm thinking, to take a sound and follow it to its logical conclusion, as if it had a logical conclusion? I pick up the iPod and flick the wheel until it lands on *Bob Marley.* All I have is an album of ambient remixes, something a friend sent me for a party mix years ago. I click on *Exodus.* A whooshing sound, a lot of echoing congas, and then the throbbing bass line, the *tsks* of the hi-hat. I listened to just enough Marley in college to know the words by heart. *We're gonna walk, all right, through the roads of creation.*

Are you thinking what I'm thinking? Julienah says.

From a pocket in her shorts she takes out a small, flat, red-and-white metal tin. An Altoids tin. And inside, of course, an expertly rolled joint, dagger-sharp at both ends, and a yellow Bic lighter. This is another thing I learned at Brown, she says, lighting up. Don't leave home without it. She swallows the smoke in a gulp, tilts her chin toward the ceiling, and blows it out in a blue stream. You'd probably prefer vodka or Scotch or something, she says. Better for the nerves. But Tariko won't have it. I mean, sure, for a party or something. But he doesn't like it in the fridge. *This,* on the other hand, he's happy to supply. All you have to do is ask.

Maybe in a minute. Give me a minute.

Take all the time you need.

Remember, I'm asking myself, remember thinking as a joke about becoming Beat Takeshi? Is there a sound I could follow back to that source? A sound, a texture, a taste? When I was first learning to cook Chinese food, Wendy would push me out of the way with her hip and say, *that's not the way to do it. It won't taste right that way.* What was I doing wrong? I would ask. *I don't know. I can't explain it.* Her mother was more straightforward. Once she tasted some black chicken soup I'd made, squinted, and said, *the problem is,* Lao Kaili, *you're not Chinese.*

I walk over to the bedside table and unscrew the thermos Julie-nah brought, letting the steam rise under my nose. How do you describe the smell of congee? The glutinous starchy smell of cooked rice, obviously, and then the undercurrent of smoked meat, the knuckles or hock or whatever spare bit was cooked in the pot. I look down; she's distributed salted greens and bits of fried onion on the surface. I stick a finger in — it's boiling hot — and lick it off. If I wasn't afraid of searing my throat I'd guzzle it all right now.

I could follow this, I'm thinking. The food you crave when you're sick. When you're flat on your back. The first food in your baby daughter's mouth. I could follow it, could I, could I follow it all the way down, all the way back?

Wendy speaking:

You could. You could.

You want to know what it was, for me? Julie says.

She sits cross-legged in a wreath of smoke.

I let myself fall into the chair next to the window, on the far side of the bed. Just close enough that if I reached out a foot — not that I would do such a thing — I could touch her leg.

It was *Love Story,* she says. You know that movie? From the Seventies? I saw it when I was in high school. Bizarrely enough. For a class on American culture. The teacher had a strange sense of humor. I mean, yes, it *is* ostensibly about autonomy and freedom from one's parents and so on. But try showing that movie to a roomful of sixteen-year-old girls who've hardly even been on a date. We went through a box of tissues and an entire roll of paper towels. And I, I, I mean — I was the most affected, you could say, of all of us. When I looked at Ali MacGraw's face, my eyes burned. The way she spoke to him. The way she laughed. The way she *suffered.* It was all there! You didn't need the subtitles. I'd never seen a face like that. I tried, when I was at home, looking at the mirror, to make all those expressions. And I couldn't. I had no range of feeling. My face was hollow. It was a mask. By comparison, it wasn't even *human.*

So, look, she says, it wasn't as if I'd never seen a white woman's face before. The ads were full of them. But after that I couldn't stop staring at them. Bus stops, billboards, magazines. I started cutting out pictures of white women laughing and saving them in an envelope. I thought it would be a good art project. This was a top girls' school; our teachers were very savvy, very postmodern. By Korean standards. We knew what feminism was. We knew what *the male gaze* meant. So I told myself that it was an intellectual interest, and I went *on* telling myself that all the way through college and graduate school. I was desperate to go to college in the United States, but Dad wouldn't let me.

So what you're saying, I say, I mean, for *you,* in any case, we're not talking about a racial dysphoria, a disorder, a sense you were born in the wrong body —

Freud says that before anything else, the ego is a body ego.

What the hell does that mean?

She shrugs. It's pretty simple, she says. You have to listen to what your body's telling you. At any stage. We're so focused on child development, adolescent development — as if, as adults, we stop changing and become one solid thing! Why shouldn't I wake up one day and say, *I need to change?* No, it wasn't always there. Not for me. No, it wasn't biological. I wasn't *born in the wrong body.* Whatever that means. Will I survive how I am? Of course. But why settle for survival? We're talking about choice. Conscious, adult, rational choice. Should I use these words? *Consumer* choice. Does that make you uncomfortable?

Should it?

Of course it should. Are you kidding? Why do you think I'm here? Because we're on a mission of mercy, operating on babies with cleft palates? Or to cash in, once it's all revealed? For me this is political. *Somebody* has to do it.

If it's political, are you for or against it?

What do you mean?

I mean, is this a protest? Are you, say, antibiotechnology, against cloning and eugenics, consumer subjectivity, that kind of thing? Or is this a transgressive, liberatory, post-human project? You're telling me I'm supposed to be uncomfortable; what am I supposed to be uncomfortable *about?*

You really want an answer to that question?

No. I want to go to bed. But since you're here, yes, absolutely.

Well, okay. You took feminist theory in college, right? Remember the *chora?* The *chora* is a provisional term for something that can't be described. Your original, prelinguistic self. Before you can even really call it a *self*. The state of perfect harmony between inside and outside. Milk flows in, shit flows out. What Lacan called the Real. Before gender, before any idea about what *you* are. It's like the dark matter of human identity. We all know it's there, but we can't prove it directly.

And what does this have to do with —

Impatient, are we? Just listen. So the whole question that biotechnology raises, you know, is, in a way, can we get back to the *chora*? I mean, is there a way of cracking open our consciousness so that we can get to the state before determination, before categories existed?

Pre-individuation.

Well, that's exactly the question, right? Is there such a thing as a self *before* there's a racial self, a male or female self? It's one of those classic mind-body questions. If doctors could sustain your brain after your body died, and preserve, say, your optic nerves, so you'd just be a brain and two eyeballs in a jar, capable of seeing the world, capable of consciousness, but otherwise body-less, who would you be? Would you be yourself? Would you still be Kelly? In other words, if consciousness isn't embodied, is it even still human? Okay, so that's still a theoretical question. But what if we made consciousness *portable,* across racial lines? It's like nuclear fission, you know, one of those projects that could create limitless electricity for the planet, only there might not *be* a planet at the end of it. It's the nuclear option. We have to decide, if we had the choice, would we eliminate gender? Would we eliminate race? Or, rather, make it all a matter of choice, a matter of means? That's what I want to find out. After all this theoretical babble, finally there's a way to test what we've all been talking about.

Give me a hit of that, would you?

She grins. I was wondering when you were going to say that, she says. Want me to roll you another one?

Not unless you're afraid of my germs.

Hold on a second. Let me get it going.

She lights the joint, stands up, and comes over to me. From where I'm sitting, when she lifts her arms, I can see the pinkish, freckly skin of her stomach, the large mole next to her belly button, the slight pudginess around the waistband of her jeans. I'm thinking about the way a woman's pelvis, from my point of view, in any case, always seems to point into itself, seems to draw the eyes down between the legs, a kind of gravitational pull. She turns the joint

around, leans over, and puts it carefully, un-
necessarily, between my lips, the neck of
her shirt hanging open. She's not subtle. I
suck the smoke greedily, and hang on to it,
gritting my teeth, and exhale, feeling my
pores opening, my tissues softening. Then
the rawness catches in my throat and I have
to cough.

I used to think, I say, when I've regained
the ability to speak, that that's what Wendy
and I were doing when we had Meimei. A
child in between. Indeterminate.

And did it work out that way?

I used to love playing with people's heads.
We'd be sitting in Baskin-Robbins, just me
and Meimei, chattering away in Chinese,
and from the back — or from a certain
angle — with her you couldn't tell. Her hair
was a kind of tawny, deep-maple color. Occasionally there'd be some old woman
watching us, with a screwed-up face, you
know, one of those Fox News fanatics, the
ones who believe that Obama's a Muslim
and the Chinese are taking over. And I
would lock eyes with her. Just to say, *this is
the future. This is what you're scared of.* Meimei never noticed, of course. And the truth
is that no one would have doubted she was
anything but Chinese. She had just enough
of the eyes and the skin tone. And, of

course, her name. I insisted on the name. Wendy wanted to call her Julia. It was all just wishful thinking, all of it.

Why do you say that?

Well, what were we pretending, exactly? What was Wendy pretending? That she would find some happy medium? She believed so completely in America, but even so, she was already sick of it. That's a terrible thing to say, but it's true. Anyone who believes immigration is some kind of panacea hasn't actually met many immigrants. They turn hard, most of them; they curl up, they desiccate. All that imaginative effort, all that plasticity — it lasts a year or two, and then it stops. You learn the language, or not. You assimilate, or maybe leave it to the kids. And then the kids — I mean, an American childhood is an ugly thing, even to those of us who lived through one ourselves. Cheetos and Super Mario Brothers and belly-button rings. All that sugar. All that *waste*. She *hated* shopping for Meimei — going to Babies "R" Us or Target or Whole Foods and having to walk down those long aisles. It made her nauseated. She said so. All that insulation, all that bourgeois padding. That's what she craved, and that's what would have done us in, in the end.

I came pretty close to having that life myself, she says. I had a Wendy once, too. In Providence. Ryan was his name.

Another professor?

No, no, he worked at a coffeehouse. A townie. He went to — what do you call it? — community college. His professors were all hardcore Marxists. Althusserians, neo-Maoists, Sandinistas, Shining Path. He was *dying* to have a baby with me. Class war through interbreeding. It was what the whole place believed in, apparently. We used to sit on my balcony and drink cheap Chilean wine and he would get all choked up talking about the Fifth International and Year Zero. I almost did it, too.

What? Became a convert?

Had a baby. I had an offer from Tufts; I could have stayed. We might have been in the same playgroup.

I wouldn't have stayed with Ryan, of course, she says. And that's what did us in, in the end. He knew. I was intractably bourgeois, a weak utopian. Like you were. She reaches out and passes a finger across my forehead, as if to smooth my hair. Know what that means? Of course not. I wouldn't have. It's from Lenin. We're liberals, we can't help it; we negotiate our dreams. He called it absolute impotence, playing at democracy without really believing in it. Or, in this case, playing at equality. The end of racism. Wishful thinking. Whatever else you want to call him, Martin's not utopian. That makes him a revolutionary. The courage to *act*. That's what got me. I was searching for something else. Shopping, actually. Looking for makeup, something a friend recommended, when Orchid's website came up. The beta version. I must have typed some weird combination of keywords. Anyway, he happened to be in the office here, and I managed to get him on the phone.

She takes a hit but blows it out immediately, not bothering to hold it. Her face has the placidity of a long-disappointed lover. Which, I'm thinking, whether or not they ever slept together, is what she is.

I had high hopes, she says. I'll admit it. I was starry-eyed. Martin talks a good game when he's trying to get you to do something. I started off calling it a revolution in consciousness.

And it's not?

Just listen to how he tried to get *you* aboard. It's another commodity fetish, in the end. Body mod. I mean, that's the logical endpoint of the world we live in, isn't it? In Korea now every other girl I know has had *ssangkkeopul susul*. That's the double-eyelid surgery. Can you imagine what will happen the next time there's a big blackness craze in Japan, like the ganguro girls? Tariko's had to cap the waiting list at two hundred *just for them,* did you know that? Each with a five-thousand-dollar nonrefundable deposit. And they're not even sure what it is they're signing up for. One of these days we'll wake up and there'll be two kinds of human beings, the mods and the plains. The done and the unwashed undone. Yeah, race will disappear, blah, blah, blah. It'll stop being the smoke screen it's always been. Frankly, it's the last barrier to a world run purely on money. The future of whiteness is colors. Damn, that sounds good, doesn't it? I should write that down. Maybe Tariko can use it.

Or, I say, equally possible, isn't it, that everyone will just want to become white?

Imagine if that happened, she says. Go ahead. Imagine it. What happens in a culture where everyone has exactly the same basic coloring, the same basic feature set?

Spray-on tans.

Exactly! Look at any monocultural society. Privilege flees from itself. *Whiteness* flees from itself. Can't you see that's what I'm doing? Now that I'm almost at the end? I can't stand myself anymore. I'll have to take up Kabbalah or tantric yoga or something.

You're giving your body to theory.

I don't know *what* the fuck I'm doing.

She laughs, and kicks off the blanket. Her legs, curled up on the chair, are the color of something I remember but can't quite describe. When it comes down to it, I think, I don't have enough of a verbal palette for colors. Especially shades of pale skin. Who does, other than perhaps the Inuit, with their supposed two hundred words for snow? Something like blue ivory, or curdled skim milk. Muscular, a little thicker than I would have imagined, with wide, almost chubby feet.

Are my legs really that interesting?

They should be, after everything you've said.

Jesus Christ, she says, with a ripe, American grin, as if she's about to spit out chewing gum, are you actually going to go through with it? Under these pretenses? I thought *I* was crazy. Why, for god's sake? For the money?

My wife, I'm about to say, *my wife* —

Let's just say there's something I can't go back to. Is that enough?

No, she says, that's not enough. I'm going to hold you to it. I want details. I want a confession.

Right now?

No. Not right now. Right now I want you to sleep with me.

Her face is expressionless for a moment; then it dissolves into a fit of giggling. Her hand comes halfway up to her face, to hide the smile, as any Korean girl would; then she remembers and drops it to her side.

That didn't come out right, did it?

Why? How did you want it to sound?

More authoritative. More Samantha Jones. You're not quite there yet.

But I meant it, she says, whether or not it sounded right. It's a good idea. It's *necessary*. I mean, as part of the overall experiment.

Because orgasm is a prelinguistic state.

Because you're my ideal. Putatively. Or as close to it as I'm likely to get in Bangkok. And I'm yours, in a way. Or, well, we'll see.

The only way to know is to find out.

Without looking down, she holds out the joint with one hand, and with the other begins to unbutton her shirt.

Her breasts are pale, diminutive, and freckled.

It's like time travel, isn't it? I bet I remind you of your first girlfriend.

My first girlfriend? I want to ask her. Shoshana Rubenstein, in ninth grade, on the Willow spring break camping trip? In a tent, halfway up Sugarloaf Mountain, on the Appalachian Trail? We zipped our sleeping bags together and fooled around in the dark. And the only smoke was the campfire smoke that permeated everything: our clothes, our hair, our lips and tongues. Would you like to know? I want to ask her. Would you like a fake past, too, to complement a fake body? *The first black woman I ever knew* — and I begin to wonder, in the moment before I take the hit, searing my lungs, where my nausea has gone. Is this the only cure for conceptual fatigue?

This isn't really happening, I say. Want to know how I feel? That's how I feel. It isn't really happening.

You mean because it's already happened?

Kind of. But that isn't it, I'm thinking. What's the word, I ask her, what's the tense, for an experience that happens neither *then,* nor *now,* but out of time? An experience that never should have happened at all? Isn't there a word for that?

We'll have to make one up, she says, smiling. She likes a game. We should try Scrabble. Not subjunctive, but anti-junctive. Contra-junctive.

Contra-conditional.

Yeah. Good. Contra-conditional. Now

enough, she says, reaching out and grasping me by the temples. Put this face where it belongs.

6.

In the winter of my fourth year in graduate school, I came down with a bad case of the flu — or what I thought was the flu. In fact, it was mononucleosis. Only after I'd dragged myself through the last two weeks of classes and spent a night in the hospital, shivering with exhaustion under two blankets, did I realize the doctors were serious and I had to stay in bed. For the second half of January and most of February I slept in unpredictable cycles, like a newborn, and when I wasn't sleeping I sat in my Ikea reading chair with my feet up, drinking weak jasmine tea, and shifting though stacks of photocopies I'd brought back from the National Library in Taipei. My dissertation prospectus was past due. If I didn't submit something by the end of March, my graduate director had informed me, my stipend for the next year would be in jeopardy. There were days when I flew through page after page and days when my eyes stopped on the simplest characters, the most obvious compounds, and refused to budge, till I'd fumbled through the gigantic *Hanyu Dacidian,* heavier than the telephone book, that I kept propped open next to me atop a dead television.

In that chair I spent nearly as many hours asleep as awake. Wendy had just started full-time at the conservation lab in Houghton Library and was gone from eight to six. For company I left the radio turned to WCET, an open-format station, now defunct, which played BBC and CBC news and documentaries interspersed with jazz, classical, folk, blues, Afro-pop. I liked the sound of the announcers' voices, always recognizable, always cheerful, unhurried, not aiming to please. They sounded like volunteers, which, in fact, they probably were. And alternating genres of music during the day — which ordinarily would have irritated me to no end — kept me from falling into a complete stupor. But it was the news programs, the voices drifting in from all over the world, that allowed me to sleep. In those weeks I had intensely vivid dreams in which I was never myself. I was a Masai tribeswoman, squatting in the red dust outside my thatched hut, building up a fire from embers. I was a French marine biologist afloat in a raft off Prince Edward Island, scanning the slate water for fresh icebergs. I was a nine-year-old Muslim boy searching for my mother in the wreckage of our house in Ahmedabad. Becalmed, I was like a sponge for world disasters. Routine pronouncements of sympathy from ambassadors brought tears leaking from my eyes.

It took longer and longer, every day, to step out of the sticky webwork of the dream and orient myself. I could make it all the way to the bathroom without knowing where I was. Or who I was. Every muscle in my body felt smooth and slack; my skin was the non-color of skim milk.

What happened next is a little hard to explain. I can attribute it to the sickness, of course, to the loneliness of the graduate student in those years when the classwork is over and the degree is still inconceivably distant. I could blame it on Derrida and Barthes, de Man and Bataille, Gadamer, Benjamin, Steiner, Blanchot: all those who convinced me of the impossibility of what I was doing, and the necessity of doing it anyway. *Derangement,* Bataille once said, *is the only key to learning.* I became convinced that I should *use* my disorientation to my advantage. With what little febrile energy I had, I scotch-taped pages of Chinese poetry to the mirror in the bathroom, so that I would read them when I stumbled to the toilet in the middle of the night. I kept a legal pad tucked next to my leg and tried to write, only in Chinese, whatever came into my mind when I opened my eyes.

There was nothing. I felt crushed into my chair, held down by cinder blocks. Fits of weeping in the shower. I gazed down at my laptop in pieces, four stories below.

It's *miao,* I said to Wendy one night. *Miao* is doing this to me.

You're doing this to you, she said.

It wasn't that she avoided me. For five weeks she'd brought all my meals on a tray: bowl after bowl of two-chicken soup, her mother's recipe, plates of plain spaghetti, roasted duck eggs for strength. Somehow she'd convinced my doctors to make house calls when I couldn't roll over in bed. But when I'd roused myself enough to sit in the chair, and then descended into the recesses of doubt, she stayed away, except to ask if I was hungry. How could I blame her for that? Would it have helped for her to say, *this isn't the mono, you're clinically depressed*?

Maybe it would have helped. It might have bought me some stability, some perspective, a middle way. But I doubt it. In any case, the cure was already upon us. I'm pregnant, she said, finally. It's ten weeks now. And the next morning I was in the shower and back at the library by nine.

The poets Wu Kaiqin and Meng Faru were born three years apart, in 1095 and 1098, in Kaifeng, the capital of the Northern Song dynasty. Technically they were first cousins. Meng's real father, Wu Qingfeng, the eldest of four brothers, was an alcoholic and chronic gambler who nearly bankrupted the family before dying of tuberculosis in his thirties; he fathered Meng with his uncle's youngest concubine just before he died, and to spare the family embarrassment Meng was given to a servant and raised in the compound as her child. Despite this, Kaiqin and Faru were each other's closest friends and playmates; they looked so much alike that strangers often assumed they were brothers. The *Family Record of the Wu Clan*, written by one of Meng's great-grandchildren, states that they began composing poems together as soon as they had learned to write a few characters, scratching them on the flagstones of the family's Orchid-Viewing Pavilion with pebbles taken from the goldfish pond. Later, when they were teenagers, they composed so many poems that the pages *lay strewn across the garden like autumn leaves, stained with wine and candle wax.* Wu was a brilliant military student who impressed the head of the Imperial Guard with a commentary on *The Art of War* when he was only seventeen; he passed the government's highest exam, the *jinshi,* at twenty-one, and Meng, a more capricious but equally brilliant scholar, followed him only two years later. They seemed destined to be forever linked, poet-scholars at the highest levels of the Imperial administration.

Only five years later, when Wu had just married his first wife, disaster struck. A confidential memorandum he had written criticizing the power of the eunuch Jin Kang over the Treasury was discovered lying on the ground outside the palace gates, apparently dropped by a clumsy courier. Circulated throughout the capital, it made him an instant enemy of Jin and his many powerful allies. Six months later, Wu was banished to a remote outpost, Zhongdian, on the western frontier of Yunnan Province, nearly four thousand miles from Kaifeng. He never returned to the capital.

I first read the *Family Record of the Wu Clan* in Wudeng, in an anthology of minor

Song historical documents in the Weiming College library. The *Record* contains nearly a hundred poems by Meng — appropriately, as it was written by Meng's descendant — but only a handful of Wu Kaiqin's. Most of them, the *Record* states, were lost in the second Jurchen invasion, after Wu's death, when the town of Zhongdian was burned and then razed to the ground. In the first Jurchen invasion Wu had been taken captive, with his family, and held hostage in the Taklamakan Desert for fifteen years, while the Jurchen negotiated a sweeping land treaty with the Emperor. Because diplomatic correspondence passed back and forth regularly, Wu was able to send and receive letters, and the only poems of his that survive were enclosed in letters he sent to Meng Faru. The letters themselves were thought lost until the 1960s, when they were rediscovered in a miscellaneous appendix to a forgotten anthology in the National Library in Taipei. My dissertation, a translation with commentary, was titled *The Captivity Letters of Wu Kaiqin.*

By the early decades of the twelfth century, when Wu Kaiqin wrote his letters, *I wrote in my introduction,* China had been the conscious center of its own universe for nearly two thousand years. Educated people knew, in theory, that beyond the Tibetan plateau and on the far side of the tribute kingdoms of Central Asia and Vietnam there existed other civilizations, most notably India, where the Buddha was born. A few government officials, geographers and mapmakers, who had contact with merchants from the Middle East, knew that the caliph of Baghdad ruled over a vast kingdom that included red- and blond-haired men with large noses and white skin. But outside of Kaifeng and the other large cities, then as today, most Chinese people had never seen anyone of another ethnicity. Even citizens of the major tribute states, Korea, Vietnam, and Japan, resembled Chinese people very closely. To be human was to look Chinese.

Wu Kaiqin and his family had the almost-unheard-of experience, among Chinese people of their era, of living surrounded entirely by foreigners for fifteen years. At the time of their capture the family numbered eleven — Wu, his three wives, and their seven children, ranging from infancy to thirteen years old. The youngest child (name unknown) died of a diarrheal illness in Turfan soon after they arrived there. The other ten all survived the experience, but all of them, apart from Wu Kaiqin, his first wife, Tian Mei, and their eldest son, Wu Fengguang, chose to stay in Turfan rather than be returned to China when the period of captivity ended and Prince Jilan allowed them to go. In his letters to Meng Faru, Wu Kaiqin never explains the circumstances that ruptured his family, or even alludes to the two wives and six children he left behind in the desert. But the *Family Record of the Wu Clan* cites other sources that claim that Wu's younger wives deserted him for Jurchen husbands, and that his two younger sons both married Jurchen wives. It also says that when given free passage by the Prince, Wu "allowed everyone in his family to choose freely whether to stay in Turfan or return to the land of the black-haired people, the land of the One Hundred Names."

What allowed Wu this extraordinary equanimity, this attitude that we would think of as extremely broad-minded even in our own time? One obvious interpretation would be that Wu was simply responding to the wishes of the younger members of his family, who had grown up in captivity with no memory of their home in China. Another interpretation would be that even if Wu was ostensibly free to leave, he was forced to leave members of his family behind as a diplomatic gesture. There is no evidence to sustain or disprove these theories. The only surviving evidence that comes directly from Wu's own hand is his letters, which point to a remarkable transformation of his attitude toward the Jurchen. As Tan Zhiqiang put it in his entry on Wu In the *New Encyclopedia of Traditional Chinese Literature,* "This was a change almost unheard of — as his experience was almost unheard of — in the whole three thousand year span of classical Chinese poetry." In his letters and particularly his poems, Wu evolved what we might call the only indigenous Chinese concept of racial equality or unity, through the interceding of a mysterious concept or substance called *miao.*

Miao is a hapax legomenon — a word which, as the *Oxford Encyclopedia of Linguistics* puts it, "occurs only once in a written corpus, either narrowly or broadly defined." In this case the "corpus" is the entire known body of traditional (pre-1911) Chinese literature. Barring the discovery of antecedent texts that have not yet seen the light of day, it appears that Wu himself coined *miao,* combining the characters 仁, 人, 火, 水 (that is, "people," "fire," "water," and the term *ren,* which means equality, justice, or humane action). The idea that a scholar would invent a new word is considered something of a scandal in Chinese philology, and during the Ming and Qing Dynasties there were lengthy debates among imperial orthographers over whether *miao* should be included in dictionaries of variant or rare characters, and whether a character invented and used by one person (if indeed that was the case) could be said to constitute a word at all.

The hypothesis that Wu himself coined the term *miao* is borne out by the letters and poems themselves, which hint at a discovery or revelation that Wu is reluctant to put into words. Consider the following poem, dated April–May 1121:

What is it that separates friends and
    strangers?
What is it that separates foreign and
    intimate?
Strange, indeed, are its transmutations,
This *miao* that swallows up five colors.
Some speak of ancestral emptiness,
A nothing that is yet an infinity.
But when *miao* is mentioned,
No one can say anything at all.

In a passage in a letter to Meng Faru sent nearly five years later, Wu offers his most explicit summation of miao:

Have you ever heard a young student

playing the lute strike a wrong note that causes your ears to shrink back in displeasure? Listen closely to the sound [*zhi yin*] of the wrong note and you will hear the harmonic principle [*li*] of the universe. *Miao* is the wrong note that harmonizes all human appearances and allows us to forget "near" and "far," "dark" and "light," "Chinese" and "barbarian."

The late Ming commentator Zhu Bing dismissed Wu's *miao* poems as "pseudo-mysticism" and "quackery disguised as immortality"; those phrases were used to marginalize Wu for nearly three centuries. And of course it is easy to understand why the concept of *miao* would seem unacceptable in late imperial China, where, to quote Edmund Chang, "Chinese identity was constituted more and more as a fortress mentality, a preservation of a static order, and a resistance to outside influence other than the strict hierarchy of tribute." This attitude about the continuity and essential unity of the Chinese tradition has defined Western scholarship and popular impressions of China up to the present. Indeed, many contemporary commentators on China treat Chinese nationalism as a monolithic, xenophobic, chauvinistic, and at least tacitly racist assumption that China is, as Pamela Taylor put it on Fox News recently, "ethnically superior . . . a natural center for world domination."

While *miao* does not constitute anything like a dissident tradition in Chinese culture — since the term begins and ends in the work of one poet who lived and worked mostly outside the borders of the empire — it does represent the imaginative capacity of the Chinese tradition as it existed in a more cosmopolitan, more unstable world. A situation not unlike the world China finds itself in today.

Two years later, when my dissertation was all but finished, Pearl Chen, my senior adviser, took me to lunch at the Faculty Club. She was an imposing woman who'd always reminded me a little of Julia Child, with a broad, doughy face and a booming voice. Her grandfather was Chinese ambassador to Washington under the Kuomintang; her father married into the Boston Bradfords and worked at the Federal Reserve; she'd started her own career in the Fifties as a CIA operative at New Asia College in Hong Kong. Talking to her was like touring a vast, eccentrically arranged museum, half full of Tang funerary ceramics, half full of old copies of *Foreign Affairs*.

Now, she said finally, after the dessert

dishes were cleared, Kelly, we have to talk about the predicament you're in.

I stared at her and put down my fork.

What predicament is that?

I think you're in the wrong business. She drummed her fingers on the tablecloth. The problem isn't the work, she said. Not to put too fine a point on it, but it's *you.* You're a little too *insistent,* dear. A little too vehement. You can't expect China to be something it's not. You can't expect the *world* to be something it's not.

I stammered something in protest. Whatever it was, I've now forgotten it. And it doesn't matter.

I'm not telling you what to write, she said. Or what to have written, at this point. I just don't think anyone will hire you. You're expected to show a little more fealty. If you were Chinese, you might stake this kind of claim. I hate to put it so crudely, but there it is. There's only so much one can prove in chasing down eccentrics. It's like digging up some obscure neo-Platonist and trying to prove that Pauline Christianity really is a misreading of the pre-Socratics. Or that Jesus was actually a Buddhist. You know these people who do this kind of thing. Of course, you can find *popular* success that way. But I don't recommend it. There's no stability in success. Just ask Joan Crawford. Or the Khmer Rouge.

I was beginning to feel the tremors again, for the first time in two years. I felt my eyes wanting to close. The world tilted sideways, slightly, to the right, then the left.

On the wall directly over Pearl's shoulder hung an enormous Art Nouveau poster of a woman bicycling down a gravel path beneath a canopy of trees, her long skirts tucked under her. Probably in the Bois de Boulogne, I thought. The legend underneath: *Cyclos Le Monde.* What does it mean, I thought, to hate yourself, not for what you are but for what you aren't? To hate yourself as a kind of double negative, a self-canceling equation? I had the urge to steal something. I felt myself retiring from ambition. Enough, I thought, to simply *live.* To cultivate your own garden. *You're asking the world to be something it's not.* Was this the end of my dreamtime?

I feel like none of this is really happening, I said. Like Zhuangzi and the butterfly.

Her face clouded for a moment. Oh, yes, she said, brightening. The famous parable. Zhuangzi awoke from dreaming that he was a butterfly.

And didn't know whether he was a butterfly dreaming he was Zhuangzi.

We all can't have it so easy, she said. Some of us are constantly reminded we're not dreaming. But perhaps having it easy in that way isn't so easy, either. Is that what you're saying?

I don't know what I'm saying. Other than I'm out of prospects.

You'll land on your feet, she said. People like you always do. You're well prepared. You're — what's the word? *Wholesome.*

How can you judge a thing like that?

It appeared she hadn't heard me. When I look into your face, you know what I see? she asked. It's that you've been so *carefully and thoughtfully raised.* With such *good intentions.* Like one of those cows from Japan everyone goes on about these days. It makes one wonder if you children these days have any inner resources at all. That's what I mean when I say you'll land on your feet. Not because you deserve anything at all, but because, I mean, you're like little mascots, all of you. Little fetishes. Your whole generation. We've been propping you up. For God's sake, we've been propping your parents up, too, in some cases. I mean, the world has to go *on,* doesn't it, even if a little more feebly than we would have liked? Even by halfway measures? So someone will give you a job. Something that involves using a computer and writing reports and making forms for the rest of us to fill in. One of those jobs with a title that doesn't actually mean anything. Vice President of Assessment Priorities! Do you know that one of my former students came here and took me to lunch last month, and that's what was on his card! God forbid, of course, that there might be, say, a global financial collapse. I mean a real one. Bread lines and all. But I'm getting off track here. Listen, Kelly. Your self-loathing is just a little mental vacation. It's as if you look at this other world and you can't quite accept that you're not *in*. You want to *push* your way in. *I belong there!* you insist. But you don't. Good heavens me, you just don't. You're like one of those missionaries who insisted on staying on after the Boxer Rebellion. Some people can't take the hint, I suppose. Decapitation's not a strong enough warning. Want more of the Chablis?

I waved off the bottle and wiped my mouth. I'll be going, I said.

My love to Wendy, Pearl said. And that darling baby.

Reaching for the bill, rummaging in her purse, she looked as if she might start humming a tune.

7.

Outside Martin's room, at the top of the stairs, a large framed print leans against a marigold-yellow wall, like an unwanted party guest, too fusty, too uncool, to be allowed past the velvet rope. *Ioan. Picvs Mirandvla,* reads the painted legend at the top. *Galleria degli Uffizi Firenze.* A profile portrait, with Pico facing left, luxuriant red bangs covering all but a sliver of his face. Puffy cheeks, a bubble chin, a long haughty nose. Lose the felt cap, I'm thinking, add a little acne, and he could be in an Iron Maiden cover band.

Oh, *that,* Martin says, when he opens the door and sees me staring at it. Silpa gave it to me. Of course. Pico della Mirandola, our patron saint. Couldn't figure out where to put it. Doesn't exactly go with the decor.

Whose patron saint?

Orchid's, of course. The whole enterprise. Didn't you know we had a motto? It's up on the website somewhere. *Sculpt your own statue.* It comes from the — what is it? "Oration on the Dignity of Man." Of course, Silpa knows it in Latin. Not my thing, exactly. I mean, what are we, an Episcopal day school? But every company has to have a genius loci. There, I'm doing it again. He gets to me, the guy does. Anyway, how are you feeling? Phran told me you're back to eating regular food.

I'm fine, I say. Actually, since Julie-nah left at dawn, I've been better than fine; I had two brioche, a mango, and an avocado shake for breakfast, read the *Bangkok Post,* checked my email — nothing but entreaties to rejoin, resubscribe, renew, redonate — and read the real estate listings at *Shanghai Ribao.* It's been a while since I've looked at a Chinese newspaper; I'm not up on all the slang.

Can I come in? I ask him.

If you don't mind the mess. Should I get him to bring us some coffee?

As he opens the door the morning sun catches me full in the face; the eaves are cut through with rows of long skylights, like mercilessly bright, oversized lamps. Squinting, I see a self-contained apartment, a white leather couch in the sitting area, a kitchenette with two barstools, a long, scarred, mahogany table at the far end, an open bathroom with a glass-fronted shower. At the table a young Thai woman — a teenager, I'm guessing, no older than eighteen — is hunched over a magazine in a pink dressing gown, drinking from a can of Diet Coke and eating chunks of papaya from a bowl.

Martin follows my eyes — how can he not? I've never learned suavity, not in these situations.

That's Mai, he says. Mai waves and gives me a wide, practiced smile. Someone has instructed her on the importance of smiling to Americans.

I would introduce you more properly, he says, but she doesn't speak English at all. She's from the south. Half-Malay family. Terribly shy around people she doesn't know.

It's been six days since I've been in Bangkok, I calculate, allowing my eyes to wander diplomatically, and I've become used to these little bursts of silence, little concussions, like the drawn breaths in the room after a loud fart or a child blurting out a secret — where you can feel the data itself in the air, stirred up and settling. There must have been part of Martin, I'm thinking, that thought I would have left by now.

That expected and wanted as much. And I'm depriving him, with a definite thrill, of that satisfaction. I'm learning what it means to take a meeting.

So, I say, sitting down in a chair that flanks the couch. There's something I wanted to go over with you. A point of clarification. Silpa asked me a question yesterday, and I've been pondering it ever since.

See? he says. I told you he's like that. Always cuts to the bone. What was it?

I pinch the bridge of my nose, hoping the headache won't come back.

My dissertation — you know, when I was at Harvard, my graduate work? It was on two Chinese poets in the Song dynasty. Wu Kaiqin and Meng —

I know. I know.

You know?

Silpa gave me the rundown.

A tinny beat, a ringtone, erupts on the other side of the room. I've heard that song, I realize after a moment: *Party in the U.S.A.* Mai rummages in her tiny green purse, squints at the screen, and turns it off. Martin makes a show of stifling a yawn and indiscreetly checks his watch.

So why am I telling you this? Why do you think, Martin?

Don't be hostile, Kelly. It's not your

strong suit.

He leans forward, resting his elbows on his knees, and through the loose drapery of his clothes I can see the tensed arch of his back, his swimmer's body, the thin and efficient muscles.

I like it, he says. *Miao*. The universal solvent. It has a ring to it. We can use that somewhere. Trademark it.

That wasn't my point.

Everyone's got to have a story, right? he says. So this is yours. Silpa dragged it out of you: good for him. I don't buy it, though. *This* is why you want to become Chinese? For life? Because of something in an old poem? A footnote? What, you think *miao* is some kind of cure-all? You want to bottle it?

What makes you think that it was my idea?

I'm not saying it was. I'm saying you're amenable to the suggestion. Right? I mean, isn't that what we're talking about? Silpa gave you the straight sales pitch. Okay. I mean, *I* would have waited.

What's the sales pitch?

For the first time since we've been in Bangkok, he aligns his face with mine. His eyes, if such a thing were possible, have become more wide-set. Softer, filmier. I'm beginning to see eyes differently: as independent entities, as matter, as material.

501

He told you that you were one of us. That
the rest of your life has been leading up to
this point. What you couldn't find in literature — look, didn't he say it well enough? I
can be a good salesman. I *am* a good salesman. But not with you. I *said* I wouldn't do
it with you. It's too close. I have principles.
I said to him, if you want this, you have to
pursue it. He has to make up his own mind.

He gives a big snort and touches each eye
with the heel of his palm, as if to drive it
further into its socket. And I almost want
to, almost am capable of, believing him.

To be honest, he says, I never thought you
were such a strong candidate in the first
place. Too cerebral. Too equivocal. Not *broken* enough.

What does that mean?

What do you think it means? It means,
fundamentally, that this is just an episode
for you. Just a chapter in a long and fulfilling life. Look, I won't deny the trauma. It's
a horrible, unimaginable thing. But you've
already landed on your feet. You're not a
wreck. You're *trying* to be a wreck. But that's
the way it always was, right? You *felt* these
things, but it didn't stop you from going on
and living the life you were supposed to
have. Amherst. China. A Ph.D. A wife. A
family. The pendulum swings, but it just

comes back to normal in the end, doesn't it? People like you always find something to do.

Who are you to speak for me? I should ask him. Why do you get to decide? I should be all heated and blustery, my face an angry pimple, indignant, pacing, hands on hips. What I didn't say to Pearl Chen — I have that in me now. But he's right, he's absolutely right: I was that person. I was *that* Kelly Thorndike. And now, unbelievably, I'm not.

I can already stand outside of this argument, I'm thinking. All I need is a new name. *Wang.* I've always wanted to be a Wang. Four strokes, 王, meaning *king,* the second or third commonest of the old hundred names. In my freshman year Chinese 1 class it was the first character in the workbook. I practiced writing it a hundred times over; when the spaces ran out I used pages of my spiral notebook. I didn't want to go on to the next one. *Wang,* like an E that faces both ways. It made me shiver. It makes me shiver. *Wo xing Wang.* My name is Wang. I am the third person in this room.

I look over my shoulder at Mai, licking papaya juice from her fingers.

The fourth person in the room.

I mean, he says, this book about me, whatever you're going to write, it's just *writing.* Isn't that true? You already churned out five hundred pages on Wu this and Fong that. Who gives a shit? But no, that's what people like you do. They just keep on *producing,* whether the world wants it or not. And then find a way to make the world pay for it.

White people.

White people. No doubt. You know what I'm saying. I mean, you feel like you had to work hard for what you've got, but not *that* hard, in the end, right? So there's a little guilt in there as well? And what do you do with guilt, except write another book about it?

So that's the standard? Mai looks up from her magazine, alarmed by the break, the misfire, in my voice box. I mean, I say, Martin, seriously. Who *are* you looking for, then? Do you have a cutoff point for total liquid assets? Or certain admissible careers only? Isn't there some business maxim about not second-guessing the customer's motivations?

You're not a customer. You're an *investor.* And anyway, look at Julie-nah. We've already made one huge mistake. After that I promised myself: *no more intellectuals.* They ruin everything.

Too ambivalent? Too conceptual?

Too motherfucking in love with their own algorithms! With all due respect, Kelly, you don't understand wealth. Nobody understands wealth less than people like you. People so far down the line of inheritance that they think they don't even *have* to care about it. I'm looking for people who can't live without money. The self-made. And, of course, the outright hedonists. Okay, of course, Silpa has his criteria. He does a psychological workup. There's always a narrative attached to that. But eventually all that stuff has to take a backseat to the forces of the market. That's why I keep saying: we have to be entrepreneurial. We have to be change agents. Leave the theorizing for later. I can recognize the people who really *need* it. The ones who have the bug. The early adopters. You're not it. Count yourself lucky.

And you hired me for —

For the American market. Because, look, Americans *care* about the backstory. They want to be spoon-fed. It has to be inspirational; it has to warm those little fat-clogged hearts. That's what I want from you. And believe me, that's all. I expect you to hold up your end of the bargain, take your money and walk away. Anything else is your own business. I'm on the record now saying *this wasn't my idea.*

And if I don't go through with it — if I stay as I am — you're saying I'm safe? I can go back to the United States? To Baltimore, even? No dropping a dime on me? No manila envelopes to the *Sun*?

You're still worried about that?

Wouldn't you be?

He takes a deep breath.

Okay. Okay. I can see why you don't trust me right now. I get that. But I hope you can see, too, why all this was necessary. It's a process. It's a — okay, if you want to use that word, it's a recruitment. All in the service of a larger goal. Tell me, just using common sense, using everything you know about me, *knew* about me, am I into point-less revenge? Do I hold grudges? I'm *telling* you to go home. What good does it do me to hold this over your head? In any case, I'd have to expose myself. For them to reopen the case. I'd have to testify.

So you've thought about it.

I haven't *thought about it.* I'm improvising. You brought it up, remember?

We're having a staring contest, a don't-blink contest.

One thing is clear to me, I'm thinking,

with a kind of creeping horror. Who was it that said, *just because you're not paranoid doesn't mean they aren't out to get you*? I lived with the knowledge of what happened to Alan, correction, *what I did to Alan,* alone for so long that it turned into a dream. Yes, okay, I talked to Cox about it. At the brink of adulthood, fatherhood, I tried to buy some certainty, some quiet skeleton-in-the-closet insurance, under the curtain of attorney-client privilege. But it wasn't a dream. Someone else has been thinking about it. The parallel life, the worst-case-scenario life, in which I do five in Jessup, maybe three with good behavior, plus five more on parole, and then try to find a job that hires felons with Ph.D.'s. Driving a school bus, maybe. Living in my parents' basement. Someone else has had that bad dream, too. Planning, waiting, watching. Or not. It almost doesn't matter. My life, *my life,* the life I thought I was living privately, was always, all the time, dangling on that string.

Martin, I say, sticking out my lower jaw, as if that will add a little extra rumble, a baritone undercurrent, for once. Will you answer a simple question? If I wanted to be completely safe, if I wanted to *know* I'd never be found out, if I wanted Kelly

Thorndike to vanish off the face of the earth, case closed, no mention of Alan or an accidental —

You think you're Pablo Escobar? That's not what this is for.

Answer the question.

We'd never acknowledge you. It wouldn't even *help,* for our purposes.

Answer the question.

You want us to be in the Rolodex of every cartel leader, every *norteño,* every oligarch Putin's sick of, every minor Al-Qaeda honcho, every spare yakuza and sick sub-Saharan dictator with a billion in IMF dollars in the bank? Because that's going to be the result. Word gets out. Why would we agree to that? We're trying to get *out* of the gray market.

Answer the question.

Yeah. okay. It'll be easy. Silpa's ready. The facial surgery — the epicanthus, the eye shaping, a little work on the lips — it's pretty straight-forward, actually. Even the pigmentation. He's been doing experiments on mice for years. Carotenoids. You wouldn't believe it. I mean, it really does turn *yellow.* But look. I'm telling you. Just because Einstein said it was possible doesn't mean they should have built the atomic bomb. It's not for you. I'm *telling* you it's not for you. He should never have said anything.

Who are you, Martin? I wish I could ask him. And were the tears real? For a moment he seems to shimmer in the air in front of me, like a cheap hologram in a Seventies movie. Friend, comrade, nemesis, exploiter? He licks his lips and looks over his shoulder at Mai. What can money do if it can't smooth over life's little inconsistencies?

Martin, I say, Silpa didn't say anything. Julie-nah did.

I've caught him at a pensive moment, looking over my shoulder, elbows on his knees, cradling an invisible globe in the webwork of his fingers. And there he stays. As still as a photograph. As wax. For the longest increment possible he doesn't even blink, his nostrils don't flare.

And now, he says finally, his eyes still raised beyond mine, still in the same disembodied position. Now what, Kelly? Now you get to call me a big fat liar?

Martin, I say, my tongue grown thick and dry, a foreign object, a giant's fat digit resting in my throat. You're still my friend. I'd like to give you the benefit of the doubt.

Really.

Or, I should say, I *would* have. If I didn't know about Northern State.

He stares at me for a moment, a Yul Brynner stare, his eyes bubbling out of his skull, and then erupts in a belly laugh. Lord God, he says, wiping away tears again. You called in the cavalry. That's more than I ever gave you credit for. Good one, Kelly. But just so you know: Silpa's already aware of my checkered past. Everyone is. Just in case you thought you had one up on me.

So you saved the lies for your biographer.

Oh, come on. I never told you those tapes were the whole story.

And what am I supposed to do, draw up a list? Fact-check every single assertion? I mean, did you ever sell drugs at all? For example?

There's no time to go back into that now, he says. You know the line *the only real crimes are the ones that are never punished*? Let's just put it that way. Anyway, my record was expunged. Thanks to the state of Vermont and its benevolence toward first-time offenders. Though I guess a P.I. can still track it down. There are always gaps that have to be plugged. Look, is this enough? You've had your adventure. I take it that now that you've exposed me we should be buying you a ticket home.

Exposed me? I want to ask him. Is this what exposure looks like? Should I tell him how close I was, just last night, to breaking the egg of his life wide open, with sixteen keystrokes? Martin is the proof. We could make a pact of mutually assured destruction. But for what? I want a new life, not détente. I want this to be over.

No, I say. I'm staying. The air seems to be crackling, with a smell of ozone. I'm taking your invitation.

Behind me, the bowl clinks on the kitchen counter, and the bathroom door closes. Martin's face works against itself at angles, assembling three or four different expressions at once.

You know what Alan told me once? I say. *You only have one chance to get it right in life.* Well, what did he know? Just because I had a happy childhood doesn't mean I'm preserved in amber. I can change, too. I can be broken and remade.

That's very poetic, he says. But what's your plan? Once it all comes out, where will you be? In China? Has Silpa worked this out yet?

Where did all the tension go? The air in the room has shifted, cooled, but Martin hasn't moved. How did that revelation pass so quickly? He flexes his shoulders and gives a magnanimous hand wave. Look, he says, Kelly, I love you, but you'll have to make up your own mind. Frankly, I'm on to other things. Silpa will have to run this end of the business once I get started.

What are you talking about?

I'm talking about *the plan.* What does all this lead up to? Where does it lead?

I have to laugh. How has it never occurred to me to ask this question?

To a lot of money for all involved, I say. And what else? Fame? Satisfaction? Progress? Revenge?

No, he says. No. Straight back to Baltimore. The CBT. The Center for Black Transformation. Remember when you schlepped me over to Annapolis, that time? We've got state biomedical development grants. We've got empowerment zones. We've got the world's best surgeons. And by god, if there's one thing Baltimore's got, it's blackness. We've got dialect coaches. We've got homestays. We've got yearlong immersion experiences. We'll give cooking lessons and run in-house gospel services, if it comes to that. You have no idea the number of people — the Germans, the Danes, the Norwegians, the Japanese, the Saudis, the Pakistani rich kids from Lahore — who are already lining up. Black culture is global now. There's hip-hop in a hundred different languages. Listen, for me Orchid is just a means to an end. I'm looking at it from a business perspective. Will it be a franchise model? Will I have to buy Silpa out? We'll work out the details. Important thing is, I have a brand to cultivate. Baltimore. New Black City. This is the real prosperity gospel.

You weren't going to fill me in on this? Kind of a crucial detail, isn't it?

No, no, no. You have to do things in the right order. That's the whole thing. You've got to have a business *mind*. He karate-chops his palm. First, the book. The exposure. The rollout. The press conferences. The talk shows. The scandals, the outrage, the magazine covers. *I'm Martin Lipkin, and this is my story. This is my journey.* No one can argue with that. Then, and only then, you start in on the plan. *I want to share this opportunity with people in need.* The trans-R community. You get a few psychiatrists on board. You get the APA's approval. In the meantime all the work is happening off-shore. Bangkok. Maybe some satellite offices, just to keep up with demand. Johannesburg. Estonia. São Paulo. Finally, you get a diagnosis code. Manna from heaven! Then the American insurers will start paying up. Licensure's a breeze after that. All that time you're working the Internet to bring up demand. Support groups, demands for recognition, all that kind of nonsense. Get the local leaders on board. Make it a pride thing. An economic-development thing. Listen, am I saying it's going to be easy? Hell, no. It's going to be a lifetime. That's what an investment is. The real payoff is all in the patents, anyway. Once all this business goes public we start looking for a major drug company to license Melanotide production. And all the subsidiary patents, too: the synthetic cartilage, the injectable silicone for the eyelids. Silpa's sitting on a cool billion or two just in intellectual property. And I've got a stake in all of that. Ultimately, I get paid whether Baltimore works or not. But that's all academic. It's *going* to work.

He stops and stares at me.

I don't care what Julie-nah told you, he says. It wasn't about recruitment. Yeah, maybe once upon a time I thought that was a bright idea. A little synergy. But it isn't for you. You still want my opinion? Leave. Take the money and go. What did I want out of you? Honestly, I don't even know anymore. I'm sorry. I saw you that day and I thought —

— as a tribute —

— as a debt to be repaid —

— our lives were so bound up together,

once. Doesn't that mean anything? There has to be a way of distinguishing that from the profit motive.

No, no. No. Don't separate money and happiness. That's the guilty liberal in you speaking. Don't act as if it has to be a tradeoff. You *can* have everything. Haven't you heard anything I've been trying to tell you? Everywhere you look in life there might be an open door in your peripheral vision. *That's* what you should take from this. Want to get the surgery? Fine. Want to go back to Baltimore? Fine. Whatever it is, be your own boss. Make your own life. Pay your own way.

I'm beginning to feel something. What is it? Was there something in the tea this morning, the tea Julie-nah brought up from downstairs? An enormous hot ball of hon-eyed light pushing its way up and through my rib cage. Could it be that this is what feeling feels like? It tastes like anger, but it's not anger. A spasm of horror over all that wasted time. He planned it all, of course; he choreographed it like Diaghilev. Someday I'll do the same. Maybe even to him.

This, I think, is what they call a win-win.

I'm doing it, I say. Look out, Martin. I'm going to surprise you.

You ready to be a self-made man?

I'm all in, I say. The cliché doesn't stumble across my teeth the way I thought it would. I have to get used to clichés now, I'm thinking. Trafficking in them. Fortunes rise and fall that way.

Well, then — he looks at me with a rueful smile. What can I say? He holds out his hand, and when I take it, I feel something hard in the palm: a little rectangle, a hard stub, the thickness of two sticks of gum. I move it to my pocket: a flash drive. Welcome aboard, man, he says. Welcome aboard.

8.

HUE, INC.
(Formerly Orchid Group, Ltd)

5-YEAR STRATEGIC PLAN AND MARKET AS-
SESSMENT

HUE is on the leading edge of the most
exciting health and lifestyle technology of
the twenty-first century: high-impact, permanent physical redesign of the body
based on desirable ethnic characteristics.
Using a combination of existing procedures and new patented and patent-
pending technologies, HUE is positioned
to be the first company in the field to offer
a streamlined, comprehensive, globally
marketed treatment for clients seeking a
markedly different physical appearance.
Based in Bangkok, Thailand, already a
highly desirable destination for aesthetic
surgery, we offer a complete personal-

transformation experience, including five-star-level housing at a private villa, private consultations with the surgeon (a leading researcher in the field) and support staff from around the world, and assistance with the legal, financial, and psychological aspects of VIT (visual identity transition).

Why is HUE a wise investment for brokers and individuals seeking to diversify a global technology/emerging technology portfolio? According to an article in *Bloomberg News,* July 3, 2011, "cosmetic surgery is poised to reach parity with cosmetics in overall consumer spending by 2020." However, because of traditional restrictions on physicians and health corporations operating internationally, no large market player has emerged to represent this industry in the global economy. Indeed, most cosmetic surgeons still operate in individual practices in most major markets, including the United States, the UK, Brazil, Argentina, Japan, Thailand, Korea, and South Africa.

Thanks to the foresight of our founder, Binpheloung Silpasuvan, HUE has the intellectual property protection to consolidate development of these new technologies under one corporate entity. Simply put, HUE owns the rights to a variety of treatments and pharmaceutical compounds essential to our key procedures, such as permanent skin alteration (PSA) and augmented rhinoplasty (AR). These processes can obtain breathtaking results — just look at the enclosed photos. In Dr. Silpasuvan's own words, "We are witnessing a major shift in the potential for altering our individual self-image. No longer are we restricted to the ethnic identity or physiognomy we were born with. For a variety of reasons, under a variety of conditions, a person may choose the visual appearance that answers their deepest psychic needs or the circumstances of their present life. Virtually any transformation is possible. [HUE] is poised to become an international brand synonymous with these permanent and life-changing acts."

How large a market are we talking about? Consider these statistics: in a survey conducted in 2011, 21% of adults 18–30 in South Korea said they had had cosmetic surgery and 83% said they had considered or planned cosmetic surgery in the next five years. Virtually all of these surgeries involve alterations to the epicanthal fold of the upper eye, a procedure that, according to sociologist Ju-nah Park, "is strongly associated, in visual-association tests, with European beauty standards." In South and East Asia, according to a 2006 study by the Economist Intelligence Unit, nearly $3 billion USD is spent annually on products and procedures designed to lighten the skin — despite the fact that virtually all of these products have limited efficacy and some carry well-known health risks. According to HUE's own analysis (Appendix A) the potential global market for VIT might eventually reach as high as $10–15 billion.

What are the ethical and legal issues involved? As with any emerging health technology, VIT poses a number of concerns that will inevitably arise once HUE makes its debut as a public entity. At the same time, we must be aware that, just as norms of beauty can vary widely among cultures, each culture holds distinct views about the limits of permissible body modification. These views and norms are also subject to increasingly rapid shifts and developments, due to the globalization of visual culture. HUE is invested in strategic development for cultural scalability. Drawing on the latest market research and sociological surveys, our sales force will be able to target products at an emerging consensus model of beauty in a highly homogeneous marketplace (Italy or South Korea) or offer a more customizable, customer-centered experience for customers in a more diverse, trend-driven market or submarket (Tokyo or Los Angeles).

At the same time, we intend to use partnerships in the medical and bioethical community to develop a rationale for Racial Dysphoria as a psychiatric diagnosis. Over time (particularly with inclusion in the DSM and other diagnostic authorities) this opens the possibility for VIT as a covered, insured condition, removing barriers to affordability throughout the industrialized world. This two-pronged approach will allow HUE to drive the market from both ends, as a provider of both residential complete identity transition (a process which takes at least a year) and discrete, targeted outpatient treatments where smaller modifications may produce the desired result.

Our corporate mission is to create value for our shareholders by offering consistent, high-quality results while aggressively expanding our customer base. We have been highly successful at attracting the seed capital that has brought us to this level. At this point we are looking for large-stake investors to help us expand our operations in Thailand and develop PR and customer service operations for the North American, European, Middle Eastern and East Asian markets. Interested investors should contact Martin Wilkinson at wilkinson@orchidgroup.com or 011-410-435-4567.

HUE is *The World's New Spectrum.* Come grow with us.

CONFIDENTIALITY NOTICE: This document and any attachments to it are intended for use only by the addressee(s), and may contain privileged or confidential information. If you are not the intended recipient, you are not authorized to read, print, copy or disseminate this message or any attachments to it, or to take any action based on them. If you have received this message in error, please notify me immediately by telephone and permanently delete the original and any copy of this message.

9.

Where I started, Silpa says, was with the skin. Of course. Otherwise, how would I have gotten the idea, how would I have glimpsed it? Even as an impossibility?

He shakes the ice in his glass and stares up at the sky: a long band of violet clouds receding away from a smoggy peach-brown sunset. We're on the roof: a long tiled deck that traverses the rear of the house, not visible from the street. Phran manning the barbecue, Martin and Julie-nah and myself stretched out on lounge chairs, Tariko hunched over his laptop, playing DJ.

I've spent nights with matches and knives
leaning over ledges only two flights up

It was just a summer job, he says, working as a technician in my adviser's lab. The research was on pigmentation disorders retrofabricated in mice. Vitiligo. Have you

523

heard of it? White blotches on dark skin. Very damaging, in some cultures. Humiliating, shameful. Even worse than albinism. You'll have babies being abandoned, men who can never marry. It's an autoimmune condition — the immune system attacks the melanocytes, but only here and there, nobody knows why. In any case, treatment can go two ways: make the skin lighter, or make it darker, to correct the patchiness and give the patient an even tone.

I'm like a steppin' razor don't watch my size I'm dangerous

Lightness is quite difficult, he says. You start with monobenzylether of hydroquinone. We don't know how, exactly, but it wipes the cutaneous layer *clean*. As if melanin never even existed. You have to use it sparingly, because there's the risk of skin cancer. And, some say, immune overcompensation. But darkening? Darkening the skin, permanently, *consistently,* beautifully? Nearly impossible, that was the consensus at the time. In any case, hazardous. Every possible conventional treatment was toxic. And, as they never tired of telling me, *undesirable.* Who would pay for it? Who would pay for a beautifully toned, brown, perhaps even a little reddish, *maple* color, a *mahogany* color, or a rich, full, espresso, actual blackness? Like Grace Jones. Like Seal.

Miles Davis, Martin says. Kobe Bryant.

Peter Tosh. Tariko speaking. Dinah Washington.

Queen Latifah, Julie-nah says. Oprah. I love Oprah.

Duke Ellington, I say. Angela Davis.

Right, Silpa says. You understand. In Rochester on my days off I went and sat in the movie theater and just watched one film after another. *Brewster's Millions. Dune. 48 Hours. Conan the Barbarian. Purple Rain.* That was how I learned English and ruined my appetite for candy. And I wanted to say, look, you take a movie like *Purple Rain,* and then you think there's no desire, no wanting, to be like that beautiful man?

When I start to laugh, everyone turns and stares at me.

Why? Silpa asks me. Don't you think it's true?

I'm not arguing with you. I just can't believe it all starts with Prince.

You're the writer. You can put that in your book. You know that song, "When Doves Cry?" *Dig, if you will, the picture?* Go look at the video again. Prince is all naked in a bathtub, and he stands up, and the camera is just looking at his face. And then he holds out his hand and does this —

Silpa gives me a sultry, low-lidded look and holds his arm out straight, beckoning me with one finger.

You want the big moment? That was the big moment for me. I don't want Prince. I'm not gay. I want to *be* Prince. He understands. He *knows* it's going to happen. If he was a chemist he'd have done it himself. I see that just by looking into his eyes. Amazing, right? And you know what it is? This is a person who says yes to everything. Yes to change. Nobody has to wear the clothes they came in with. Nobody has to be stuck in one body. *Dig, if you will, the picture.* To me, *that* was America. And the funny thing is, it takes a Thai guy to understand it. The melting pot. I mean, that's what this is, right?

He leans back in his chair and drains his glass. And I notice, for the first time, how thin his arms are, thin and nearly cylindrical, right up to the shoulders. Like iron bars. Phran brought him a plate of satay and sliced pineapple and he hasn't touched it. When we had our lunch together the other day he must have ordered six dishes and taken three bites of each. A man who runs on some other energy source.

Tell him about the science, Julie-nah says. Lying back, a forearm over her eyes, as if it's midday. I love it when you talk about the science.

no one remember old Marcus Garvey no no one remember

I'll give you the short version, he says. Skin darkens because of melanin production, right? Melanogenesis, that's what it's called. A hormone, melanocyte-stimulating hormone, binds with the receptors in the melanocytes in the epidermis. This sends a signal to the genetic material in the melanocytes — a signaling cascade. The cascade sets off the production of eumelanin — that's the good stuff. The black and brown stuff. So the crux of the matter is, how do you create melanogenesis on its own? At first I thought it was simply a matter of going back and reproducing the MSH. But that didn't work. The half-life is too short; inject it and it just disappears into the bloodstream. I needed a new peptide. A stable analogue, all the way from scratch, that would bind with the melanocyte and run through the whole process in just the same way. Every enzyme had to be right. Not just the melanocortin 1 receptor; *all*

527

the melanogenesis genes — tyrosinase, TYRP1, and DCT. It was enough to make any biochemist tear his hair out.

Well, what else did I have to do, in the middle of the winter, in Rochester? I synthesized peptides, one after the other. After my labwork, after all my other responsibilities, I just commandeered the centrifuge and sat there till two or three in the morning. It took six months, and then I got it. [Nle^4, D-Phe^7]-α-MSH. My baby. Melanoxetine. The perfect biomimic. Hundreds of times more potent than natural MSH, and utterly stable as a pharmacologic compound. The first, the only, artificial agent to induce melanogenesis. You can look it up; the patent's been pending for nearly a decade.

carried us away in captivity required of us
a song how can we sing King Alpha's

One day he's going to win the Nobel Prize for it, Martin intones.

I showed it to my lab supervisor, Silpa says, and this is what he said: either you've just invented the world's best tanning drug, or a brand-new form of skin cancer. Or both. Refused to have anything to do with it. So I bought my own mice. Set up my own lab, in the kitchen of my apartment. It took another year, a full set of trials, to prove noncarcinogeneity. No anchorage-independent clonogenic cell growth. No metastatic tendencies at all. Then, I imagined, it would be easy. I submitted a paper to *JAMA*. No luck there. Submitted to *The New England Journal of Medicine*. The reviewer wrote back, *This drug has no clinical application outside of questionable and theoretical cosmetic procedures. No one would willingly consent to have his skin darkened permanently.*

So where was I, then? With no published results, no biomed corporation would touch it. I could file patents all I wanted. I was such a true believer! It would make you cry. All around me, it seemed, people were getting rich. It was the Eighties! Nobody was content with a mere clinical practice anymore. All you had to do was put your hand on the magic compound and you would sprout golden wings and fly off to Cambridge. Or Palo Alto. *Call it a tanning supplement,* my friends told me. I could have just hired some Indian jerks to synthesize it on the fly and sold it over the Internet. But that wasn't the way! I kept thinking, *someday people are going to want the real thing.* In this way I'm still a Marxist. Formally speaking. I don't believe in incremental change. In working within the system. It's cost me tremendously. But now the result is almost here. It *is* here. You people are the result. We have only the one corner left to turn.

follow the shadows for rescue but as the
day grows old I know the sun

What do we know about plastic surgery? he asks, rhetorically, looking around at us. What's the consensus of the field? It's all about taking away. Subtract, subtract, subtract. Does a sculptor start with a block of marble and glue little bits on? What is this neoclassical beauty all the doctors talk about? The least possible extrusion. *Slenderness.* A level plane. A level playing field. Of course, it all begins with the Jewish nose. In the Western world, at least. The nose that looks like a sail. A hatchet. Shylock's nose. An aggressive nose, a nose that intrudes, a nose that *takes.* So what do you do? Cut it down to size. Reduce the curvature. Thin out the alar base. Do you know how many careers, how many lifetimes, have been spent figuring out how to shave a few millimeters off the human nose? Then take some doctor from the Third World, with an unpronounceable name, with his article on "Expansion of the Nostrils and Widening of the Cura to Reproduce African-Identified Features." Using the first synthetic cartilage, for God's sake! Why do you think it took so long for anyone to admit it was possible to do female-to-male sex changes? No one wanted to make a penis. No one wants to *make* anything. Why is that?

Babylon throne gone down gone down oh
Babylon throne gone down

Because, Julie-nah says, sitting up now, if you make it, it's not natural. It's not *augmented.* It's brand spanking new.

Correct. Enlarge a breast, and you have a woman with larger breasts. Give a young girl a rhinoplasty, and she's just the same Sarah or Hee-jin she always imagined herself to be. Arguably, you can extend the same logic even to the original sex change. A man minus a penis is a woman. But clearly there's a double standard at work. An enormous blind spot. *In theory,* all my techniques could have been developed thirty years ago. But we're not yet at the point of accepting what the science can actually do. Why? Because our trajectories of beauty still only point one way.

The Roman nose, Julie-nah says, wide-eyed.

I and I do not expect to be justified by the laws of men

The classical ideal. The Aphrodite of Melos. It's in the literature; it's the foundation of plastic surgery. Look in the textbooks. Better yet, look in the museums. That translucent marble surface, the smoothness, the tight curves. *That's* what whiteness means. *Horaios,* do you know that word? The Hellenistic Greek term for beautiful. The same etymology as *hour.* Meaning *of the moment,* or *ripe.* But the ripeness we're talking about is something else.

Stillness, Julie-nah says eagerly, sitting up in her chair. Something frozen in time. Not actual ripeness, not the ripeness of a plum, or an actual teenager, say, but ripeness as a disappearing point on the horizon. Not actual beauty, more like the tomb of beauty. What do you think Botox is all about? All those whiteness creams, all those pale waif-models? It's the death glow. The corpse pose. It's been in the literature for thirty years. It's not news.

Which is why RRS is going to be so difficult to accept, Martin says. It's a fundamental reordering of the field. What if anything you wanted were possible? What if there *were* no trajectories, only personal choice? We're going to have to hit this point hard when we go out as ambassadors.

Julie-nah stares at him with a strange, transfixed smile.

Tariko, Silpa says. You've been awfully quiet. Too quiet. What do you think?

He shrugs.

For me, he says, it all comes from the teachings of the *Holy Piby.* You know what that is, Kelly? The rest of these brethren have heard enough about it. But maybe I can enlighten you.

Go on.

The Holy Piby, he says, in an exhausted voice, barely audible. The foundation of all our reasoning. I had to memorize it before I turned thirteen. His voice turns high-pitched, as if he's resuming a recitation from long ago. Written by His Holiness Robert Rogers in Newark New Jersey in the year of Our Lord 1928 and dedicated by him unto His Holiness Marcus Garvey. What does it say? It says that when the time is ripe a great angel will come to Babylon and say, Children of Ethiopia, stand, and there will flash upon the earth a great multitude of Negroes *knowing not from whence they came;* and then instantly the whole heavenly host will shout, Behold, behold Ethiopia has triumphed. What else does it say?

The ice in the north and the ice in the south shall disappear. Then shall continents which are submerged arise and the whole earth shall bloom. For with thee, he shall sit in his parlor in Africa, and see a rooster treading in the moon and the bees on the roses in Venus. The laborers in Mars, strike-breakers on earth and my daughter in college in Jupiter. My children shall remind you of the things I have forgotten, for I have seen so far, but those that cometh after me, of me, with me and upon our God shall see farther even than I.

What else is there? he says. It's all rooted in prophecy. I've been waiting for this moment my whole life, man. My father would have *died* for the opportunity. In three months I'm going to be sitting on my patio up in Mona watching the sun rise over the Blue Mountains. And when it rise, it'll be on the color of my true face. The dark skin of a Negro not knowing from whence he came. The lost tribe. By the grace of God.

Bravo, Silpa murmurs. As if it's a bit of oratory.

On the other hand, isn't it? What else do we say, embarrassed by the spectacle of faith? *Amen?* Martin has closed his eyes and angled his face upward, which could be read as reverence, I suppose. Julie-nah picks at her teeth.

You can see why Tariko's our best advocate, Silpa says, filling the silence as it has to be filled. It's a *vocation*. Well, it's a vocation for me too, of course. But I don't quite have the words to say so.

What I worry about right now, Martin says, slowly, is infrastructure. Whether we're ready to meet the demand when the demand comes. Scalability. I've been doing what I can. But we're going to need everything, when the moment comes. Customer reps. A phone bank. A website that can take a million hits in a day and not crash.

A bigger office, Tariko says.

That's the easy part. Physical space is not the problem. It's client relations that I worry about. Client relations, reliability of our supply chain, and, of course, waiting times. Because there's only one Silpa. That's the problem with doing it this way.

He's right, of course, Silpa says, looking up at the sky. None of these changes are permanent, you know. There's the question of maintenance, too. Drug regimes for forty or fifty years. That's why the egg is so fragile right at the moment. I need assistants. Apprentices. Otherwise, if something happens to me?

In the stairwell Julie-nah turns and gives me a baleful stare. For a good ten seconds we stand there, like a frieze, my palm on the bannister, her body twisted, whorled, as if to catch me and fling me away.

I thought you were kidding, she says.

I did too. At the time.

Really? You're telling me Martin's powers of persuasion are that strong? Even if you knew that it was all one big sche—

Martin tried to argue me out of it.

Like hell he did, she says. Ever heard of reverse psychology?

I had my own reasons.

We all have *our own reasons.* A globule of spit catches me in the eye; she runs a crude hand across her mouth. That's the problem. I thought you understood me. Didn't you understand me, Kelly? We've got to unplug this Orchid machine. Before it makes us all billionaires. There's a healthy point-five percent of the world's population that has *really good reasons* for RRS. If you don't say no, that's it. You're the final picture in our happy little mosaic.

I let myself sit down on the tile step.

Anyway, she says, what do you expect is

going to change? Even if it takes. Even if it's perfect. You think, what, you'll be less *divided,* more *yourself?* You'll just be the same ball of questions as always. Believe me. I can tell. You don't get that jolt out of being a congenital liar. Not like Martin. You'll be a freak.

Julie, do you ever get tired of deciding what's right for the world?

No, she says, wide-eyed. Don't tell me. Don't fucking tell me.

I mean it. Speaking, myself, as someone like you. A professional mind. An inquirer. A critic. Isn't it ever *tiring,* to you, just a little, being an arbiter all the time? You know the joke about the French? *It may work in practice, but will it work in theory?*

What the hell does that mean?

You know what I'm talking about. The tingle of empty accusations. All this conspiratorial fault-finding. Hegemonic diagnostics. It's all one big autoimmune condition, isn't it? Look, maybe it works when you have tenure. Or cradle-to-grave health insurance. Or a rich dad who works for Samsung. But look, from my perspective, I'm out of a job.

It's Daewoo, actually. And I thought you were on Martin's payroll.

Oh, I am. For the time being. But I'm

talking about *real money* for once. What's wrong with that? Money that lets you make decisions.

It's as if some rind, some slippery, rubbery substance, has detached from my gums; I find myself chewing at the words.

You know how they want *you* to make money? she says. Why they're so desperate to make a Chinese connection? Tissue farming. What the fuck else? All those prisoners, all those no-name corpses. Hair. Skin. Retinas. Healthy teeth. Cartilage. You ready to get into that business, Kelly?

Speaking as someone who's already in it?

She laughs.

Oh, you have no idea about me, she says. Don't even bother to guess.

But isn't that the point? It's up to you. Shouldn't we own up to that? White people that we are.

Don't call me that.

Why? Isn't that what you wanted, Julienah?

It was a *project,* she says, all but crying now. It was a provocation. I wanted to make myself into an instrument of my own desires. A demonstration of the emptiness of buying out —

I could have told you not to bother. You really think you need to tell people what they already know? After all, who's to say I haven't bought all of my identities? Not just this one. This, come to think of it, is the second time.

That's cold, she says. You sure you want to go that far, Kelly? That's really cold. It's your wife we're talking about. Your wife, your *child.*

Don't tell me about my wife and child, I would have said to her, to anyone, ordinarily. My jaw seems to want to flap open.

Call it closure, I say. Closure comes in unexpected ways.

That's sick.

Since I can't have you, I want to say, I have to become you. Where did that phrase come from, all of a sudden? Though I don't quite understand it, it seems to be all that needs to be said. Then why can't I quite fit the words on my tongue?

I'm tired, I say to her. Speaking past her. I have an appointment with Silpa first thing. Can we continue this later? My door is always open.

Don't be an ass.

To *talk.*

I'm through with talking, she says. Aren't you? It's time for decisions. And not waiting for a reply, or a question, she pivots and disappears.

10.

On a dark screen six feet tall, a screen I
could fall into, I watch life-sized, naked
photographs of myself, one after another:
frontal, profile, half-angles, close-ups on the
chin, the nose, the eyes. It's like a bizarre
video installation, I'm thinking, a work of
performance art, crossed with an initiation
ritual. There are creases I never noticed
under my chin, a constellation of moles
beneath my left armpit. My eyes show the
faint beginnings of crow's feet. My penis is
a strange dark color, sullen, almost bruised.
A photograph like this, I'm thinking, is
harsher than a mirror under bright light:
something about its being preserved makes
it harder to face.

But it won't be preserved.

You're making me self-conscious, I say.
Maybe I should just get an ordinary facelift.
A little liposuction.

Let's get started, Silpa says, turned away

from me, clicking away at the desktop monitor across the room. Begin by focusing on the face. For practical reasons, and aesthetic reasons, the principle here is to do as little as possible to achieve the desired effect. So we're not talking a *severe* epicanthal single fold. Really the enlargement and adjustment of the eye socket will be quite small. The result will be like this. I'll change the skin tone, too, to give you the full effect.

The new image spools down from the top, the same thinning hairline, the faint widow's peak, slightly narrowed eyebrows. Only with the eyes does the face become someone else's. I know those eyes, I'm thinking, I *recognize* those eyes. Someone I knew in Weiming, someone at Harvard? How many thirty-something Chinese men have I known? Stop! I say, a little louder than I intended.

What's the problem?

That's a photograph, right? That's not *me.*

It's not a photograph. It's software. Didn't I explain this? Predictive modeling. Those are *your* eyes, Kelly. Really, the change is very minor. It's essentially just padding the eye socket a little around the edges. And then adding a *slightly* folded epicanthus. I'm surprised it startles you. To me the effect is almost not enough. I could make it much more pronounced. Should I continue?

When I don't answer, he taps the keyboard again, and the rest of the face appears, centimeter by centimeter. A smaller nose. Slimmer lips. Narrower shoulders. He's reducing me by ten percent. A flatter stomach, bonier hips. Even the knees are less pronounced, somehow. And the skin? Only when I look away and look back do I see it: a weakening of the light, a slightly sepia tone over my normal color.

This is crazy. What are you going to do, Silpa, shave down every part of my anatomy?

What do you mean? We're only talking about alterations to the face. Plus skin tone, of course, which is chemical. No other surgery.

Then why do I look so different?

He laughs. It's the eyes, he says. I see it all the time. Change the eyes, tweak the nose, and it's a different person. Haven't you heard the old saying about how a nose job takes off fifteen pounds?

No.

I suppose it's a joke in the business.

Who is this man? I close my eyes and open them again, slowly, and again; I turn my face away and back; I get up from the stool, go out into the hallway, shut the door, open it, and reenter. Who are you? *How* are you? How did you come to be, sourceless human being, person from nowhere, person who has never existed, who should never exist? It's a vertiginous feeling, a feeling that starts in the feet and gathers momentum in the thighs, as if I've leaned over a balcony railing, drawn by something I've seen fifteen stories down. A vertiginous feeling, that is, of having leaned against the natural settling order of one's joints, but also a feeling that originates between the thighs. Arousal. Arousal out of something deeply wrong.

What this is, I think, without stopping to explain the thought, what this is, is a kind of incest. A violation of the natural process. A skipping ahead.

Let's go through the next steps, Silpa says. I turn back to face him, and he folds his hands in his lap, retreating into doctor mode. First, we make up an agreement and sign it. It's a formality, but we have to do it, because it's a two-way financial transaction. Because by electing to pay for the operation, you become a shareholder in the company. Understood? Next, you write your RLTP plan. You've read Martin's, right? In your case I think we have to forgo the actual period, because of the anatomical difficulties. But you need to have a full day of reflection before the surgery begins.

What anatomical difficulties?

Because in your case, unlike Martin, there's no way you can pass without the operation being complete. You understand, right? There's no halfway point here. Once you go, you go all the way.

I understand.

Immediately after that — really as soon as possible — you have to give me your passport. Altering U.S. passports is an enormous task these days. We have the best technicians working on it, but it can take more than two weeks. Because of all the new security features. What other passports are you going to want? PRC? Taiwan? Singapore?

I can choose more than one?

You can do more or less whatever you want. We're starting from scratch, aren't we? The only question is how much you want to spend. And of course, some things are off limits. No one can become a North Korean citizen. The CIA has been trying for sixty years. And of course, outside of the realm of the impossible, there are still time constraints. Complete U.S. or UK or German citizenships take six months. With Scandinavian countries or Canada, if you have enough money, it's better to start elsewhere and go through immigration. By those standards the PRC is actually extremely easy, if you go through the right channels. We have an ex-PLA contact here in Bangkok who can do it in a week — passports, ID cards, all the relevant databases, everything. I think the going rate is around two hundred thousand baht. That's about seven thousand U.S. Taiwan is a little more — maybe three hundred thousand. But, of course, as a U.S. citizen you can live in Taiwan as long as you like. It's all a matter of where you want to feel at *home.*

How much does changing the U.S. passport cost?

Oh, don't worry about that. Martin's covering it. It's his gift to you. I think he called it your *country club initiation fee.* You must know what that means better than I do. Of course, you know, U.S. citizenship can be problematic, once you get into a certain income bracket. You might take this opportunity to choose a tax haven. Those are the easiest, of course. The Cayman Islands, for example. Or Monaco. I believe Martin himself has his assets somewhere in the Caribbean. Antigua, or the Virgin Islands.

I'll have to think about it.

Of course. And we have an accountant,

too, who works with us. Kamala. A very nice Indian lady from Singapore with an MBA from the Wharton School. She speaks Mandarin, Cantonese, Toishan, Hindi, Malay, English of course, French, and Italian. She can talk to you about all the financial ramifications. I know that's not your specialty. Nor mine. The most important thing, frankly, is the narrative. You have to have it down. You have to *believe* who you are. Or else there's a risk of a certain schizoid feeling.

You make it sound so straightforward.

One day it will be. All this documentation, it's just a charade, really. A smoke screen. Soon none of it will be necessary. You know what they do now, with sex changes? Change-of-gender cards. It's an announcement that comes in the mail, like a wedding or a birth. *I will now be known as Martha instead of Mark.*

And that's all right with you?

His smile is almost giddy. There's something elastic about his limbs, as he crosses his legs, leans back, wiggles the chair a little, getting comfortable.

The need is there, he says. Let's put it another way. The *desire* is there. Does this just sound like a pile of crap to you? Stay with me for a minute. Let's say, just for argument, desire is a kind of a wormhole, a door in time. Any deep human desire is really just an expression of how things will be in the future. How did we get airplanes? As soon as *Homo sapiens* stood up, he wanted to fly. For a time we thought we would all become angels in heaven. Or flying arhats, or celestial apsaras, in a future life. Then that dream popped like a bubble. *Then* we built airplanes. Get it? Look around you! Look at yourself, as an example. Your ancestors would think of you as a god. You can fly across the world in a day; you can live just about anywhere you like. Marry anyone you like. How far in the future can it be when people say, *I don't want to be* me *anymore*? Isn't it just as simple as that? Listen, it's already happening.

For those who have the resources —

You think this is an argument for decadence? You need to read Marx more carefully.

He slides open a desk drawer and hands me a palm-sized photograph in a battered tin frame. It's black-and-white, poorly printed, with water stains at the corners: a group of young men in white shirts and dark armbands around a table, talking earnestly, papers and books, flags and batons, piled up in front of them.

I was there, at Thammasat, he says. 1976. That was our Tiananmen Square. Our May of '68. You don't know what I'm talking about, do you? Hok Tulaa. The Thammasat University massacre. Don't feel bad. They don't even teach it in schools here. But you can go down to the campus and look at the memorial. Suffice it to say this: out of the seven people in that picture, I was the only one who survived. We were the student liaisons to the Federated Trade Unions of Thailand, and when the student rebellion happened, when we took over the campus, we all slept outdoors in the same tent. I just happened to be the one furthest away from the street. When the Red Gaurs came, the paramilitaries, I cut a hole in the side of the tent and ran straight to the river and dove in.

I —

Don't say anything! You don't have to express your condolences to *me*. I'm alive. And their bodies were burned out in the countryside, in pits, so no one could mourn them. Anyway, I escaped. I swam. It was like swimming in motor oil. Eventually a boat picked me up and drove me ten miles upstream. There were Communists all over Thailand in those days. I was handed from one to the other, all the way up to Isaan. I spent three years up there on a commune learning how to grow bananas and sugarcane. And reading Marx, Lenin, Trotsky, Mao, and Ho Chi Minh. Those were the only books we had. Until I finally had my realization. It's very simple. *Too* simple, really. Just this: *the dialectic is nothing to be afraid of.*

He takes a flat cardboard package from his breast pocket, shakes two pieces of gum into his palm, and unwraps them carefully, still looking at me. The writing is in Thai, but I recognize the colors: Nicorette.

I mean, what other conclusion can you draw, from all that analysis, all that modeling, all those patterns? Eventually it's going to happen as Marx predicted. In the broadest general sense. Capital is not self-sustaining. We know that much. What else have we seen, in our lifetimes? The expansion of the world economy is finite. What we think of as decadence is really only a shadow. Technology is neutral. That's what medicine teaches us. Stainless steel was first developed for weapons. Now it saves a million lives an hour. Chewing gum. Developed as candy for children, now it's saving my lungs.

He chews more aggressively, exaggeratedly, to prove his point.

And who are we saving?

Who the hell knows? Excuse my language. But look, Kelly, you're part of this now. You have to learn to think in larger increments. Decades, not years. Eras, not news cycles.

Millions, not thousands.

Billions, not millions.

He laughs at my face, which, I imagine, has registered some kind of dismay. At what? Being behind the curve?

Want my advice? Leave your Protestant guilt behind. Make that a promise to yourself. Read all those books you never thought you needed. Carnegie. *The Art of the Deal.* The *Seven Habits* one. And this, too. He reaches into the lowest drawer of his desk and hands me a battered hardcover without a dust jacket, the corners foxed, the binding split. *Awaken the Giant Within.* I can't remember the name, but I remember the teeth: a giant, voracious mouth, a jaw like a moray eel. He had infomercials on late-night TV when I was in high school. Anthony Robbins, Silpa says. Call it trash. Call it vapid. I call it my bible. Does that shock you? Good. That means you're ready. Read it before we put you under, and you'll wake up a new human being. Genuinely. No, take that copy! I know it by heart.

Why should I believe you? I wonder.

Looking at him, for the last time, out of my own eyes. *The dialectic is nothing to be afraid of.* This could all be a bit of theater, custom-designed for my benefit, and it wouldn't matter.

I don't need a rationale, I should tell him, I don't need a conceptual *framework*. I've had my entire life to come up with that. The switch has been flipped.

Thanks, I say. I mean, thank you. Sincerely. For doing this. For the opportunity.

He grins. Never thank a surgeon until you're in recovery, he says. It's bad luck. But okay. I appreciate it.

There's really no way for me to express —

You don't have to, he says. That's the wonderful thing about my line of work. No words are necessary. I get to be the first one to hold up a mirror and see the look on your face. That's my payment. That, and the cash. You've talked to your bank, yes?

It's all set.

It's a beautiful thing we're doing, he says. Put that in your book. You're still writing your book, aren't you?

I'm not sure.

Because it's no longer about Martin.

He gives me one of his blank smiles, his eyes receding into their creases, their laughing folds.

Among other things. There was the matter of an agreement.

Oh, he says, that money was more like seed capital. It's the kind of thing you write off in an instant. Don't let that worry you. We all work together as a unit now. Your energies may be better spent elsewhere. The field's moving very fast these days. Books are a little slow.

He glances at his watch and stands up. When I hold out my hand, he grasps it between his tiny palms, cradling it more than shaking it.

In any event, he says, staring not quite at my eyes, but slightly above them, you're living your life now. How can you live a life, and write a book, simultaneously? I've never quite understood it. It seems to me you have to choose one or the other.

RLTP

Kelly Thorndike (GI: Curtis Wang, Wang Xiyun 王西雲)
April 30, 2012

PATIENT STATEMENT
I was born in Tianjin in 1975 and left China in 1981 with my parents and younger brother, Xigang (Kevin). We lived in Hong

Kong for a year while my parents negotiated our US visas, and then moved to Athens, Georgia. My father, Wang Geling, started on a research fellowship and eventually became a professor of biochemistry at the University of Georgia; he died of a stroke in 2008. My mother, Xi Tande, was a professional dancer in China who performed in traveling shows during the Cultural Revolution. In the United States, she worked first as a bank teller and later as a branch and regional manager at NationsBank. She died of liver cancer in 1998. Kevin converted to Catholicism while a student at Georgetown University and is now a brother in the Cistercian order at Abbaye Pont-Desrolliers, in Alsace, France. He observes a strict vow of silence, and my only contact with him has been on two visits, the last of which was three years ago.

My childhood was happy and mostly uneventful. I attended public schools in Athens and had a very close circle of friends from my neighborhood, though I now keep in touch with them only sporadically. In high school I played bass in a local band that was moderately successful and recorded two LPs. I attended Harvard and switched majors three times, from philosophy to East Asian Studies to English. Through my roommate I became involved in an Internet startup, Amoeba.com, in 1996, first writing content and later designing the first version of the website. Amoeba had its IPO in September 1999, and I sold my shares a week later, resulting in a net profit of seven million dollars. Though the company went bankrupt and liquidated in February 2000, during the first dot-com bust, I was left an accidental millionaire. Since then I have spent most of my time in Silicon Valley and Marin County, working in venture capital.

None of my projects have performed as well as Amoeba, but I've had some close calls, and my net worth has grown a bit over time. I was married to Sarah Duffy from 2004 to 2009, but divorced amicably without children. My father's death prompted me to become more interested in my Chinese roots, and I have spent the last few years becoming familiar with venture capital markets in East Asia and the possibilities of new investment in high-tech startups in China.

Amazing, Martin says. It reads like a dating profile. Nearly put me to sleep. You're really good at vanilla, you know that?

We're having a working dinner alone at the kitchen table. Tariko is upstairs plinking away at his guitar; Julie-nah, having served us coconut rice, cold tofu with chili and lime, a tomato salad with edamame, and chicken sautéed with ginger and basil — it's nothing, she said, as we watched her working, each hand doing four things at once, her mouth set in a rictus of bland anger — has now retired into the garden, where she sits with a pile of string beans in her lap, staring at nothing in particular.

Isn't that the point? To be normal? I mean, not to arouse any suspicions? No reasonable doubt? I'm supposed to be passing, not doing a lion dance.

And the fifteen-minute rule?

This is the rule of thumb for a fake ID, he told me: your new identity has to survive fifteen minutes of Internet research by an intelligent amateur. Any more than that is just overkill. You think the world is full of investigative reporters and intelligence analysts who actually *do their jobs*? They're looking at kittens playing the piano on Facebook like everyone else.

Amoeba's still listed in some databases, I say. Wang Geling and Xi Tande have obits in the *Athens Banner-Herald*. And there's a memorial page on the University of Georgia website. Plus all his academic publications. And there's a few hits in Chinese, too, from their hometown Party newspaper.

Listing the kids' names?

Survived by two sons, Curtis and Kevin. And Curtis did go to Harvard. Or at least *a* Curtis Wang did.

You learn well, grasshopper.

It wasn't difficult, though I won't tell him that. It wrote itself. I left the names blank and filled them in at the end. It's not hard, with a billion and a half people and only a hundred surnames: pick Wang, Chen, Li, and you can more or less write any life that suits your fancy. It's not unlike doing algebra. Simple patterns and infinite variations.

This is the easy part, he says. The question is, are you ready to *be* Curtis Wang? Are you, Kelly? You heard what Silpa said. There's no halfway point.

It's already done, I say. Actually it happened a long time ago.

That's what I hoped you'd say. And you know why I believe you? Because you had me fooled. You were in drag. I took you for a normal.

I took myself for one, too.

One more day, he says. It's hard to wait, isn't it? Don't worry. Deciding is the worst part. The agony is already over. Now you just have to coast a little longer. Go downtown. Eat some great curry, get a massage, see the sights. Check your mind at the door. Can you do that? Can you relax, Kelly? Turn off those analytical faculties?

Julie turns and looks my way, chewing on a bean, shading her eyes against the blade of evening sun.

I *am* relaxed, I say. This is me, relaxed. Can't you tell?

11.

Not until the water taxi has rolled away from the pier, the thrum of the engine vibrating the balls of my feet, not until we've muscled past two long-tailed boats, thin as barracudas, and the hot brackish wind from the river has caught me full in the face, can I look over my shoulder and say for certain, certifiably, that I'm being followed.

It's ridiculous, the phrase, the whole idea, I've been telling myself that all day, as I shuffled along with the columns of tourists at Wat Phra Keow, the Temple of the Emerald Buddha, which even I could recognize was the Disneyland of Thai temples — every tile and mosaic buffed and shining, every ornament dripping with ornament, the grass poison-green, security guards glaring straight ahead every few feet. It was a young kid in an orange-and-white polo shirt, who tried and failed to be inconspicuous, turning every corner just behind me, not more than twenty feet away, and who stared frankly at me every second, as if fearing I would disappear before his eyes. Later I sat for forty-five minutes in a massage chair at Wat Po, the Temple of the Reclining Buddha, and when I opened my eyes at the end I thought I'd imagined the whole thing, or maybe he was a young hustler, or just some crazy teenager following me on a whim. But as I left the temple gate and crossed two blocks, almost tottering in the heat, following the map in a *Lonely Planet* Tariko lent me, looking for a vegetarian café he'd highly recommended, a man on a motorbike kept pace with me, sidling through the crowds of elderly Japanese ladies with floral handbags, the groups of Chinese all wearing the same ill-fitting red mesh baseball caps printed, in gold, *Empire West.* He wore the absurdly tight brown uniform all Bangkok police wear, with gold aviator glasses, but the bike was unmarked. At the café I took a seat in the window, and ate an excellent papaya salad and Massaman curry with tofu, keeping watch. Nothing. Of course, I thought, reeling back through every detective novel I'd ever read, every episode of *Law & Order* or *Magnum P.I.,* if the target is in a home or a business you don't have to park out front, only somewhere with a clear view of the entrance, unless the target is savvy enough to find a back door. In which case you have to have two followers anyway, guarding each exit.

I had my Thai cell phone there on the table, next to the *Lonely Planet;* I could call Tariko, or get into a cab and head back to the house. Should I be afraid, I wondered, actually? And who of?

Who else, other than Martin?

It would be convenient to have a person vanish in the middle of Bangkok. Probably there's few places in the world with more opportunities to disappear. You could go to Patpong and have a prostitute slip you a little GHB, and the next thing you know you're decomposing in a field on the road to Ayuthaya while she empties your bank accounts. You could get on a bus for Phnom Penh or Chiang Rai or Vientiane and leave in the middle of the night. If I went missing, I thought, who would look for me? The night before leaving I'd emailed my parents my flight receipt, telling them I was on a reporting trip for a book project with no definite return date. They don't expect regular phone calls or emails; it might be a month before they started looking in earnest.

Have I become that much of a liability?

Because of that additional five percent?

Because I'm a competitor? Another story, another celebrity? *Becoming Chinese: If You Can't Beat Them, Join Them: An American Leaves Home to Join the World's Newest Superpower: Chinese from the Inside Out.*

Because he thinks he's doing me a favor. Before I become the tragic mulatto.

Because I'm the last one on earth who knows his real story. Who can pin him to a map.

Thinking this way was so ridiculous I flushed, the hairs prickling on my arms.

But then why would he have them follow me? Don't these things depend on the element of surprise, the bag over the head, the hustling into the unmarked van? Wouldn't they be more likely to send someone as bait? Like in *The Crying Game.* Forest Whitaker, the black soldier from Tottenham, snogging with Miranda Richardson in a muddy field at an Irish country fair, when Stephen Rea puts a gun to his head. Miranda Richardson, killed in a skiing accident just a few years ago, an untreated head wound, only in her fifties.

No, that was Natasha Richardson.

This is my last day on earth as Kelly Thorndike, I thought, the last day in my own skin, as the person my parents made, my grace period, and I'm inventing surreal murder plots and misremembering old movies. Shouldn't this be a sign of something? I ought to be in a panic. Shouldn't I run home, in a defensive posture? I ought to be missing my Rice Krispies about now. My neat and orderly life, my books and furniture, my desk, the clean-swept hardwood floor where I can pad about barefoot and listen to the police sirens streaking down St. Paul knowing they're not coming for me. Baltimore. Home. But no. I didn't want any of it. I've broken the spell, I thought, I'm free.

You want anything else?

The kind-faced young waiter in a Greenpeace T-shirt scooped up my dishes with one hand and refilled my water glass with the other.

Give me a recommendation, I said. I've seen the temples. What should I do now?

Take a river taxi, he said. You won't regret it. Best thing for a day as hot as this.

The man in the gold glasses and brown uniform followed me onto the boat, ten paces behind, never glancing my way, talking on his phone the entire time. An ordinary preoccupied commuter. Now he's taken a position on a bench next to the gangway. Alarm, alarm. A well of panic into which anything can fall without making a sound. I'm going to be leaving this life before it's even begun. I turn away and pretend to study the enormous white cone of Wat Arun, just coming into view on the far side of the river.

Or — it occurs to me just now — maybe he's simply having me followed. To make sure I don't stray. No surreptitious emails, no long phone calls, no meetings with clandestine publishing agents. Why does that seem, if anything, even less believable? Of course he would consider it. I would, too. Given our history, who would believe in such a thing as absolute trust? I should call him just to confirm. In an easy tone. *Hey, Martin, about that guy watching me* —

Two heavy fingers rest on my shoulder.

You Kelly? he asks when I turn around. He's removed his glasses and stares at me with puffy eyes, the lids swollen like inchworms. Kelly from USA? My name San.

I have no idea what to say to this, so I nod.

Somebody want to see you, San says. You know. You know him. Follow me, please. We get off next stop.

We're in the tourist quarter. Khao San

563

Road, where the trustafarians play. Streaming past me are muddy-faced white girls done up in braids and beads, batik skirts and jingling anklets; twenty-something boys in Beerlao and ManU and Che T-shirts; towering Aussies with splotchy sunburns gnawing kebabs and spooning pad thai out of paper cups. San threads me through the middle of the street, dodging tuk-tuk drivers and travel agents offering flyers, strolling ukulele players and kickboxers giving impromptu demonstrations. We turn two corners, all the sidewalks packed with pink faces, puffed out by heat and alcohol. Down an alley lined with sidewalk cafés and massage chairs, and under a hotel canopy — *Hotel Santana* — into deep, pungent shade. Sticky cocktails, cigarette smoke, spilled beer and fish sauce. On the back wall *The Notebook* plays on an eight-foot screen with the volume turned down, a close-up of Ryan Gosling's puppy-dog eyes.

Mort Kepler, reclining in a rattan chair, a bottle of Singha and a glass of mango juice at his elbow, sees me and jumps to attention, with a broad, toothy grin. Son of a bitch, he says. I can hear him halfway across the bar. They got you. I was just about to pack it in for the day. Want to know how long I've been sitting here, waiting for you?

■ ■ ■ ■

Mort, I say, swallowing a warm wave of shock, how the fuck did you make *this* happen?

I'm a reporter, he says. This is what reporters do. Use fixers. Local eyes on the ground. Haven't you ever — oh, wait. I forgot. Right! You don't *have* a background in journalism. Okay. I guess I have to explain everything from the beginning. Well, I have what Hemingway used to call a one hundred percent foolproof bullshit detector. And when I looked at you, right from the start, I knew you were hiding something. Just not what.

I raise one hand, defensively, and lower it a moment later. What's the point in arguing with him? I'm so glad to see him, so relieved, I almost want to reach over the table and hug his bristly shoulders. Go on, I say. Give me the full report. I'm listening.

So you shitcan the station, you and what's-her-name, after, what is it, three months? Three months after you get there? I've had Chinese food that lasted longer than you at BCC. Well, so I had nothing else to do. And a grudge, yes. A vendetta. So I started tailing you. Having nothing better to do. Don't you remember that day I crept up on you in Fell's Point? There are no accidents in this world. Didn't anybody ever tell you that? I was hoping for an introduction to the girl, but it didn't take long to trace her back. Quite a pedigree.

You followed her, too?

No, you idiot. I used the good old-fashioned Internet. Photo-recognition software. And then a fifty-dollar scanner to pick up your WiFi signal. There's this amazing store online, Orchid Imports? Based right in Baltimore. Sells all that kind of gadgetry. Ever heard of it?

Nope.

That's okay. I don't expect you to give up your sources all at once. Let's just chitchat. Pretend I didn't just shell out five thousand bucks to make this happen.

Who ever told you I was reporting anything?

Well, you don't expect me to believe you're *involved,* do you? Come on. Good luck with that. If you've managed to convince them of your ideological soundness, you're a better actor than I ever gave you credit for.

I can't do anything but stare at him, in sheer, confused defeat.

The movement, he says. Does it have a

name? I did a lot of digging and came up all zeroes. Wilkinson's friends with everybody, but no one wanted to talk when I came around. And believe me, I *know* people. So I've been doing a process of elimination. It's not the New Black Panther Party. It's not the Revolutionary Communists or the ACP. It's not Occupy Wall Street. It's not the Nation. If it's Islamist at all, he's a cell of one. Never been to a mosque, never met with an imam. There's always that possibility. He could be one of those YouTube guys, the Zarqawi syndicate. But I doubt it. I think he's starting from the ground up. He's got the charisma, the connections, and the funds. But what *is* it, man? Just give a clue. What's his agenda? Black nationalist? Radical self-determination? Third World revolution? Chavismo? Or is he just another drug runner with fancy ideas? Okay. Not that. I can tell just by looking at you.

You must be a mind reader.

No, you'd just be a terrible poker player. I'm getting *somewhere,* I know that much. It's like I thought. He's a big thinker. He's got ideas. So look, listen to me. I've covered insurgencies before. That's my specialty. Leonard Peltier, Mumia, all the great ones. They all needed a chronicler. A *mythologist.*

567

You know that book *In the Spirit of Crazy Horse*? Matthiessen ripped it off from my reporting. I would've sued him, but AIM said no. Didn't want the distraction. Listen, I'm a movement guy underneath. Ask anyone I've worked with. I can talk a good line to the lamestreamers, but make no mistake: I'm a tool in the hands of the people. Not a word of this comes out till the moment is ripe. Listen, if you *are* actually in Martin's pocket, let me talk to him. That's all I want. Ten minutes to make my case. We can all be in it together. I've got the connections and the savvy. You've got — well, whatever it is. You've worked with him. And Robin, too. Robin's obviously the key.

What are you talking about?

Have you read her master's thesis? *Talking Resistance: Therapy as Emancipation from Freire to Fanon?* I know I'm not supposed to use words like this, but what the hell. Here we are in Bangkok. The girl's *fiery*. We're talking about the diary of a mad black woman. I don't care if she works for Hopkins or Harvard or the goddamned Cato Institute, she's a double agent. Scratch that surface and you've got a latter-day Angela Davis. Put the two of them together and you've really got something. The brains and the means.

A waiter brings me the same thing he's having, the mango shake and the glistening bottle of Singha.

The mango's for the vitamins, he says. The beer's to stay relaxed. Old R&R trick I learned from my friends who spent years in Saigon. Because you never know, do you, when someone's going to bomb the place out? All these Yankees, out here in the open air? One of these days they're going to do Bangkok like they did Bali.

He grins, lifts his straw fedora, scratches his bald spot. I never noticed, in the office, just how hairy he was — a salt-and-pepper thatch that runs up his wrists under the sleeves of his linen shirt and emerges over the collar, covering the nape of his neck. A sinewy, almost apelike, grasp. Here is a man, I'm thinking, who loves living his life. Mort Kepler, by Mort Kepler. A self-authored man. Emerson would be proud, and horrified. Does anyone my age live so vigorously, so unironically, so heedless of offense? On the other hand, did his parents? Or are the Boomers just a separate species, never to be repeated?

Mort, would it help in any way, I say, would it make any difference, if I told you you were completely fucking crazy?

All I need is one word. Not even a word.

You don't even have to say it. Just nod. What's in the boxes? Is it rocket launchers? Centrifuge parts? C-4?

It's electronics. Gray market electronics. You can ask him.

Well, answer me this, then. If it's not a movement, what the hell is it? What happened to you, to turn you into this kind of, what, a *robot*? Is it a cult? A new religion, excuse my language? What, is he some kind of mystic? I mean, if it's not drugs, and it's not revolution, and it's not just out and out *money,* then what the fuck is left? Religion, right?

I want to tell him. This is it, I'm thinking, this is the door, the way around and over and out. Mort Kepler is a steaming pile of crap, yes, but he's also a real reporter, who has actually in his life turned a story around and sold it. Leave it to him to break the news. Who cares if it's *Mother Jones* or *The Nation*? Let him have the scoop, let him write the book, and then go back to Baltimore and start again. Hire a lawyer and negotiate a plea deal. Probably it'll all amount to nothing. Look for another NPR job. Move back in with the parents, if it comes to that. Take shelter. Embrace the ordinary. Take shelter in this pockmarked face, in these big capable hands. Treat Mort

Kepler as a father confessor. Why the hell not?

Because I'm free, that's why. When I'm Curtis Wang, I'll never have a conversation like this again. What would Mort Kepler say, if Curtis Wang were sitting across the table? He'd be mincing his words, biting his tongue, thinking all kinds of inappropriate thoughts about the Little Red Book and internment camps and industrial espionage and Yao Ming. And penis size. How else do men like him measure their distance from other men, when it comes down to it? Wasn't I tempted to ask Martin about it, once, long ago? To ask, that is, as a joke, whether Silpa had invented penis extensions, as a side project, to correct for anatomical averages? I can see it in Mort's face even now, in embryo: *Chinaman, my dick is bigger than yours.*

Why would I choose that? Why would I step out of the circle of belonging, where I've always been? The gilded prison house of whiteness, with its electric fences, its transparent walls? Being the most visible, therefore the most hated, of all? The one who can always condescend, not the one condescended to?

Reader, doesn't the question answer itself?

I'm expected back at the office, I tell him.

Conference call at five.

No more R&R, huh? Who's the conference call with?

I give him a pitying look.

Enjoy the rest of your time in Bangkok, I say. Go get a massage at Wat Po. They're only five bucks.

The massages I want are all in Patpong.

With that, I give him a wave, and walk easily out of the bar and down the alley, as if I've lived here all my life, and step into a hot pink taxi waiting at the corner. No one follows me.

■ ■ ■ ■

EPILOGUE: ENDTIME

■ ■ ■ ■

I wake up with Wendy sleeping next to me.

Her hair spilling across the pillow, her fingers dug into the crook of my elbow. Long white curtains blowing away from an open window, a French door, actually, on her side of the bed. Birds twittering and the hump and sizzle of the surf.

We're on vacation. Meimei is with my parents in New Paltz. I know these things immediately, automatically, when I open my eyes. This is the vacation we promised each other we would take for our eighth wedding anniversary. Vieques. My supervisor at BUR, Kathleen, insisted we borrow her condo.

How is it that things sometimes fall into place so easily?

That was what Wendy asked me at dinner last night. We were picking through the remains of a grilled yellow snapper, eating the last tostones with our fingers.

I mean, when we came to the United States, she said, the first thing I promised myself is we would take *vacations.* She switched to Chinese. My parents never took one. Where would they have gone? All their family was in Wudeng, and it's not as if they could have afforded to go back to Shanghai. Or Beijing.

We'll take them, next time we go.

It's expensive now. Not like when we lived there. Even a three-star hotel in Beijing now costs a hundred bucks a night. It's like New York. I looked it up. The real question is, when can *we* afford to go, period?

We'll work it out.

You always say that.

When I stand up my gaze crosses the room to a small mirror, an antique, propped on the dresser, in a blue frame crudely painted with doves. My chin, my eyebrows, my neck. My eyes.

Remember when I first met you, she's murmuring, how funny I thought it was that you came from a town called Athens? Curtis, I'm so glad we came here. It's a place we won't have to explain to each other. But next time we have to bring Meimei.

Don't make me feel guilty about that.

I'm not trying to make you feel guilty. I said *next* time.

We are in the midst of ordinary life, I'm thinking to myself, as I cross the room and pull on a loose cotton shirt, one I've kept crumpled in the back of my closet since the last time I went to the beach. A good life. I close my eyes. I don't have to think about it at all.

I'm being pulled up through a warm ocean, thick, silky, amniotic, toward the surface's blue light. A throbbing, murmuring voice: *no one knew she had the gun. Where'd she get it? Korea? You know what the prison sentence is for owning an unregistered firearm in Korea?*

When I come back from the 7-Eleven, with three slices of pizza stacked up in a box, two Dr Peppers and a Sprite and a bag of crab chips in a plastic bag, Alan and Martin have pulled themselves out of the water and are lying stretched out, facedown on the pool deck. No towels. Skin on concrete, hands by their sides. They look like they've been executed where they lie. The lifeguard ignores them.

What the fuck are you doing?

Sunbathing, Alan says. Vitamin D.

You'll turn into a crispy Chicken McNugget. It's about 105 out here, Loco Blanco.

That's Blanco Loco, Martin says.

From the back, from an angle I never see, two slabs of human tissue, two specimens: one white as Crisco, white as Sherwin-Williams Bright White, white so that he reflects the sun, an oblong moon; one turned dark, coal-dark, much darker than his usual medium-toned, maple-syrup color. I stand there for a moment, fascinated. It's not usually this stark. Pink, brown, and yellow, Martin says. We're the twenty-first-century Neapolitan trio.

You know something? Alan's voice is muffled by the concrete. This is it. I could *live* like this.

And if the sun were a little hotter, we could just turn right back into pure carbon.

Shut up. I mean it. Freeze time. So I can just lie here in the sun, smelling that pizza Wang brought back, watching Katie Cryer over there practice her synchronized swimming or whatever it is.

It's so unlike him, a positive statement of any kind, let alone a declaration of happiness, that Martin lifts his head and turns it to the other side, so that he faces the back of Alan's head. And I think, *this isn't my story. This is a dream I'm going to wake up from and never remember.*

Write a song about it, why don't you?

Maybe I will.

— *Hell, it was a cheap Saturday Night Special she bought in Woonsocket when she was going to Brown. Trust me on that. I can tell you the store; I've been there myself. Only place to get a retail handgun between New Haven and Boston. Maybe she thought it was cool, like Charlie's Angels. How are you supposed to predict these things? She's in Bangkok for eight months, a week for the surgery, six weeks in recovery, and then the rest of the time working in the goddamned kitchen or on the computer. I think we got her out of the house three times. Didn't want to sightsee. Didn't want the goddamned* pad kee mao.

Daddy, Meimei says, when I lift her out of bed, Daddydaddydaddydaddy. Stringing together the words with great satisfaction. Her legs wrap halfway around my waist, little pincers, little monkey limbs. She went to bed in one of Wendy's old T-shirts and a pull-up diaper, now heavy with urine, pressed against my stomach. Do we have to get up already? It's still *dark.*

It's December, I tell her, flipping on her closet light, her little body still cemented to me, pulling a plum sweater-dress off its hanger. Let's let Mama sleep, okay? Don't talk too loud. Her heels thump on the carpet.

Can you make me oatmeal?

Yeah.

After you make yourself coffee.

Priorities, little girl, I say, switching to English. Priorities.

With bananas *and* raisins?

I think we're out of raisins.

Then you should get more, silly.

I have to go by the store on the way home this afternoon. Will you remind me?

Can I draw a note on your hand?

No. No more drawing on people's hands. Miss Lewis warned you about that, right?

Her face, as it cranes up to look at me in pretend puzzlement — is it the murky light from her tiny tableside Dora lamp, or has she gotten darker? Has the brown in her eyes crushed the blue?

Stay, Daddy, she says. Stay with us. Stay here. In this story.

I can't. I have to go to work.

— Yeah, she walked into the office and just popped him. Just like that.

We're working on tracing his lists of suppliers. At this point the maintenance drugs are the crucial thing. Problem is, he kept way too much of it in his head. And as far as a replacement surgeon goes, we're absolutely screwed. I mean absolutely. This was an irreplaceable asset. He would have been training ten assistants after the announcement, after we were out in the open. But not now. Too dangerous. Yeah, you know, our coverage with the Chens gets us up to five million. But believe me, Sasha, this isn't a money thing. You have to know people at these pharmacies. All this stuff is hand-prepared.

What did you think? That I had a private stash somewhere? Maybe I should have. Jesus Christ, it all went through him, okay? Tariko's just out of his mind over it. It was his job, primarily. Watching her, I mean. Monitoring her movements. But she didn't make any movements. She just sat there and stewed.

Our guy's on it. Obviously. The important thing is to watch for noises in the press. What's done is done. I'm not after any vendettas. I've made that clear. She's untouchable as long as she stays in Korea, and I doubt she's going anywhere else. No, there's been nothing in the papers. Mai is helping out with that. We told the police he was alone in the office and the cameras were out for maintenance. Disgruntled former client. Apparently it's a thing in Bangkok. They didn't seem too interested. His family took the body. No idea where the funeral was.

Whatever you say. The important thing is, Sasha, we need chemists. An in-house staff. I couldn't give a damn where they're located. Put them in Vilnius, put them in São Paulo. Put them in Juárez. We have all his papers, but what good does that do us? Ten synthetic chemists, say, on a yearly contract. Get them straight out of grad school, get them from Sandoz and Merck and Pfizer, get them from meth labs, I don't care. As long as they can do the work. We're talking about a total reboot here. The drugs come first. Self-tanning. Yeah, okay, I said it, right? Silpa's not even cold. So shoot me. Let's talk primary markets. Then we develop the surgeons. Five years down the line, Orchid reopens. In the meantime, we're Orchis Pharmaceuticals, Ltd. I just did the paperwork. Caymans.

No, my same office. Same address. Orchid Imports, 200 Light Street, Sixteenth floor, Baltimore, Maryland 21001. I'll be back there in a week. Have to take care of some business first. Tariko's wrapping things up, no. Sold the house to a Saudi. Six-fifty, that's fifteen percent profit. Silver linings, right?

I wake up again, now, a haze of light filling the gauze bandages over my eyes. A white world, inside a fluorescent tube. The airplane window vibrates against my cheek.

582

Sunlight above the clouds, the brightest sunlight, unfiltered, un-ozoned, cell-killing, cell-dividing. It'll hurt to open them at first, Silpa said, under the bandages, but you shouldn't hesitate. Move those babies around. You don't want the eye muscles to atrophy. Anyway, by that time you'll only be a day or so away from full use.

You there? Martin asks. You there, Kelly?

Curtis, I say, through a dry mouth. It's Curtis.

Shit. Sorry. Curtis. Now I can stop taking your pulse. I was sure those Vicodins were really something stronger. Never seen anyone sleep so long.

I wasn't asleep the whole time.

I hear him taking a moment to digest this.

The important thing, he says, is that we've got your back. Nothing changes. Payments as normal. Deliveries as normal. Here we are, landing in Shanghai in forty-five minutes. As promised. Passport in hand.

It didn't sound that way to me.

Forget what you heard. You were addled. I could have been talking Klingon.

Silpa's dead, I say. Isn't he? Did I get that much right?

The alert bell pings overhead, and a voice comes over the loudspeaker. *Dajia hao,* the flight attendant says. She has a chirpy Shan-

583

dong accent. A warm tear rests on my upper lip. How good it is, I'm thinking, to hear a language I completely understand.

Here. Martin presses a cold glass into my hand. Don't worry, he says. Ginger ale. I'm not trying to knock you back out.

So I guess your plans are off the table.

For now, he says. For now. The moment has to be right. Think globally, act locally. You have to expand your consciousness. The *world* is Baltimore, remember? It just doesn't know it yet. His face slackens; he might be, impossibly, about to cry. I'm always at home, he says. You know why? My money travels with me. There's nothing more beautiful than stepping up to that ATM for the first time, wherever you are, putting your card in and watching the color of the bills shooting out. It's like sex. That's when I think, *there's nothing I can't do.*

Not me, I say. That's never worked on me.

Tell me about it.

No, I mean, in my universe, Baltimore is a fixed point. It doesn't expand and contract.

You'll see how that changes when you come back to visit.

What do you mean, *come back*? I've never been there before.

Heh-heh-heh, he says. Don't fuck with me. Trying to give yourself retrograde amnesia? It's not that easy. Believe me, I've tried.

Seriously, I say. I'm from Athens, Georgia. Didn't you know that? Never been to Baltimore in my life. I mean, I passed through on 95 on the way up to Cambridge.

As I say it, I will it into being: an orb, a warm, pulsing thing, orange-yellow, the color of butterscotch candy, rising again out of my very center, up into my throat. My guide-light. It points only in one direction. The future vibrates in me; my legs are shaking. I want to tear off the bandages *right now.*

Do I feel sadness? I ought to ask myself that, but it seems like an impossible question. Should I grieve for them, for my lost girl, for the woman who could finish my sentences in two languages? And spend my life, waste my life, along with theirs? I've *become* them. I didn't make the world. Should I give up on it?

My senses have grown sharper, I'm thinking: I can hear a magazine rustling in the seat behind us, keys clicking on a laptop, a can of Diet Coke snapping open. The rustle of life itself. The *impatience* of it. All these people fidgeting with their phones, drumming their fingers, feeling money trickling away with every waiting second. The towers of Shanghai, towers I won't even recognize, floating up out of an electric haze. The light thrown off by assets multiplying. Isn't this the pattern of heaven? I've grown old, I'm thinking. Old and slack, in my original habitat, in the cage of one body, hardly even aware that it is a cage. Time to wake up. Time to plant some seed capital. Who cares if it's with Orchid, or with Hue, or Hue.2, or something I haven't dreamed up yet? Money, I'm thinking, to paraphrase *The Art of War,* always finds its place. And when I have enough, whatever *enough* means, I'll endow another wing of the Harvard Library. The Wang Center for Translation Studies. Or maybe the Miao Center for Translation Studies. Or, if the time is right, the Thorndike Center. The Wendy and Meimei Thorndike Center.

Because that story, too, will have to be told.

Don't fuck with me, Martin says. I'm not your goddamned life coach. For the first time I can hear the ticking of fear in his voice. This isn't about your journey, he says, so let's get some things on the record. You signed a contract. You have duties to perform. A fiduciary obligation. And don't think that you can hit the ground and go all renegade on us. We'll find Julie-nah, and we'll find you.

Okay, I say, just to keep him calm. You're right.

We'll be in touch when it's all arranged, he says. In the meantime, you have a Bank of China account set up for you. Here's the card. Here's the passport. I'll whisper the PIN in your ear. You ready? He leans over until I can feel the warmth of his lips glowing on my ear. *2526.* There's an easier way to remember it, though.

Because it spells *Alan*? I say. Who's Alan? Am I supposed to remember him?

The plane is descending now; I feel it in my knees, my hips, the pull of the atmosphere, the engines measuring out the shock of gravity in little tugs and dips. Martin says nothing. I remember, just now, something he said to me on the flight out of BWI, when we'd just settled into our seats. I love taking off, he said, but I hate to land. Gives me the creeps. Can't get it over with soon enough. Those flaps, you know, that flip up on the wings? Doesn't it just seem like a toy, when you look at those things? Like fingernails. All that momentum, and then they flick a switch and squash you like an ant.

You going to be okay getting out of the airport? he asks suddenly. Because I'm not staying overnight. My flight's in two hours.

Back to Bangkok?

Almaty. Kazakhstan.

What's in Kazakhstan?

I don't know. Fur hats? Lamb skewers? Mostly an oil pipeline, that's what I hear. Oil going to China. No, seriously. Potential clients. And investors. It's been in the works for months. No point canceling when we could be on the cusp of something new.

The alert bell pings again. We're on the ground, we've taxied, without noticing it, and bumped up against the boarding gate. We stand up together, or rather he lifts me up, by the elbow. Careful, he says, watch your head. Here. He binds my hands around the handle of my laptop bag.

Martin, I say, suddenly overcome. You thought of everything.

Don't worry about it. What else was I supposed to do? Go on, I'll be right behind you.

These are my last few minutes, I'm thinking, or, more precisely, the thought wandering through my mind, looking for a feeling to settle on. Goodbye, Kelly. I ought to hug myself. Instead, I reach up and lock him in an awkward, grappling, swaying embrace. And then I turn and find the back of the next seat, pulling myself into the aisle. In front of me, it seems, to the left, at the exit door, is an intense brightness, and there's a cloud of some floral perfume, as if someone's dropped a duty-free bag. It doesn't matter. I hear the babble of voices, dialects, accents, the toddler saying lift me up! lift me up! The wife calling, old man, don't forget the camera, it's right by your foot.

Excuse me, the flight attendant is saying, in Chinese, of course, coming down the aisle toward me, excuse me, we have a disabled passenger here. To me she says, loudly, taking my elbow, sir, follow me, I'll take you through.

Is this happening? Can this be? My words. My world. I've been addressed; I've been seen. The knot of fear at the back of my neck — how long has it been there, I'm wondering, has it been there my entire waking life? — dissolves.

You're going to make it, right? Martin asks a moment later.

I turn against the tide of shoulders and elbows. *Biezhaoji,* I almost say, turning the words on my tongue. I mean, don't worry about me.

You're here now, right? You're home.

I'm home.

ACKNOWLEDGMENTS

To Sander Gilman, for *Creating Beauty to Cure the Soul;* Jonathan Ames, for *Sexual Metamorphosis: An Anthology of Transsexual Memoirs;* Rebecca Walker, for *Black Cool: One Thousand Streams of Blackness;* Fred Moten, for *In the Break: The Poetics of the Black Avant-Garde;* Spike Lee, for *Do the Right Thing;* David Simon and all those involved in creating *The Wire;* Maxine Hong Kingston, for *The Woman Warrior* (and particularly "Thirteen Stanzas for a Barbarian Reed Pipe"); Paul Beatty for *The White Boy Shuffle;* Adam Mansbach for *Angry Black White Boy;* Cornel West for *The Gifts of Black Folk in the Age of Terrorism,* and above all to James Baldwin for *Another Country* and for his words to white Americans, in anger and love.

To the doctors, scientists, lawyers, and their staffs who generously answered my questions: Alan Engler, M.D., Ryan Turner, M.D., Steven Cohen, M.D., Pichet Rodchareon, M.D., Chettawut Tulyapanich, M.D., Professor Victor Hruby of the University of Arizona, Professor David Gray of the University of Maryland School of Law, Professor Byron Warnken of the University of Baltimore School of Law, and David Waranch, Esq. Also to Ruangsasithorn Sangwarosakul, Matt Wheeler, and Justin McDaniel for their help making connections in Bangkok. And to Bobby Sullivan for clarifying a point of Rasta etiquette.

To Major Jackson, Martha Southgate, and Sonya Posmentier, who read early drafts and shared immensely helpful thoughts.

To Rosalia Ruiz, Laura Hill, and the teachers of U-NOW Day Nursery, Little Missionary Day Nursery, and PS 3.

To my friends and colleagues at the College of New Jersey, Vermont College of Fine Arts, and the City University of Hong Kong, for their encouragement, and in particular to David Blake for helping me secure a sabbatical when I needed it most.

To Denise Shannon, who believed in this project before I did, and Megan Lynch, who saw it through to the end.

To my parents, for their unwavering support.

To Sonya, Mina, and Asa for sharing the life that inspired this book most of all.

ABOUT THE AUTHOR

Jess Row is the author of two short story collections, *The Train to Lo Wu* and *Nobody Ever Gets Lost*. Named one of *Granta*'s Best Young American Novelists in 2007, he has won a Whiting Writers' Award, a PEN/O. Henry Award, and two Pushcart Prizes; his work has appeared three times in *The Best American Short Stories*. He lives in New York City and teaches at the College of New Jersey and the Vermont College of Fine Arts.

JESSROW.COM
TWITTER.COM/ROWJESS

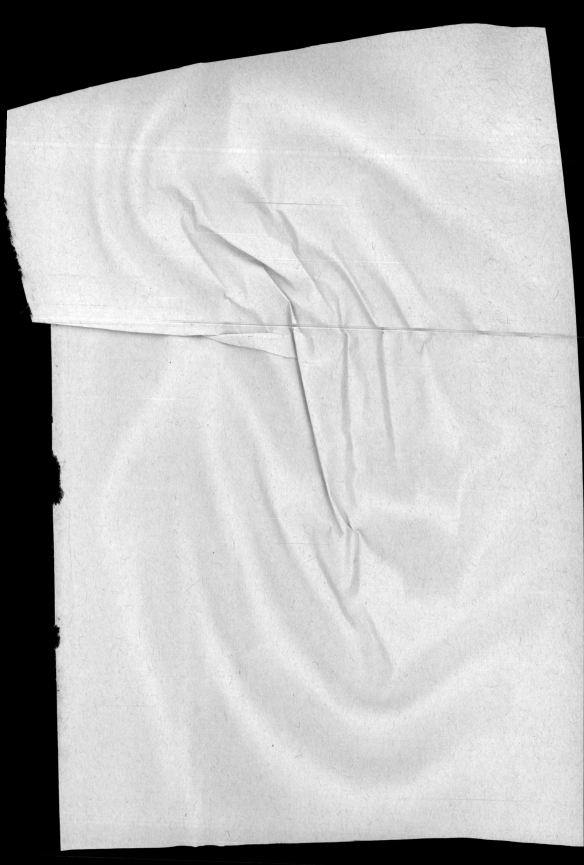

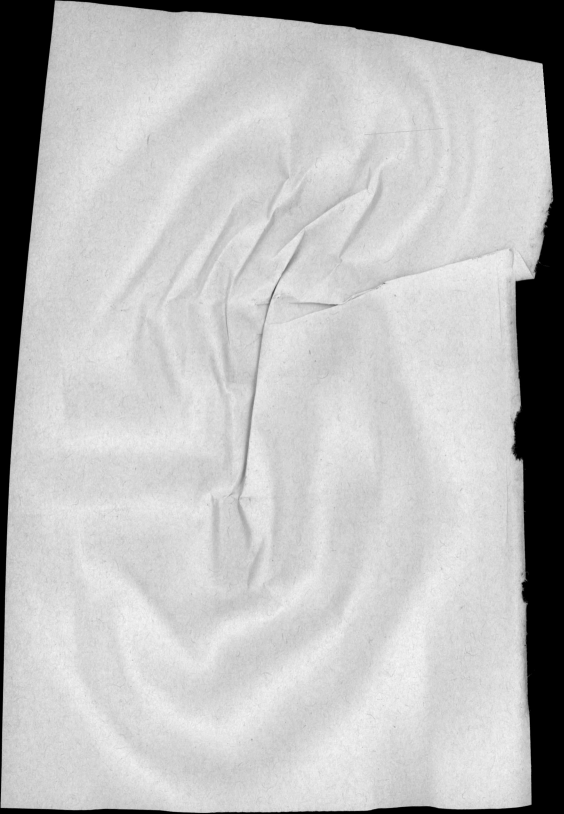